Lead Designer: Scott Gable
Designers: Dan Dillon, James J. Haeck, Chris Harris, Victoria Jaczko, Jeff Lee, Shawn Merwin, Carlos Ovalle, Kelly Pawlik, David N. Ross, Stephen Rowe, Christopher Sniezak
Additional Designers: Thilo Graf, Eric Hindley, Amanda Hamon Kunz, David Schwartz, Mike Welham
Developers: Scott Fitzgerald Gray, David N. Ross, Stephen Rowe
Editors: David N. Ross, Stephen Rowe
Additional Editor: Scott Gable
Cover Illustrator: Eric Belisle
Interior Illustrators: Eric Belisle, Julie Dillon, Domenico Neziti, Tanyaporn Sangsnit, Bryan Syme
Graphic Designers: Crystal Frasier, Scott Gable
Special Thanks to Michael Bauer and BJ Hensley
And to Frank Payne for the extra eyes
Tremendous Thanks to the support of our 315 Kickstarter backers for making this all possible. You're wonderful.

www.zombiesky.com

ISBN-13: 978-1-940372-50-1 (ebook)
ISBN-13: 978-1-940372-51-8 (hardcover)

Along the Twisting Way

table of contents

reference

This guide builds on the twelve primary servitor fey introduced in *Along the Twisting Way: The Faerie Ring Campaign Guide.*

Those twelve different fey species are presented here as options for players. They are designed to be balanced with one another and with other existing player races, so you should feel free to adventure however you please, as it should be. These player races are designed utilizing the kith subtypes introduced in *Along the Twisting Way: The Faerie Ring Campaign Guide.* Instructions are given under type in the **Traits** sidebar for each player race.

Introduction

The wind blows out of the gates of the day,
The wind blows over the lonely of heart,
And the lonely of heart is withered away,
While the faeries dance in a place apart,
Shaking their milk-white feet in a ring,
Tossing their milk-white arms in the air;
For they hear the wind laugh and murmur and sing
Of a land where even the old are fair,
And even the wise are merry of tongue;
But I heard a reed of Coolaney say,
'When the wind has laughed and murmured and sung,
The lonely of heart must wither away.'

—William Butler Yeats,
"The Land of Heart's Desire"

Welcome to the vast possibilities of Faerie! Do watch your back.

We are here not to play in the realms we know but in the realms beyond, in the unknown, seeking wonder and strangeness in unplumbed proportion. These are the places free from judgement. (Except when they're *not.*) And you have a mandate to explore and experiment. (Except when you *don't.*) And everything is as it should be. (Except when it *isn't.*)

These are the lands of the fey: delightful and fabulous, complicated and exasperating. Oh, you're in it now, my friend—delight is waiting for you behind every corner. You can't escape the delight so don't even try.

And you're here to play! How grand. You're already one of us, so you're fabulous right from the start. A complex and intriguingly unique sigil scratched upon the fabric of the multiverse. (Along with everyone else here.) You're already a part of the mystery, a supernatural being with pleasure and misery at your fingertips.

Not to worry, for there is danger enough ahead for even the most wary. For sure, there is plenty of excitement in your future. And you'll only get exactly as many chances as you need. So go find your joy, your mystery, your salvation. That's all you'll need.

Find your whimsy.

Bitterclaws

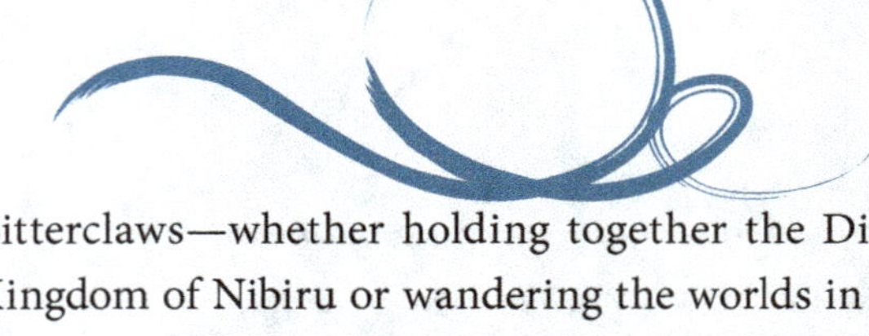

Yes, yes. I am quite apologetic! Though, I think, in time, you'll see you are blowing this whole "limb-loss" thing wildly out of proportion. It is all ultimately going to work out for the best. How many people have the proper motivation to use their feet like hands?!

—Sir Remolio Redondo Randostan VI

Bitterclaws—whether holding together the Divided Kingdom of Nibiru or wandering the worlds in sweet escape—can never shed their role as big siblings to the frenetic, infuriating gremlins. Their curse is twofold: both the love their sovereign has for gremlins and their own devotion to their utterly irrational liege. They bear these with some shred of dignity along with biting, sardonic wit.

Herding gremlins has created an overdeveloped sense of responsibility among bitterclaws. They keep careful watch of the people shuffling and events transpiring around them. They are always expecting the bad, and they prepare themselves for the worst. As a result, they have a tendency to get themselves into trouble, even when gremlins are not involved. When gremlins are about, however, bitterclaws are forced to follow their sibling's insane logic in order to get ahead of and hopefully confine ensuing mischief. Some confuse this unlucky tendency with recklessness.

Bitterclaws' genesis came from an inspired matabiri experiment, the result of an attempt to slow the destructiveness of metal-hungry gremlins. This weighs heavily on the psyche of these fey. They can't forget that Flibbertigibbet had little to do with their creation and greeted their gift by the matabiri with the glee of a child opening a birthday gift. While the matabiri infused bitterclaws with more intelligence and common sense than typically found among gremlins, the bitterclaws suspect that such traits are no more than liabilities under the rule of the Scattered Prince.

As Flibbertigibbet is torn in three, the bitterclaws are torn in two—so to speak. Motivated both by the urge to please their lord by bearing the responsibility of maintaining his demesne in his frequent absences and also by the drive to be just as carefree and rootless, embracing the wanderlust they share with the mogwoi sovereign. Their tempestuous emotions do not always blend well. The innate common sense they possess makes them insightful allies, but it is a burdensome gift in a realm of nonsense. The secret temper they try to hide sooner or later gets the better of them, perhaps influenced by the mystically tainted blood in their veins. It's uncertain how the bitterclaws developed such toxic blood: some conjecture it is the distilled resentment of the matabiri for fixing Flibbertigibbet's "mistakes" while others hold that perhaps the repressed frustrations bitterclaws have with their sovereign has comingled dangerously with their innate love and obedience for him. It grants them both a potent

weapon and a hint of the deeper and darker currents running beneath the surface.

Physical Description: Bitterclaws are much taller than their gremlin siblings but still quite small by human standards. The tallest among them reaches about 4 feet tall, but few are shorter than 3-1/2 feet. Their bodies are lean and either gray or white skinned. Some maintain a coat of white, fuzzy fur along their backs and limbs, but others prefer to shave entirely to better resemble Flibbertigibbet.

Bitterclaws are mostly bipedal but drop to all fours when particularly irritated or curious. They have an unsettling grin filled with nearly indestructible metal teeth set in an oversized mouth, so most bitterclaws avoid smiling unless they wish to terrify others. Equally disturbing are a bitterclaw's lengthy, needle-like claws.

Garb is an individual choice for bitterclaws, and some choose to do without clothing entirely. Others are more pragmatic and adopt the styles and customs of whatever land they happen to be traveling through. They make exceptions for trappings of office or of accomplishment. Badges, medals, official uniforms, and so on, are worn with pride and well-maintained with studious care.

Society: Within Nibiru, bitterclaws serve as wardens of a massive asylum, but no one has the keys. While they do their best to meet their sovereign's expectations, things eventually go wrong, and it's the bitterclaws who shoulder the blame.

Two bitterclaws in a room bicker like an old married couple. Larger groups of bitterclaws often transform into an assembly of cantankerous, hissing

BITTERCLAW TRAITS

Bitterclaw characters possess an assortment of traits all their own.

- ***Ability Score Increase.*** Your Dexterity score increases by 1, and your Intelligence score increases by 2.
- ***Languages.*** You can speak, read, and write Common and Sylvan.
- ***Size.*** Bitterclaws stand between 3 and 4 feet tall and weigh about 60 pounds. Your size is Small.
- Speed. Your base walking speed is 25 feet.
- ***Type.*** Your type is fey. Spells and effects that specifically target humanoids do not affect you. You also gain the mogwoi subtype (see **Appendix**).

- ***Bitter Blood.*** Your blood is a psychoactive poison to humanoids. A humanoid who deals damage to you with a melee slashing or piercing weapon must succeed on a Constitution saving throw or be poisoned until the start of their next turn. The save DC is 8 + your proficiency bonus + your Constitution modifier.
- ***Darkvision.*** As a creature of unnatural realms, you have superior vision in dark and dim conditions. You can see in dim light within 60 feet of you as if it were bright light, and in darkness as if it were dim light. You can't discern color in darkness, only shades of gray.
- ***Natural Attacks.*** You have a claw attack that deals 1d4 slashing damage and a bite attack that deals 1d4 piercing damage. You are proficient with these attacks, which are considered light melee weapons with the finesse property.
- ***Remarkable Bite.*** Outside of combat, you are able to bite through most unattended nonmagical objects given enough time. The GM determines how long it takes to bite through an object, and whether doing so requires one or more Strength checks.
- ***Sense Metal.*** You can sense metal objects up to 60 feet away from you.
- ***Touched.*** You have advantage on saving throws against being charmed, and magic can't put you to sleep.

curmudgeons. These arguments lull in order to cobble together plans and sometimes even to enact those plans, but often they do not survive the mischief of the gremlins and the capricious attention of Flibbertigibbet himself. Bitterclaws expect such failure and then jockey to place the blame and retain their position or even gain promotion.

Flibbertigibbet assigns ranks and offices arbitrarily, often making up nonsensical titles and giving them out when he is breezing through his demesne. He even allows some bitterclaws to make up their own titles and treats the whole event with his variety of pomp and circumstance within strangely grand ceremony. Then, without providing any explanation of what the title means or is responsible for or how it ranks, Flibbertigibbet is gone again.

Bitterclaws divide themselves roughly into the Titled and the Untitled. Titled bitterclaws form a loose council that convenes regularly in the Divided Kingdom to maintain the demesne and enact Flibbertigibbet's will, but they usually just argue for days about what the sovereign's will actually is. Sometimes, when a particular bitterclaw is given obvious favor and preference by Flibbertigibbet, the individual gains enough respect from his brethren to take a more active leadership role. Other bitterclaws then fall in line, though often begrudgingly.

A major quirk of the bitterclaws is their obsession with destiny. As a bitterclaw ages, they grow increasingly concerned with achieving their hidden ambitions, making their mark, and fulfilling an important purpose. Some are fortunate enough to be given missions by Flibbertigibbet himself and throw their all into achieving their "destined" quest. Most give in to their wandering urges sooner or later and seek out their personal meaning—a task often destined for catastrophic failure. Still, those bitterclaws that feel they've uncovered their purpose, either rightly or wrongly, are powerful forces throwing their considerable will behind their destiny.

Whether by accident or by matabiri design, there are noticeably more bitterclaw men than women. This limits their birth rates and makes mated pairs rare. Relationships are brief and filled with squabbling, and resulting children are raised by usually one parent who hardly ever forms much of a bond with their offspring.

Relations: It is difficult to faze a bitterclaw. Even the most erratic gnome is downright stodgy compared to a gremlin. As such, bitterclaws rarely take offense to others' behavior. Bitterclaws are too focused on their own aims to worry much about others, but if an outsider interferes with their plans, a bitterclaw's moody temperament becomes abruptly dangerous.

The mood swings of a bitterclaw can become tiresome for others. When bitterclaw plans are going well, they are confident and almost cocky. When things turn against them, they are withdrawn and passive aggressive. Bitterclaws curiously prefer the company of non-fey whenever possible. They find the relative stability of other creatures refreshing.

Alignment and Religion: Most bitterclaws tend toward neutral alignment, but chaos is a part of their nature as well. Their petty, grandiose schemes make them seem selfish at times, but their disinterest in arguing moral politics is refreshing to some.

Bitterclaws find gods to be curious things as Flibbertigibbet is the only deity-like creature they perceive. Most don't see the point in worshipping gods, but there are exceptions. Those bitterclaws who find a sense of purpose in the service of a deity make the most passionate—and dangerous—sort of zealots.

Adventurers: Most bitterclaws take up adventuring sooner or later, driven by wanderlust. They usually need help to fulfill their personal plots and are capable of working with anyone, even if they can't stand them; most have spent years negotiating with their own kind and gremlins after all.

Bitterclaws are uncomfortable with leadership but are used to having it thrust upon them. Nonetheless, they ease comfortably into support roles. Bitterclaws overcome by their violent tempers embrace combat roles. While some bitterclaws hear the call to service from the gods or other masters—other than Flibbertigibbet—they tend to feel ill-suited for such roles, but they are used to being burdened.

Age: Bitterclaws persist for anywhere from 101 and 201 years before fading away to become part of Nibiru once more.

Female Names: Bellay, Dizzi, Ferrana, Hebbri, Morra, Ossriana, Rozz, Teggray, Zennix.

Male Names: Azzo, Cellan, Evanssam, Grezzel, Jorry, Linnzo, Nossam, Pergged, Syllbert, Vorennzo.

SUBCLASSES

The fey provide an array of unique qualities and perspectives for creating interesting new characters. Consult your GM before applying these subclasses to other races.

CIRCLE OF THE WEEP
(DRUID: DRUID CIRCLE)

Some bitterclaws find the perfect randomness and brutality of nature so soothing, they opt to never leave—and destroy any who would attempt to corrupt, control, or establish "order" in their flawless domains. A weep is a bitterclaw who has melded their savage form with natural magic to become nature's perfect assassin.

BONUS PROFICIENCIES

When you choose this circle at 2nd level, you gain proficiency with simple and martial weapons. In addition, you gain proficiency with poisoner's kits.

VIRULENT POISON

Starting at 2nd level, creatures that are affected by your poison—either poison you deliver or poison delivered in your wild shape forms—have disadvantage on Constitution saving throws to resist the poison.

POISONOUS WILD SHAPE

Also at 2nd level, you can use your Wild Shape to become a beast of up to challenge rating 1, as long as it can deal poison damage or inflict the poisoned condition. You must still follow the other limits on the Wild Shape table.

TOXIC WEAPONS

Starting at 6th level, your natural claw and bite attacks are infused with poison. In addition to the normal damage, your claw and bite attacks, either in your natural form or your wild shape form, deal an additional 1d6 poison damage. When you reach 11th level as a druid, this additional damage increases to 2d6 poison damage.

POISONOUS SNEAK ATTACK

Starting at 10th level, you gain the ability to strike at your foes' most sensitive areas. This works as the rogue feature of the same name. You deal an extra 1d6 damage at 10th level, an extra 2d6 at 14th level, and an extra 3d6 at 17th level. If your attack deals poison damage, you can choose to make the extra damage from Sneak Attack poison damage. The target must succeed on a Constitution saving throw against your druid spell save DC or take twice as much poison damage as your Sneak Attack dice.

LINGERING POISON

Starting at 14th level, when a creature fails its Constitution saving throw against your Poisonous Sneak Attack, it gains the poisoned condition. At the end of each of the target's turns, it makes a new Constitution saving throw, ending the condition on itself on a success.

COLLEGE OF CHAOS CHEMISTRY
(BARD: BARD COLLEGE)

Most bard colleges place emphasis on magic through a mixture of performance, lore, and skill-at-arms. Bitterclaws do things a bit differently though. They emphasize study and knowledge of course, but they focus their magical exploration and learning on the mixing of chemical reagents.

Whereas most bards inspire their allies with tales of derring-do or rousing songs or bawdy limericks, you hand your allies flasks of steaming, bubbling liquids or simply splash them on targets to use your spells and features. Instead of casting spells through music, you throw together reagents to dramatic effect, leveraging the power of alchemy.

Although bitterclaw colleges rarely take on non-bitterclaw students—as such students rarely complete their studies—chaos chemists of other races are not unheard of.

EARLY ADMISSION

When you join the college of the chaos chemist, you do so at 1st level. Make the following changes to the normal bard abilities:

- Instead of gaining proficiency with three musical instruments, you gain proficiency with the herbalism kit and alchemist's supplies.
- Instead of gaining a lute or other musical instrument as starting equipment, gain an herbalism kit.
- You gain proficiency with Dexterity and Intelligence saving throws instead of Dexterity and Charisma.
- You can use an herbalism kit, poisoner's kit, or alchemist's supplies instead of a musical instrument as your spellcasting focus.
- Use Intelligence to figure your Spellcasting DC and attack rolls instead of Charisma.
- Use Intelligence to figure your Bardic Inspiration uses instead of Charisma. You hand over or throw vials of stimulating tonics to perform Bardic Inspiration.

INVIGORATING INSPIRATION

Starting at 3rd level, when a creature uses your Bardic Inspiration die to add to a roll they just made, they also gain temporary hit points equal to the number rolled. If they roll a 1 on the die, they take 1 point of poison damage instead of gaining temporary hit points.

REST IN A BOTTLE

Starting at 6th level, your Song of Rest ability is actually you mixing quick chemical formulations to assist in your recovery and that of your allies. A creature can drink the concoction during the rest to heal normally, as per Song of Rest. If they do not use the concoction during the short rest, they can keep it and use it as a bonus action, up until the next time they take a short rest. The concoction only works for them, healing the number of points that it would have if they had used it during the short rest. You can only make up to ten of these concoctions during a short rest, each for a different target.

FEEL THE BURN

Starting at 14th level, when you use your action to cast a bard spell using a spell slot, you can target one creature within 30 feet of you with a splash of your chemical mixture. The creature must make a successful Dexterity saving throw against your spell DC or take damage equal to 1d12 + the slot level. You can choose to make this damage any of the following: acid, cold, fire, lightning, poison, or thunder.

MISCHIEF DOMAIN
(CLERIC: DIVINE DOMAIN)

You are so attuned to the chaos and mischief around you that you've become a living embodiment of those forces: a literal priest of mischief. Flibbertigibbet often grants to you little paragons of chaos your abilities, though other powers and deities may also step in if it suits their needs to turn bitterclaw clerics loose on the unsuspecting world.

MISCHIEF DOMAIN

You are granted the following domain spells.

MISCHIEF DOMAIN SPELLS

Cleric Level	Spells
1st	*disguise self, hideous laughter*
3rd	*invisibility, misty step*
5th	*bestow curse, hypnotic pattern*
7th	*confusion, polymorph*
9th	*animate objects, mislead*

MISCHIEF MAKER

When you choose this domain at 1st level, you gain proficiency in two of the following skills: Deception, Sleight of Hand, and Stealth. In addition, you gain proficiency with disguise kits and your choice of one gaming set.

CHANNEL DIVINITY: SOW CHAOS

Starting at 2nd level, you can use your Channel Divinity to create confusion in the minds of your foes. As an action, you speak gibberish. All humanoid enemies that can hear you within 30 feet must succeed on a Charisma saving throw, or they are distracted for 1 minute or until they take damage. While distracted, the target has disadvantage on Wisdom (Perception) checks, they cannot take reactions, and attack rolls against them are made with advantage.

CHANNEL DIVINITY: ILL LUCK

Starting at 6th level, you can use your Channel Divinity to give an enemy worse luck in combat. As an action, you point at one creature within 60 feet. That target must make a Charisma saving throw. If the target fails, for 1 minute it has disadvantage on attack rolls and rolls twice for the damage of any successful weapon attack, taking the lower of the two damage rolls. The target may use an action on its turn to attempt another Charisma saving throw to remove the effect.

SPLITTING HEADACHE

Starting at 8th level, once on each of your turns, when you damage a target with a weapon attack, you can deal an extra 1d8 psychic damage. When you reach 14th level, the extra damage increases to 2d8.

WREAK HAVOC

Starting at 17th level, you can use a bonus action (if it is your turn) or a reaction (if it isn't your turn) to force an enemy within 60 feet to reroll an attack roll, saving throw, or ability check before the GM declares whether or not the roll hit or succeeded. If you do, the new result replaces the old one. Alternatively, you can use this feature to apply disadvantage on a creature's passive ability check score as a reaction or bonus action after an ability check is rolled against that score (such as a check using Stealth against a passive Perception score) but before the values are compared. You can use this feature a number of times equal to your Wisdom modifier (minimum 1). You regain all uses of this feature after finishing a long rest.

RAPSCALLION
(ROGUE: ROGUISH ARCHETYPE)

The manic madness of Flibbertigibbet inspires you, and you yearn to follow in the footsteps of the clown prince of the fey. You've studied the pranks. You've listened to the legends. You have the skills. Now it's time to show the world—regardless of how much damage and mayhem you might inflict.

COMBAT MISCHIEF

Starting at 3rd level, you can use the bonus action granted by your Cunning Action to force a creature you can see within 30 feet of you to make a Wisdom saving throw (DC 8 + your proficiency bonus + your Dexterity modifier). On a failed save, you trigger a practical joke against the target. You describe the joke, and the target is knocked prone or is deafened for 1 minute (your choice, and depending on the nature of the joke). A deafened creature can repeat the saving throw at the end of each of its turns, ending the effect on itself with a success.

MISCHIEF AND MAYHEM

Starting at 9th level, when you use your Combat Mischief feature, you can also impose the blinded or poisoned conditions. A blinded or poisoned creature can repeat the saving throw at the end of each of its turns, ending the effect on itself with a success.

STUNNING JAPE

Starting at 13th level, when you use your Combat Mischief feature, you can also impose the stunned condition. A stunned creature can repeat the saving throw at the end of each of its turns, ending the effect on itself with a success. If you use this ability with Combat Mischief, you cannot do so again until you finish a long rest.

DIE LAUGHING

Starting at 17th level, you can attempt to kill a creature with your Combat Mischief feature. If the target creature has 150 hit points or fewer and fails the saving throw, it dies. If you use this ability with Combat Mischief, you cannot do so again until you finish a long rest.

ROADRUNNER
(RANGER: RANGER ARCHETYPE)

Most think of Nibiru as a dangerous realm, but you have walked its shifting and winding pathways to learn the nature of that place. Your peers know you as one of the Roadrunners, and Nibiru is your second home.

NIBIRU EXPLORER

Starting at 3rd level, whenever you are in Nibiru, you gain all the benefits of your Natural Explorer class feature. You do not need to have traveled for an hour or more in Nibiru to gain these benefits.

ROADRUNNER'S PRESENCE

At 7th level, you add the following benefits to your Natural Explorer class feature after traveling for an hour or more in any of your favored terrains or while in Nibiru:

- You and your group can move stealthily at a normal pace.
- You instantly know if you have been affected by any magical effect that would cause you to lose your way.
- You have advantage on Wisdom (Perception) and Wisdom (Survival) checks when you make those checks in your favored terrain or in Nibiru.

ROADRUNNER'S STRIDE

At 11th level, any companions within 30 feet of you who can see and hear you gain the benefit of your Land's Stride class feature.

ROADRUNNER'S PORTAL

At 15th level, you gain a measure of control over the paths you walk, letting you step easily from world to world. When you are walking the paths of Nibiru and acquire one or more steps toward finding your way, you can use the *teleport* spell to allow you and your companions to immediately reach your destination. When you roll on the table to determine your chance of a teleportation mishap, you treat your destination as if it was very familiar, regardless of how well you really know it. Once you use this feature, you must finish a long rest before you can use it again.

ZEALOT OF FLIBBERTIGIBBET (WARLOCK: OTHERWORLDLY PATRON)

Though Flibbertigibbet is far from being the most powerful of the fey lords, he might be one of the most cunning and mischievous. He has bestowed power upon you in aid of some scheme or plot—but what that plot is and how you fit into it remains beyond your understanding.

EXPANDED SPELL LIST

Flibbertigibbet lets you choose from an expanded list of spells when you learn a warlock spell. The following spells are added to the warlock spell list for you.

FLIBBERTIGIBBET EXPANDED SPELLS

Spell Level	Spells
1st	*bane, hideous laughter*
2nd	*detect thoughts, magic mouth*
3rd	*bestow curse, nondetection*
4th	*confusion, greater invisibility*
5th	*animate objects, scrying*

FRENETIC PRESENCE

Starting at 1st level, your patron grants you the ability to disrupt the minds and bodies of lesser creatures as an action. All creatures within 10 feet of you must make a Wisdom saving throw against your warlock spell save DC. On a failed save, a creature is charmed or poisoned by you (your choice) until the end of your next turn.

Once you use this feature, you can't use it again until you finish a short or long rest.

PART OF THE PLAN

Starting at 6th level, you can play a practical joke on a creature that dares to harm you. When you take damage from a creature within 15 feet of you, you can use your reaction to set up a practical joke and force that creature to make a Wisdom saving throw against your warlock spell save DC. On a failed save, the creature is knocked prone or is blinded, deafened, or poisoned until the end of its next turn (your choice, and depending on the nature of the joke).

You can use this feature three times. You regain all expended uses when you finish a long rest.

MIND HIJACKER

Beginning at 10th level, Flibbertigibbet infuses you with overwhelming strength of mind. You are immune to being charmed. Whenever another creature attempts to charm you, you can use your reaction to force that creature to make a Wisdom saving throw against your warlock spell save DC.

On a failed save, the creature is overcome by irrational anger and spends its next turn engaging in one of the following courses of action (your choice):

- The target moves toward you by the shortest and most direct route, ignoring any danger that would result in immediate death. For example, the target could be compelled to take damage by running through an area of open flame but not to enter a pool of lava.
- The target attacks you in a manner of your choosing—usually involving making the attack in the worst possible way. For example, the target might throw a melee weapon, target you with a spell that does not affect creatures of your type, and so on.
- The target is overcome by stammering and shivering, imposing disadvantage on its next d20 roll made before the end of its next turn.

SPLIT ASPECT

At 14th level, you draw on the power of Flibbertigibbet to split yourself into two identical aspects. As an action, you create a second identical body that appears in an unoccupied space within 5 feet of you and lasts for 1 minute. Your clothing and gear is not duplicated, but you can decide which body retains certain items and gear when you split (including having one body retain all your gear and the other body appear naked if you wish). You can choose to end this effect early as an action.

The new body rolls initiative when it appears, and you control both bodies as a single creature. Each body takes its own actions and is aware of the other body's actions and thoughts. Your new body and your original body each have hit points equal to half your current hit point total before you split (rounded down). When this effect ends, your second body disappears. Any gear on your second body returns to your original body, and you add the current hit point total of both bodies to determine your current hit point total.

At 16th level, the duration of this effect lasts for 10 minutes. At 20th level, the effect lasts for 1 hour.

Once you use this feature, you must finish a short or long rest before you can use it again.

BACKGROUNDS

The following backgrounds are especially common in bitterclaws. At the GM's discretion, other appropriate races may have access to them.

BANISHED FROM NIBIRU

You were once one of Flibbertigibbet's favored bitterclaws, running grand schemes and pushing plots to their hilarious and disastrous conclusions. Then you made an unforgivable mistake—or at least took the blame for one. But Flibbertigibbet cut ties with you, and that's all your brothers and sisters need to know. Usually, you'd be killed for such an indiscretion, but you were simply banished instead—told to never return to Nibiru on pain of being separated into three aspects that won't go back together again.

Devastated, you now walk through numerous worlds and preternatural planes as you yearn for your home—and as you wonder whether your banishment is legitimate or whether this might just be part of one of Flibbertigibbet's plots.

Skill Proficiencies: Performance, Survival

Languages: Two of your choice

Equipment: A bag containing three trinkets claimed on your travels, along with 13 cp, 2 gp, and an iron coin with a bite taken out of it

BANISHMENT

You can work with your GM to decide the exact nature of your exile, or you can choose or roll on the following table to determine the reason for your banishment.

d6	Banishment
1	You played a prank that caught Flibbertigibbet off guard.
2	You told a joke about Flibbertigibbet that got back to him, and he did not appreciate it.
3	You have no idea what you did, but Flibbertigibbet's anger was most memorable.
4	Without meaning to, you kind of killed a group of adventurers who were supposedly important to one of Flibbertigibbet's schemes.
5	Flibbertigibbet asked you to do something and you forgot. Or you ignored him because you didn't feel like it. Or both.
6	You made a joke to one of Flibbertigibbet's aspects, and he laughed hysterically. But then he was interrupted by his second and third aspects, who embarrassed the first by telling him the joke wasn't funny.

FEATURE: JOKESTER FOR HIRE

Having hung out with Flibbertigibbet and his inner circle, you have a gift for jokes and dark humor. When you start cracking funny, people can't help but listen and laugh. By offering to entertain for an evening, you can earn free lodging and food of a modest or comfortable standard wherever you travel. You can also learn rumors or gain information from the locals when your performance is done, as determined by the GM. Unfortunately, your best comedic material tends to run to insults, and while people can laugh at themselves for one night, follow-up shows in the same area tend to get stale. Or violent.

SUGGESTED CHARACTERISTICS

Those banished from Nibiru tend to be loners, never

able to wholly fit in with their new environments and companions. So though you always carry yourself with humor, that humor has a dark edge—and often an undercurrent of cruelty.

d8	Personality Trait
1	Everything in life is funny if you look at it the right way.
2	I can find a joke for every situation—whether the situation warrants it or not.
3	I use humor to hide how much my exile hurts me.
4	A prank is the best way to make a friend or kill an enemy.
5	I joke only when among others. Those who catch sight of me when I'm alone see the darkness in me.
6	Though I love playing jokes on others, I grow uneasy if anyone tries to make me the butt of their humor.
7	My connection to the multiple aspects of Flibbertigibbet makes me partial to the number three.
8	I seek out any creature with a connection to Nibiru, hoping for news of my lost home.

d6	Ideal
1	Humor. Without the unexpected madness of comedy, existence would be futile. (Chaotic)
2	Creativity. I need to engage fully with the world to maintain my edge. (Any)
3	Honesty. A good joke will show you the truth of things. (Good)
4	People. I don't care about politics, ethics, or morality. All that matters is making people laugh. (Neutral)
5	Cruelty. At the heart of every joke is a sharp word, and mine are the sharpest. (Evil)
6	Healing. I need to get over what I've lost, and seeking comfort in my new surroundings is the only way to do so. (Any)

d6	Bond
1	I will dedicate every waking moment to seeing my banishment undone.
2	I seek out experience at all times, looking to find laughter in new things.
3	Having been disowned by my fellow servants of Flibbertigibbet, I'll show them who's the funniest of them all.
4	Flibbertigibbet remains my idol and master, and I will make him proud.
5	Having renounced my connection to Nibiru, I attach myself to each new place I find in the hope that it will feel like home.
6	I left a person or thing I care about in Nibiru, and I will do anything to get it back.

d6	Flaw
1	I'll do anything for a laugh, and I don't care who I hurt.
2	Sometimes my jokes are a little too honest, but I get as much satisfaction from anger as from laughter.
3	I engage in hedonistic pastimes that I believe will expand my mind.
4	Hoping to prove my loyalty, I'll do anything for a fellow bitterclaw.
5	My sense of having been betrayed by Flibbertigibbet leaves me unable to trust anyone.
6	My need to laugh means that I take nothing seriously—including self-preservation.

FAVORED OF FLIBBERTIGIBBET

You did something that impressed Flibbertigibbet so much that he . . . they . . . the trio decided to promote you. At least you think they promoted you. Things can get very confusing when it comes to deciphering Flibbertigibbet's plans. But however it happened, you've earned a reputation as one of the best and brightest of the bitterclaws. Now you just need to live up to that.

Skill Proficiencies: Deception, Sleight of Hand

Languages: Two of your choice

Equipment: A wooden token given to you by

Flibbertigibbet, 10 gp, and a key that fits one of the many side doors in the Confluence (but which opens no lock you've ever tested it in)

ACCOMPLISHMENT

In order to gain Flibbertigibbet's trust, you did something that impressed him—even if you're not entirely sure what it might have been.

d6	Accomplishment
1	You ran a scheme that helped further one of Flibbertigibbet's goals. You have no idea what goal it was, but Flibbertigibbet seemed quite pleased.
2	Having thought for a long while on what you did to earn Flibbertigibbet's favor, you've been forced to conclude that you didn't do anything—you've been set up by someone.
3	A joke you played on another bitterclaw was so funny that one of Flibbertigibbet's aspects died laughing. You're now not sure whether the favor granted you is a setup for Flibbertigibbet to take revenge.
4	You won favor for the sheer number of pranks you've played, but that's made you realize that no individual prank was funny enough to win Flibbertigibbet's notice.
5	You saved Sweet Tooth Greta from some threat, marking you as unusually heroic. Unfortunately, you fear that Flibbertigibbet now expects you to be braver than you actually are.
6	You became known for pulling off legendary schemes whose risks claimed many of your companions. But what no one knows is that many of those schemes were actually the plans of those fallen companions, and you've been taking credit for their work for years.

FEATURE: RUN OF THE PLACE

Flibbertigibbet has made you one of the temporary rulers of Nibiru. He gave you a key that fits one of the doors in the Confluence (but which has so far failed to work), and that was that. There's no power that comes with the title and even less responsibility, though some of the denizens of Nibiru might recognize you as a ruler. The key is a symbol of authority for them, and as long as you possess it, the denizens of Nibiru will act favorably toward you (as determined by the GM). Additionally, other fey might recognize your station as a ruler of Nibiru, granting you advantage on Charisma checks at the GM's determination.

SUGGESTED CHARACTERISTICS

The favored of Flibbertigibbet wear an air of superiority that often hides deep-seated fear and paranoia, for all who claim that favor have heard tales of how hard it is to keep it. Rumors speak of favored bitterclaws that are subsequently banished when Flibbertigibbet deems their service unsatisfactory. Dark tales tell of one temporary ruler who was torn into three pieces by frenzied folk of Nibiru hoping to see if they could make a lesser Flibbertigibbet. For many of the favored, the fear of failing their fey lord more than balances out any benefit.

d8	Personality Trait
1	I would rather play and have fun than rule anyone, and I hope no one catches on to that.
2	I prefer to be on the move, seeing things rather than sitting around and talking.
3	I smile because it makes me feel better, even when it makes others uncomfortable.
4	I speak my mind when talking about trivialities but always hide my true thoughts and desires.
5	I secretly yearn for power, and earning the favor of Flibbertigibbet is the first step to seizing it.
6	My lack of understanding of what I did to earn favor makes it hard to accept gratitude from others.
7	I embrace the favor granted to me and grow angry when others don't treat me with respect.
8	I know that others covet my special relationship with Flibbertigibbet, and I see enemies everywhere.

d6	Ideal
1	Logic. It is my duty to seek purpose in randomness. A prank with no point is a poor prank. (Lawful)
2	Balance. The chaos of existence must be tempered by the control of those in charge, and that's me. (Neutral)
3	Power. The favor that grants me power is a gift, and I will work hard to show myself worthy of it. (Any)
4	Fun. I have the power to trick others for my own amusement, and it gives me joy. (Evil)
5	Subterfuge. I am positive that Flibbertigibbet favored me by mistake, and I need to keep a low profile so no one notices. (Neutral)
6	Charity. I was miserable as a victim of circumstance, and I will use my authority to help others who are likewise victimized. (Good)

d6	Bond
1	I hold to the throne of Nibiru even if that throne is one of lunacy.
2	Flibbertigibbet is my sovereign and master, and I will do his bidding no matter what.
3	I have risen to power on my own, and I will maintain this power on my own.
4	I am devoted to the bitterclaws of Nibiru, and they will follow me.
5	The favor given to me by Flibbertigibbet is the secret result of others' actions, and they won't let me forget it.
6	I always felt like an outcast, and I will use my favor to make others rue the days when they shunned me.

d6	Flaw
1	This favor proves that I have no equal in Nibiru.
2	The weight of responsibility gives me more satisfaction than anything else I've ever done.
3	I secretly loathe Flibbertigibbet and fear that this favor has been granted to test me.
4	Even before being granted favor, I knew that the multiverse revolved around me. This just makes everyone else realize it too.
5	My friends don't treat me with the respect I deserve, but they'll come around eventually.
6	The favor granted to me is actually owed to an old companion of mine, and I couldn't care less.

ADDITIONAL OPTIONS

The following options are available to bitterclaws. At the GM's discretion, other appropriate races may have access to some of these new rules.

EQUIPMENT

Bitterclaws have developed the following equipment according to their specific needs and utilize them to particular effect.

Claw Guard. Similar to a cestus, this leather bracer covers your forearm, wrist, and mid-finger, but the claw guard goes further and has leather and metal caps extending to all but the tips of lengthy claws. You must be a bitterclaw to wield a claw guard effectively; if you aren't, you can only use it as an improvised weapon. The claw guard reinforces the strength of your sharp claws, allowing you to attack with them in a wider variety of ways. Each time you attack with a claw guard, you choose whether it deals bludgeoning, piercing, or slashing damage.

Nibiru Lockpick. This jagged metal tooth is set onto a small wooden handle carved in the vague shape of a gremlin. Given sufficient time, a Nibiru lockpick can saw through almost anything, combining the indestructible property of gremlin teeth with their total lack of regard for subtlety. This lockpick can be used to attack unattended objects within 5 feet. It automatically hits and deals 1d2 slashing damage when used this way. Tiny objects can be destroyed by this damage; larger objects reduced to 0 hit points by a Nibiru lockpick have up to 3 cubic inches of material removed.

Razor Puzzle Box. This 5-inch metal toy conceals blades under moving panels. Disarming and opening it requires a successful DC 15 Intelligence check, which can be made with thieves' tools. A small object such as a potion fits inside. While open, it can attach to a latch or joint as a trap. When attached as a trap, it can be noticed with a successful DC 15 Intelligence (Investigation) or Wisdom (Perception) check. Anyone using a trapped item or failing to open the box must make a DC 15 Dexterity saving throw, taking 3d6 slashing damage on a failed save or half as much damage on a successful one.

BITTERCLAW EQUIPMENT

Item	Cost	Weight
Nibiru lockpick	60 gp	—
Razor Puzzle Box	40 gp	1 lb.

FEATS

Bitterclaws have evolved a style all their own and are quite fond of the following feats.

NATURAL FIGHTER

Prerequisites: Bitterclaw

You are well versed in fighting with tooth and claw, granting you the following benefits:

- Increase your Strength or Dexterity score by 1, to a maximum of 20.
- Your bite and claw attacks use a d6 for damage.
- When you engage in two-weapon fighting, if you make your second attack with your bite or your claws, you can add your ability modifier to the damage of that attack.

SHARP-TONGUED

Prerequisites: Bitterclaw

Flibbertigibbet is the master of insults, and your worship of his sharp wit grants you the following benefits:

- Increase your Charisma score by 1, to a maximum of 20.
- If you are proficient with the Insight or Intimidation skills, you can add double your proficiency bonus to ability checks involving those skills.
- You can use a bonus action to insult an intelligent creature you can see and that can hear and understand you. You make a Charisma (Intimidation) check opposed by the creature's Wisdom (Insight) check. If your check succeeds, the creature has disadvantage on any d20 roll it makes until the end of its next turn. You can use this feature three times. You regain all expended uses when you finish a short or long rest.

SPLIT PERSONALITY

Prerequisites: Bitterclaw

Your long admiration for the divided nature of Flibbertigibbet's aspects has allowed you to split your focus and concentration, granting you the following benefits:

- Increase your Intelligence or Wisdom score by 1, to a maximum of 20.
- You need to sleep for only 2 hours during a long rest, allowing you to perform light activity for the duration of the rest.
- You are immune to being charmed.

BITTERCLAW WEAPONS

Name	Cost	Damage	Weight	Properties
Simple Melee Weapon				
Claw guard	25 gp	1d4 special	2 lb.	Finesse, light, special

Black Hats

Yes, my lamb, it is as safe as your darling mother's arms. You are my dear friend, and I won't ever harm you. I swear it by the Painted Lady's unchanging face and form. Now drink it all down. Every drop. You'll feel so much better forever after.

—Argin Atisch

Black hats are tricksters without mercy or restraint, given over to their darker urges. These wayward cousins of the far darrig are not content to dawdle with illusion and glamor. Rather, they tap into darker forces, raising necromantic terrors to spread fear and suffering. Gone is the ubiquitous red hat, only to be replaced with one dyed black with shadowstuff, giving these fey their name. Exiled and living under the rule of the Painted Lady, the black hats perfect their strange rituals and dark arts in the benighted caverns of Aralu.

Physical Description: The darkness tainting the spirit of the black hats has also twisted their form. With the slightest glance, one can see some of the traits of goblins mingling with that of their far darrig cousins.

Unlike goblins, black hats can grow hair upon their heads and faces. Their lank hair is typically jet black but can gray quickly in some, turning stark white as the years progress. Their skin is ashen and prone to wrinkles, making them appear aged beyond their years—even desiccated. A black hat's pointed ears stick out from the sides of their head, and the tips often fold over or carry scars from battles and other misfortunes. Their eyes are a sickly yellow as are their long, crooked teeth, often showing within unnerving smiles.

Their spindly, emaciated bodies twist and lurch from the bottom of their feet to their oversized heads. Black hats are rarely taller than 3 feet, though their hunched forms often make an individual seem shorter than their actual height, and they average about 30 pounds. A black hat's twisted and awkward frame hides surprising physical strength, and many who have underestimated these strange small creatures have paid for the mistake with their lives.

Society: In the dark, endless caverns of Aralu, the black hats congregate in fluid confederacies of up to several dozen individuals. They do so for mutual protection against other denizens of the plane and to conspire in their foul necromantic rites. These groups are rarely harmonious for long and are often plagued with power struggles, petty arguments, and destructive vendettas. In truth, a black hat will readily sacrifice a fellow in the pursuit of arcane knowledge and other sources of power. They maintain their far darrig cousins' love of mischief and often engage in elaborate campaigns of terror against enemies or rivals. These machinations are no mere pranks and often end in a trail of blood and bodies. Torture and terror are high comedy to the twisted black hat mind.

Relations: Black hats find goblinoids extremely useful. They make great underlings and have a delightfully vicious streak. Bugbears, in particular, are admired for their ability to sow fear, but most black

hats favor the stealth and cunning of kobolds and occasionally form alliances with them to access their trap expertise. Dwarves are often targeted by black hats in order to ingratiate themselves to potential goblinoid allies. Gnomes remind black hats overly much of their far darrig cousins and the fey courts and are often murdered on sight. Half-orcs are favored targets as black hats enjoy cowing those larger than they are. Halflings are often lucky or brave enough to resist a black hat's magics and are often granted a grudging respect. Black hats have been known to befriend halflings of more malevolent bent. Their relationship with humans is often complex: they are the most common target of the black hats' pranks and the most prolific victims of their necromantic experiments. However, given that humans are relatively easy to corrupt and often succumb to dark temptations, black hats find them to be useful servants. More rarely, exceptional humans are treated as equals and allies, at least until their usefulness has run its course.

Alignment and Religion: The majority of black hats are irredeemably evil. Any chance to change these foul creatures is typically washed away in the pursuit of their necromantic arts, mangling any sense of mercy,

BLACK HAT TRAITS

Black hat characters possess an assortment of traits all their own.

- ***Ability Score Increase.*** Your Intelligence score increases by 2, and your Strength score increases by 1.
- ***Languages.*** You can speak, read, and write Common and Sylvan.
- ***Size.*** Black hats stand between 2 and 3 feet tall and weigh about 30 pounds. Your size is Small.
- ***Speed.*** Your base walking speed is 25 ft.
- ***Type.*** Your type is fey. Spells and effects that specifically target humanoids do not affect you. You also gain the gnomekin subtype (see **Appendix**).

- ***Black Cap.*** You possess a special black hat that you created and that maintains your connection to your magic. You can use your hat as a spellcasting focus, even if your spellcasting class doesn't normally have access to that feature. If you lose your hat, you can't use your Gloomweaver trait or cast any necromancy spells until you retrieve it or create a new one. Creating a new hat requires 1 month of work and 50 gp. As long as you wear your black cap, you have resistance to necrotic damage.

  If lost or stolen, the hat magically teleports to you at the following dawn even if it is on another plane of existence. As long as you don't have your hat, other black hats are hostile toward you and might even attack.
- ***Darkvision.*** Accustomed to dwelling in gloom, you have superior vision in dim and dark conditions. You can see in dim light within 60 feet of you as if it were bright light and in darkness as if it were dim light. You can't discern color in darkness, only shades of gray.
- ***Gloomweaver.*** You know the *chill touch* cantrip. When you reach 7th level, you can cast the *fear* spell once with this trait and regain the ability to do so when you finish a long rest. Intelligence is your spellcasting ability for these spells.
- ***Gnomekin Magic.*** You can cast the *enlarge/reduce* spell once per day without expending a spell slot but only to enlarge yourself. You increase in size up to two steps, to a maximum of Large (which doesn't otherwise alter the spell's effects).
- ***Illusion Resistance.*** You have advantage on saving throws against illusions and ability checks made to recognize them.

compassion, or even basic empathy. Creatures are tools to serve their twisted humor in either life or death. There are those rare souls that are more selfish than cruel, remaining neutral. However, such neutrality typically gives way to evil as the years roll on and dark taxations take over. Black hats are only rarely lawful in bent as ethical ambiguity is an advantage when dealing with the petty stratagems of their own kind. While a good number of black hats embrace the depraved liberty of chaos, the typical black hat is neutral evil. Most black hats are de facto servants of Jasmine, though the relationship hinges on mutual benefit and fearful respect of her power rather than anything that can be called loyalty. Some black hats delve into utter animalism and the pursuit of occult power, becoming servants of evil gods, demon lords, or worse, especially if that entity has power over death or undeath.

Adventurers: Black hats are not content with their lot in Aralu. Many band together to go adventuring, and even join members of other races, especially to increase personal power and search for necromantic texts, artifacts, and trinkets. Such a transient existence also allows them to indulge in their dark humor and depraved experiments with a wider range of subjects and move on when their misdeeds are discovered. Many black hats practice the arcane arts, often specializing in necromancy or shadow magic. A few walk the path of divine power, making pacts with dark gods. Even those martially inclined black hats mix their physical strength with magic. Many are drawn to the straightforward role of assassins, mixing bladework, poison, and the dark arts with terrifying glee.

Age: Black hats mature at a similar rate to gnomes, reaching adulthood at 40. They can live to fantastically old age with the oldest among them claiming to have seen the passage of millennia.

Female Names: Bracken, Cinder, Illthorn, Nightshade, Twistil, Umbra.

Male Names: Bogrin, Gravenail, Grist, Hobknacker, Lubberfend, Vex.

SUBCLASSES

The fey provide an array of unique qualities and perspectives for creating interesting new characters. Consult your GM before applying these subclasses to other races.

BIG BOSS
(FIGHTER: MARTIAL ARCHETYPE)

A black hat specialized in working with other humanoids sometimes ends up in charge thanks to their fey cleverness, ruthlessness, and magic. As a big boss, you are obligated to provide support to others in combat and to grant them a share of any rewards. But in exchange for this leadership, you gain the ability to whip your allies into a frenzy. You're the boss. For now at least.

GET IN HERE AND FIGHT

Starting when you choose this archetype at 3rd level, you can inspire your allies into bloodthirsty combat. When an ally within 5 feet of you makes an attack with a melee weapon, you can use your reaction to grant advantage on the attack roll. You can use this feature a number of times equal to your Charisma modifier (minimum of 1). You regain any expended uses when you finish a long rest.

BIG PRESENCE

Starting at 7th level, your potential involvement in combat is often enough to get foes thinking twice. You gain proficiency in the Intimidation skill if you do not already have it, and you can add double your proficiency bonus to any ability check you make using that skill.

In addition, your allies have advantage on Charisma (Deception, Intimidation, or Persuasion) checks made against any creature within 30 feet of you.

SHOUTED ORDERS

Beginning at 10th level, your ability to motivate your allies with a well-timed word grants them swiftness and insight. As an action on your turn, you can shout at an ally within 30 feet of you, allowing that ally to use a reaction to move up to its speed without provoking opportunity attacks. This feature has no effect if your ally cannot hear you.

ALL OF YOU GET IN HERE AND FIGHT

Beginning at 15th level, your ability to incite fury into your allies intensifies. When an ally within 10 feet of you makes an attack with a melee weapon, you can use your reaction to grant advantage on the attack roll.

In addition, whenever a hostile creature has you and at least two other creatures that are hostile to it within 10 feet of it, that creature has disadvantage on attack rolls and Wisdom saving throws.

BONE DOMAIN
(CLERIC: DIVINE DOMAIN)

Black hat clerics delving too deeply into the secrets of necromancy find their bodies and magic tainted by death. As a follower of the domain of bones, you are a bonecaller—able to summon undead to you, even as your own body twists into the stuff of nightmares.

BONE DOMAIN

You are granted the following domain spells.

BONE DOMAIN SPELLS

Cleric Level	Spells
1st	*false life, inflict wounds*
3rd	*blindness/deafness, darkness*
5th	*animate dead, bestow curse*
7th	*black tentacles, death ward*
9th	*hold monster, planar binding*

BLESSINGS OF BONE

At 1st level, necrotic energy hardens your body and grants you magical sight. You gain darkvision out to a range of 60 feet. If you already have darkvision, you increase its range to 120 feet.

In addition, your bone structure hardens and reshapes itself. When you aren't wearing armor, your AC equals 13 + your Dexterity modifier.

CHANNEL DIVINITY: CONJURE UNDEAD

Starting at 2nd level, you can use your Channel Divinity to tap into necromantic energies and summon undead to your side. As an action, you cause a number of Medium humanoid skeletons or zombies (your choice) equal to your proficiency bonus to appear in unoccupied spaces within 30 feet of you. This number increases to double your proficiency bonus at 7th level and triple your proficiency bonus at 15th level. Undead you summon disappear after 10 minutes or if they are reduced to 0 hit points.

UNDEAD RESISTANCE

Starting at 6th level, when you or a creature within 30 feet of you takes bludgeoning, piercing, or slashing damage, you can use your reaction to grant resistance to the creature against that instance of the damage.

POTENT UNDEAD

Starting at 8th level, undead under your control attack with more precision and strength. Whenever you create an undead with a necromancy spell or summon undead with your Channel Divinity feature, the undead gains the following benefits:

- The creature's hit point maximum is increased by an amount equal to your cleric level.
- The creature deals an extra 1d4 necrotic damage on all successful attacks.

MASTER OF UNDEATH

Starting at 17th level, you can use an action to shroud yourself in a powerful necromantic aura that extends 30 feet from you and lasts for 1 minute. This aura reduces any bright light within it to dim light. Additionally, you and any undead within the aura that you have created or summoned or that are under your control are draped in deep shadow. Creatures that rely on sight have disadvantage on attack rolls against creatures draped in this shadow.

While the aura lasts, you can use a bonus action to command an undead within the aura and under your control to attack one creature. The undead adds your Wisdom modifier to the attack roll and deals an extra 3d10 necrotic damage on a hit.

After using this feature, you must finish a long rest before you can do so again.

CIRCLE OF BLIGHT
(DRUID: DRUID CIRCLE)

When druids fall to corruption, their magical connection to nature twists and poisons the land around them. You and other blighted druids are creatures of hate who see all life as fodder. No longer drawing strength from the purity of nature, you instead gain power from its destruction. Many of your circle are evil, but whispers speak of tragic druids who have turned their backs on the circle out of horror and who now strive to find their way in the world.

BONUS PROFICIENCY

When you choose this circle at 2nd level, you gain proficiency with one martial weapon of your choice.

WITHERED GROVE

Starting when you choose this circle at 2nd level, you gain the ability to create a withered grove in a 5-foot-radius sphere centered on yourself. The sphere moves with you and is visible as a dark haze.

You use a bonus action to create the withered grove, which lasts for 1 minute. It ends early if you are incapacitated or if you choose to end it (no action required). While the withered grove is active, you gain the following benefits:

- You have resistance to necrotic damage.
- Mundane plants (but not plant creatures) in the area wilt and die. If you are at half your hit points or fewer, you regain hit points equal to your Wisdom modifier (minimum of 1) at the start of any turn in which this effect kills living plants. To continue regaining hit points on subsequent rounds, you must move to bring more living plants within the area.
- Any beast or plant creature that enters the area for the first time on its turn or starts its turn there must succeed on a Wisdom saving throw against your druid spell save DC or be frightened until the start of your next turn. While frightened in this way, a beast must take the Dash action and move away from you by the safest available route on each of its turns unless it has nowhere to move. When you activate the withered grove, you can have it ignore any creature of your choice that you can see.

You can use this feature twice. You regain all expended uses when you finish a short or long rest.

DRAIN THE LAND

At 6th level, the strength of your withered grove feeds your hatred. While that effect is active, you can make a weapon attack as a bonus action.

Further, you can drain magical energy from the land as your withered grove defiles it. If your withered grove lasts for its full duration, you regain expended spell slots when it ends. The spell slots you regain can have a total number of combined levels equal to half your Wisdom modifier (rounded down, to a minimum of 1).

RAPID DECAY

Starting at 10th level, the radius of your withered grove expands to 10 feet, and you can infuse the area with your magic to cause instant decay. At the start of your turn, you can expend one spell slot to deal 1d8 necrotic damage per level of the spell slot to every creature you choose within the area of your withered grove.

UNSTOPPABLE BLIGHT

At 14th level, your withered grove has a radius of 20 feet. While it is active, your weapon attacks deal an extra 1d8 necrotic damage.

At the start of your turn, you can choose to draw strength from the decay caused by your withered grove. Until the end of your turn, you regain hit points equal to half of any necrotic damage you deal on your turn. Once you use this ability, you can't use it again until the next time you activate your withered grove.

COLLEGE OF REGRET
(BARD: BARD COLLEGE)

Few creatures steep themselves in bleakness more profoundly than black hats, and the first college of regret originated in the depths of Aralu. You have weaponized your despair and self-loathing, striking at the hearts of your foes to shake confidence and drain will, fulfilling your insidious ethos.

BONUS LANGUAGES

When you join the college of regret at 3rd level, you learn three languages of your choice, the better to sow regret among a wider range of creatures.

DIRGE

Also at 3rd level, you learn to demoralize and sap the resolve from your foes. When a creature that you can see within 60 feet of you makes a saving throw or an ability check, you can use your reaction to expend one of your uses of Bardic Inspiration, rolling a Bardic Inspiration die and subtracting the number rolled from the creature's roll. You can choose to use this feature after the creature makes its roll but before the GM determines whether the saving throw or ability check succeeds or fails. The creature is immune if it can't hear you or if it's immune to being charmed.

AGGRESSOR'S LAMENT

At 6th level, when an enemy within 60 feet of you damages you or any of your allies you can see, you can use your reaction to expend one of your uses of Bardic Inspiration and roll a Bardic Inspiration die. The foe must make a Wisdom saving throw against your bard spell save DC. On a failed save, the creature takes psychic damage equal to the roll of the Bardic Inspiration die times your Charisma modifier and has disadvantage on its next attack roll or ability check. On a successful save, the creature takes half as much damage and doesn't suffer disadvantage.

CRUSH HOPE

Starting at 14th level, you can cause a creature within 60 feet of you to suffer a catastrophic loss of confidence and will. As an action, you expend one of your uses of Bardic Inspiration to force a creature to make a Wisdom saving throw against your bard spell save DC. On a failed save, the creature gains two levels of exhaustion or one level of exhaustion on a successful one. The creature is immune if it can't hear you or if it's immune to being charmed.

Once you target a creature with this ability, you can't target the same creature again until you finish a long rest.

DARK REAVER
(FIGHTER: MARTIAL ARCHETYPE)

You blend blade skill with the necromantic arts, creating a swift, fluid fighting style. The darkness infuses your weapons, causing wounds more grievous than would seem possible. You harvest the bodies, of course, and supply them fresh to your fellows for research and ritual.

CHILL WEAPON

Starting at 3rd level, you can use a bonus action to channel the cantrip *chill touch*. When you use the Attack action on the same turn, the weapon you attack with becomes a conduit for the *chill touch* cantrip. The first time you hit with that weapon before the end of your turn, you hit with the *chill touch* cantrip in addition to the normal weapon damage.

VAMPIRIC WEAPON

Starting at 7th level, you can use your weapon attacks to drain the life from your enemies and strengthen yourself. When you hit using the Chill Weapon feature, you can declare that attack to be a vampiric attack. You regain hit points equal to half the necrotic damage dealt by your *chill touch* cantrip. Once you use this feature, you can't use it again until you finish a short or long rest.

EXECUTIONER'S WEAPON

Starting at 10th level, you can infuse the very essence of death into your weapon as an action. You can then make one weapon attack. If you hit a creature with the weapon attack, the target must succeed on a Constitution saving throw or fall unconscious until the end of its next turn. The save DC equals 8 + your proficiency bonus + your Charisma modifier. A creature automatically succeeds on its saving throw if it has previously succeeded or failed on a saving throw against your Executioner's Weapon in the past 24 hours. At the end of the unconscious target's next turn, it awakens but must make a Constitution saving throw again. On a failed save, the target takes 6d6 necrotic damage.

ENDLESS DARKNESS

Starting at 15th level, when you hit with an attack using your Chill Weapon, you can use this feature. If you do, the target is blinded unless it succeeds on a Constitution saving throw against the save DC of your Executioner's Weapon. At the end of each of the target's turns, it makes a new saving throw, ending the blinded condition on a success.

SUPERIOR DARK POWERS

Starting at 18th level, whenever you deal necrotic damage with your *chill touch* cantrip or your Executioner's Weapon feature, the target's hit point maximum is reduced by the amount of necrotic damage it takes. If you reduce a creature's hit point maximum to 0, it dies.

Additionally, your Executioner's Weapon deals an additional 4d6 necrotic damage when you hit a target, before it rolls its saving throw.

TOXIC SHADE
(ROGUE: ROGUISH ARCHETYPE)

A gift for handling poisons, and a focus on their use and refinement, seems second nature to you. Contract killers with no skill for subtle infiltration, dabblers in alchemy, apothecaries gone bad, and practitioners of ancient cultural traditions in which potent poisons abound: your colleagues come from wide and far. And the black hats of Aralu are well known for their ability to brew deadly toxins.

TOXIC TOUCH

When you choose this archetype at 3rd level, you gain proficiency with the poisoner's kit. Additionally, you can use the bonus action granted by your Cunning

Action to apply a dose of poison to one slashing or piercing weapon or up to three pieces of ammunition.

POTENT POISON

Starting at 3rd level, you learn to increase the potency of your poisons. Whenever you deal poison damage with a weapon attack, that damage ignores resistance to poison.

DEADLY RESIDUE

At 9th level, your weapons always carry a lingering trace of the poisons you wield. When you hit a creature with a weapon attack, the creature takes an extra 1d8 poison damage. You can deal this extra damage only once per turn.

Additionally, any creature that takes poison damage from your weapon attack has disadvantage on Wisdom checks until the end of your next turn.

DEFT POISONER

At 13th level, your poisons can affect even the hardiest of creatures. Whenever you deal poison damage with a weapon attack, you can choose to reroll a number of dice for that poison damage equal to your Intelligence modifier (minimum of 1).

Additionally, whenever you would deal poison damage with a weapon attack, a target with immunity to poison has that immunity temporarily negated to take poison damage equal to the number of damage dice you roll for the attack's poison damage.

KISS OF DEATH

Starting at 17th level, your poisons can leave their victims reeling and unsteady. Until the start of your next turn, a creature that fails a saving throw against your poison can't take reactions and suffers one of the following conditions of your choice: blinded, deafened, poisoned, or prone. If the poison you use doesn't allow a saving throw, the target must make a special Constitution saving throw to avoid this effect (DC 8 + your proficiency bonus + your Intelligence modifier).

On a successful save, the target is affected by your poison but doesn't suffer any additional conditions and can take reactions as normal. A successful saving throw also means the creature is immune to this ability until you finish a short or long rest.

BACKGROUNDS

The following backgrounds are especially common in black hats. At the GM's discretion, other appropriate races may have access to them.

GRAVEDIGGER

The grim reality of life is that one day it ends. And someone should be there, ready to provide comfort and dignity. Someone should fulfil the wishes of the departed and comfort those left behind.

From literal gravediggers to death-worshiping priests, characters with this background see to the final needs of the deceased. You might be clinical and detached with a focus on research or a bent toward hard logistics of interment and disposal. Or you might concentrate on the spiritual needs of the bereaved, comforting them in their time of loss, offering assurances of some greater purpose. You might be well-respected for your efforts or regarded as a second-class citizen, forever marked by your long association with the dead.

Skill Proficiencies: Intimidation, Religion

Tool Proficiencies: Alchemist's supplies, disguise kit

Equipment: A disguise kit, a book of diverse funerary customs, 5 sticks of incense, a set of common clothes (stained with earth, ash, or incense), and a pouch containing 15 gp

FEATURE: AT HOME WITH DEATH

Your vocation makes you comfortable around the trappings of death and those near the end of their lives. You are familiar with nearly any culture's funeral traditions, general information on the deities of death and the afterlife, and the most commonly occurring undead (such as ghouls, skeletons, and zombies). At the GM's discretion, mysterious cultures or religions might be beyond your expertise. Even then, you can likely find parallels to the strange traditions in more familiar societies or scattered folklore.

Additionally, you can expect lodging and shelter from any organization that sees to the deceased. However, other groups might find your past or profession disconcerting, depending on local attitudes.

SUGGESTED CHARACTERISTICS

Gravediggers can be grim and brooding individuals who see all the living as clients-in-waiting. Others might be vivacious and bright with a strong appreciation for life and a confidence in a pleasant hereafter. However, they all hold a deep respect for the dying and the dead and believe in safeguarding a soul's journey. They almost always have a negative view of undeath as an unnatural halting to an orderly transition or as a gross disrespect shown to the bereaved.

SPECIALTY

While you had exposure to all of the many talents required for preparing a corpse for peaceful rest, there was one aspect of the work which appealed to you most. Choose a specialty or roll one on the Specialty table.

d8	Specialty
1	I enjoy placing the dead securely within their final resting places, be it grave, mausoleum, or sprawling catacomb.
2	I prefer to be of comfort to the living left behind, ensuring safe places to grieve and confidence that loved ones are cared for.
3	I am fascinated with the complex arts of body preservation, whether embalming corpses for viewing or mummifying remains for the ages.
4	I seek to provide religious counsel because I know death isn't the end of existence.
5	I focus on methods of bodily destruction, such as burning or dissolving, for local tradition or for concern of disease or undeath.
6	I oversee the construction and placement of stones, monuments, or even vast complexes, so the dead can be remembered.
7	I see it as my sacred duty to prevent the dead from being defiled, whether from grave robber or necromancer.
8	I obsess over esoteric funerary practices, such as feeding remains to animals or transmuting loved one's corpses into jewelry.

d8	Personality Trait
1	I guiltlessly feign whatever religion makes people most comfortable because I know even deities fear death.
2	I always require payment for my services and take from the dead what I choose if they have no living to reimburse me.
3	I enjoy having one-sided conversations with the dead as a corpse is the perfect listener.
4	I am morbidly curious and bizarrely excited about anything related to dying or death.
5	I dress in somber clothes as if in mourning and sometimes even give myself a corpse-like appearance with makeup.
6	I seek vengeance on anyone who grossly defiles the dead but recognize what is disrespectful to one culture might not be to another.
7	I wish to learn all there is to know about the afterlife, so I can provide the living with a greater understanding of what awaits them.
8	I purposefully seek to defy stereotypes and preconceptions surrounding people who handle the dead.

d6	Ideal
1	Callous. I believe death is the best solution to problems with the living. (Evil)
2	Guardian. It is my sacred duty to ensure the dead's eternal rest is left undisturbed. (Lawful)
3	Charity. When someone dies unexpectedly, I try to ensure their dependents are cared for. (Good)
4	Respect. I endeavor to hear and fulfil even my worst enemies' final requests. (Lawful)
5	Hedonist. I have seen too much sadness and death and now wish to live life to its fullest. (Chaotic)
6	Hypocritical. While I counsel strangers to be accepting of death, I will do anything to save myself or those I care about. (Any)

d6	Bond
1	I come from a long, storied line of morticians, and my family name is synonymous with the practice.
2	Someone I love is chronically ill or dying from a mysterious condition, and I cannot bear to lose them.
3	I failed the person who trained me, and they became an undead abomination as a result. I must do something.
4	I keep a reliquary of someone I loved and believe I can talk to them through it.
5	I see each and every client as family and treat them as I would my parent or child.
6	I sometimes meet with Death but am unsure if it is a deity, hallucination, or trick.

d6	Flaw
1	I see little issue with charging inflated prices for my expert services.
2	I believe I know what the dead would want better than their living relations.
3	I have a secret and shameful fascination with undeath and even contemplate such an existence.
4	I prefer the aroma of rot to more generally pleasant smells, and I often stink of death.
5	I enjoy making people uncomfortable and reminding them of their looming, unavoidable death.
6	I am acclimated to working at nights and find myself lethargic or uncomfortable during daytime hours.

PRISONER

You spent a significant portion of your life incarcerated. Perhaps you were lawfully jailed as punishment for your crimes, or you might have been born into slavery before escaping to a life of adventure. You might have come from an even darker place, such as the torturous depths of Aralu, the Gaol of Always—and you wonder now if you can ever truly be free of that past.

You know that memories of harsh conditions, cruel overseers, and cutthroat inmates will always color your perception. But the scales of justice maintain balance in all things, and your past affords you a keen appreciation of all that you have. You understand the true value of a trusted confidant, a warm meal, and a safe bed. Above all, you know there isn't much the world can throw at you that you can't survive.

Skill Proficiencies: Intimidation, Persuasion

Tool Proficiencies: Your choice of one type of musical instrument or one type of gaming set, and your choice of one of the following artisan's tools: calligrapher's supplies, cook's utensils, mason's tools, smith's tools

Languages: One of your choice

Equipment: A musical instrument (one of your choice), a set of common clothes, a trinket that reminds you of family or an ally from your past, and a pouch containing 5 gp

FEATURE: STRETCHED THIN BUT STRONG

Your time imprisoned or enslaved forced you to learn the absolute limits of your endurance. Now you can push yourself to the edge of exhaustion without going over. You can engage in one additional hour of light activity during a long rest without spoiling your rest. You can also travel for one additional hour per day before you are at risk of exhaustion. Once you use this ability, you can't use it again until you finish a long rest.

Additionally, you have a handful of contacts from your time on the inside who you can call upon for minor aid. Work with your GM to determine who your contacts are and where they reside.

SUGGESTED CHARACTERISTICS

Depending on experience, each prisoner's personality can bear a multitude of scars. Many are hard individuals, loath to show weakness for fear of losing respect and putting themselves in danger. Others become fawning or sycophantic, always looking for someone else whose shadow they can safely stand in. Above all else though, every former prisoner knows how to survive. No matter what outward form the past takes, a prisoner has a core of iron that refuses to bend.

d8	Personality Trait
1	I always track the passage of days, marking them on walls, my armor, or scraps of parchment.
2	Fear means respect, so I go out of my way to make sure others fear me.
3	I keep quiet and try desperately to avoid attracting attention.
4	Sometimes I try something new for no other reason than that I can.
5	I form tight bonds with those who live in close proximity to me and push all others away.
6	I always try to identify the leaders of any social group and attach myself to them.
7	There's nothing wrong with doing the dirty jobs as long as they get me through to tomorrow.
8	I prefer being indoors with solid walls to set my back against. Open spaces make me nervous.

d6	Ideal
1	Freedom. I know what it means to have your freedom taken away, and no one will ever do that to me again. (Chaotic)
2	Righteousness. My past mistakes taught me the importance of making the right choices. I won't waste that lesson. (Good)
3	Debt. I'll pay what I owe to society even if I'm no longer in chains. (Lawful)
4	Friendship. The people near me can help me get through anything, and I'll be sure to return the favor. (Neutral)
5	Survival. You'd be surprised what a person can live through. (Any)
6	Station. I'll earn the respect of everyone—or beat respect into them if I must. (Evil)

d6	Bond
1	Someday I'll see the place where I was imprisoned reduced to rubble and dust.
2	I was born a slave to a kind master, and I hope one day to repay that kindness.
3	Those who imprisoned me know I've escaped, and every day brings them closer.
4	I willingly went into prison searching for a lost treasure, and it's still there somewhere.
5	I won't suffer slave owners, consequences be damned.
6	A rival killed the person who kept me safe when I was imprisoned. One day, I'll avenge them.

d6	Flaw
1	I can't grasp how to live outside of incarceration anymore, so I never fit in.
2	Though I'm no longer a slave, I fall into the pattern of following others rather than speaking up for myself.
3	I take even the slightest disagreement as a grave insult. Violence is never far behind.
4	I'll back down from just about any cause if the threat of being sent back to prison looms.
5	The place I was held was the stuff of nightmares, and I still see it in my sleep. Sometimes when I wake, I'm not entirely sure I've gotten away.
6	To escape from prison, I had to betray someone close to me. Others know my secret, and I avoid staying in any place too long as I try to keep ahead of the truth.

ADDITIONAL OPTIONS

The following options are available to black hats. At the GM's discretion, other appropriate races may have access to some of these new rules.

EQUIPMENT

Black hats have developed the following equipment according to their specific needs and utilize them to particular effect.

Araluan Robe. These robes, woven of giant spider silk and dyed black, are commonly worn by the black hats of Aralu. The tight silken weave, darkened by wisps of shadow-stuff, are resistant to snags and tears, and its smooth material slides easily from the clutches of hunting predators. You have advantage on Dexterity (Acrobatics) checks and Dexterity saving throws you make to avoid or escape a grapple while wearing the robe.

Bleeding Onyx. Gathered from volcanic caverns in Aralu, this onyx's normal glossy black color is shot through with veins of crimson. When you use bleeding onyx as a material component for a necromancy spell that creates undead, the spell requires twice the usual value but is also more potent. The spell creates the undead with a fleeting resistance to a cleric's power to Turn Undead. The first time the undead must make a saving throw against Turn Undead, it has advantage on the saving throw.

Bone Dust. Bone dust is a special alchemical preparation of the cleaned bones of a deceased creature that is dead no more than 24 hours at the time of preparation. This dust is a potent hallucinogen and a source of information about the creature's death.

A tin of bone dust remains viable for up to 1 week. To use the dust, you must inhale it, taking 10 minutes to process the entirety of the tin. Surreal, ghostly hallucinations then appear and converse with you about the afterlife for 1 hour. Unless you succeed on a DC 13 Constitution saving throw, you have disadvantage on Wisdom (Perception) checks, and you become incapacitated until the visions fade or you notice an obvious potential threat such as a creature with a drawn weapon. As the hallucinations fade, you witness the consciousness of the creature, from whom the bone dust was made, from the final minute before its death. You can ask one question about the creature's death and gain an accurate answer. The answer is limited to what the creature knew at the moment of its death and can't include speculation about anything after its death or impart new information to the deceased. If only partially inhaled, the bone dust has no effect.

Corpse Money. Coins looted from the pockets of the dead carry traces of necromantic energy. When enhanced by black hat secrets, these coins can afflict non-fey with the malaise of a lost soul.

If you are a black hat, you inflict the forgetfulness of the underworld upon any creature who accepts the corpse money from you. Once you and the creature can no longer see or hear each other, the creature must succeed on an Intelligence saving throw to remember any details of your appearance or of the conversation, including whatever you might have purchased with the money. The save DC equals 8 + your proficiency bonus + your Charisma modifier. Additional effects, at the GM's discretion, might include a general feeling of doom and forgetfulness for details and minor events.

The effects of corpse money last for 10 days or until all the money leaves the target's possession. Entering an area affected by the *hallow* spell or similar effects ends the forgetfulness immediately. Once the effect ends, the target of the corpse money can recall you normally. Constructs, fey, and undead are immune to the effects of corpse money.

Poison, Gnawing Death (Injury). The formula for this virulent poison is known only to the black hats. Some say it contains darkness drawn from the Shadow Plane, but the recipe is guarded jealously. Gnawing death wracks the body and mind of its victim, causing pain and maddening hunger pangs. It can be applied to a melee weapon or up to three pieces of ammunition. Applying the poison takes an action. Once applied, the poison retains its potency for up to 1 minute before drying.

A creature hit by the poisoned weapon or ammunition must succeed on a DC 15 Constitution saving throw or take 2d4 poison damage and become poisoned for 1 minute. If it was already poisoned by gnawing death poison, it then becomes recklessly aggressive as long as it is poisoned; it no longer has disadvantage on attack rolls from the poisoned condition and instead attacks against it have advantage. If it was already reckless due to gnawing death poison, then it attacks the nearest living creature every round that it remains poisoned, attempting to kill and devour any nearby creature unless physically restrained from doing so or unless the poison is removed or it receives *greater restoration*.

Poison Reservoir Hilt. This delicate alchemical and mechanical modification can be made to any piercing or slashing weapon with a hilt or handle. A weapon with a poison reservoir hilt has a secret compartment that holds a single vial of poison. The reservoir can be filled as an action by carefully pouring a vial of poison into the compartment. As a bonus action, you can activate a secret switch which releases the poison, coating the blade of the weapon. Black hats typically fit their sickles with such hilts for easy application of gnawing death poison. A poison reservoir hilt can be detected with a successful DC 20 Intelligence (Investigation) or Wisdom (Perception) check. A weapon with a poison reservoir hilt costs 50 gp more than normal.

BLACK HAT EQUIPMENT

Item	Cost	Weight
Araluan robe	200 gp	1 lb.
Bleeding onyx	twice normal	—
Bone dust	100 gp	—
Corpse money (coin)	350 gp	—
Poison, gnawing death (vial, 1 dose)	2,000 gp	—
Poison reservoir hilt	+50 gp	—

FEATS

Black hats have evolved a style all their own and are quite fond of the following feats.

MORTICIAN

Prerequisites: Black hat, the ability to cast fear with your Gloomweaver trait

You draw on the dread energies of your fellow black hats to imbue a corpse with a mocking semblance of life. While you are within 30 feet of at least two other black hats, you can use your Gloomweaver trait to cast the *animate dead* spell using your black cap as focus, in place of the material component. Once you use this ability, you can't use it again until you finish a long rest.

POISON MASTER

Prerequisites: Black hat, proficiency with the poisoner's kit

Your skill with poisons is unsurpassed, and grants you the following benefits:

- Increase your Dexterity or Intelligence score by 1, to a maximum of 20.
- When you roll for poison damage, you can treat any 1 on a damage die as a 2.
- Whenever you apply a dose of poison to a weapon, you can choose to apply a second dose at the same time. If you do so, any creature subjected to the poison has disadvantage on its saving throw against the poison's effects.
- When you make an Intelligence (Nature) check to extract poison from a creature, you are subjected to the poison only if you fail the check by 10 or more.

STOIC

Prerequisites: Black hat, Wisdom 13 or higher

You are inured to fear and can swallow the worst of its effects in times of need. At the start of your turn, if you are frightened, you can choose to suppress the condition for a number of turns equal to your Wisdom modifier (minimum of 1). While the condition is suppressed, you aren't considered frightened, and this time counts against the condition's duration. Once you use this ability, you can't use it again until you finish a short or long rest.

TERRIFYING PRESENCE

Prerequisites: Black hat, proficiency in the Intimidation skill

You can amplify another creature's terror to bring its nightmares to life. Whenever you cause a creature you can see within 60 feet of you to become frightened, you can use your reaction to force the creature to make a Wisdom saving throw (DC 8 + your proficiency bonus + your Charisma modifier). The creature takes 3d6 psychic damage on a failed saving throw or half as much damage on a successful one. On a successful saving throw, the creature is immune to this ability until you finish a long rest.

Darklings

There exists a truer darkness, and it flows in when fear leads to apathy and ignorance. This darkness is tyranny. However, like the deepest black, it can be banished with only a small glimmer of light. This light is reason.

—Zheddo the Bluetongue

Darklings emerged from a battle for their very existence against a powerful, unknowable Adversary—victorious but at great cost. The appearance of the Adversary unleashed the cascade of the darklings' long-forgotten history, a history where they were almost and perhaps should have been obliterated. Shades whisper to them from all corners of the sprawling, shadowed city-state of Zussael, promising knowledge, power, and truth if only the darklings would trust them, listen, and obey.

To protect itself, the Darkling Dominion has shunned many of the traits that once made it great. But with ancient spirits haunting the walls, looking for willing ears to hear them, the grand matriarch knows destroying what the darklings once were is the only way to save them.

Physical Description: Darklings are tall, lean, and tough creatures whose coloration varies with the shades of twilight. Their skin may be dusty violet, deep blue, or a smoky gray, but it is always somewhat muted and shadowed. Hair colors range from white to black and many deep, dusky shades of various colors in between. Men tend to be shorter than women, though just as hardy. Darklings are roughly equivalent to humans in size and weight: averaging 5–6 feet tall and 160 lb.

Darklings have long, pointed ears as well as goatlike horns sprouting from their brow. Women tend to have longer, sharper horns that curl slightly overhead while men's horns are shorter and taper into blunted ends.

The eyes are the only aspect of a darkling that isn't muted or faded. Indeed, darkling eyes glow a solid, jewel-like color: sapphire blue, topaz yellow, amethyst purple, or—much more commonly now—a bright, ruby red.

They walk on cloven-hoofed hind legs and have thick, red-tipped tails that they use for balance.

Darklings favor clothing and adornments that are both luxurious and keep their lower limbs unhindered: cloaks, togas, stolas, and kilt-like wraps are common garments as are gold and silver jewelry and ornamental bits of armor. Zussael has lost much of its rich and powerful legacy but some still lingers in how its residents carry themselves.

Society: The life of a darkling is highly regimented, dangerous, and often lonely. Their matriarchal society has links to forgotten power and expansion they have yet to even fully remember, and it seems they have rebuilt their species from ashes before. And they are determined to do so again. Their grand matriarch does whatever is necessary to preserve her people and their way of life, but survival in such circumstances can resemble tyranny.

Darklings are raised under strict martial law. Upon reaching adulthood, all darklings serve a 20-year term of public service, such as in Zussael's military, regardless of social class or gender. Military officers are judge and jury when laws are broken. Minor offenses might be resolved with compulsory public service or temporary imprisonment or—in times of conflict—forced conscription, but graver offenses leave the offender with only two choices: exile or death.

Darkling women occupy most of the higher echelons of power in the city-state with their rank and influence—and that of their subsequent family—determined by both their matrilineal ancestral power and by the individual darkling's performance in her mandatory military term. Most of the men fill supportive or artisanal roles and enjoy a little more flexibility in their choice of work than women as long as they do not attempt to step too far beyond their status. Darkling men with exemplary military performance records can find themselves in powerful

DARKLING TRAITS

Darkling characters possess an assortment of traits all their own.

- ***Ability Score Increase.*** Your Dexterity score increases by 2, and either your Charisma or Wisdom score increases by 1.
- ***Languages.*** You can speak, read, and write Common and Sylvan.
- ***Size.*** Darklings are about the same size and build as humans. Your size is Medium.
- ***Speed.*** Your base walking speed is 30 feet.
- ***Type.*** Your type is fey. Spells and effects that specifically target humanoids do not affect you. You also gain the shadow subtype (see **Appendix**).

- ***Darkling Magic.*** You know the *ray of frost* cantrip. You can choose to use it as a melee spell attack in which case it takes the form of a shadowy blade. You can make opportunity attacks with it as a blade. Charisma is your spellcasting ability.
- ***Darkvision.*** Your people's home on the Shadow Plane has granted you superior vision in dim and dark conditions. You can see in dim light within 120 feet of you as if it were bright light and in darkness as if it were dim light. You can't discern color in darkness, only shades of gray.
- ***Self Control.*** You know yourself. Choose to have advantage on saving throws against being charmed or against being frightened.
- ***Shadow Born.*** You have resistance to cold damage and vulnerability to radiant damage.
- ***Sunlight Sensitivity.*** While in direct sunlight, you have disadvantage on attack rolls, as well as on Wisdom (Perception) checks that rely on sight.

positions as well, but these are the exceptions, and even these often have a powerful matriarch working in the background to elevate her son.

Power means wealth and influence of course. These are worthy enough ends for members of most any society, but in Zussael, it means something else too: a glimmer of protection against the Grand Matriarch's Hidden Blades. While a darkling exhibiting signs of the Curse is doomed no matter the social status, enough power can shield certain family idiosyncrasies for quite some time while the Blades and the soldiers busy themselves hunting the lower strata of Zussael for deviants. As with everything else in darkling society, power plays and shadowy intrigue are only a veneer atop the constant fear lurking in everyone's minds, wondering who will be taken by the Curse next and whether it will be a neighbor, a family member, or themselves.

Arranged marriages are the norm among darklings as is a non-negotiable two-child policy; same-sex marriages are required to adopt. Marriages are usually orchestrated by the matriarch of a family who barters with other families of her rank for the best placement of her children. The "best" placement is with families who have lost few relatives to the Curse; despite no evidence to indicate it, there is an unspoken assumption among darklings that the Curse has some form of generational bias in whom it takes. As much as possible, the two families ensure the betrothed darklings do not meet prior to their wedding ceremony. Weddings are opulent, darkly beautiful affairs meant to showcase the wealth and taste of the participating families; the betrothed are decorated figureheads and nothing more. In times of too-fast population growth, most darkling adults remain single and cohabitate with siblings or others in their trade or with secret lovers. Divorce is permitted in truly difficult marriages as darklings aim for loveless marriages not torturous ones. Hatred is as bad as love in keeping the Curse at bay.

There is no real poverty in Zussael thanks to strict population limits and emphasis on work efficiency and productivity. Darklings refusing to work or shirking their duties are eventually suspected of falling to the Curse. These darklings either shape up or disappear.

With some notable and drastic exceptions, most darklings accept these draconian social policies. From birth, they are not given a chance to perceive their limitations as anything but normal. The sanitized histories taught to them as children omit much of their true history—and not just the lore the Adversary brought them. Few young darklings know the artistic, curious, and egalitarian society of the Darkling Dominion prior to the Adversary and Moaro's corruption.

Scientific and magical advancement is Zussael's specialty, and these arenas—along with their advanced techniques in war—keep the populace busy and carefully monitoring trade filtering into its markets. As isolated as darklings are, their efficiency and single-minded effectiveness has allowed them not only to survive surrounded by horror but to keep Zussael thriving as a dark jewel in an ocean of shadows.

Relations: Darklings are in a tentative alliance with the grue beyond Zussael's borders, a state of affairs that is a grim testament to the grand matriarch's desperation. Apart from a kinship with shimmer dogs, darklings have few races they could truly call allies in Zussael—but visitors, clients, acquaintances, these darklings may have in spades.

Beyond the denizens of the Shadow Plane, darklings can be off-putting to races intimidated by their appearance and cold demeanor. Races tied to shadow can make for either rivals or comrades. Elves can be drawn to the darklings' contrast of tightly controlled emotion, but darklings are just as likely to see elves as flighty wastes of immortality. Dwarves distrust the convoluted and otherworldly history of the darklings. Gnomes find them wholly unappreciative of their pranks, but half-orcs, tieflings, and halflings sometimes sense a kindred spirit in exiled darklings, though a darkling is likely to deny it.

Alignment and Religion: Most darklings are lawfully aligned out of necessity. The grand matriarch's laws are harsh, but they keep the darklings safe. The unwholesome acts sometimes necessary to accomplish this make it difficult for most darklings to be truly good, but their motivations prevent them from being wholly evil either. Darklings are nothing now if not pragmatic, and they realize, regardless of lofty moral ideals, that things simply must be the way they must.

Some darklings find comfort in the worship of deities of mercy, magic, strength, and the night, seeking forgiveness and salvation from the Curse and from Moaro. Moon deities are almost universally shunned due to the moon's terrifying effect on darkling beasts and Moaro herself.

Adventurers: Adventuring darklings are often exiles fleeing the Hidden Blades for exhibiting signs of the Curse (true or not). Some are banished—or choose to leave—simply for indulging in social anathema like overly emotional displays, secret marriages or children, consorting with ancient spirits, or attempting to spread the truth of darkling history. A few are actually agents of the city-state, seeking the planes for foils to the Curse or tracking Moaro's fractured consciousness on the Material Plane.

Darklings blend magical and martial might well, making them well suited to roles that support this, including inquisitorial roles if tending toward faith.

The Willful & the Wise

You could say there are two types of darklings: the willful and the wise.

The "willful" darklings live precarious lives within Zussael. Their emotionally demonstrative natures constantly draw suspicion, and they often find themselves hunted by the Hidden Blades or taking the Silver Path to whatever fate has in store for them. Leaving is often their only recourse, and outside of Zussael, characters of other races often find these darklings more personable than their more reserved kin.

The "wise" darklings rarely leave Zussael unless under orders from the grand matriarch or her agents. Possessed of the practiced calm necessary to thrive in the shadow city without drawing the wrong kind of attention to themselves, these darklings often find a different sort of danger.

Classes with emphasis on chaos and emotion such as barbarians are rare. Monks are not unusual as the rigid structure of darkling life makes them particularly suited to such discipline. Curiously, while sorcerers and warlocks are commonly called among darklings, they are frowned upon or worse, for darklings hold a deep mistrust of the source of these classes' powers. Only slightly less suspected are psychically endowed darklings, and woe to any darkling that appears to be channeling the ancient spirits responsible for the darklings' current state.

Age: Darklings achieve maturity at 15, though must then spend a mandatory 20 years in public service, such as in the Zussael militia. They tend to live to 300 years or beyond.

Male Names: Andreas, Carras, Gero, Hatzis, Kyrill, Myles, Panagi, Stevano, Xanthus.

Female Names: Burou, Dianthe, Elissa, Io, Lilah, Nasica, Rhea, Tabith, Voleta.

Subclasses

The fey provide an array of unique qualities and perspectives for creating interesting new characters. Consult your GM before applying these subclasses to other races.

Child of Moaro
(Sorcerer: Sorcerous Origin)

When Moaro became the monster she is now, deformed by the ancient spirit magic of your distant darkling past, a connection was also opened for others. You too have felt the intrusion of the shadowy spirits. Though you were not corrupted to the extent Moaro was, you find you can tap into that power, molding it to perform feats of magic. You are of the Children of Moaro, and you are held at a distance from civilized darkling society.

Dark Infestation

Starting at 1st level, you know the languages Abyssal and Infernal. Additionally, you know *chill touch*. It doesn't count against your number of sorcerer cantrips known.

DEATHLESSNESS

Also at 1st level, when damage would reduce you to 0 hit points but not kill you outright, you can use your reaction to make a Constitution saving throw. The save DC is 10 or half the damage dealt, whichever is higher. On a success, you are instead reduced to 1 hit point. Once you use this feature, you can't use it again until you finish a short or long rest.

TOUCH OF DARKNESS

At 6th level, when you cast a spell that deals acid, cold, fire, lightning, necrotic, or thunder damage, you can spend 1 sorcery point to change the damage type to cold or necrotic instead. Additionally, whenever you cast a spell that deals cold or necrotic damage, either as a result of this feature or because the spell normally does so, that spell deals additional cold or necrotic damage equal to your Charisma modifier (minimum 1).

When you cast any spell that deals cold or necrotic damage, you also gain resistance to that type of damage for 1 minute.

FROZEN TRANSPOSITION

At 14th level, you gain the ability to switch places with a target of your spells. When you deal cold damage to a creature within 60 feet, you can use a bonus action and spend 2 sorcery points to switch places with the target. The target is restrained by ice in your previous location until the end of its next turn. The ice can be broken as an action.

CLOAK OF HORROR

Starting at 18th level, you can don a cloak of horror as a bonus action by spending 4 sorcery points. This cloak lasts for 1 minute or until you fall unconscious. An enemy that starts its turn within 5 feet of you must make a Wisdom saving throw against your spell save DC. On a failed save, the enemy takes 4d10 psychic damage and becomes frightened until the cloak disappears. On a successful save, it takes half as much damage and is not frightened. At the end of each turn, the enemy makes a new Wisdom saving throw. On a success, the frightened condition ends for that creature, and it is immune to your cloak for 1 hour.

DESOLATE SCAVENGER (WIZARD: ARCANE TRADITION)

The Plains of Desolation are fraught with danger, but to an enterprising mage like yourself, they are also experimental playgrounds, tying shadow into magical energy. Most desolate scavengers are darklings.

SHADOW AFFINITY

Beginning when you select this arcane tradition at 2nd level, you learn the *minor illusion* cantrip. If you already know this cantrip, you learn a different wizard cantrip of your choosing. The cantrip doesn't count against your number of cantrips known.

CONSUME SHADOW

When you choose this school at 2nd level, you gain the ability to consume a creature's shadow. As an action, you may attempt to consume the shadow of a creature you can see within 30 feet of you. The creature must succeed on a Charisma saving throw against your spell save DC or have its shadow devoured. If the creature fails on this saving throw, you consume its shadow. You gain a number of temporary hit points equal to 5 + half of your wizard level. On each of your turns, while the target's shadow is consumed, you can use a bonus action to prevent the creature from taking a reaction until the start of your next turn. The creature's shadow returns after the creature finishes a long rest. A creature that succeeds on its saving throw cannot be affected by Consume Shadow until after you finish a long rest.

SHAPE SHADOW

At 6th level, you gain proficiency with two sets of artisan's tools of your choice. You can use an action to create an inanimate object that you could create with any artisan's tools you are proficient with—but made of shadow. This object can be no larger than 3 feet on a side and weigh no more than 10 pounds, and its form must be that of a nonmagical object that you have seen.

The object disappears after 1 hour, when you use this feature again, or if it takes or deals any damage. If the object is exposed to bright light, it fades away after 1 round.

DARK ILLUSIONS

Also starting at 6th level, Intelligence checks made to recognize your illusion spells in dim light or darkness are made with disadvantage. Likewise, creatures in dim light or darkness have disadvantage on saving throws against your illusion spells and against your Consume Shadow feature.

SHADOW BOLT

At 10th level, you gain a new attack option that can be used with the Attack action or as a bonus action. This attack is a ranged spell attack with a range of 120 feet. You use your wizard spell attack bonus. Its damage is 1d10 + your Intelligence modifier, and its damage type is cold or necrotic, which you choose when you make the attack. You have advantage on Shadow Bolt attacks against creatures whose shadow you have consumed with your Consume Shadow ability.

SHADOW DOMINANCE

Starting at 14th level, a creature whose shadow you have consumed with your Consume Shadow feature has disadvantage on the saving throws of any spells you have cast that require it to make a saving throw, and you have advantage on spell attack rolls against that creature.

OATH OF THE PEACEKEEPER (PALADIN: SACRED OATH)

Peacekeepers comprise the elite police force of the darkling world. You conquer and harness the unquiet forces churning within you, using that energy to bring calm to the world. An exemplar of the grand matriarch's law and order, you and your fellow peacekeepers ensure the terrible echoes of the former darkling world are muted.

TENETS OF PEACEKEEPER

Though the exact words and strictures of the Oath of Peacekeeper vary, paladins of this oath share these tenets.

Restraint. First, remain peaceful yourself, except when reason fails. Even in action, avoid unnecessary upset or emotional outbursts.

Boldness. Those who willingly break the law threaten to unleash the Curse and destroy all that remains of darkling society. There is no time for hesitancy when confronting them.

Pragmatism. Emotional attachments can get in the way of the painful actions necessary to keep chaos from destroying Zussael. Always keep the big picture in mind, even if it demands small, distasteful deeds.

Duty. Be responsible for your actions and their consequences, protect those entrusted to your care, and obey those who have just authority over you.

OATH SPELLS

You are granted the following oath spells.

OATH OF THE PEACEKEEPER SPELLS

Paladin Level	Spells
3rd	*protection from evil and good, sanctuary*
5th	*see invisibility, zone of truth*
9th	*nondetection, phantom steed*
13th	*dimension door, locate creature*
17th	*dominate person, hold monster*

CHANNEL DIVINITY

When you take this oath at 3rd level, you gain the following two Channel Divinity options.

Shadow Weapon. As a bonus action, you can summon a weapon made of pure shadow. This weapon can take the form of any martial melee weapon that you are proficient with. For 1 minute, you can wield this weapon, adding your Charisma modifier to damage rolls made with that weapon (with a minimum bonus of +1). This weapon counts as a magical weapon for the purpose of affecting creatures immune or resistant to nonmagical weapons.

If you are wielding a physical weapon, you can also summon your shadow weapon around it, adding the shadow weapon abilities to the properties of the physical weapon. You can't alter the physical form of a weapon this way.

You can also use a spell slot to power this Channel Divinity option. You expend a spell slot to summon your shadow weapon for 1 minute per level of the spell slot used.

Keep the Peace. As an action, you exude an aura of peace and lawfulness. All creatures of your choice that you can see with 30 feet of you must make a Charisma saving throw. On a failed save, a creature becomes incapacitated for 1 minute. A creature attempts another Charisma saving throw at the end of each of its turns to break the effect. If a creature or its allies are attacked or take damage, the effect automatically ends.

AURA OF CALM

Starting at 7th level, your calming presence gives succor to your allies. When an undamaged ally within 10 feet of you is damaged, they gain temporary hit points equal to half your paladin level. At 18th level, the range of this aura increases to 30 feet.

SHADOW SMITE

Starting at 15th level, when you use Divine Smite and Improved Divine Smite while wielding your shadow weapon, use d10s instead of d8s for the additional smite damage.

SHADOW SENTINEL

At 20th level, you can assume the form of a shadow guardian of your realm. You can use your action to gain the following benefits for 1 hour:

- You can teleport to an unoccupied space you can see by spending an amount of your movement equal to the straight-line distance.
- You gain truesight out to 90 feet. You can see in normal and magical darkness, see invisible creatures and objects, detect visual illusions and succeed on saving throws against them, and know the original form of a shapechanger or a creature transformed by magic.

Once you use this feature, you can't use it again until you finish a long rest.

PATH OF SHADOW

(BARBARIAN: PRIMAL PATH)

Darklings that follow the Path of the Shadow Warrior explore the relationship between intense emotions and shadow, which some believe leads to the very edge of the Curse. You use you emotions to fuel your battle prowess but must hide your feelings or risk discovery by the Hidden Blades. Foes find you disquieting in combat since you appear as pure darkness and make little sound. Although other creatures learn this wisdom, the prolonged exposure to Shadow that is required makes the path almost unheard of among most other races.

DECEPTIVE APPEARANCE

When you select this path at 3rd level, you gain proficiency in the Stealth and Deception skills. If you already have proficiency in either of these skills, instead you gain proficiency in another skill from the barbarian list. Additionally, you have advantage on Charisma (Deception) checks to hide your emotions.

SHADOW'S CHILL

Beginning at 3rd level, your shadow envelopes you and your equipment when you rage, shrouding your features in darkness and offering you additional power. You do not cast a shadow, and you are not recognizable by sight when you rage. While raging, the first creature you hit on each of your turns with a melee weapon attack takes extra damage equal to half your barbarian level. Each time, you can choose for this extra damage to be cold or necrotic damage.

SHADOWY WARD

At 6th level, your shadow offers you protection, and you can share this protection with allies. While raging, you gain resistance to all damage, except fire, lightning, and radiant damage, and you gain immunity to necrotic damage. Also while raging, you can use your reaction to grant another creature you can see within 30 feet of you resistance to necrotic damage until the beginning of your next turn.

CHARGE THROUGH SHADOWS

At 10th level, you can charge through the shadows to attack your foes. When raging in dim light or darkness, as a bonus action, you can teleport up to 60 feet to the closest unoccupied space adjacent to a foe you can see. The foe must be one beyond your reach. You have advantage on the first melee attack you make against that foe before the end of the turn.

Additionally, you have resistance to necrotic damage even when not raging.

SHADOWS' VENGEANCE

Starting at 14th level, when you take damage from a creature that is within 5 feet of you, you can use your reaction to cause the creature to be blinded until the beginning of that creature's next turn. At the start of your next turn, the creature makes a Constitution saving throw (DC 8 + your proficiency bonus + your Charisma modifier). On a success, the blinded condition ends on it.

SHIMMERLING
(RANGER: RANGER ARCHETYPE)

Many darklings forge bonds with the enigmatic shimmer dogs of Zussael, but some bonds run deeper. You have developed a deep friendship with a shimmer dog, enjoying a freedom of emotion unknown to most darklings, and your shimmer dog companion also becomes stronger with the partnership.

SHIMMER DOG COMPANION

At 3rd level, you and a young shimmer dog form a permanent empathic link (use the challenge rating 1/2 version of the shimmer dog below). Your companion has their own agency and motivations, but the bond only forms between two that have the same alignment, are otherwise compatible, and have similar goals.

Your companion gains proficiency in all saving throws and proficiency in two skills of your choice that you are proficient in. Their proficiency bonus is +2 and increases by 1 at 5th level in this class and every four levels thereafter. Your shimmer dog companion gains a Hit Die each time you gain a level beyond 3rd, increasing their hit points. Your companion acts on your initiative. Like any creature, they can spend Hit Dice during a short rest to regain hit points. When you gain the Ability Score Improvement class feature, your companion's ability scores can increase in the same manner and with the same restrictions. These benefits persist through each of your companion's forms.

You receive the benefits of your companion's empathic link. Your shimmer dog companion can no longer form an empathic link with another creature while you are bonded in this manner.

If the shimmer dog dies, your connection allows you to bring them back to life as long as the body is intact. Spending a short rest and 1 Hit Die to share your life force with them, reviving them with 1 hit point. If the shimmer dog is dead and the body not intact, you can spend a long rest communing with the spirits to return your companion to life with full hit points.

YOUNG SHIMMER DOG

Small fey (shapechanger), any alignment

Armor Class 13
Hit Points 18 (4d6 + 4)
Speed 30 ft.

STR	DEX	CON	INT	WIS	CHA
12 (+1)	16 (+3)	13 (+1)	12 (+1)	10 (+0)	10 (+0)

Saving Throws Dex +5
Skills Acrobatics +5, Stealth +5
Senses darkvision 90 ft., passive Perception 10
Languages understands Common and Sylvan but can't speak
Challenge 1/2 (100 XP)

Keen Hearing and Smell. The young shimmer dog has advantage on Wisdom (Perception) checks that rely on hearing or smell.

Shapechanger. The young shimmer dog has three forms—humanoid, animal, and a hybrid—and they can polymorph between forms as a bonus action. Their statistics are the same in each form. Any equipment they are wearing or carrying isn't transformed if they polymorph between humanoid and hybrid form but can be absorbed or borne by the new form if they polymorph between animal form and either human form or hybrid form. They revert to their animal form if they die.

ACTIONS

Bite. *Melee Weapon Attack:* +5 to hit, reach 5 ft., one target. *Hit:* 6 (1d6 + 3) piercing damage. If the target is a creature, it must succeed on a DC 11 Strength saving throw or be knocked prone.

Empathic Link (1/Day). The shimmer dog chooses another shimmer dog or darkling they can see, establishing an empathic link with the chosen creature that allows them to track the creature's emotional state. If the linked creature is a darkling, they have advantage on saving throws to resist the darkling curse. If the darkling is transformed into a darkling beast as a result of the curse, the empathic link survives, and the shimmer dog can use it to influence the darkling beast's emotional state, as the GM determines. The empathic link can be renewed for the same creature or switched to another creature when the shimmer dog finishes a long rest.

PROTECTIVE BOND

Beginning at 7th level, your shimmer dog companion gains the Pack Tactics trait of the shimmer dog. Your companion gains resistance to cold damage, and you lose your vulnerability to radiant damage. (For shimmer dog traits, see *Along the Twisting Way: The Faerie Ring Campaign Guide.*)

MAGICAL BOND

Starting at 11th level, your shimmer dog companion adds their proficiency bonus to their weapon damage rolls and gains the Luminescence and War Shadow abilities of the shimmer dog. Once your companion has used its War Shadow, it must finish a short or long rest before it is able to use it again. The War Shadow's save DC is equal to your spell save DC.

You gain the ability to cast *calm emotions* once without expending a spell slot. You regain the use of this spell when you finish a long rest.

PERFECTED BOND

Beginning at 15th level, your shimmer dog companion gains resistance to bludgeoning, piercing, and slashing from nonmagical attacks not made with silvered weapons.

If you and your companion are each within 5 feet of the same foe, your companion can use their reaction to hamper that enemy's attack when you are hit, causing it to deal half damage against you. You can similarly use your reaction to hamper that enemy's attack against your companion.

You gain the ability to use your companion's War Shadow ability. Once you have used it, you must take a short or long rest before you are able to use it again.

WAY OF TWILIGHT
(MONK: MONASTIC TRADITION)

To steel themselves against the temptations of the spirits, some darklings apply their natural self-discipline to monastic training. You learn to make peace with your shadows, using them against the darkness. Due to the culture and isolation of these monks, few non-darklings are taught these techniques, but twilight monks of other races are not unknown.

SHADOW TECHNIQUE

Starting when you choose this tradition at 3rd level, you can use your shadow to attack your opponent when you spend ki. You can designate one of the attacks from your Flurry of Blows as a shadow attack. A shadow attack counts as magical for the purpose of overcoming resistance and immunity to nonmagical attacks and damage. You can additionally impose one of the following effects on that target:

- It cannot take reactions until the end of your next turn.
- It must succeed on a Constitution saving throw, or its speed becomes 0 until the end of your next turn.
- It must succeed on a Wisdom saving throw, or it has disadvantage on Dexterity saving throws, and opportunity attacks against it have advantage until the end of your next turn.

SHADOW BOXING

At 6th level, you learn to impair your opponents by attacking their shadows. Once on each of your turns, when you hit a creature with an attack, you can spend 1 ki point to attack the target's shadow. A creature such as a vampire that casts no shadow is immune to this feature. The damage dealt by attacking the target's shadow is either cold or necrotic (your choice) instead of its usual type, which you can choose at the time of the attack. You can impose one of the following effects:

- The target must succeed on a Constitution saving

throw, or its level of exhaustion increases by one step. At the end of the target's next turn, it can make another Constitution saving throw, losing that level of exhaustion on a success.

- The target must succeed on a Wisdom saving throw, or it is frightened until the end of your next turn.
- The target must succeed on a Dexterity saving throw, or it is restrained until the end of your next turn.

REACHING SHADOW

At 11th level, when you take the Attack action, you can use your shadow to extend your attacks with unarmed strikes and monk weapons. You can spend 1 ki point to have your reach extend by 5 feet or 3 ki points to have your reach extend by 10 feet until the beginning of your next turn.

HARRYING SHADOW

At 17th level, you can use a bonus action to stretch your shadow to distract and harry an enemy within 30 feet until the start of your next turn. Attacks against that enemy have advantage.

BACKGROUNDS

The following backgrounds are especially common in darklings. At the GM's discretion, other appropriate races may have access to them.

CORRUPTED SOUL

Perhaps you were possessed by a demon once, and some fragment of that unclean spirit lies dormant within you still. A nexus of pure evil might have tainted you in the womb, or your distant ancestors could have traded the purity of their descendants for a quick path to power. Whatever its source, your soul is twisted now around a shard of darkness.

As a corrupted soul, the darkness in your nature need not dominate you, but it colors all that you are and do. Those around you eventually become aware that something is wrong with you, and your relationships can become strained. You might find yourself a pariah, striking out on your own. Or you might learn to disguise your secret nature, guarding the truth carefully even as you refuse to embrace the darkness within you.

Skill Proficiencies: Deception and one of Arcana, History, or Religion

Tool Proficiencies: Disguise kit

Languages: Choose one of Abyssal, Deep Speech, Draconic, Infernal, or Undercommon

Equipment: A disguise kit, a set of traveler's clothes, a holy symbol or other badge of a society or organization, and a pouch containing 10 gp

FEATURE: CONCEALED CORRUPTION

The concealed nature of a corrupted soul's inherent darkness allows you to subvert taboos without immediate reprisal. Once per adventure or during downtime, you can ignore one restriction or taboo related to a class, organization, or culture to which you belong without any consequences. For example, a paladin corrupted soul could undertake one act outside their oath without being in violation of it, a cleric could commit blasphemy with no direct repercussions, or a druid could use a metal shield for a short time.

If someone from the relevant class, organization, or culture witnesses your transgression, this immunity crumbles. You might still avoid direct penalties for the action (such as a paladin retaining their paladin status and features), but censure from the organization might follow at the GM's determination. Depending on the organization and the transgression, penalties might range from penance to incarceration or expulsion or even a death sentence. Work with your GM to determine what organization's taboos you can subvert and what the penalties for doing so might entail.

SUGGESTED CHARACTERISTICS

Corrupted souls often bear some mark of their inner darkness. Sometimes that mark is physical, but it more commonly manifests as behavior. Paranoia, mistrust, fear of outsiders, and an insular nature are common among corrupted souls. Conversely, some corrupted souls wear a mask of righteousness, whether to disguise their true evil or to aggressively hold that evil at bay.

d8	Personality Trait
1	I hang on what people say and sometimes read too much into their choice of words.
2	I feel at home in dark places others would shun, such as deep caves and catacombs.
3	Representatives of churches and temples make me uneasy.
4	Rituals of all kinds fascinate me for reasons I don't understand.
5	I find myself most comfortable around people like me—outsiders who live on the fringe.
6	Strangers make me uneasy. Anyone could be hunting me.
7	I say little, but I watch constantly.
8	I always have a quick excuse at the ready.

d6	Ideal
1	Redemption. I want my destiny to be my own, so I'll find a way to rise above my nature. (Any)
2	Service. I know better than most that good only thrives when people choose to do what is right, despite what stands in the way. (Good)
3	Wanderlust. I must keep moving. Staying in one place too long draws too much attention. (Chaotic)
4	Loyalty. Salvation lies in finding people you can trust. (Neutral)
5	Entitlement. I carry a legacy of power, and I will have my due. (Evil)
6	Duty. Because it's so easy for me to break commitments, they are that much more important to uphold. (Lawful)

d6	Bond
1	There's a secret locked away that explains my dark nature, and I'll stop at nothing to find it.
2	I love to subvert the laws and codes I'm supposed to uphold and will do so whenever I can get away with it.
3	I'm desperate to purge the evil from my being and will do nearly anything to accomplish this end.
4	My greatest desire is to gain control over the corrupted power within me.
5	Anyone I trust enough to share my secret with becomes worthy of protection at all costs.
6	A magical site or relic created the corruption within me, and I know that one day I'll have to return to it.

d6	Flaw
1	Someone from my past knows the truth of my nature, and they're hunting me.
2	My body is marked with a physical brand that reveals the evil within me.
3	My corruption sets me at odds with someone I care about, no matter how I try to make amends.
4	I lose track of time sometimes and find I've been doing things I don't remember. Other times, I speak in languages I don't understand.
5	I have a hunger to consume some unnatural substance (blood, flesh, grave-dug earth, and so on) that's difficult to ignore.
6	I have no problem letting others pay the price for what I've done . . . and it's happened before.

SOLDIER OF ZUSSAEL

You serve (or once served) in the military forces of the darkling grand matriarch. In your time, you helped protect Zussael from the beasts that are the product of the darkling curse, as well as external threats. If not still ongoing, your service might have ended honorably or otherwise, and you might have served in any number of capacities. However, all soldiers of Zussael share a number of common points of training and outlook.

Skill Proficiencies: Insight, Intimidation

Equipment: Manacles, a chain, a lock, a signal whistle, a set of common clothes, and a belt pouch containing 10 gp

FEATURE: COMMAND PRESENCE

Your training and experience as a soldier of the grand matriarch has made projecting authority as instinctive and automatic as breathing. Any Charisma (Intimidation) or Charisma (Persuasion) check you make against another darkling is made with advantage.

SUGGESTED CHARACTERISTICS

The soldiers of Zussael share a dedication to service and duty that makes them stalwart warriors and staunch allies—but many expect their allegiance and camaraderie to be rewarded by fealty rather than true friendship. Whether their commitment to their city is a thing of the past or an ongoing duty, all soldiers of Zussael are marked by their service and by the darkness that service has exposed them to.

d8	Personality Trait
1	My face is like a mask, and I am considered cold even by my fellow darklings.
2	I am haunted by the memory of hunting down a family member who succumbed to the curse.
3	I do my duty with courtesy and good humor and see no point in being gloomy.
4	I take my time when making my mind up about someone. And once I do, I rarely change my opinion.
5	I live for excitement and danger and often struggle to conceal that passion.
6	I do not speak the names of those turned by the darkling curse once they are gone.
7	Past battles haunt me, and I am constantly alert no matter where I am or what I'm doing.
8	I am known among my fellows for my dark humor.

d6	Ideal
1	Protection. I live to protect my people—even from themselves when necessary. (Good)
2	Vigilance. I keep watch even on the behavior of my superior officers, and they know it. No one is above suspicion. (Lawful)
3	Fearlessness. My penchant for derring-do is seen as both a blessing and a curse by my comrades. (Chaotic)
4	Initiative. When my suspicions are roused, I act. It is better to be safe than sorry, even if my comrades don't always admire my zeal. (Evil)
5	Independence. I do my job as dispassionately as I possibly can, favoring no one. (Neutral)
6	Misgiving. I am constantly distracted by thoughts of the families of those I have driven from the city and the knowledge that they may hate me for what I am. (Any)

d6	Bond
1	I will not hesitate to lay down my life to protect the defenseless.
2	My fellow soldiers can call on me whenever the need arises.
3	My true love remains in Zussael and has my pledge of protection.
4	I know that some of the darklings I have driven out of Zussael did not succumb to the darkling curse, and I will make amends to them one day.
5	I obey any lawful order from a superior officer, even after leaving my soldiering days behind.
6	I bear a secret that could lead to the ruin of my home.

d6	Flaw
1	I become preoccupied with the emotional outbursts of my companions and will watch them closely for days afterward.
2	On occasion, I notice some physical characteristic or mannerism in my enemies that reminds me of a loved one, making it almost impossible for me to strike them.
3	I never forget an insult and will not let it go until my pride is avenged.
4	The playful excesses of other fey drive me into a fury.
5	I cannot pass up an opportunity for a practical joke, regardless of the situation.
6	I often wake in a cold sweat after dreaming that the darkling curse has turned me.

ADDITIONAL OPTIONS

The following options are available to darklings. At the GM's discretion, other appropriate races may have access to some of these new rules.

EQUIPMENT

Darklings have developed the following equipment according to their specific needs and utilize them to particular effect.

Darklight. This oily substance is made from peat dredged from mires within the Shadow Plane and refined into smooth, black grease. Darklight is usually carried in small metal tins. As an action, you can daub darklight over the sides of a lantern or other solid, light-radiating vessel and reduce its light radius. Each daub reduces the light radius of the item by 10 feet until it emanates no light at all. One tin has enough darklight to reduce 100 feet of light radius. Despite its greasy appearance, darklight is difficult to ignite.

Darkling Warning Cloth. This fabric, traditionally for girdles but also used in robes and cloaks, includes alchemically resonant silver thread. This thread shrinks tangibly when unpredictable magic or spirits are active nearby. Whenever the wearer is within 30 feet of either a conjuration, evocation, necromancy, or transmutation spell or a celestial, elemental, fey, fiend, or undead creature of a kind that wasn't present the previous round, the wearer can feel it subtly shift. The pattern of reacting threads can be examined as an action to determine which school of magic or type of creature caused it with a successful DC 13 Intelligence (Arcana) check. The cloth doesn't react if a trigger is obscured by a solid object, but it does react to unseen and ethereal creatures and spells. A set of clothing made from darkling warning cloth costs 750 gp more than normal.

Shimmering Tea. Made from specially cultivated herbs and flowers growing in Zussael's gardens, this purple tea has a faint, sparkling sheen to it when brewed. The tea is highly valued among darklings for its calming properties and its use in the emotion training of darkling youth. If you are a darkling, you can brew and drink shimmering tea in a process that takes 10 minutes to gain advantage on saving throws against spells and effects that would give you the charmed or frightened condition (or that have already given you that condition). The tea's effect lasts for 1 hour.

Spirit Paper. These papers are highly illegal in Zussael, and possession of them is cause for banishment or death. No two are exactly the same: some appear torn from an ancient book while others are fresh scribbles on torn paper. The contents differ as well with some discussing historical events of unknown origin and others the lineages of forgotten families or maps of places no one remembers existing. All have notes written on them that are arcane shorthand to reach specific spirits.

While you are able to read and reference a spirit paper, you have a +2 bonus on any ability check related to learning about, conjuring, contacting, negotiating with, or controlling a specific celestial, elemental, fey, fiend, or undead detailed in the paper. The bonus also applies to the save DC of spells you cast related to the aforementioned. When you cast a spell such as *conjure fey* that could conjure the named individual but which isn't guaranteed to, you can make an ability check using your spellcasting ability to ensure you reach that specific spirit. The spirit paper bonus applies to this check. The DC is determined by the GM, but unless the spirit is unusually hard to contact, it is typically equal to 10 + half the creature's challenge rating. The spirit must otherwise be a suitable target for the spell, abiding by challenge rating limits, creature type restrictions, or other limitations.

In addition, you also gain a +1 bonus on saving throws against the spells and abilities of that spirit while you possess the paper. A spirit paper's price depends upon the prominence of the spirit it details: minor (challenge rating 2 or lower), lesser (challenge rating 3–6), major (challenge rating 7–10), or greater (challenge rating 11 or higher).

DARKLING EQUIPMENT

Item	Cost	Weight
Darklight	10 gp	1/2 lb.
Darkling warning cloth	+750 gp	—
Shimmering tea (serving)	10 gp	—
Spirit paper, minor	200 gp	—
Spirit paper, lesser	500 gp	—
Spirit paper, major	1,100 gp	—
Spirit paper, greater	2,500 gp	—

FEATS

Darklings have evolved a style all their own and are quite fond of the following feats.

DARKLING SKIRMISHER

Prerequisite: Darkling

You have become a capable close-quarters combatant. You gain the following benefits:

- You can make unarmed strikes with your horns and hooves. These attacks use your Strength modifier and deal 1d4 piercing damage (horns) or 1d4 bludgeoning damage (hooves).
- Whenever you hit a creature with an unarmed strike from your horns, you can force it to make a Strength saving throw (DC 8 + your proficiency bonus + your Strength modifier). On a failed save, the creature is knocked prone.
- Whenever you make an unarmed strike with your hooves against a prone creature, you don't provoke opportunity attacks from that creature for the rest of the turn, whether you hit or not.

FRIEND OF THE LIGHT

Prerequisite: Darkling

Your sensitivity to light is less daunting than that of most darklings. You do not have the Light Sensitivity racial trait, and your Wisdom increases by +1.

SHADOWRIDER

Prerequisite: Darkling

While in dim or dark conditions, you can cast the *misty step* spell. Once you cast it, you must finish a long rest before you can cast it again. Choose either Intelligence, Wisdom, or Charisma as your spellcasting ability for this spell.

SPIRITCALLER

Prerequisite: Darkling

Whether willingly or not, you break the darklings' greatest taboo—you commune with spirits. You gain the following benefits:

- Increase your Charisma score by 1, to a maximum of 20.
- You have advantage on Charisma saving throws to avoid being possessed.
- You can add your Charisma modifier to any Intelligence checks.

SPIRITWALKER

Prerequisite: Darkling; the ability to cast at least one spell

Heedless of the supposed "risks," you welcome spirits into your life, quietly calling them to exert their influence. You gain the following benefits:

- If a hostile creature moves to within 5 feet of you, you can use your reaction to move 5 feet without provoking opportunity attacks.
- If you are caught by surprise, you can use your reaction to add your Charisma modifier to your AC until the start of your next turn.
- If you succumb to an effect that allows you to repeat a Wisdom saving throw to end that effect, you have advantage on the saving throw.

Far Darrig

Oh, your sword*! I thought you were saying you were* bored*. Anyway, yes, got it right here! Even sharpened and polished it up for you real nice . . . and don't look at me like that! I am insulted you'd imply with your stinky eyes that I'd ever put all of our lives in peril, during a pivotal battle against a dire foe, all for the sake of a theoretically hilarious prank!*

—Wink Stubbins

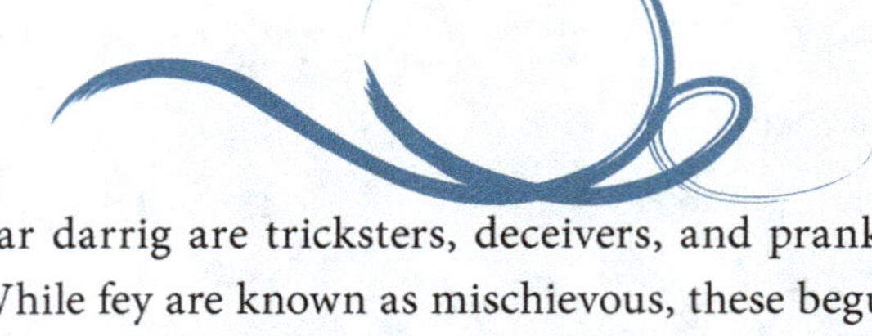

Far darrig are tricksters, deceivers, and pranksters. While fey are known as mischievous, these beguiling folk's acts of deception and fraud put other fey to shame. Guile and trickery are like music to the far darrig, and they love to dance. Even the most benevolent of them is not above pulling practical jokes on friends or strangers for amusement.

Physical Description: Standing around 3-1/2 feet tall, far darrig are spindly of frame and long of limb. Their fingers and toes are long and graceful. Their faces are sharp and angular, ranging from aquiline to rodent-like, and their ears rise to slender points. They are quick to smile, showing long, perfect white teeth. Far darrig complexion always has a red cast to it, usually quite pale though, which lends to their moniker of the "red folk," but their eye color runs the typical range, plus the odd outlier such as violet and gold. Though their hair runs a gamut of colors, red is the most common. A far darrig is never seen without its tall, round-brimmed hat, which is always red.

Society: Within the courts of the fey, the far darrig are common, though they are not always welcome. Many far darrig may pay lip service to the laws of the fey courts, taking chances that skirt as close to the line as possible without drawing the wrath of their sovereigns. This makes them equal parts entertaining and exasperating. Still, many far darrig feel great loyalty to their courts and clans. While they may tease and prank at others' expense, they are protective of kith and kin.

Far darrig tend to be loners but at times come together to feast and drink and outdo one another with boasts and tales of the wild pranks they've played.

Relations: Far darrig get along well with gnomes. They harbor feelings of kinship for their lost cousins but feel pity for their fading from the fey. Elves are looked upon favorably and respected for their grace and magical abilities; half-elves are treated as elves but with more caution due to the taint of their human blood. Far darrig are not fond of dwarves, finding them stiff, stodgy, and ripe targets for their pranks. Half-orcs are also viewed as easy targets with their quick tempers and often slow wits making them easy targets for trickery. Halflings are often considered friends by far darrig, who are taken by their charm and hospitality, and far darrig often form mutually beneficial relationships with halfling neighbors. Their relations with humans are complex. Humans have a great deal of variability, and a far darrig finds that unpredictability vexing. They often pull their pranks and tricks on humans simply to determine what sort of individual they're dealing with before making proper introductions. As for the black hats, far darrig look upon those lost brethren with equal parts disdain and sorrow.

Alignment and Religion: With their predisposition toward trickery and deceit, most far darrig are of chaotic alignment. Lawful far darrig are rare and typically serve a charismatic sovereign. These lawful or less chaotic far darrig abide by the rules of their court, unleashing their wit and wiles only on enemies or those outside the fey ranks. Far darrig are quite obsessive about their jokes, and their pranks can be cruel at times, but they rarely cause serious injury or death, even among humanoids, whom most fey deem lesser beings. Neutrality and goodness are both paths the far darrig walk with the former trotted with greater frequency than the latter. True evil among these fey is rare as they know the fates of those walking the dark paths.

Adventurers: Given their knavish natures and willingness to risk much for their pranks, it is no wonder that many far darrig end up adventuring. Their magical talents make them excellent arcane spellcasters, and a fair amount delve into the more obscure realms of magical and psychical practice. Their

FAR DARRIG TRAITS

Far darrig characters possess an assortment of traits all their own.

- ***Ability Score Increase.*** Your Charisma score increases by 2, and your Constitution score increases by 1.
- ***Languages.*** You can speak, read, and write Common and Sylvan.
- ***Size.*** Far darrig stand between 3 and 4 feet tall and average nearly 40 pounds. Your size is Small.
- ***Speed.*** Your base walking speed is 25 ft.
- ***Type.*** Your type is fey. Spells and effects that specifically target humanoids do not affect you. You also gain the gnomekin subtype (see **Appendix**).

- ***Darkvision.*** Accustomed to sneaking through the shadowy corners of the world, you have superior vision in dim and dark conditions. You can see in dim light within 60 feet of you as if it were bright light and in darkness as if it were dim light. You can't discern color in darkness, only shades of gray.
- ***Gnomekin Magic.*** You can cast the *enlarge/reduce* spell once per day without expending a spell slot but only to enlarge yourself. You increase in size up to two steps to a maximum of Large (which doesn't otherwise alter the spell's effects).
- ***Illusion Resistance.*** You have advantage on saving throws against illusions and ability checks made to detect them.
- ***Illusory Instinct.*** You know the *minor illusion* cantrip. When you reach 3rd level, you can cast the *disguise self* spell once with this trait and regain the ability to do so when you finish a long rest. Charisma is your spellcasting ability for these spells.
- ***Magic Hat.*** You possess a special red hat that you created and which maintains your connection to your magic. You can use your hat as a spellcasting focus even if your spellcasting class doesn't normally have access to that feature. If you lose your hat, you can't use your Illusory Instinct trait or cast any illusion spells until you retrieve it or create a new one. Creating a new hat requires one month of work and 50 gp.

  Once per day as an action while you wear your hat, you can cause it to display psychedelic colors. Each creature that can see the hat must succeed on a Wisdom saving throw against DC 8 + your Charisma modifier + your proficiency bonus or be charmed by you until the start of your next turn. While charmed, it can't move and is incapacitated.

  As long as you don't have your hat, other far darrig "disbelieve" you, ignoring you as if you don't exist.
- ***Supernatural Ally.*** Once per day as an action, you can magically pull a beast out of your hat into an unoccupied space within 5 feet as if you had cast *conjure animals*. You can conjure only one beast, and its challenge rating can't exceed one-third your level.

size and stealthy nature make them excellent rogues. They have a natural knack for storytelling and bravado, which often leads them to become bards.

Age: Far darrig mature at a similar rate to gnomes, reaching adulthood at 40. They can live to a fantastically old age with the oldest among them claiming to have seen the passage of millennia.

Female Names: Dulcina, Gelsey, Jigs, Nissa, Sebille, Zanna.

Male Names: Branduff, Carbry, Duffy, Eflann, Oddwig, Wix.

SUBCLASSES

The fey provide an array of unique qualities and perspectives for creating interesting new characters. Consult your GM before applying these subclasses to other races.

COLLEGE OF THE PIPER (BARD: BARD COLLEGE)

You possess a beguiling power over the minds of beasts, and the secrets of your songs are guarded closely by the far darrig of your college, who have a particular fondness for charming rats.

Legend holds that a human woodsman tricked the far darrig pipers into revealing to him their enchanting songs and brought this secret back with him to his homeland, offering his services as a rat catcher and a beast tamer to villages afflicted by plague or threatened by roving wolves. Bards of all stripes hunted the world for the piper as his legend spread, and those who found him formed a bardic college to contain and control those fey secrets.

Some say that your people still search for the guileful piper and try to trick those who have learned your secret songs into giving up the knowledge—permanently. Others say that the piper's power over beasts could be turned against mortal minds, a thought that has turned many villainous bards to study the pipe.

BONUS PROFICIENCIES

When you join the college of the piper at 3rd level, you gain proficiency in three skills of your choice and with one wind instrument of your choice, such as a horn, a pipe, or a pan flute.

BEGUILER OF BEASTS

At 3rd level, you learn the *animal friendship*, *animal messenger*, and *enthrall* spells if you didn't already know them. They don't count against the number of bard spells you can know. If you already know one of those spells, you learn another bard spell of a level you can cast. You can cast any of these spells without expending a spell slot by expending instead one use of Bardic Inspiration and playing a wind instrument that you are proficient with for 1 minute. You can also target a swarm of beasts instead of a beast when you cast *animal friendship*. You can charm the beast or swarm even if it has immunity to the condition, but such a beast or swarm has advantage on its saving throw against your spell.

Additionally, as a bonus action, you can choose one beast or swarm of beasts charmed by you. Until either the charmed condition ends, you are no longer on the same plane of existence, or you choose another target, you have a telepathic link with the target. You can use your action to take total and precise control over the target. Until the start of your next turn, the creature takes only actions that you choose, and it doesn't do anything that you don't allow it to do. During this time, you can also cause the creature to use a reaction, but this requires you to use your own reaction as well.

CONJURER OF BEASTS

At 6th level, you learn the spell *conjure animals* if you don't already know it. It is a bard spell for you but doesn't count against the number of bard spells you know. If you already know it, you instead learn another bard spell of a level you can cast. You can cast it without expending a spell slot by expending two uses of Bardic Inspiration and playing a wind instrument that you are proficient with for 1 minute. You can conjure a swarm of beasts with *conjure animals* as a beast of its challenge rating.

SPEAKER OF THE WILD TONGUE

Also at 6th level, you gain the ability to comprehend

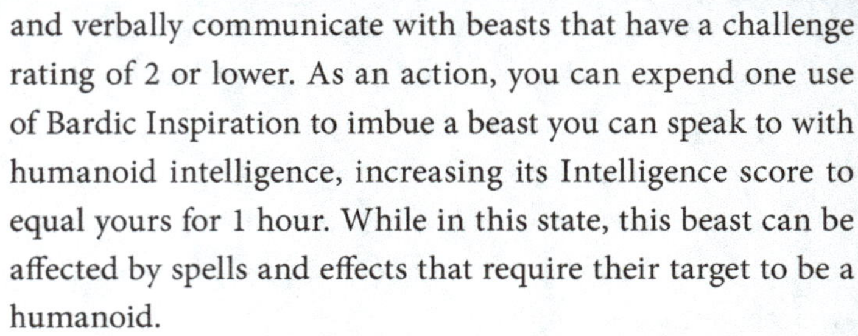

and verbally communicate with beasts that have a challenge rating of 2 or lower. As an action, you can expend one use of Bardic Inspiration to imbue a beast you can speak to with humanoid intelligence, increasing its Intelligence score to equal yours for 1 hour. While in this state, this beast can be affected by spells and effects that require their target to be a humanoid.

At 14th level, you can communicate with beasts of any challenge rating.

BEGUILER OF THE MASSES

At 14th level, you learn the spell *charm person* if you didn't already know it, and it doesn't count against your number of bard spells known. If you already know it, you instead learn another bard spell of a level you can cast. Regardless of whether you learned it from this feature, you can cast *charm person* without expending a spell slot by playing a wind instrument that you are proficient with for 1 minute. While casting the spell in this way, you can expend and roll a Bardic Inspiration die. You can cast the spell as if you had cast it using a spell slot of a level equal to the result of the die. On a result of 10 or higher, the spell affects all creatures that you can see of your choice and that can hear you within 30 feet.

Additionally, you can choose one creature charmed by you as a bonus action. Until either the charmed condition ends, you are no longer on the same plane of existence, or you choose another target, you have a telepathic link with it. You can use your action to take total and precise control over the target. Until the start of your next turn, the creature takes only actions that you choose, and doesn't do anything that you don't allow it to do. During this time, you can also cause the creature to use a reaction, but this requires you to use your own reaction as well.

GLADE GUARDIAN
(FIGHTER: MARTIAL ARCHETYPE)

The far darrig know too well that illusions and magic can't solve every problem, so the glade guardians arose to keep their settlements safe from more tangible threats. As a glade guardian, you draw upon the power of the Veil to mark an area of the world as yours, becoming a potent force for the defense of your people.

GUARDIAN'S STAND

Beginning when you choose this archetype at 3rd level, you can use a magical technique to take limited control of the Veil in an immediate area called a stand.

You use a bonus action to create your stand, which lasts for 1 minute. Your stand is a 15-foot-radius area centered on your space, which doesn't move with you once you create it. The radius of your stand increases to 20 feet at 5th level, 25 feet at 7th level, 30 feet at 10th level, 35 feet at 15th level, and 40 feet at 18th level.

While you are within your stand, you gain the following benefits:

- You have advantage on any saving throw or ability check made to resist any effect that would force you out of your stand.
- If you are charmed, frightened, or possessed by another creature or if you are subject to an effect that fails to work on creatures immune to being charmed, you can use your reaction to suppress the effect until the start of your next turn. The time suppressed counts against the duration of the condition or the effect.
- At the start of your first turn within your stand, you gain temporary hit points equal to your fighter level. These temporary hit points last until your stand ends.
- If you end your turn outside the area of your stand, your stand ends immediately.

You can use this feature twice. You regain all expended uses when you finish a short or long rest.

UNWAVERING GUARDIAN

Starting at 7th level, when a creature targets any creature or object other than you that is within your stand with an attack or a spell, you can use your reaction to force the attack or spell to target you instead. You add half your proficiency bonus to your AC against the attack or to any saving throw you make against a spell. This is in addition to any proficiency bonus you are normally allowed on the saving throw.

ONE WITH THE STAND

At 10th level, while you are within your stand, you gain blindsight with a radius of 10 feet. As a bonus action, you can magically teleport to any unoccupied space within your stand. You have advantage on the next attack roll you make during the same turn that you teleport.

DEADLY STAND

At 15th level, while you are within your stand, your weapon attacks are magical, and you add your Charisma modifier (minimum 1) to the damage of your weapon attacks.

FINAL STAND

At 18th level, if you drop to 0 hit points while within your stand, you automatically stabilize at the start of your next turn and regain 1 hit point. If an effect would cause you to die outright while within your stand, you drop to 1 hit point instead. Once you use this feature to avoid death, you can't use it again until you finish a long rest.

Additionally, while you are within your stand and you are at half your hit points or fewer or when you are within 5 feet of two or more foes but no allies, your weapon is infused with the power of the Veil and deals an extra 4d8 psychic damage. You can deal this extra damage only once per turn.

MIRAGE WALKER

(RANGER: RANGER ARCHETYPE)

Taking up the mantle of the mirage walker means confronting the deceit that enshrouds all existence. As your understanding of the Veil grows, you learn to defy its hold on you and your companions. Eventually, you can turn it against your foes, using it both as a weapon and as a shield against those who seek to do you harm.

SHIFTING MIRAGE

At 3rd level, you learn to take hold of and alter the Veil in your immediate vicinity. As an action, you cause the terrain within 15 feet of you to become one of the terrain types chosen for your Natural Explorer feature. The specific terrain within the affected area does not change, but you treat that area as if it were one of your favored terrains. This effect moves with you, and lasts for a number of hours equal to your Wisdom modifier (minimum 1).

Additionally, at 3rd, 5th, 9th, and 13th level, your growing understanding of the Veil grants you access to illusion spells. These spells count as ranger spells for you but don't count against the number of ranger spells you know.

MIRAGE WALKER SPELLS

Ranger Level	Spell
3rd	*silent image*
5th	*mirror image*
9th	*major image*
13th	*phantasmal killer*

PART THE VEIL

At 7th level, you learn to let the Veil imbue your attacks, granting an edge against your opponents. When you hit a creature with an attack, the creature takes an extra 1d8 psychic damage. You can deal this extra damage only once per turn. If a target takes psychic damage from this feature and is currently affected by one or more illusion spells, you can dispel one illusion spell of 4th level or lower on the target. If the target is affected by multiple illusions, you choose which one to dispel. Once you dispel an illusion from a target, it is immune to the dispelling portion of this feature until you finish a short rest.

MIRAGE COMMAND

At 11th level, your command over the Veil surrounding you grows stronger. Choose one of the following effects:

- You can ignore the effects of cover caused by terrain.
- If terrain causes an area to be lightly obscured or heavily obscured, you can ignore that terrain's effects on your attacks.
- You can ignore difficult terrain caused by magical manipulation of an area.

You can use this benefit only once per turn.

You can use this feature a number of times equal to your Wisdom modifier (a minimum of once). You regain all expended uses when you finish a short or long rest.

TWISTED IMAGE

At 15th level, when a creature you can see targets you with an attack, you can use your reaction to force the attacker to make a Wisdom saving throw against your ranger spell save DC. On a failed save, the attacker redirects the attack to a different target of your choice within 30 feet of you, resolving its attack against the target you chose.

A creature that succeeds on the saving throw against this feature can't be affected by it again until you finish a long rest.

OATH OF FAERIE

(PALADIN: SACRED OATH)

Although rare, some far darrig bear a strong sense of order and goodness, faithfully serving good sovereigns of Faerie and utilizing their humor and pranks to impart important moral lessons. These fey are sometimes noticed by more whimsical gods, often associated with magic or children, who make them shining lights of laughter and wonder. As a faerie knight, you still possess the far darrig love of illusion and tricks, unlike most paladins. But you use such guile only with the best of motivations and with the intention of restoring goodness.

TENETS OF THE FAERIE

The tenets of the Oath of the Faerie are in many ways less strict than those of the Oath of Devotion and the Oath of the Ancients, encouraging trickery and deception to achieve the greater good. Though the code allows faerie paladins to do as they see fit, all faerie paladins share these tenets.

Be Swift. Act quickly and decisively, but temper your speed with guile.

Be Kind. Do not deceive the innocent; save your trickery for the evils of the world.

Be Clever. Outsmart your enemies, eschewing open combat for a decisive end behind the scenes.

Be Yourself. Constant trickery can weigh on the soul. Delight in showing your true colors to your friends and companions.

OATH SPELLS

You are granted the following oath spells.

OATH OF FAERIE SPELLS

Paladin Level	Spells
3rd	*disguise self, silent image*
5th	*invisibility, mirror image*
9th	*blink, major image*
13th	*greater invisibility, hallucinatory terrain*
17th	*modify memory, seeming*

CHANNEL DIVINITY

When you take this oath at 3rd level, you gain the following two Channel Divinity options.

Humbling Prank. You can use your Channel Divinity to trick an enemy, imposing an awkward circumstance. As an action, you create an embarrassing illusory effect on a creature you can see, such as soiling the mayor's pants or causing a tyrannical king to shout out a swear word or declare his love for Oberon during a speech. The creature must succeed on a Charisma saving throw or have the illusion appear real, which imposes disadvantage on all the creature's attack rolls and Charisma checks for 1 minute. On a success, the effect is revealed as an illusion, and the creature does not have disadvantage.

Exit Stage Left. You can use your Channel Divinity to cause you and your allies to disappear in a cloud of colored smoke. As an action, you flourish dramatically, forcing each hostile creature within 30 feet of you to make a Wisdom saving throw. For each creature that fails its save, you and all allied creatures within 30 feet of you become invisible for 1 minute. An individual invisible creature becomes visible if it attacks or casts a spell. For a hostile creature that successfully saves, you and your allies are still partially hidden by the smoke, which heavily obscures the area in a 30-foot radius around you for 1 minute or until a wind of moderate or greater speed (at least 10 miles per hour) disperses it.

AURA OF SEEING

Beginning at 7th level, your familiarity with illusion magic lets you easily reveal the truth to others. You and friendly creatures within 10 feet of you automatically succeed on saving throws to see through illusions, and you all have advantage on Intelligence (Investigation) or Wisdom (Perception) checks to find secret compartments, doors, or similarly concealed objects or rooms.

BASTION OF KINDNESS

Starting at 15th level, your outward positivity and strength makes you even more resilient in the face of danger. The first time a creature attempts to attack you in combat, it must succeed on a Charisma saving throw equal to your spell save DC. On a failure, the creature cannot attack you until the start of its next turn, and you have advantage on the next Charisma (Deception) or Charisma (Persuasion) check you make against that creature.

REALMS OF ILLUSION

Beginning at 20th level, you can emanate an aura of shimmering illusion, casting doubt on everything your enemies see.

As an action, you create an illusory form as if you had cast *disguise self*, except that the form can recreate any creature no larger than a 20-foot cube. Any creature attempting to discern your true form has disadvantage on its Intelligence (Investigation) checks to do so. This form lasts for 1 minute, during which time you also radiate an aura of bright, colorful light in a 30-foot radius and gain the following benefits:

- At the start of each of your turns, you can cast *silent image* as a bonus action.
- Enemy creatures in the aura have disadvantage on Intelligence (Investigation) checks and Intelligence saving throws.
- Whenever a hostile creature fails an Intelligence (Investigation) check or an Intelligence saving throw while in the aura, that creature is stunned until the end of its next turn.

After using this feature, you must finish a long rest before you can do so again.

PHANTASM
(SORCERER: SORCEROUS ORIGIN)

The varied potential of the multiverse drifts through the planes, sometimes concentrating in special places or within individuals. You might have been trapped in a plane composed of unreal energies, such as the Shadow Plane or any of the Preternatural Planes. Or perhaps a great burst of illusion magic suffused the area where you were born, and that magic settled into your blood.

DETECT ILLUSIONS

Starting when you choose this origin at 1st level, you can use a bonus action to attempt to identify any illusion you can see. Until the start of your next turn, you automatically recognize any illusion for what it is. You don't know what caused the illusion or what its exact effects are—only that it is an illusion.

FORCE OF PERSONALITY

Starting at 1st level, when you aren't wearing armor, your AC equals 10 + your Dexterity modifier + your Charisma modifier.

Additionally, you can use your reaction to add your Charisma modifier as a bonus to a Wisdom saving throw you make. You can't use this feature again until you finish a long rest.

TENACIOUS ILLUSION

Starting at 6th level, you can bolster the effect of any illusion spell you cast. Any creature that makes a saving throw or an ability check to disbelieve or resist the illusion does so with disadvantage. You can't use this feature again until you finish a short or long rest.

UNCERTAINTY FIELD

Beginning at 14th level, you can spend 1 sorcery point as a bonus action to create a shifting field of phantom images in a 15-foot-radius area around you. The field moves with you and lasts until the start of your next turn.

Any creature you designate that enters the area for the first time on its turn or starts its turn there must make an Intelligence saving throw against your sorcerer spell save DC. On a failure, the creature loses sight of you, treating you as invisible until the start of your next turn. If the saving throw fails by 5 or more, all of the creature's allies that are also within the field appear to be you as long as you are treated as invisible. If the creature has no allies in the field, it sees an illusory image of you 10 feet from your actual location. The effects of the field end for a creature that leaves the area.

PHANTASMAL BEING

At 18th level, you have immunity to psychic damage and necrotic damage.

As a bonus action, you can spend 2 sorcery points to become shady and insubstantial until the start of your next turn. During this time, you can pass through objects and creatures as if they were difficult terrain, and you have resistance to bludgeoning, slashing, and piercing damage from nonmagical attacks. If you end your turn in a solid object, you take 5 (1d10) force damage, and you are pushed to the nearest open space at the start of your next turn.

While in this phantasmal form, you can't talk or manipulate objects, and any objects you were carrying or holding can't be dropped, used, or otherwise interacted with. You can't attack or cast spells.

As an action, you can instead use this ability on an ally you touch. If you do so, you can't use it on yourself until the start of your next turn.

RED HAT
(WARLOCK: OTHERWORLDLY PATRON)

The mystic properties of a far darrig's red hat are notorious, but not all such hats manifest their magic the same way. You have made contact with your patron inside the strange, extradimensional interior of your hat. The nature of your patron is entirely speculation, though none can deny its power.

EXPANDED SPELL LIST

The patron you make contact with inside your hat lets you choose from an expanded list of spells when you learn a warlock spell. The following spells are added to the warlock spell list for you.

RED HAT EXPANDED SPELLS

Spell Level	Spells
1st	*bane, sleep*
2nd	*blindness/deafness, silence*
3rd	*dispel magic, slow*
4th	*arcane eye, freedom of movement*
5th	*modify memory, wall of force*

WARLOCK'S HAT

Your red hat functions as a hat as well as a small extradimensional space that can hold 8 cubic feet of material weighing up to 80 pounds.

In addition, your hat is magically adhered to your head. If any creature other than you attempts to remove it, the creature must succeed on a Charisma saving throw equal to your spell save DC. On a failed save, the creature cannot remove your hat by any means for 24 hours. If you are ever separated from your hat, you can summon it back onto your head as a bonus action as long as it is on the same plane of existence.

ENGULFING HAT

Starting at 6th level, you can use your red hat as an offensive weapon. As an action, you can attempt to shove your hat over the top of a Large or smaller creature's head. This forces the creature to succeed on a Dexterity saving throw equal to your spell save DC or have the hat engulf its face. While engulfed by the hat, the creature is blind, cannot take reactions, and has disadvantage on saving throws against your warlock spells. The hat stays on the creature's face for 1 minute or until the creature or another creature succeeds on a Strength check against your spell save DC to remove it.

PROTECTIVE HAT

Beginning at 10th level, your hat protects you from certain magical effects. While wearing the hat, your thoughts can't be read by telepathy or any other means unless you allow it.

Additionally, when a creature casts a spell that requires you to make an Intelligence, Wisdom, or Charisma saving throw, you can use your reaction to gain advantage on that saving throw. Once this feature is used, you must finish a short or long rest before you can use it again.

OTHERWORLDLY PRISON

Starting at 14th level, you can capture a creature in your hat for a short period of time. As an action, you can cause any creature that has both failed its saving throw against your Engulfing Hat feature and currently has the hat on its face to disappear into the hat with a puff of red smoke. While inside your hat, that creature is incapacitated, cannot take damage, does not need to breathe, and does not age. The creature can attempt a Charisma saving throw equal to your spell save DC at dawn each day, ejecting itself out of your hat on a success. Another creature in possession of your hat can pull out any creature stuck in the hat with a successful Strength check against your warlock spell save DC. You can remove the creature from your hat in the same fashion you would remove a stored object, either by reaching into the hat and calling the creature to mind or by turning your hat inside out and spilling out all its contents.

BACKGROUNDS

The following backgrounds are especially common in far darrig. At the GM's discretion, other appropriate races may have access to them.

COUNCIL MEMBER

You were a member of your community's ruling council. You might have been young for the position, or you might be older than most other far darrig wanderers—but for whatever reason, your time on the council is now over. During your service, you enjoyed great status among your people, and you forged many connections with the ruling councils of other far darrig communities. However, the circumstances surrounding your decision to give up your seat could have repercussions.

Skill Proficiencies: Deception, Persuasion

Tool Proficiencies: One musical instrument of your choice

Languages: One of your choice

Equipment: A musical instrument (one of your choice), a set of fine clothes, a badge or other symbol of office, and a pouch containing 25 gp

FEATURE: CONNECTED ACROSS THE HORIZON

While most far darrig dwell in the Preternatural Planes, many have migrated to the Material Plane and settled there. Council members of various far darrig settlements keep in touch with one another, forming a slow, informal, and most useful network of contacts. You can send messages through this network using secret signs and drop locations, and you can expect shelter and basic aid from most far darrig you encounter.

SUGGESTED CHARACTERISTICS

The council members of the far darrig all navigate the halls of power within a society that doesn't believe halls actually exist. They understand the importance of laws, tradition, and belief, counterpointed with the eventual goal of universal disbelief. As might be expected, many such characters develop conflicting ideas and quirks along the way.

d8	Personality Trait
1	I try to always put my best foot forward.
2	My former station demands respect, and I expect all around me to understand that.
3	Manual tasks are beneath me.
4	I have advice to give on every topic, and I'm eager to share.
5	Even if I'm no longer a community leader, it's important to look the part.
6	Manners are all well and good, but actions speak louder than words.
7	I am always evenhanded in managing disputes.
8	I enjoy getting to rub elbows with different kinds of people. It's important to understand how the common folk feel.

d6	Ideal
1	Belief. The Veil must be lifted, and adherence to the old ways is how it will happen. (Lawful)
2	Equity. My position carries great responsibility, and I pursue it fairly. (Neutral)
3	Change. Broad experience is the best teacher. (Chaotic)
4	Benevolence. Those around me are counting on me, and I won't let them down. (Good)
5	Power. There must be a reason I'm always in charge. (Evil)
6	Unity. Together we can accomplish the impossible. (Any)

d6	Bond
1	I cherish my sterling reputation.
2	The debt I owe the one who helped me escape the destruction of my old home can never be repaid.
3	I take the time to help the less fortunate whenever I can.
4	I attained my position by stealing my predecessor's cap and throwing it away.
5	It is my duty to protect those around me.
6	A jealous rival ousted me from the council.

d6	Flaw
1	I follow the laws of my people, even around folk who don't understand those laws.
2	Anyone less powerful than me isn't worth my time, but I can't let it show.
3	My fondness for gold often gets the better of my judgment.
4	It's easy for me to treat my allies as my subordinates.
5	I've become too used to the perks of power.
6	I'm quite jealous of other powerful leaders.

CRIMSON CHANGELING

You were born to ordinary mortal parents, but in the early days of your life, you were switched with a false child and taken to live with the far darrig. In observance of their strange beliefs, the red folk took you in as family, raising you and gifting you with a red hat of your own.

Living among the far darrig, you have learned the rudiments of their strange cultural philosophy. You understand that the nature of the world around you is an elaborate ruse. The red folk's teachings granted you a general familiarity with the workings of magic and with illusion in particular. And though you lack the capacity to truly manipulate the ever-present illusions around you, you know how to twist expectations and use them to your advantage. People are primed to believe whatever they see or hear, and you can easily find the leverage to make them believe what you want them to.

Skill Proficiencies: Arcana, Deception

Tool Proficiencies: Disguise kit

Languages: Sylvan

Equipment: A disguise kit, a red hat (in a style of your choice), a set of traveler's clothes, a memento from your far darrig family (a pebble or other worthless trinket that appears to be a wondrous bauble), and a pouch containing 10 gp

FEATURE: SEEING IS BELIEVING

Having grown up surrounded by illusions, you find that sniffing them out has become second nature to you. When you use an action or a bonus action to examine a phenomenon that you suspect to be an illusion, you automatically succeed on any Intelligence (Investigation) check you are normally allowed. If the illusion effect doesn't allow such a check, you have no greater ability to see through it than anyone else.

SUGGESTED CHARACTERISTICS

Life among the far darrig leaves a mark, and those they capture resemble the red folk in personality more than they do ordinary mortals. Crimson changelings find the truth to be a fluid thing, and while they might not deliberately try to deceive those around them, such deceit comes as naturally to them as breathing. Likewise, if they're not careful, many such changelings slip into the habit of dismissing very real things as illusions.

d8	Personality Trait
1	When asked questions, I often make up stories instead of giving truthful answers.
2	I sometimes ignore things that would otherwise demand my attention.
3	The color black, particularly in clothing, makes me uneasy.
4	Magic that deals with the dead frightens and angers me.
5	I'm more comfortable on the road or in smaller settlements. Large cities have too many solid walls hedging me in.
6	I sometimes speak to people who aren't there because I'm so used to my adopted family being around even if I can't see them.
7	Physical objects fascinate me, and I can lose a great deal of time fiddling with things that don't vanish when I touch them.
8	I love to challenge my friends' views of the world.

d6	Ideal
1	Dedication. The only constant is tradition. Everything else is smoke and shadows. (Lawful)
2	Family. Nothing is more important than those closest to me. (Neutral)
3	Travel. There's so much to see beyond the next hill. I know that something out there will eventually let me make sense of the world. (Chaotic)
4	Service. It's hard to get by alone, so I try not to let anyone be truly alone when I'm around. (Good)
5	Mischief. What good is knowing the world is a lie if I can't make the lie work in my favor? (Evil)
6	Aspiration. I want to make a lasting impact on the world—something I know is real. (Any)

d6	Bond
1	I'll stop at nothing to take revenge on the black hats that killed my family and drove me into hiding.
2	The teachings of the red folk still resonate with me, and I hope to find others who will study the Veil with me.
3	I'm searching for lore that will help my family unravel the secret nature of the world.
4	I want nothing more than to find a magical relic that lets me wield my own innate illusion magic as I have none of my own.
5	My companions are like my family, and I'll do anything I can to protect them.
6	Because of me, my far darrig family became black hats. They're still hunting me.

d6	Flaw
1	I am terrified of the undead and have great difficulty facing them.
2	My skin has taken on a faint red hue from my time with the far darrig, and I will go to any length to hide it.
3	I can't ever just tell the whole truth. I always mix in a bit of a lie, no matter how small.
4	I occasionally forget that other people take the idea of "personal property" so seriously.
5	I am slow to trust others because of how I was stolen as a baby.
6	I can't imagine anyone getting the better of me through deceit. I'm just too good at spinning lies.

DARK HUNTER

You are no stranger to the evil that lives in the shadows of the multiverse. You've seen the corruption that can take root and turn good beings into monsters, and you've been trained to root it out. Perhaps you are a far darrig warden who hunts the traitorous black hats. Or you might be one of the few to survive a vampire's predations and lived to tell the tale. Whatever its source, your sense of duty—or your sense of vengeance—now sees you stand between the darkness and the innocent.

Choose a creature of darkness, such as undead, fiends, dark fey, or aberrations. Creatures of that type are your sworn enemies, though you'll stand up to any foul beast that seeks to prey on those who dwell in the light. One of these creatures might have attacked you, or perhaps you survived the destruction they wrought on those you loved. Whatever the creature and for whatever reason, you have become the thing they will learn to fear.

Skill Proficiencies: Arcana, Survival

Tool Proficiencies: Poisoner's kit

Languages: One of your choice of Abyssal, Deep Speech, Infernal, Sylvan, or Undercommon

Equipment: A poisoner's kit, a hunting trap, a dagger, a set of traveler's clothes, and a pouch containing 10 gp

FEATURE: AGAINST THE SHADOWS

You recognize subtle signs of corruption, either because of long study or a sinister familiarity with creatures of darkness. Whenever you spend an hour or more in the presence of dark creatures or in the vicinity where those creatures prowl or lair, you begin to catch their telltale signs. These are subtle enough to not fully give a creature away but sufficient to alert you to its predations in the area. If you attempt to gather additional evidence, you can expect shelter and mundane aid from good-aligned organizations.

SUGGESTED CHARACTERISTICS

Brooding or jumpy. Scarred or vigilant. Dark hunters always bear some mark of the things they've seen and fought, whether physical or psychological. They are often practical, decisive, and intolerant of frivolity. Some dark hunters might bear hidden hypocrisy or ulterior motives for their hunts while some might simply be too jaded to relate well with others.

d8	Personality Trait
1	I don't talk much—the better to keep an eye out for trouble.
2	When night falls, I can't help but keep my back to a wall and one eye on the shadows.
3	I never turn away a sincere offer of help.
4	I never give up once I'm set on a goal.
5	I suspect the motives of anyone who shows me kindness.
6	Simple solutions are usually the best ones.
7	I try to be sociable to avoid alerting my prey that I'm on to them.
8	When I notice that other people are trying to hide something, I call them on it.

d6	Ideal
1	Competition. I'm clearing out my rivals as efficiently as I can. (Evil)
2	Obligation. Why do I do this? Because I'm the only one who can. (Any)
3	Honor. I swore an oath to beat back the darkness. (Lawful)
4	Life. People shouldn't have to live with the fear of being hunted. (Chaotic)
5	Greater Good. What it costs me doesn't matter. It's worth it. (Good)
6	People. I made a commitment to the people I care about, and that's all that matters. (Neutral)

d6	Bond
1	Those who saved me from monsters died to keep me safe, and I'll carry on in their memory.
2	Anyone who takes up arms against the darkness will be my ally.
3	Most people have no hope of standing against the things I've seen. I fight so they don't have to.
4	I have sworn vengeance against the specific creature that attacked me or my loved ones, and I won't rest until I find it.
5	I can't forget how dark monsters left my home in ruins, and I will rebuild it someday.
6	The creatures I hunt took something of great value. Nothing else matters but getting it back.

d6	Flaw
1	I see evil in every shadow, and there are shadows in every room.
2	I'm quick to judge others because I've seen how far they can fall.
3	My worst fear is becoming the thing I hate. I'll do anything to avoid that fate.
4	I overlook deeper meaning in pursuit of my prey.
5	I secretly hope that the things I hunt will put an end to me.
6	A few fellow survivors know that my actions drew the monsters that destroyed our home, and I fear that others will find out.

ADDITIONAL OPTIONS

The following options are available to far darrig. At the GM's discretion, other appropriate races may have access to some of these new rules.

EQUIPMENT

Far darrig have developed the following equipment according to their specific needs and utilize them to particular effect.

Far Darrig Coat. This long coat is woven of lightweight but durable fabrics and adorned with large buttons. Though a far darrig coat is not armor, your armor class when you wear it without armor is 11 + your Dexterity modifier. It is sewn with a number of cunningly hidden pockets, giving you advantage on Dexterity (Sleight of Hand) checks made to hide objects within.

Far Darrig Shillelagh. This knob-ended stick is typically crafted of blackthorn or oak, often from root wood to increase the weapon's durability. The end is hollowed and filled with lead for added weight and striking power. This weapon is traditionally used in duels between far darrig. It doubles as a walking stick.

Whenever you attack with the far darrig shillelagh, you can choose to make the attack roll with disadvantage. If you accept this disadvantage, even if your attack misses, the target of your attack has disadvantage on its next attack roll to hit you before the start of your next turn. A non-proficient wielder can use a far darrig shillelagh as a mace.

Promise Coin. This gold piece is octagonal. One side bears the image of a hat and the other a grinning face. Writing in Sylvan around the outer edge of the hat side reads "A promise made, a bargain fair, this coin buys fey favor; oath breakers beware." Far darrig give this coin to a creature owed a favor. The coin is a promise to keep the bargain and help the bearer of the coin at a later date, either personally or through proxies. When you display the coin to a fey that is neither neutral evil nor chaotic evil, you get a +1 bonus on any Charisma check made to influence that fey, so long as the coin is not given to the fey. The coin can instead be used to buy a service from such a fey, but the GM decides whether or not the fey agrees to the exchange and what manner of service the fey is willing to provide. A merchant won't allow you to walk out of the shop with the entire stock but might loan out a needed item. A warrior won't die for the coin but might fight as an ally in one battle with reasonable apparent odds or perhaps delay an opponent long enough for you to escape.

Trapped Puzzle Box. Far darrig prize their secrets as much as a good joke. The puzzle boxes they craft

FAR DARRIG WEAPONS

Name	Cost	Damage	Weight	Properties
Martial Melee Weapon				
Far darrig shillelagh	30 gp	1d6 bludgeoning	3 lb.	Special

are much like those of other races but with penalties should someone attempt to open them without proper cunning. Solving the puzzle requires three successful DC 10 Intelligence (Investigation) checks before three failed checks. Attempting each check is an action. Upon the third failure, the puzzle resets itself (the count of both successes and failures returns to 0) and activates the trap. Succeeding by 5 or more counts as two successes and succeeding by 10 or more solves the puzzle. Traps contained in this puzzle box are simple pranks, such as a loud alarm going off. Some may be loaded with hidden bladders that spray the offender with something noxious, such as skunk musk. Each puzzle has a different trap decided at creation (and approved by the GM). Opening the box without solving it requires a successful DC 15 Dexterity check with thieves' tools. The trap triggers automatically if this Dexterity check fails.

FAR DARRIG EQUIPMENT

Item	Cost	Weight
Far darrig coat	120 gp	3 lb.
Promise coin	15 gp	—
Trapped puzzle box	15 gp	1 lb.

FEATS

Far darrig have evolved a style all their own and are quite fond of the following feats.

FEINTING ATTACKER

Prerequisites: Far darrig, proficiency in the Deception skill

Your careful study of a foe grants you an edge in combat. The first time you attack a creature on your turn, you can use your reaction to gain advantage on the attack roll.

PIERCER OF THE VEIL

Prerequisites: Far darrig, the ability to cast at least one illusion spell of 3rd level or higher

You have a profound talent interacting with the Grand Illusion, an ability to accept—or not—as your needs demand. You gain the following benefits:

- Increase your Charisma score by 1, to a maximum of 20.
- As an action, you can expend one spell slot of 3rd level or higher (or one use of a 3rd-level or higher innate illusion spell) to dispel an illusion spell you can see within 60 feet of you. You must have successfully identified the target spell as an illusion by some means. The spell ends, and you gain temporary hit points equal to twice the spell's level.

VEIL ADEPT

Prerequisite: Far darrig

The illusory threads of the Veil infuse your red hat's substance, granting you greater control over illusions. You gain the following benefits:

- You can use your Illusory Instinct trait to cast the *disguise self* spell once and regain the ability to do so when you finish a long rest.
- When you reach 5th level, you can use your Illusory Instinct trait to cast the *invisibility* spell once and regain the ability to do so when you finish a long rest.
- When you reach 7th level, you can use your Illusory Instinct trait to cast the *major image* spell once and regain the ability to do so when you finish a long rest.

VEIL SAVANT

Prerequisites: Far darrig, the ability to cast at least one illusion spell

Your study of the far darrig philosophy of the Veil grants you keen insight into the nature of illusions. You gain the following benefits:

- Increase your Intelligence score by 1, to a maximum of 20.
- Whenever you perceive an illusion that allows an Intelligence (Investigation) check to determine its nature, you can make the check as a reaction.
- When you cast an illusion spell, you can add double your proficiency bonus to your spell save DC for that spell. Once you use this ability, you can't use it again until you finish a short or long rest.

Fir Bolg

The Hunt echoes in our blood like a howl in the night. When we were strong, it sang eternal, picked up anew by another before it could ever fall silent. Now, we fade, and the song dies with us.

—Mallt-y-Nos, the Dog Mother

They are conquerors conquered and hunters hunted, but the proud backs of the fir bolg have not yet broken beneath centuries of injustice. Once, they were the fearsome avatars of the Wild Hunt's savage power. Someday, they may be again.

These fey are not what they once were, but they are too stubborn to die. Their connection to Annwn is broken, taking the might of the Wild Hunt with it. The betrayal of the túatha dé danaan shattered the tribes' greatest leaders. A terrible curse forces those fir bolg capable of giving birth to choose between their minds and parenthood, and the fir bolg numbers dwindle. The tribes are divided. Their outlook is grim, and they work tirelessly to survive. They fight without restraint or fear, for they know their enemies are many and their days few.

Yet there is hope. Sláine, the Gray King, neither alive nor as dead as he should be, has returned, and in him kindles anew the power of the Wild Hunt, birthed from the fir bolg themselves. In a time to come, the fir bolg may stand, tribes united under the banner of the Gray King, and unleash the Wild Hunt once more against the fools who dared attempt to bring them to heel.

Physical Description: Fir bolg possess a sinewy grace granted by the tight, chiseled musculature of their bodies and the fluidity of their movements. They resemble elves somewhat with their angular faces and long, pointed ears, but fir bolg are both taller and bulkier. Their skin color is always some shade of gray, ranging in tinge from yellow to blue or green. Many fir bolg shave their heads, but they can grow lengthy hair in earthy colors: muddy brown, clay orange, foliage green, or stone gray. Fir bolg have hunters' eyes: yellow, orange, and red are common hues, but just as many are nearly black.

Tattoos are popular adornments among the fir bolg. In fact, they often wear more tattoos than clothing. Designs are usually nature motifs or badges of hunting prowess. Inks tend to be bright to call attention. It isn't unusual for fir bolg to create intricate designs from their many scars, even creating new ones to help map the scars together.

Society: Fir bolg are tribal folk led by their fiercest and canniest hunters. These leaders are effectively tiebreakers and champions now—the storied leaders of old long gone. The fir bolg have so thoroughly scattered into small, nomadic groups that governance is simple. Most tribes number fewer than a hundred, and those numbers continue to shrink as the birthrate plummets, lifebringers bearing only one child before their transformation into cŵn annwn, barring twins.

Apart from the unusual fir bolg of Solitude, the tribes are nomadic hunters who move with their prey. Conflicts with other tribes over territory happen but are seldom resolved with violence despite fir bolg aggression; with their numbers dwindling, even hated rivals are loathe to kill one another. Spars to first blood are popular and frequent sources of a fir bolg's network of scars.

Fir bolg are a warlike people, but they do not throw their lives away carelessly. If they can best a foe with intimidation or guerilla warfare to diminish losses, they will do so; if direct combat is the only choice, then they face it without fear.

Families are complicated for the fir bolg. Lifebringers transform into cŵn annwn after childbirth, thus only ever bearing one child; twins are truly spectacular and good omens. As such, parenthood is seen as something avoided as long as possible, but the pressure to preserve their race weighs heavily on the fir bolg. After transforming, cŵn annwn walk a precarious balance between losing themselves to the hound or becoming cù sìth, tools of the Morrigan. The choice is difficult, and no easier is the fir bolg duty to put down any cù sìth, despite once being a proud member of the tribe.

FIR BOLG TRAITS

Fir bolg characters possess an assortment of traits all their own.

- ***Ability Score Increase.*** Your Constitution score increases by 2, and your Wisdom score increases by 1.
- ***Languages.*** You can speak, read, and write Common and Sylvan.
- ***Size.*** Ranging in height from 5 feet to more than 6 feet tall, fir bolg bear a resemblance to elves but are stockier and more muscular.
- ***Speed.*** Your base walking speed is 40 feet.
- ***Type.*** Your type is fey. Spells and effects that specifically target humanoids do not affect you. You also gain the fomorian subtype (see **Appendix**).

- ***Darkvision.*** Owing to the necessities of the hunt, you have superior vision in dark and dim conditions. You can see in dim light within 60 feet of you as if it were bright light, and in darkness as if it were dim light. You can't discern color in darkness, only shades of gray.
- ***Keen Hearing and Smell.*** You have advantage on Wisdom (Perception) checks that rely on hearing or smell.
- ***Mark Prey.*** When you hit a creature with an attack, you can choose to mark it as your prey until you mark another creature as your prey. You always know the direction to your prey as long as it is within 30 feet and have advantage on Wisdom (Survival) checks made to track it.
- ***Survivor.*** Your people have always made their homes in the wild places of the world. You have proficiency in the Survival skill.

Fir bolg have a powerful connection with nature and its creatures. Much of their upbringing revolves around learning plants, animals, stones, and the weather. A fir bolg earns their first tattoo when they hunt and slay their first prey; fir bolg children are not considered adults until they can participate in hunting parties. Tattoos are typically earned for feats of strength, endurance, or cunning, for felling a great beast or for slaying foes of the tribe.

Relations: Fir bolg associations with other fey or other races tend to be terse at best and hostile at worst. The fir bolg despise the sídhe and the Morrigan's other servants and attempt to kill them on sight. Weak cultures—those the fir bolg view as softened by civilization—are seen as valid raiding targets for supplies. Those strong enough to earn fir bolg respect may be considered for trading or worthy of a glorious war. Against their most hated enemies though, a fir bolg will put aside any enmity to rally against them.

Alignment and Religion: Spiritual fir bolg revere nature itself or totemic or natural spirits. They consider hunting a sacred ritual, and many of their traditions and rites of passage involve a hunt in some way. To kill a creature without both expressing gratitude for its return to nature and then making use of its carcass is considered immoral. The gruesome displays some fir bolg make of their prey—preserved heads, bone jewelry and adornments, trophies—are not just about prowess but are used out of respect of the creature they slew. Fir bolg believe that when a slain foe is honored, its spirit and strength live on and make the fir bolg stronger.

The fir bolg began as servants of the Wild Hunt, but over time, more and more, they are becoming the Wild Hunt itself. As a consequence of this and their shattered history, they have undergone a shift in their cultural temperament. Where once they were honorable beyond reproach and dedicated to their people and families, now they are more fractured, torn between serving community and their own self-preservation, and the family unit no longer exists as it did. Most fir bolg are decidedly neutral, only held together by the hunt and loyalty to their individual, small tribes.

Adventurers: Unsurprisingly, most fir bolg prefer the martial classes, especially barbarians, fighters, and rangers. They have a strong spiritual side too, however, and they also count many druids among their number. Arcane classes have the stink of the Morrigan about them so are viewed with suspicion and prejudice. And as a war-like race, skalds are highly regarded.

Age: Like their elf cousins, fir bolg reach physical maturity in their late teens, like humans. They can live as long as 750 years, though most die far younger.

Female Names: Almedha, Caryse, Elin, Glesig, Indeg, Lynwen, Nia, Perweur, Sian.

Male Names: Bledwyn, Derog, Folant, Harri, Kevenard, Moried, Owein, Rhisiart, Talorg, Vauhan, Ysfael.

SUBCLASSES

The fey provide an array of unique qualities and perspectives for creating interesting new characters. Consult your GM before applying these subclasses to other races.

CIRCLE OF THE WILD HUNT (DRUID: DRUID CIRCLE)

Some fir bolg focus on their connection with the natural world by embodying the traits, drives, and instincts of the wolf. You integrate with local wolf (or other canid) populations—ensuring the prosperity of your extended family. Harmony is not your priority, and your lands prove threatening to settlers and explorers.

CIRCLE SPELLS

You are granted the following circle spells.

CIRCLE OF THE WILD HUNT SPELLS

Druid Level	Circle Spells
3rd	*see invisibility, web*
5th	*fear, haste*
7th	*dimension door, faithful hound*
9th	*hold monster, mislead*

PACK TACTICS

Beginning at 2nd level when you choose this circle, you take on the combat instincts of the wolf. You have advantage on attack rolls against a creature if at least one of your allies is within 5 feet of the creature and the ally isn't incapacitated.

BEYOND DOG AND WOLF

Also at 2nd level, you add the following creatures to the list of Wild Shape forms you can take at the indicated levels.

Druid Level	Creature
2nd	blink dog
4th	death dog
6th	feyhound
9th	winter wolf
12th	cŵn annwn
15th	cŵn wybyr
18th	cù sìth

HOWL

Beginning at 6th level, you can use your action to howl to any wolves (and other canids) within 5 miles of you and understand their responses. Those you contact this way can communicate the general direction and distance between you and the nearest source of food or water. A wolf's ability to communicate limits how specific its directions can be: such as, "West of you, near the creek." As well, a wolf's definition of food covers a wide range of options, from herd animals on the move to caches of rotting carrion.

You must be outdoors to use this ability.

HOWL FOR WARNING

At 10th level, you can use your Howl ability to ask for information about danger in the area around you. All wolves (and other canids) within 5 miles of you report the presence of threats they have encountered or avoided, giving the monster type if this would be detectable by a wolf's senses (for example, the smell of undead). A wolf can provide information only on threats it has encountered within the previous 48 hours. Wolves cannot single out an individual creature within a group unless something distinctive to their senses (for example, the smell of an infected wound) sets that creature apart from others.

Evil canids who hear your howl might respond to you with misleading information or use your howl to track you.

You must be outdoors to use this ability.

HOWL FOR AID

Beginning at 14th level, you can use your Howl ability to call for assistance from wolves (and other canids) within 5 miles of you. The type and number of canids are appropriate to the environment and at the GM's discretion, as is the length of time it takes them to arrive. The wolves will fight alongside you, though they might flee if one or more of them is killed. They will not attack your companions unless provoked, though they are not charmed.

Evil canids who hear your howl might respond to you with misleading information or use your howl to track you.

You must be outdoors to use this ability.

COLLEGE OF SILENCE
(BARD: BARD COLLEGE)

Fir bolg know the danger of idle words: careless tongues have shattered armies, secrets shared in bad faith have toppled empires. While the minstrels of mortals openly share knowledge and lore through music, you and the other warrior-poets of the fir bolg keep secrets locked away behind oaths of binding, communicating in silence through gesture and innuendo. Known as silent skalds, you use words like sacred weapons—to be brandished only when prepared to kill.

BONUS PROFICIENCIES

At 3rd level, you gain proficiency with medium armor, shields, and martial melee weapons.

If you're proficient with a melee weapon, you can use it as a spellcasting focus for your bard spells.

FIGHTING STYLE

Also at 3rd level, you adopt a style of fighting as your specialty. Choose one of the following options. You can't take a Fighting Style more than once, even if something in the game lets you choose again.

Defense. While you are wearing armor, you gain a +1 bonus to AC.

Great Weapon Fighting. When you roll a 1 or 2 on a damage die for an attack you make with a melee weapon that you are wielding with two hands, you can reroll the die and must use the new roll, even if the new roll is a 1 or a 2. The weapon must have the two-handed or versatile property for you to gain this benefit.

Protection. When a creature you can see attacks a target other than you that is within 5 feet of you, you can use your reaction to impose disadvantage on the attack roll. You must be wielding a shield.

SILENT SKALD

At 3rd level, your bard spells no longer require verbal components, but you must be able to perform somatic components instead. Additionally, creatures do not have to hear you in order to gain the benefits of your Bardic Inspiration, but they must be able to see you.

If you choose to cast a bard spell of 1st level or higher using its verbal component, you can expend one use of your Bardic Inspiration to make the spell harder to resist. Roll a Bardic Inspiration die and choose one of the following: add the number rolled to your next attack roll for the spell, add the number rolled to the damage the spell deals to one target, or subtract the result from one saving throw made against the spell. After casting the spell, you can't take actions or reactions until the end of your next turn.

EXTRA ATTACK

At 6th level, you can attack twice, instead of once, whenever you take the Attack action on your turn.

SONG OF PERFECT SILENCE

Starting at 14th level, whenever you give an ally a Bardic Inspiration die, you can expend an additional use of Bardic Inspiration to help your ally remain quiet and also steal the voices of nearby creatures. Your ally has advantage on Dexterity (Stealth) checks with advantage until they speak or spend the Bardic Inspiration die you gave it. Also choose a number of creatures within 5 feet of your ally equal to your Charisma modifier (minimum 1) and roll a Bardic Inspiration die. Each of those creatures must succeed on a Wisdom saving throw or have its voice stolen for a number of rounds equal to the result of your roll. The save DC is equal to your spell save DC.

A creature with a stolen voice cannot speak and cannot cast spells that include a verbal component. A *remove curse* spell immediately restores its target's voice as does any other spell or magic that removes a curse. Additionally, you gain 5 temporary hit points for each voice you steal.

GLORYHOUND
(FIGHTER: MARTIAL ARCHETYPE)

Gloryhounds revel in landing killing blows against foes. By displaying grisly trophies of your most powerful prey, you bolster your own strength and ego.

KILLING RUSH

Beginning at 3rd level, the thrill of killing an opponent spurs you to a rampage. Whenever you reduce a hostile creature to 0 hit points, you gain advantage on attack rolls made before the end of your next turn.

GRISLY TROPHIES

Starting at 7th level, you can use your action to collect a body part (such as a tooth or claw) or a piece of clothing or armor from a dead creature that you fought within the last 24 hours and then use a bonus action to display that trophy on your person. While the trophy is visible on your person, your successful weapon attacks deal an extra 2d6 damage to any creature that has the same type or tag as the creature you gathered your trophy from, and you have advantage on Charisma (Intimidation) checks made against those creatures. You can display only one grisly trophy at a time. The extra damage dealt to creatures that share a type or tag with your trophy increases to 3d6 at 11th level, 4d6 at 15th level, and 5d6 at 19th level.

THRILL KILLER

Starting at 10th level, while you have advantage on attack rolls granted by your Killing Rush feature, you cannot be charmed or frightened, and you also have advantage on Intelligence, Wisdom, and Charisma saving throws.

FETISH COLLECTOR

Starting at 15th level, you can use your Grisly Trophies feature to display up to three items at a time, and you gain advantage on Wisdom (Insight) checks and Wisdom (Perception) checks when interacting with any creature that shares a type or tag with a creature you gathered any grisly trophy from.

GUERRILLA
(RANGER: RANGER ARCHETYPE)

The massive, regimented armies of empire trample smaller armies with ease but stumble against foes who strike like vipers and fade too quick back into the wilderness. As a guerrilla, you have no use for "rules of war" or "honorable" combat. You know the only rule is to survive.

GUERRILLA SPELLS

Starting at 3rd level, you learn an additional spell when you reach certain levels in this class, as shown on the Guerrilla Spells table. The spell counts as a ranger spell for you, but it doesn't count against the number of ranger spells you know.

GUERRILLA SPELLS

Ranger Level	Spells
3rd	*expeditious retreat*
5th	*blindness/deafness*
9th	*meld into stone*
13th	*confusion*
17th	*mislead*

NATURAL AMBUSHER

Also at 3rd level, you have advantage on Dexterity (Stealth) checks while within your favored terrain. If you aren't in your favored terrain, you can use your action and expend one ranger spell slot to treat the terrain you're currently in as your favored terrain for 1 hour per level of the spell slot spent.

FRIGHTFUL AMBUSH

Starting at 3rd level, when you hit a creature with a weapon attack and it didn't know your location at the start of the current turn, the creature must succeed on a Wisdom saving throw or be frightened of you for 1 minute. The save DC is 8 + your proficiency modifier + your Dexterity modifier. The creature repeats this saving throw at the end of each of its turns, ending the effect on itself on a success. Once you have used this feature, you can't use it again until you finish a short or long rest.

SKIRMISHER

Starting at 7th level, you are adept at striking with surprise and retreating without a trace. When you hit or miss with a weapon attack on your turn and had advantage on the attack roll, you can take the Disengage or Hide action as a bonus action. If your attack hits, the target has disadvantage on Wisdom (Perception) checks until the end of your next turn.

Starting at 15th level, you no longer have to use a bonus action to take the Disengage or Hide action when you use this feature for the first time on your turn.

SKIRMISH LEADER

Starting at 11th level, when one of your allies within 60 feet of you hits with a weapon attack on their turn while having advantage, the target has disadvantage on Wisdom (Perception) checks until the end of that ally's next turn. If the target already had disadvantage on Wisdom (Perception) checks from this feature or your Skirmisher feature, you can use your reaction to cause the attack to deal an additional 3d8 damage. At 15th level, this extra damage increases to 4d8.

MASTER AMBUSHER

At 15th level, when you hit a creature with a weapon attack in the first round of combat, it must succeed on a Constitution saving throw or be incapacitated until the end of its next turn. The save DC is 8 + your proficiency modifier + your Dexterity modifier.

PATH OF THE PREDATOR SOUL
(BARBARIAN: PRIMAL PATH)

Fir bolg are fearsome hunters, but some have a stronger sense of the mystic bond between predator and prey. As a predator soul, you easily impose your will on lesser creatures and absorb the strength of your slain prey.

BLOOD FEAST

Starting when you choose this path at 3rd level, you gain strength and vitality from your fallen foes. When you reduce a hostile creature to 0 hit points while you are raging, you gain temporary hit points equal to your Constitution modifier + your barbarian level (minimum 1). These temporary hit points last until expended or until the end of your rage.

BESTIAL SOUL

At 3rd level when you adopt this path, you gain the ability to cast the *animal friendship* and *speak with animals* spells but only as rituals.

COERCE PREY

Beginning at 6th level, you can use your innate predatory instincts to force lesser creatures to submit to your will. You have advantage on Wisdom (Animal Handling) checks to calm or intimidate an animal and on Charisma (Intimidation) checks against any creature you have hit with a melee attack since your last long rest.

HUNTER'S INSTINCT

Starting at 10th level, you sense weakness as easily as a predator smells its prey. When a hostile creature within 5 feet of you moves away from you, you can use your reaction to move up to your speed to follow that creature.

In addition, you have advantage on Wisdom (Perception) and Intelligence (Investigation) checks to find or track any creature you have hit with a melee attack since your last long rest.

GORY FINISH

Starting at 14th level, you kill enemies with such ease and ferocity that you terrify lesser creatures. When you reduce a hostile creature to 0 hit points with a melee weapon attack, each hostile creature within 30 feet of you must make a Wisdom saving throw (DC 8 + your proficiency bonus + your Charisma modifier). Each creature that fails is frightened of you for 1 minute. While frightened by this feature, a creature must take the Dash action and move away from you by the safest available route on each of its turns unless there is nowhere to move. If the creature ends its turn where it doesn't have line of sight to you, the creature can make a Wisdom saving throw against the original DC. On a successful save, the effect ends for that creature. A creature who saves against this feature is immune to it for 24 hours.

PATH OF THE SPEAR (BARBARIAN: PRIMAL PATH)

The spear has always been the chosen weapon of your people, even taking on a spiritual status. You wield it as though you were born to it, applying this ecstatic martial tradition to focus your explosive strength in destroying your enemies.

LUNGING ATTACK

Starting when you choose this path at 3rd level, you can use a bonus action to increase your reach for any melee attack you make with a spear to 10 feet. This benefit lasts until the end of your turn, and it can't be used on an attack made as a reaction.

PARRYING DEFENSE

Beginning at 6th level, you master the ability to knock aside the attacks of your foes with your weapon. You gain a +1 bonus to your armor class when wielding a spear with two hands.

FAR STRIKER

Beginning at 10th level, if you move at least 10 feet before making a ranged attack with your spear, the range of that attack increases to 40/120 feet.

HEART SEEKER

Starting at 14th level, you know how to hit your enemies for maximum harm. Your spear attacks score a critical hit on a roll of 19 or 20.

BACKGROUNDS

The following backgrounds are especially common in fir bolg. At the GM's discretion, other appropriate races may have access to them.

RAISED BY WOLVES

Whether by ill luck, fate, or cruel design, you were left on your own at birth. Then the wolves came. These were no ordinary beasts though, rather the cŵn annwn—fir bolg transformed and trapped in animal form by an ancient curse. Still possessing some of the intelligence of their former selves, they were able to keep you alive and protect you with a ferocity no fir bolg could have matched. In the years since, you learned the ways of the wild with a depth and thoroughness few can understand.

Though you form deep and lasting bonds with your companions, your upbringing sets you apart from them on a fundamental level. You will always feel most at home under an open sky or a

forest canopy with loam and leaves beneath your feet.

Skill Proficiencies: Nature, Survival

Tool Proficiencies: Herbalism kit

Equipment: A leather bag filled with tokens of your early life (leaves, stones, small bones, teeth, and so on), a set of common clothes, an herbalism kit, and 5 gp

FEATURE: SLEEP ANYWHERE

Thanks to your upbringing, you have developed the ability to lie down and get a decent rest virtually anywhere, suffering no ill effects or exhaustion. As long as you take no damage from the environment or weather, you can curl up on the ground and rest for any length of time with no difficulty.

SUGGESTED CHARACTERISTICS

Characters raised by wolves have a wildness to their nature that can never be completely hidden, no matter how much time they spend among "civilized" folk. Though they seek out the company of others to recreate the pack structure they grew up in, they crave solitude in equal measure—especially when it's time to hunt.

d8	Personality Trait
1	I sometimes go days without speaking—and do so only begrudgingly.
2	I have a number of canine social habits, such as brushing against people I like and sniffing strangers.
3	At no other time am I happier than when I am hunting wild game.
4	Something about items in containers transfixes me. I often unpack bags and boxes for no apparent reason, leaving the contents strewn around after inspecting them.
5	I have never fully adjusted to the sleep cycle of others and will become nocturnal within a couple of days if left to my own devices.
6	I love engaging in horseplay wherever and whenever I can.
7	Monetary wealth doesn't have the same value to me as items I can directly use.
8	I am fascinated with the moon and am drawn to groups and cultures that venerate it.

d6	Ideal
1	Mercy. I have a habit of picking up stray or orphaned animals and raising them, viewing this act as payment for how the wolves raised me. (Good)
2	Discretion. Sometimes my quarry is too swift or powerful. I am quite comfortable walking away from fights I can't win. (Neutral)
3	Optimism. If I am beaten down by life one day, that doesn't mean it will happen the next day as well. (Chaotic)
4	Possession. If I can take it, it's mine. (Evil)
5	Power. Questions of right and wrong don't concern me when it comes to who rules. The ability to dominate one's peers should be the sole requirement for leadership. (Evil)
6	Community. As long as I'm part of a strong group, I don't mind someone else being in charge. (Any)

d6	Bond
1	The pack that raised me and the land they call home will always be foremost in my heart.
2	My companions are my pack now, and I will defend them without a thought—for good or for ill.
3	Whenever I can, I patrol a specific region that I consider my territory, clearing it of threats to my primacy or to the natural order of things.
4	I am protective of the most defenseless of my packmates, responding with fury toward anyone or anything that might do them harm.
5	I have a particular item, whether a valuable treasure or a favorite old bone, that I always keep buried near my current location. If it ever goes missing, it will cause me a great deal of anxiety.
6	Outside my closest companions, I am far less likely to bond with people than with the mounts and other animals serving them.

d6	Flaw
1	I react to being cornered with hostility, even when it is done by accident.
2	I am utterly without any sense of decorum.
3	I dislike children that aren't my own and see no point in being subtle about it.
4	I have little use for clothing and shed it when it becomes uncomfortable—regardless of my surroundings.
5	I accept that fighting for dominance in any social group is just how things are done.
6	I bathe only often enough to maintain good health, leaving me with a musky odor that some find offensive.

ADDITIONAL OPTIONS

The following options are available to fir bolg. At the GM's discretion, other appropriate races may have access to some of these new rules.

EQUIPMENT

Fir bolg have developed the following equipment according to their specific needs and utilize them to particular effect.

Hunter's Pigment. This pigment, derived from fairy dust, is bluish when pure but can be combined with local ingredients to provide camouflage in any environment. If you are a fir bolg or proficient with disguise kits, you can apply it with 1 minute of effort. It gives the wearer advantage on Dexterity (Stealth) checks to avoid being seen. If you are a fir bolg wearing hunter's pigment and roll a 4 or lower on the die for a Dexterity (Stealth) check to avoid being seen, you can treat the result as if you had rolled a 5 on the die. The pigment lasts for 8 hours before fading.

Poison, Deathglow (Ingested/Injury). Fir bolg harvest venom from large, bioluminescent wasp-like vermin. The poison causes victims to uncontrollably shake and sweat, and their perspiration glows with a soft green radiance. Poisoned creatures leave traces of glowing sweat behind them, making each easier to track over long distances. The poison is effective when consumed or when applied to a melee weapon (or up to three pieces of ammunition). Applying the poison takes an action. Once applied, the poison retains its potency for up to 1 minute before drying.

A creature who consumed an entire dose or is hit by the poisoned weapon or ammunition must succeed on a DC 12 Constitution saving throw or become poisoned for 8 hours. As long as it is poisoned, it exudes glowing sweat. The glow might be blue, green, or violet, depending on the breed of vermin used. The glow negates all benefits of invisibility and sheds dim light in a 10-foot radius. Sighted creatures can track the glowing sweat without making an ability check. At the end of every hour it is poisoned, the creature makes another saving throw. On a successful save, the poisoned condition ends.

Quicksnare. The fir bolg grow and collect a living vine that reacts to fast movement by tightly constricting. The plant can be used to rapidly set effective snare traps. Setting a quicksnare trap is an action. A creature can notice the quicksnare trap with a DC 15 Intelligence (Investigation or Nature) or Wisdom (Perception or Survival) check. The ability check DC to spot quicksnare is increased by 5 in forest or jungle terrain. The skill check DC is decreased by 5 in urban terrain. It can be rendered harmless as an action with a successful DC 15 Dexterity check with thieves' tools or DC 15 Wisdom (Survival) check. If the ability check exceeds the DC by 5 or more, the quicksnare can be collected without ruining it and can be reused.

Quicksnare can only affect a single Large-sized or smaller creature. Quicksnare constricts around the limb or other part of a triggering creature's body entering its 5-foot square. A creature can avoid the grasping quicksnare with a successful DC 15 Dexterity saving throw. On a failed save, the creature cannot move from the square until it is free of the snare. If the creature's save failed by 5 or more, the creature is also restrained. A creature can use its action to make a DC 15 Strength check, freeing itself or another creature within its reach and ruining the quicksnare on a success. A creature can escape with a successful DC 15 Dexterity (Acrobatics) check as an action. Quicksnare can be attacked (AC 15, 10 hit points, immunity to psychic damage). At the GM's discretion, if there is a tall object or structure nearby, the quicksnare lifts the creature up to 10 feet off the ground.

Trackless Slippers. Trackless slippers are special lightweight footwear made of leather and wood that fir bolg craft to aid in concealing their tracks. While you wear trackless slippers, you can cover your tracks as you move to increase the DC of Wisdom (Survival) checks made to track you by 5. Thanks to the assistance of the slippers, covering your tracks this way doesn't slow your movement.

Wild Call. The wild calls of the fir bolg can take many forms, but most are carved of wood and resemble whistles or horns. When it is created, a wild call is made for a specific type of creature with the beast creature type ("wolves" is an acceptable target, "canids" is not).

When you sound a wild call as an action, it emits a sound that draws members of that species closer if they hear it. If you are in an environment where the selected animal lives and your game uses random encounters, then the next random encounter within the area is automatically one or more of the appropriate animal. Additionally, you have advantage on your next Wisdom (Survival) check made to track or locate an animal of the appropriate type.

FIR BOLG EQUIPMENT

Item	Cost	Weight
Hunter's Pigment	100 gp	1/2 lb.
Poison, deathglow (vial, 1 dose)	750 gp	—
Quicksnare	150 gp	10 lb.
Trackless slippers (pair)	150 gp	1 lb.
Wild call	10 gp	1/2 lb.

FEATS

Fir bolg have evolved a style all their own and are quite fond of the following feats.

CHARIOTEER

You have trained and drilled in the deadly practice of attacking from a moving chariot. You gain the following benefits:

- Increase your Dexterity score by 1, to a maximum of 20.
- While in a chariot, you gain a +2 bonus to armor class.
- While in a chariot, if you move at least 20 feet straight toward a target and then hit it with a melee weapon attack on the same turn, that attack is automatically a critical hit.

If you are driving a chariot, you can wield a weapon only with one hand. If you are a rider in a two-person chariot driven by someone else, you can wield a weapon with two hands.

DEN DWELLER

Prerequisite: Fir bolg

Your senses come alive in a new way when you are beneath the ground. You gain the following benefits:

- Increase your Wisdom score by 1, to a maximum of 20.
- Air flow, dampness, and faint echoes all combine to give you an impression of what lies ahead while underground. As an action, you make a Wisdom (Perception) check, consulting the table below on a result of 14 or higher. Results on the table are cumulative, so any result also yields the previous information. Absolute silence and stillness are required of you and your companions while you make this check. It is possible for environmental factors to play tricks on your senses, as determined by the GM.

d20	Result
14–16	You can detect moisture in the air, indicating if a source of water lies ahead.
17–19	A shifting breeze lets you know whether the path widens ahead into a chamber.
20–22	You can pick up the faint scent of other creatures in the immediate area, though not whether they are currently present.
23–25	You are able to sense the faint traces of bad or poisoned air or water ahead.
26+	When you detect the scent of a creature, you are able to identify it if it is a creature you have encountered before.

Goodfellows

The baron's ebon castle? Oh my, yes. You are quite close! You should be able to see it once you reach the top of that mountain . . . though it is concealed by the mists. Anyway, you are better off walking around the peak rather than going up it. Just keep heading clockwise until you get all the way around twice, then do the same thing but halfway up the southward side. Oh . . . wait. Is it Tuesday? Okay, all of that I just said but backwards."

—Duggen Dreamheart

Are goodfellows Puck's light-hearted playmates? Meant to contrast his mother's foreboding kingdom? Or are they disarmingly innocent spies serving as Queen Mab's eyes and ears across the realms? None can be certain—maybe not even the goodfellows themselves.

What is certain is these tiny fey provide unpredictable adventure wherever they go. Their elaborate pranks and impetuous mischief can create legends talked about for generations—or lead to unforeseen tragedy for their erstwhile targets. Most goodfellows aren't intentionally malicious, but their capricious, free-spirited temperament puts them at odds with mortal empathy.

Magic is essential to the goodfellows. They pity those without it and shun as aberrations their own kind who are bereft of it. That said, very little angers these fey, but despoiling the natural places they protect incites a wrath of pranks turned deadly and hails of tiny, lethally poisoned arrows.

Physical Description: Goodfellows are tiny creatures, resembling elves in miniature. Their coloring is as vivid as nature's flora: eyes, skin, wings, and hair may be dark as ebony bark or bright as magnolias or any rainbow of hues in between.

While not androgynous, visual differences between genders are subtle. All genders may have long or short hair and few goodfellows bother with rich adornment. Most in fact reuse natural detritus they find as armor, weapons, clothing, and decoration.

Society: Goodfellows form clustered, tightly knit communities centered around particular regions of flowers but have only a loose society as a whole. Thus a single forest with several wildflower meadows within may be home to dozens of goodfellow communities. These communities are often aware of each other and engage in trade, intermarriage, or prank wars but are not beholden to one another unless Puck comes knocking and rounds them all up.

The different magical aptitudes of goodfellows, called wreaths, divide their communities into something resembling a loose caste system. Rose goodfellows, for example, are often in leadership positions while Elders are typically sages and healers. There is nothing barring a goodfellow from taking on a particular role, but time has shown certain wreaths excel at particular society functions. Clever and elaborate pranks are the best way to prove aptitude beyond wreath as the set-up, target, effect, and resolution of a prank reveals much of the mind behind it; since pranking one's own community is frowned upon, communities engage in prank wars with each other to prove themselves—after training on hapless mortals and fey of course.

For those unfortunate goodfellows born without magic—the wreathless—their role is uncertain and unpleasant. Life at the bottom of their community is typically the best they can hope for,

working as a menial laborer or servant. If very lucky, one wreathless may meet another and enjoy a family and have a fulfilling life even on the fringe of goodfellow communities. Sometimes groundbound communities (those goodfellows without wings, either by birth or misadventure) welcome such wreathless goodfellows and usher them into a different lifestyle where they are free from judgment. These are best-case scenarios however; many wreathless end up alone, shunned, or exiled.

The family unit is of major importance to goodfellows. While cavalier about relationships as a rule, after numerous trysts, a goodfellow in want of settling down will engage in a ritual originating with Poppy goodfellows to find their true, fated heartmate. The identity of this individual is delivered in a dream; sometimes the goodfellow need only acknowledge feelings for another in the community, but other times, finding a goodfellow's heartmate requires searching into other communities or embarking on a quest. Once the heartmate is found, the ritual is complete, and only death will separate them.

Same-gender relationships are as common as opposite-gender ones among goodfellows. As pregnancy is relatively easy for female goodfellows, extra children aren't uncommon, and babies may be gifted to heartmates unable to have children together. Heartmate marriages are lavish affairs and tend to bring multiple communities of goodfellows together—but they annoy Queen Mab.

Once a decision is made to keep or gift a child, it is done; that child becomes a part of the family unit.

GOODFELLOW TRAITS

Goodfellow characters possess an assortment of traits all their own.

- ***Ability Score Increase.*** Your Dexterity score increases by 2, and your Charisma score increases by 1.
- ***Languages.*** You can speak, read, and write Common, Sylvan, and Undercommon.
- ***Size.*** Resembling miniature humans with wings, goodfellows are approximately 1 foot tall and weigh only a few pounds. Your size is Tiny, your class's Hit Die type is reduced by 1 die type, and you can't use any two-handed or versatile weapon except for those designed for Tiny creatures, such as a deftbow.
- ***Speed.*** Your base walking speed is 20 feet.
- ***Type.*** Your type is fey. Spells and effects that specifically target humanoids do not affect you. You also gain the sprite subtype (see **Appendix**).

- ***Darkvision.*** As a creature of Mab's dominion, you have superior vision in dark and dim conditions. You can see in dim light within 60 feet of you as if it were bright light and in darkness as if it were dim light. You can't discern color in darkness, only shades of gray.
- ***Flight.*** You have a flying speed of 20 feet.
- ***Glow.*** You naturally shed bright light in a 5-foot radius and dim light for an additional 5 feet. If you cover your entire body, you shed only a 5-foot radius of dim light. You can't hide from vision where your light is brighter than your surroundings. As an action, you can increase the brightness up to a 20-foot radius of bright light, with dim light for an additional 20 feet, for as long as you concentrate (as if concentrating on a spell).
- ***Wreath.*** Goodfellows have no subraces, but like all others of your kind, you belong to a wreath. This is a community of goodfellows whose members all share the same magical interests and aptitudes. Choose a wreath from those provided (see **Goodfellow Wreaths**).

Goodfellow communities aid one another with child-rearing, but parents are who typically determine a child's wreath, who will introduce the child to Puck (and sometimes Mab), who instill reverence for the wild places, and who, most importantly, whisper a secret name, one never spoken again, to the baby. Goodfellow parents take a child's secret name to the grave; a goodfellow can't reveal his or her secret name, so Queen Mab and other fey cannot learn it—thus goodfellows cannot be controlled.

Besides weddings, threats to a forest or other natural place will also bring goodfellow communities together in a hurry to protect and to repel interlopers. All goodfellows are expected to serve as wardens of their homes and to respect the flora and fauna they share.

Relations: Goodfellows befuddle mortal races. They use pranks and riddles and tricks the way some might tell stories or share mementos: such methods are how goodfellows introduce themselves, engage in creative expression, and brag about their accomplishments. They get on well with gnomes. Elves may be patient with them and respect their appreciation for nature. Shorter-lived races often find them frustrating and fascinating—sometimes in the same hour. Dwarves they find dour and insulting and tend to prank mercilessly.

Alignment and Religion: Most goodfellows tend toward a free-wheeling chaotic neutral, abiding by few rules other than the guidance of their emotions and aptitudes. More are good than evil with most wishing to make the world a happier or at least more entertaining place. They are profoundly irreverent and tend to make poor religious converts, but they do have a worshipful attitude to nature that can border on spirituality.

Adventurers: Goodfellows like to form up in bands and go on adventures together. Some go on jaunts in mortal realms and like it so much they decide to stay, even if Mab won't have them back—or especially because Mab won't have them back. Exiles, wreathless, and goodfellows opposing Mab comprise the bulk of adventurers found outside Mab's kingdom.

Classes vary depending on wreath—Belladonnas, for example, are typically rogues. However, all goodfellows share a predilection for arcane spellcasting and for nature-based classes. Bards are also common. Rare are the very disciplined or devout classes, like clerics or monks, or intense ones, like barbarians.

Names: The secret names of goodfellows are complex and in an ancient language. Perhaps it was whispered to them during their creation by Puck or—more alarmingly—Mab herself, or perhaps they learned it from the trees and the animals and insects. Their everyday names, however, are often taken from flowers or trees or natural features. Goodfellows don't have formal surnames, instead using their everyday name, followed by their wreath and community name. Thus, a goodfellow may be Hazel, Poppy of Brambles-by-Oak.

Age: A goodfellow is immortal and can live forever as long as it isn't killed in some unfortunate way.

Female Names: Bonnet, Daffi, Ferna, Hazel, Jassimine, Lilliane, Nest, Posey, River, Thistle, Valeria, Yarrow.

Male Names: Ant, Chrysant, Elms, Gardennis, Indigo, Magnol, Orchis, Quill, Saffron, Umber, Willow, Zeed.

GOODFELLOW WREATHS

Goodfellows group into wreaths based on their magical aptitudes.

WREATH OF THE BELLADONNA

As part of the Wreath of the Belladona, you are naturally duplicitous, and magic associated with trickery and poison calls to your talents. Mab loves your wreath, believing that you will aid her in taking down Titania someday.

Belladonna Magic. You know the *acid splash* and *mage hand* cantrips. In addition, you can cast *detect poison and disease* once without expending a spell slot and regain the ability when you finish a long rest. Charisma is your spellcasting ability for these spells.

WREATH OF THE ELDER

As part of the Wreath of the Elder, you are fascinated by succor and suffocation, and your magic reflects those interests. Mab loves your wreath, believing that you will help her torture Titania someday.

Elder Magic. You know the *vicious mockery* cantrip. In addition, you can cast *goodberry* and *purify food and drink* once each without expending a spell slot. You regain the uses of these spells when you finish a long rest. Charisma is your spellcasting ability for these spells.

WREATH OF THE FOXGLOVE

As part of the Wreath of the Foxglove, you are drawn to luminosity and the magic that comes from within. Mab watches your wreath closely, believing that you will grant her insight into overcoming the light and love that surrounds Titania.

Foxglove Magic. You know the *dancing lights* cantrip. In addition, you can cast *expeditious retreat* and *faerie fire* once each without expending a spell slot. You regain the uses of these spells when you finish a long rest. Charisma is your spellcasting ability for these spells.

WREATH OF THE POPPY

As part of the Wreath of the Poppy, you are a dreamer and are fascinated by the state of sleep. Mab loves you because you help her watch and weave the dreams of Titania's court, which might give her the advantage she needs.

Poppy Magic. You know the *minor illusion* cantrip. In addition, you can cast *sleep* once without expending a spell slot and regain the ability when you finish a long rest. Charisma is your spellcasting ability for these spells.

Lullaby. When you sing this magical song as an action, every creature within 10 feet of you who hears you must succeed on a Wisdom saving throw (DC 8 + your proficiency bonus + your Charisma modifier) or become drowsy for 1 minute. While drowsy, a creature has disadvantage on Wisdom (Perception) checks and on saving throws against effects that would cause it to fall asleep. Once you use this ability, you can't use it again until you finish a short or long rest.

WREATH OF THE PUMPKIN

As part of the Wreath of the Pumpkin, you crave change and see magic as a means to that end. Mab loves your wreath because she believes you'll help her infiltrate Titania's realm, giving her the answers she seeks to complete her revenge.

Pumpkin Magic. You can cast the *alter self* spell without expending a spell slot but only to use its change appearance option, and you can change your size to Small or Medium. Charisma is your spellcasting ability for these spells.

WREATH OF THE ROSE

As part of the Wreath of the Rose, you delight in the magic of enchantment, enticing others to your beauty while trusting in your thorns to help keep you safe. Mab loves your wreath because you will help her destroy Titania and her ilk with your beauty and pain.

Rose Magic. You know the *minor illusion* cantrip. In addition, you can cast *charm person* and *entangle* once each without expending a spell slot. You regain the uses of these spells when you finish a long rest. Charisma is your spellcasting ability for these spells.

SUBCLASSES

The fey provide an array of unique qualities and perspectives for creating interesting new characters. Consult your GM before applying these subclasses to other races.

ARCLIGHT BOMBARDIER
(FIGHTER: MARTIAL ARCHETYPE)

Raining explosive projectiles onto your foes from the sky, you excel at softening opposition for your ground-bound allies before a fight begins. Squadrons of arclight bombardiers are often used by Mab as a first wave of attack against her foes.

RESTRICTION: FEY ONLY

While only the tiny fey known as goodfellows are instructed in the martial ways of the arclight bombardier, the secrecy of these techniques are not the only thing keeping creatures of other races from training as a bombardier. The powers of an arclight bombardier are drawn from the primordial magic of the fey themselves—and they also make heavy use of their

natural-born fey powers of flight.

For these reasons, only fey with a natural flying speed can choose the arclight bombardier. The GM can alter this restriction to fit the campaign but should still only make this archetype available to creatures that have constant access to flight, whether through a natural flying speed or through magic items.

ARCANE BOMBARDIER

Starting at 3rd level when you choose this archetype, you learn how to twist the magic of the fey into a volatile sphere the size of a pea. This tangle of arcane energy can be manipulated like a physical object, but mere moments after it leaves your hand, it explodes.

As an Attack action, you can create and use one of the following arcane explosives. Charisma is your spellcasting ability for your arcane explosives, your spell save DC equals 8 + your proficiency bonus + your Charisma modifier, and your spell attack modifier equals your proficiency bonus + your Charisma modifier. If you have a feature such as Extra Attack that allows you to make multiple attacks in the same Attack action, you can create and use an arcane explosive in place of one or more of your attacks.

Once you use an arcane explosive, you can't use it again until you complete a short or long rest.

Arcing Light: A diamond of radiant light appears in the space between your hands. You can throw the explosive at a point you can see within 60 feet of you on a surface. Once it touches the surface, beams of golden light burst from the diamond, creating an area of bright light in a 30-foot radius until the end of your next turn. All creatures within this area must make a Constitution saving throw, taking 1d4 radiant damage on a failed save as they are struck by arcing beams of light or taking half as much damage on a successful save.

After you reach 10th level in this class, if this is the first bomb you throw on the current turn, each target takes an extra 2d4 radiant damage.

Gravelbomb. A vibrating stone appears in your clenched fist. You can throw the explosive at a point you can see on a surface within 60 feet of you. Once it touches the surface, it explodes in a hail of sharp stones, and all creatures within 15 feet of that point must make a Dexterity saving throw, taking 1d6 piercing damage on a failed save or half as much on a successful one.

You can also throw the explosive at a point you can't see within 60 feet of you as long as the explosive can physically travel to that point, but creatures affected by the explosion have advantage on their saving throws.

After you reach 10th level in this class, if this is the first bomb you throw on the current turn, each target takes an extra 2d6 piercing damage.

Pepperblast. A fiery sphere appears in the palm of your hand, its condensed flames straining to break free. Make a ranged spell attack against a creature you can see within 60 feet. On a hit, the target takes 1d10 fire damage, and all creatures within 5 feet of the target must make a Dexterity saving throw, taking half as much damage on a failed save or no damage on a successful save.

After you reach 10th level in this class, if this is the first bomb you throw on the current turn, both the primary target and any secondary targets take an extra 2d10 fire damage.

Quakecrystal. A hunk of crystal forms on the back of your hand. Choose a point on the ground that you can see within 60 feet. When the bomb touches that point, the ground in a 20-foot radius around it quakes violently, turning that area into jagged, difficult terrain. Any creature in that area when you throw the explosive must succeed on a Dexterity saving throw or take 1d6 bludgeoning damage and fall prone.

After you reach 10th level in this class, if this is the first bomb you throw on the current turn, all creatures in the area must make a Dexterity saving throw, taking 3d8 bludgeoning damage and falling prone on a failed save or taking half as much damage on a successful one.

Stone-eater. A bubble of hissing acid appears at your fingertips. Make a ranged spell attack against a creature or object you can see within 60 feet. On a hit, the target takes 1d8 acid damage, and that creature's resistance to bludgeoning, piercing, and/or slashing damage (if any) is suppressed until the end of your next turn.

After you reach 10th level in this class, if this is the first bomb you throw on the current turn, the target takes an extra 2d8 acid damage, and its resistance and immunity to bludgeoning, piercing, and/or slashing damage (if any) is suppressed until the end of your next turn.

AERIAL SUPERIORITY

Starting at 7th level, while flying, you have advantage on Dexterity (Acrobatics) checks and on saving throws to avoid being restrained, knocked prone, or moved. Also, if a creature that is at least 20 feet below you but within 60 feet makes a saving throw as a result of one of your bombs, it has disadvantage on that saving throw.

ARCANE RESERVES

Also at 10th level, you can use each of your arcane explosives twice before needing to complete a short or long rest to use them again.

STEALTH BOMBER

Starting at 15th level, whenever you end your turn without having moved in that turn, you become invisible. Anything you are wearing or carrying is invisible as long as it is on your person. This invisibility lasts until you move, take damage, cast a spell, or make an attack.

Starting at 18th level, this invisibility isn't ended by attacking with arcane explosives or by moving.

CIRCLE OF THE HIVE
(DRUID: DRUID CIRCLE)

Druids that join the circle of the hive form deep bonds with creatures so small as to be ignored by the great forces of the world. You are particularly fond of bees and are likely to become a beekeeper at the edge of civilization, trading honey and fruits from your blessed orchards. Your circle lives in close-knit communes and holds to a strict ideology: the burden of power should not be borne by a single great person but by a unified group of people bound by trust and cooperation. However, some of your circle do set out on their own for a time in the name of the hive.

HIVEBORN COMPANION

Starting at 2nd level, the *find familiar* spell is added to the druid spell list for you. When you cast *find familiar*, you can only use it to summon a bee (or another stinging insect). This familiar uses hawk statistics but has no attacks. Its sting does no damage but causes a painful red welt to appear on the flesh of living creatures.

As an action, you can expend one use of Wild Shape to transform the bee into a giant wasp for up to 1 minute. This wasp obeys your commands to the best of its abilities and acts on your initiative but does not take any action unless you command it to. On your turn, you can mentally order the wasp where to move (requiring no action) and use your action to order it to take one of the following actions: Attack, Dash, Disengage, Dodge, or Help.

POWER OF THE HIVE

Also at 2nd level, whenever you deal damage to a creature with a spell attack or weapon attack, you deal an extra 1d4 damage if one of your allies is adjacent to that creature. You can deal this extra damage once per turn. This extra damage increases to 1d6 at 5th level, 1d8 at 11th level, and 1d10 at 17th level.

IMPROVED HIVEBORN COMPANION

Starting at 6th level, you no longer have to expend a use of Wild Shape to transform your bee familiar into a giant wasp, and its transformation lasts until you transform it into a bee again as an action.

Additionally, you now add your proficiency bonus to the wasp's AC, attack rolls, Dexterity saving throws, damage rolls, and its sting saving throw DC. Its attacks also count as magical for the purpose of overcoming resistance and immunity to nonmagical attacks and damage.

Finally, the wasp is now a Large creature, increasing its hit points to 16 (3d10) and increasing its carrying capacity to 300 pounds.

BEE SPEECH

Also at 6th level, you gain the ability to comprehend and telepathically communicate with bees and other insects. The knowledge and awareness of many insects is limited by their Intelligence, but at minimum, insects can give you information about nearby locations and monsters, including whatever they can perceive or have perceived within the past day.

SWARMING WILD SHAPE

At 10th level, you can use Wild Shape to transform into a swarm of insects. Using the variant Insect Swarm rules, you can choose to transform into a swarm of beetles, centipedes, spiders, or wasps. Your consciousness is fragmented across each individual creature in the swarm, and you can control each insect individually and/or as a single swarm. An individual insect can leave the larger swarm (which must remain in a 5-foot-by-5-foot space), but you lose 1 hit point at the start of each of your turns for each insect outside of the main swarm. An insect separated from the swarm has the swarm's statistics except it can't attack and it has 1 hit point. When Wild Shape ends, you can choose any of the swarm's members to return to your normal form while the rest of the swarm disappears.

HIVE MONARCH

Starting at 14th level, you can communicate telepathically with any ally within 60 feet. Whenever an ally in this area takes damage, you can use your reaction to give that ally resistance to all of that damage. When you do, you take an amount of psychic damage equal to the damage your ally takes, which can't be reduced or prevented in any way.

Additionally, whenever you cast a spell with a range of touch, you can choose any ally within 60 feet to make the spell attack instead of yourself and can cast spells with a range of self on any ally within this area. The ally must use a reaction to accept your spell or deliver a touch spell, but you still make any spell attack roll required.

COLLEGE OF THE ROSE (BARD: BARD COLLEGE)

A goodfellow bard who belongs to the Wreath of the Rose can choose this option.

All goodfellows of the Rose practice the magic of enchantment, but its bards further focus that magic through performance and song. They believe that the inevitable end goal of their magic is to control the reactions of their audience.

You gather within the black rose hedges of Mab's gardens, seeking to be closer to the beauty and pain of the magic they wield. In exchange for the use of her gardens as a place to meet, learn, and grow in your art, Mab desires only that you perform for her at court once a year—a performance no one will forget.

PERFORMER

When you join the college of the rose at 3rd level, you gain proficiency in the Performance skill if you do not already have it. If you already have proficiency in Performance, your proficiency bonus is doubled when using that skill.

ENTICEMENT

Also from 3rd level, you gain the ability to use your performance to lure a creature to you. As an action, you can start a performance that lasts until the end of your next turn. Choose a nonhostile creature within 60 feet of you that can see or hear your performance, and then expend one use of Bardic Inspiration to cause that creature to make a Wisdom saving throw against your bard spell save DC.

On a failed save, the creature is charmed by you until your performance ends. While charmed, the creature moves toward you by the shortest and most direct route, ending its turn if it moves within 5 feet of you. While the creature is charmed, the first attack roll or check you make against it is made with advantage.

ROSE'S THORNS

At 6th level, you understand how to harm creatures affected by your mind magic. Whenever you deal damage to a creature that is charmed by you, that creature takes an extra 1d6 psychic damage. This damage increases to 2d6 at 12th level and 3d6 at 18th level.

SO BEAUTIFUL IT HURTS

At 14th level, you learn to channel a performance so beautiful that it causes pain to those who witness it. When you use your Enticement feature, it affects all nonhostile creatures within 60 feet of you that can see or hear your performance. Additionally, when you expend your use of Bardic Inspiration, roll a Bardic Inspiration die. Any creature that fails its Wisdom saving throw against your Enticement takes psychic damage equal to the roll of the Bardic Inspiration die but remains charmed by you until your performance ends.

OF DREAMS AND NIGHTMARES (SORCERER: SORCEROUS ORIGIN)

A goodfellow sorcerer who belongs to the Wreath of the Poppy can choose this option.

All fey have some connection to magic, but your power is stronger than most, coming as it does from the world of dreams and nightmares. You might have been birthed by the realm of dreams itself, able to unknowingly walk its ways since you came into existence. Or perhaps you met and mingled with a living dream or nightmare.

WATCHER OF DREAMS

Starting when you choose this origin at 1st level, you can tap into the minds of other creatures to glean information from their dreams. Choose one creature you know. You see that creature's most recent dreams, which come to you as symbols and fragments, as determined by the GM. Additionally, you can ask a single question about the creature whose dreams you saw. The GM offers a truthful reply. Once you use this feature, you must finish a short or long rest before you can use it again.

DREAM MAKER

Starting at 6th level, you can cast the *dream* spell. Once you use this feature, you must finish a long rest before you can use it again.

DREAM WALKER

Starting at 14th level, you and up to eight willing creatures can enter the realm of Dream by use of a meditative ritual that takes 10 minutes to perform. Dream is the place where dreamers go when they sleep—a realm where nightmares are born and where dreams persist after a sleeper wakes. While within this realm, you are physically present in Dream and can be harmed or killed there. You can also bring things out of Dream.

While in Dream, you can seek out the dreams of sleeping creatures, shifting and changing their dreams in the manner of the *dream* spell. Additionally, you can alter a dreaming creature's perceptions of reality and the way they think, behave, and function. Doing so is dangerous though, and every dreaming mind you try to alter will present its own pitfalls, guardians, and nightmares as determined by the GM.

To exit Dream, you need to once more engage in a meditative ritual that takes 10 minutes to perform. You reappear in the same place from which you entered Dream. If you are killed or abandoned while in Dream, other creatures that accompanied you must find their own way out of that realm as determined by the GM.

Once you use this feature, you must finish a long rest before you can use it again.

MASTER OF THE DREAM

At 18th level, you have mastered the process of entering and exiting Dream. As an action, you can spend 5 sorcery points to instantly enter or exit that realm along with up to eight willing creatures. While in Dream, you can spend 2 sorcery points to gain advantage on any ability check, saving throw, or attack roll.

SHADOWFELLOW
(ROGUE: ROGUISH ARCHETYPE)

A goodfellow rogue who belongs to the Wreath of the Belladonna can choose this option.

You live or have lived in Scáthbaile and understand that shadows are not just images left behind by the light. Shadows are the reflections, echoes, and memories of the figures that create them, and you have come to an understanding with those memories and echoes. Shadows speak to you, hear your call, and treat you as a friend.

SHADOW CLOAK

Starting at 3rd level, you can draw shadows around you to help conceal yourself. While in an area of dim light or shadow, you have advantage on Dexterity (Stealth) checks.

SHADOW IMAGE

Starting at 9th level, when you use Uncanny Dodge, you can teleport up to 15 feet to an unoccupied space you can see, leaving a shadowy image of yourself behind. The shadow persists until the end of your next turn. While the shadow persists, you can use a bonus action to teleport back to it as long as its space remains unoccupied.

ECHOES FROM THE DARK

At 13th level, you gain the ability to fully tap into the memories that shadows hold. You must spend 1 hour to listen to a shadow (typically one cast by an object in a well-lit area). After which, you can question the shadow for 10 minutes about events within 30 feet of it within the past day, gaining information about creatures that have passed, weather, and other circumstances.

SHADOW SPEAKER

When you reach 17th level, you understand how to speak with shadows and can ask them to do things for you. As a bonus action while you are within an area of dim light or shadows, you can make use of one of the following options:

- Use the Attack action to shove a creature within 30 feet of you.
- Take the Use an Object action for any object within 30 feet of you.
- Use the Help action to aid a friendly creature to accomplish a task or attack another creature within 30 feet of you.

The creature or object you affect with these actions must also be within the same area of dim light or shadows.

SHRINKING VIOLET
(ROGUE: ROGUISH ARCHETYPE)

Good-natured and mischievous, you manipulate your size to hide under the feet of larger creatures, possibly as a spy and sneak for some cause or liege. Those creatures that do manage to see you are quickly dispatched with your venom.

DIMINUTION

Starting at 3rd level, you can use your action to shrink your body and all items on your person. Your weapon attacks deal 1d4 less damage for each size category shrunk (this can't reduce the damage below 1). If you drop an item, it instantly returns to its original size. Your size decreases by one category, such as from Medium to Small. Your size is halved in all dimensions, and your weight is reduced to 1/8 of normal. If you are grappled when you shrink, you can make a Dexterity (Acrobatics) check with advantage to escape as a bonus action. You remain this size as long as you concentrate (as if concentrating on a spell); when no longer concentrating, you and all items you shrunk instantly revert to your original size. If you revert to your original size in a place that does not fit

ADJUSTING FOR SIZE

The rules don't currently account for creature sizes smaller than Tiny. So for a goodfellow character to gain any benefit from the shrinking violet subclass, we just need to revisit earlier editions to add two more size categories: Diminutive and Fine.

Conveniently, size doesn't have the mechanical impact that it did in previous editions, so incorporating two new sizes is relatively straightforward. Most of what you need should already be incorporated into the subclass features. Other questions that might come up are few, such as grappling, moving through another's space, and squeezing, but these are all relative to another creature or object's size rather than based on concrete modifiers. (See **Size Categories** table below for numerical values of the new size categories.)

SIZE CATEGORIES

Size	Space	Typical Height/Length
Fine	1/2 × 1/2 ft. or smaller	Less than 1/2 ft.
Diminutive	1 × 1 ft.	1/2–1 ft.
Tiny	2-1/2 × 2-1/2 ft.	1–2 ft.
Small	5 × 5 ft.	2–4 ft.
Medium	5 × 5 ft.	4–8 ft.
Large	10 × 10 ft.	8–16 ft.
Huge	15 × 15 ft.	16–32 ft.
Gargantuan	20 × 20 ft. or larger	32–64 ft. or more

you, you either break the enclosure or are immediately ejected into the nearest unoccupied space (at the GM's discretion). If you are grappled or restrained when you increase in size, you can make a Strength (Athletics) check to escape as a bonus action.

While reduced in size in this way, creatures that are one size larger than you have a –5 penalty on Wisdom (Perception) checks made to see you. Creatures that are two sizes larger than you instead have a –10 penalty on Wisdom (Perception) checks made to see you. Creatures that are three or more sizes larger than you instead have a –15 penalty on Wisdom (Perception) checks made to see you.

Starting at 17th level, you can choose to decrease your size by two categories when you use this feature, such as from Medium to Tiny.

UNDERFOOT STEALTH

Also at 3rd level, you can end your movement in the spaces of creatures at least two size categories larger than you and hide from them by using their own bodies as cover. The creature must not have been aware of your location at the start of the turn in order for your Hide action to be effective against it.

SLUMBERING STING

Starting at 9th level, you can enwreathe your weapons with drowsy magical energy. As a bonus action, choose one weapon or piece of ammunition that you are holding. The next creature hit by that weapon before the end of your turn must make a Constitution saving throw (DC 8 + your Intelligence modifier + your proficiency bonus) before you deal damage. On a failed save, it falls unconscious for 1 minute but takes no damage from the attack. The creature wakes up if it takes damage or if another creature uses its action to wake it up. On a successful save, the target takes normal damage but doesn't fall unconscious.

Once you have used this feature, you can't use it again until you complete a short or long rest. Starting at 17th level, you can use it twice between rests.

DIMINUTIVE NIMBLENESS

Starting at 13th level, you have advantage on melee attack rolls against creatures of a larger size category than you.

SHARE SIZE

Starting at 17th level, you can choose a creature within 5 feet as an action and change its size to match yours for 1 hour. If the target is unwilling, it can make a Constitution saving throw (DC 8 + your Intelligence modifier + your proficiency bonus). On a success, it remains its current size. It can make a new saving throw at the end of each of its turns, ending the effect on a success. You can reverse the effect as a bonus action on your turn or a reaction on another creature's turn. If the target changes size and is grappled or restrained, you can choose to free it as it changes size.

If the creature is reduced in size, its size is halved in all dimensions, and its weight is reduced by 1/8 for each size category it shrunk. It also has disadvantage on Strength checks and Strength saving throws for the duration. Its equipment also shrinks, and its weapon attacks deal 1d4 less damage for each size category it shrunk (this can't reduce the damage below 1).

If the creature is enlarged in size, its size is doubled in all dimensions, and its weight is multiplied by 8 for each size category it grew. It also has advantage on Strength checks and Strength saving throws for the duration. Its equipment also grows, and its weapon attacks deal 1d4 more damage for each size category it grew.

Once you use this feature, you can't use it again until you finish a long rest.

BACKGROUNDS

The following backgrounds are especially common in goodfellows. At the GM's discretion, other appropriate races may have access to them.

MANITOU'S FELLOW

You've spent time in Manitou's Gift against queen Mab's wishes and have met the trickster lord. He showed you the way of untamed lands and the feral beauty they contain. Having roamed the lands of Manitou's Gift whenever you can, you adhere to the lessons that Mab's former lover has taught you. Of course, you now see the tame lands of Scáthbaile as the prison they truly are.

Skill Proficiencies: Nature, Survival

Tool Proficiencies: Herbalism kit, musical instrument (horn)

Equipment: Hunting horn, 5 gp worth of platinum flakes, a token from Manitou (usually a symbol of the hunt), a set of traveler's clothes, and 10 days' worth of rations

MANITOU'S REQUEST

When you first met Manitou, he granted to you the protection of his abdicated demesne (which he still maintains just enough influence over) in exchange for something. Roll or choose a request from the table below, or create a different request with the GM's approval.

d4	Request
1	Keep an eye on Mab, and make sure she doesn't go to war with Titania.
2	Protect Manitou's Gift from any encroachment from the others of Faerie.
3	Help Manitou find his daughter Pellowea.
4	One day, Manitou will ask for a favor, and you will do it, no questions asked.

FEATURE: MANITOU'S BLESSING

You can go to Manitou's Gift, and the land will provide you with succor in the form of the hunt. Manitou's Gift is a place of the wilds, and you feel at home there. You can find food, shelter, and simply exist for a time. And if you go to Hunter's Tower, you might find Manitou himself and beg his wisdom.

SUGGESTED CHARACTERISTICS

All of Manitou's fellows are shaped to some degree by the secrecy inherent in their relationship with the trickster lord—and by their fear of what might happen if that relationship is discovered by the wrong people. They are drawn to wilderness and untamed lands, and they quickly become restless in other environments, especially civilized realms where the need to hunt cannot be satisfied.

d8	Personality Trait
1	I enjoy the green and the warm so much more than the cold.
2	Animals are my friends and allies—my family. I would never harm an animal unless I had no choice.
3	I stare into people's eyes. It's just something I do.
4	I always look for a weakness or an edge I can exploit, in all situations, always trying to get the upper hand.
5	I constantly crave the thrill of the hunt, the pounding heart, the labored breath, the taxing muscles.
6	I honor the land—even speak to it—every day.
7	I avoid people, requiring instead only solitude.
8	I talk to myself all the time. I mean, I'm doing it right now.

d6	Ideal
1	Joy. To hunt gives me the greatest joy, regardless of what prey I seek, always testing my wits and my might. (Evil)
2	Preparedness. It's only a matter of time before something bad happens, but I'll be ready. (Lawful)
3	Beauty. I hunt to eat, but I live for Manitou's Gift. (Any)
4	Dedication. The living come and go, but the hunt is forever. Accept the hunt, for it is eternal. (Neutral)
5	Service. For all I've been given, it is important that I be useful, that I return something of myself. (Good)
6	Freedom. I can live like I've always wanted. (Chaotic)

d6	Bond
1	There is no lovelier place than Manitou's Gift. I spend as much time there as I can.
2	The folk of my wreath are precious, but if they knew about my time in Manitou's Gift, it would cause an irreparable rift between us.
3	Mab killed the leaders of my wreath. I will find some way to get revenge.
4	I owe Manitou a debt for saving my life. I will repay him or die trying.
5	Despite Manitou's friendship, he hurt one I hold above all, and I cannot forgive that.
6	I owe it to myself to live my truest life.

d6	Flaw
1	I've become a little wilder than I used to be and would be of no use in courtly affairs.
2	Instinct is my first response to any problem—and my instinct too often tells me to fight.
3	A wreathmate found out about my arrangement with Manitou, and I was forced to murder them to keep my secret.
4	I'm blunt, lacking any tact or subtlety. It draws attention to me in a way I don't like.
5	I have no interest in fulfilling Manitou's request of me.
6	I'm paranoid of Mab's spies, that she suspects and is constantly watching me.

PRETERNATURAL TRAVELER

Life in Scáthbaile was nice for a while, but you eventually grew tired of the shadows, the cold, and the hate your queen felt toward Titania. So you left that realm to go wandering across the Preternatural Planes (see *Along the Twisting Way: The Faerie Ring Campaign Guide*). As you walk those realms and meet their strange and unusual denizens, you stop from time to time in the hope of settling down. Still, you know it's only a matter of time before you start wandering again.

Skill Proficiencies: Insight, Survival

Languages: Two of your choice

Equipment: An explorer's pack with 20 feet of silk rope instead of hempen rope, a rose thorn from Mab's garden, a walking stick, a leaf hat, and fragments of diamond worth 10 gp

FEATURE: I'VE MET THAT FEY

Having traveled through many lands, you have met countless fey who you count among your friends—and sometimes your enemies. Each time you enter a city or demesne, you know someone in it. The GM determines how and when you meet this creature, but its attitude toward you is determined by rolling a d20. If the roll is 16 or higher, the creature is friendly toward you. On a 5 or lower, the creature doesn't like you or wants to harm you for some reason. Any other result indicates that you are aware of each other but hold neither animosity nor friendship for each other.

Additionally, the many rumors you've heard on your travels mean that you always have a good idea of where to start looking for someone. When you want to speak with a figure in Faerie, the GM will tell you the best place to seek that creature out.

SUGGESTED CHARACTERISTICS

Many preternatural travelers carry a sense of darkness and wonder, extending from the realms they have journeyed through. The things they have seen leave some preternatural travelers possessed of an unnatural calm as if nothing is capable of surprising them. Others are constantly wary and on edge, having been taught by their experiences to take nothing and no one at face value.

d8	Personality Trait
1	My moods swerve in strange directions like the winding road.
2	I love good conversation with someone new even more than talking with an old acquaintance.
3	Existence stretches ahead of me like an endless horizon, and I walk toward whatever might be waiting there with a smile.
4	I like to cause trouble as much as help end it, but I don't always think my pranks through.
5	Blazing new trails through wilderness and unsettled lands are preferable to urban areas.
6	Details of all the people I meet are kept in my journals, and I often relive my conversations in their pages.
7	Nothing brings me more joy than bringing people together through my pranks.
8	I draw detailed maps of all the places I visit.

d6	Ideal
1	Knowledge. Mab's way wasn't for me, but I still need to find a way. (Lawful)
2	Experience. I never walk the same path twice. (Any)
3	Independence. Putting down roots isn't really my thing. (Chaotic)
4	Beauty. Seeing the wondrous beauty of Faerie is what I live for. (Any)
5	Connection. Interacting and aiding others is the best way I can help. (Good)
6	Power. Collecting and leveraging secrets along the way ensures my comfort. (Evil)

d6	Bond
1	My endless wandering is the only way to stay one step ahead of the others of my wreath. We push one another to ever greater accomplishments.
2	I wander because I couldn't be with the star sprite I love.
3	I've met so many incredible creatures on my travels, and I wish to be able to meet them all again.
4	Faerie is as beautiful as it is varied, and I must protect that beauty.
5	The gathering and accumulation of knowledge is all that matters.
6	My dearest is lost out there somewhere, and I won't stop until I find them.

d6	Flaw
1	I have a hard time making friends because I don't want to stay in one place.
2	I dislike those who have settled lives, those who have chosen to "stand still."
3	I'll walk out of a place that needs my help if doing so means saving myself.
4	I typically come on strong with new folks, and doing so often gets relationships off on the wrong foot.
5	I don't really like people much at all. I mean, companionship never sits well with me.
6	I'll go to any length for the perfect prank, even if people get hurt.

ADDITIONAL OPTIONS

The following options are available to goodfellows. At the GM's discretion, other appropriate races may have access to some of these new rules.

EQUIPMENT

Goodfellows have developed the following equipment according to their specific needs and utilize them to particular effect.

Acid Flower. This weaponized plant is similar to a

blowgun, but its ammunition is a carnivorous flower bud. Medium and larger creatures have disadvantage on attacks with an acid flower due to its small size.

Beguiling Fife. When you play this fife with a successful DC 15 Charisma check as an action, it emits notes that distract one target beast that can hear it within 60 feet. The target can negate the effect with a successful DC 10 Wisdom saving throw. If a creature succeeded on its saving throw against that fife in the past 24 hours, it automatically succeeds on its saving throw. A distracted creature is incapacitated, has disadvantage on passive Wisdom checks, and approaches you for as long as you continue to play as an action each round. If this movement would take the creature through a dangerous area, it gets a new saving throw with advantage immediately, ending the effect on itself on a success. If the creature is attacked, the effect ends. Creatures engaged in combat are immune to the fife's sound.

Deftbow. This Tiny shortbow is made up of one piece of wood, about 8 inches in length. If you score a critical hit with it, double your Dexterity bonus along with the damage dice. Medium and larger creatures have disadvantage on attacks with a deftbow due to its small size.

Goodfellow Riding Bee, Queen. Goodfellows have domesticated a species of giant bees. These riding bees have been bred to respond to goodfellows; you have advantage on Wisdom (Animal Handling) checks to influence riding bees if you are a goodfellow. A riding queen bee has the same statistics has a giant wasp. A riding queen bee can be ridden by a Small humanoid or up to four goodfellows in a basket underneath (which is a type of exotic saddle).

Goodfellow Riding Bee, Worker. A riding worker bee is similar to a riding queen bee except that it is Small, it has 10 (3d6) hit points, its Strength is 7 (–2), its challenge rating is 1/8 (25 XP), and stinging is very risky for it. Whenever it stings, it must succeed on a DC 10 Constitution saving throw, or its stinger rips free, in which case it can no longer sting and it dies 10 minutes later. A trained riding worker bee stings only if a goodfellow or queen bee uses an action to command it to do so. Riding bees require a light but carefully placed exotic saddle, which keeps the rider out of the way of the bee's wings.

Wreath Emblem, Common. Gifted to goodfellow children when their magical abilities develop, this minuscule, wreath-shaped metal symbol has the imagery of the goodfellow wreath the individual has shown an aptitude for. Often worn as a cloak clasp or a brooch, this emblem is the envy and bane of the goodfellows who lack magical talents.

Wreath Emblem, Elaborate. Elaborate wreath emblems are similar to common wreath emblems except that they are intricately styled and typically made of precious metals inlaid with precious stones.

GOODFELLOW EQUIPMENT

Item	Cost	Weight
Acid flower buds (50)	1 gp	1 lb.
Beguiling fife	400 gp	1/2 lb.
Deftbow arrows (50)	1 gp	1 lb.
Wreath emblem, common	5 sp	—
Wreath emblem, elaborate	10 gp	—

GOODFELLOW WEAPONS

Name	Cost	Damage	Weight	Properties
Martial Ranged Weapons				
Acid flower	25 gp	1d4 acid	1/2 lb.	Ammunition (range 25/100), loading, special
Deftbow	35 gp	1d4 piercing	1 lb.	Ammunition (range 60/240), special, two-handed

Goodfellow Mounts

Item	Cost	Speed	Carrying Capacity
Goodfellow Riding Bee			
Queen	350 gp	50 ft.	100 lb.
Worker	100 gp	50 lb.	50 lb.

Feats

Goodfellows have evolved a style all their own and are quite fond of the following feats.

Argemone (Prickly Poppy)

Prerequisites: Goodfellow, Wreath of the Poppy

You have mastered the magic of the poppy to gain the following benefits:

- You add the *major image* spell to your Poppy Magic trait. You can cast this spell once with that trait and regain the ability to do so when you finish a long rest.
- You add the *sleep* spell to your Poppy Magic trait. You can cast this spell three times with that trait. You regain all expended uses when you finish a long rest.
- Your skin sprouts thorns and burs that make it painful to maintain contact with you. Any creature that successfully grapples you or hits you with a natural weapon or an unarmed strike takes 1d6 piercing damage. You can then use your reaction to cast *sleep* against only that creature. When you do so, roll 10d8 instead of 5d8 to determine how many hit points the spell can affect.

Darklight

Prerequisites: Goodfellow

You are able to absorb the light around you:

- As a bonus action, you can completely turn off your Glow trait, so that you shed no light. As a bonus action, you can turn your Glow back on.
- You can cast the *darkness* spell once per day without expending a spell slot. It must be centered on yourself, and you can see through the darkness you create with this feat.

Deadly Nightshade

Prerequisites: Goodfellow, Wreath of the Belladonna

You have mastered the magic of the belladonna to gain the following benefits:

- Increase your Intelligence or Charisma score by 1, to a maximum of 20.
- When you make a Charisma check, you can treat the check as if you had rolled a 15 on the d20. You can choose to do so after you roll the die for the check but before the GM tells you whether you succeed or fail. Additionally, if you are under any effect that would compel you to speak the truth or that would detect the truth of your statements, anything you say as part of the check is treated as truthful. If you must make a saving throw to speak the truth, you automatically succeed. Once you use this ability, you can't use it again until you finish a short or long rest.
- You can spend 1 Hit Die to magically produce one dose of poison, which can be delivered through ingestion or by injury. The dose of poison can be used to coat one slashing or piercing weapon or up to three pieces of ammunition and remains potent for 5 minutes. Any creature that ingests the poison or is injured by a weapon treated with it must succeed on a Constitution saving throw (DC 8 + your proficiency bonus + your Charisma modifier) or be poisoned for 1 minute.

Elderberry

Prerequisites: Goodfellow, Wreath of the Elder

You have mastered the magic of the elderberry to gain the following benefits:

- Increase your Intelligence or Charisma score by 1, to a maximum of 20.
- You add the *lesser restoration* spell to your Elder Magic trait. You can cast this spell three times with that trait. You regain all expended uses when you finish a long rest. Your magic can sap the energy from an enemy. Choose one creature within your reach. The target must succeed on a Constitution saving throw (DC 8 + your proficiency bonus + your Charisma modifier) or gain one level of exhaustion. You can use this

ability three times. You regain all expended uses when you finish a long rest.

HUMMINGBIRD

Prerequisites: Goodfellow, Wreath of the Foxglove

You have mastered the magic of the foxglove to gain the following benefits:

- Increase your Intelligence or Charisma score by 1, to a maximum of 20.
- You add the *blur* spell to your Foxglove Magic trait. You can cast this spell three times with that trait. You regain all expended uses when you finish a long rest.
- You add the *haste* spell to your Foxglove Magic trait. You can cast this spell three times with that trait. You regain all expended uses when you finish a long rest.
- You add the *slow* spell to your Foxglove Magic trait. You can cast this spell once with that trait and regain the ability to do so when you finish a long rest.

HYBRID FLOWER

Prerequisite: Goodfellow

You have the knack and aptitude for more than one kind of wreath magic. You can choose another wreath in addition to the wreath you chose at character creation. You have access to all its associated abilities.

JACK-O'-LANTERN

Prerequisites: Goodfellow, Wreath of the Pumpkin

You have mastered the magic of the pumpkin to grant you improved shapechanging ability. You gain the druid's Wild Shape ability except you can transform only into a Small or Medium beast. You use your character level to determine the challenge rating of the beast you can transform into, and you can stay in beast shape for a number of hours equal to half your character level (rounded down).

You can use this ability twice. You regain all expended uses when you finish a short or long rest.

If you already have the druid's Wild Shape feature, this feat works separately from that feature.

PLANT FRIEND

Prerequisite: Goodfellow

You are in tune with the natural world around you, granting you the following benefits:

- While you are within an area containing plant life (including grasses, trees, or shrubs), you can use a bonus action to teleport up to 30 feet to a space you can see within the same area of plant life. The path of your teleportation cannot cross over any area more than 5 feet wide that is devoid of plant life.
- You add the *entangle* spell to the spellcasting trait granted to you by your wreath. You can cast this spell once with that trait and regain the ability to do so when you finish a long rest.
- As long as you are within an area containing plant life, you have advantage on Wisdom (Perception) checks to notice anything taking place within the same area of plant life.

SPRIGHTLY

Prerequisite: Goodfellow

You are faster than other goodfellows and better at avoiding danger while in the air. Your flying speed increases to 30 feet, and you have advantage on Dexterity ability checks and saving throws made while you are flying.

TILLER

Prerequisite: Goodfellow

You have developed a connection to the earth that grants you the following benefits:

- Increase your Strength or Constitution score by 1, to a maximum of 20.
- You gain a burrowing speed of 20 feet. You can burrow through sand, earth, mud, and ice but not through solid rock. If you end your movement within the material you're burrowing through, you gain one level of exhaustion.
- Your hands are tipped with claws that can be used as a melee weapon attack. Your claws deal 1d4 slashing damage and have the finesse property.

Kitsune

Around every corner, beneath every rock, and past every horizon is a mystery. Sometimes you guess the ending before you get there, but sometimes it defies your most fevered dreams. I'm not going to waste my life with people who only seek answers or, worse, who can't muster enough curiosity to care.

—Mokuren "Ren" Kamura

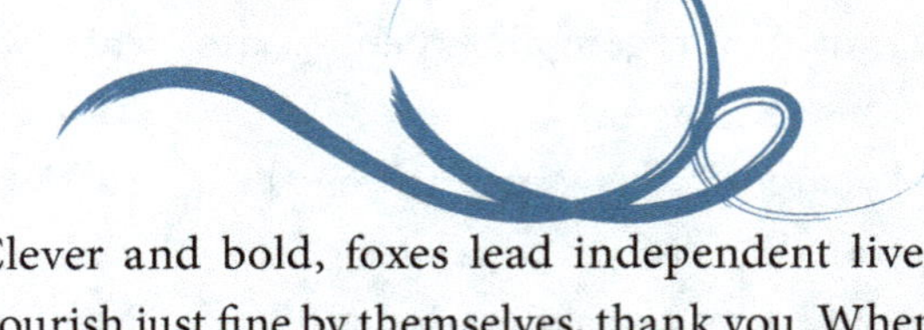

Clever and bold, foxes lead independent lives and flourish just fine by themselves, thank you. When a fox reaches a century of age, it transforms into a fey known as a kitsune, opening a new chapter—one of many to come—in a life much more complex than a mundane fox could ever know.

A kitsune is every bit as charming and witty as a typical fox but enhanced by magic and greater intelligence. With age, kitsune grow extra tails and uncover new stages of enlightenment and powerful sorcery. A kitsune's journey is long and full of new challenges, but intuition and magic act as their guides, pushing the kitsune into new life milestones with each new tail. These challenges are simple enough at first but grow more daunting with time. Only the strongest kitsune ever reach the pinnacle of their enlightenment: a ninth tail.

The spiritual side of the kitsune is important to them but is not a side outsiders ever see. As part of their development, kitsune are driven to interact with others. Early in maturity, these interactions are often driven by mischief and a desire to test boundaries and elicit reactions. Later, their dealings with outsiders become more curious, seeking knowledge and forming bonds. The outside world carries many dangers for kitsune however; their history is rife with betrayals, hunts, and mistrust from outsiders who do not understand them or are confused and frightened by their changing natures. Once a kitsune becomes consumed with bitterness and revenge, there is no turning back.

Kitsune characters possess an assortment of traits all their own.

- ***Ability Score Increase.*** Your Dexterity score increases by 2, and your Charisma score increases by 1.
- ***Languages.*** You speak, read, and write Common and Fox—a unique language that allows kitsune to communicate with true foxes as well as others of their kind.
- ***Size.*** An adult kitsune is slightly more than 3 feet long, and weighs about 20 pounds. Your size is Small.
- ***Speed.*** Your base walking speed is 40 feet.
- ***Type.*** Your type is fey. Spells and effects that specifically target humanoids do not affect you. You also gain the yokai subtype (see **Appendix**).

- ***Bite.*** Your sharp teeth grant you a bite attack that deals 1d4 piercing damage. You are proficient with your bite attack, which is treated as a light melee weapon with the finesse property.
- ***Darkvision.*** Your fey heritage provides you with superior vision in dim and dark conditions. You can see in dim light within 60 feet as if it were bright light and in darkness as if it were dim light. You can't discern color in darkness, only shades of gray.
- ***Dextrous Tail.*** You have one tail. You can use your tail to hold and manipulate objects as easily as you could with a hand. You can also use it to provide somatic components for spells. You can't use your tail to wield shields or to attack with weapons (other than those specifically designed for it). At 3rd level and every odd level thereafter, you grow an additional tail, to a maximum of nine tails.
- ***Fox Magic.*** Choose *dancing lights* or *minor illusion*. You know the chosen cantrip. You can also cast *speak with animals* once per day. Feats can allow you to cast other spells with this feature. Charisma is your spellcasting ability for these spells. Casting any of them requires your star ball as a spellcasting focus (see below).
- ***Keen Smell.*** You have advantage on Wisdom (Perception) checks that rely on smell.
- ***Quadruped.*** You move on four legs and have paws instead of hands. You cannot hold items such as weapons, shields, or implements, and you cannot wear armor or other items unless they are modified to fit your form.
- ***Shapechanger.*** At character creation, you can choose the form of a Small or Medium humanoid race and choose a unique appearance for an individual of that race. You can use your action to assume that unique appearance. In humanoid form, your speed becomes 30 feet, and you lose your Bite, Dextrous Tail, Keen Smell, and Quadruped traits. Each time, you can choose to retain your tail or make it disappear until you return to fox form. By concentrating for 10 minutes (as if concentrating on a spell), you can change your humanoid form (but not its race). You can change your humanoid form's appearance, including height, weight, facial features, sound of your voice, hair length, coloration, and distinguishing characteristics, if any. You can make an Intelligence (disguise kit) check to create a disguise this way even without a disguise kit. At 3rd level, you can alter your humanoid shape in 1 minute.
- ***Star Ball.*** You can use a stone as a spellcasting focus even if your spellcasting class can't normally do so. It must be magic or have sentimental value to you and be no larger than a few inches in diameter. While attuned, the star ball can be made to cling firmly to your forehead or the base of your throat, and it cannot be targeted or stolen while attached. Attaching or detaching a star ball is an action. The star ball is a required spellcasting focus for your Fox Magic feature. Magic star balls can serve a variety of functions, such as weapons and armor, as described in *Along the Twisted Path: Magic Guide*.

Physical Description: A young kitsune resembles a slightly larger fox. Their coloration is typical of foxes, from a vivid red or orange to brown, black, or snowy white. Kitsune do carry themselves with a regal air and compose themselves with more intelligence than a typical fox, but these differences are slight. As kitsune age, they gain multiple tails, marking their fey nature immediately.

Kitsune also possess a humanoid shape chosen when they learn to transform as fledgling fey. For most kitsune, this form is static and is indistinguishable from a normal member of their chosen race. Kitsune tend to keep similar coloration between their forms or at least hints of it. They may choose to keep their tails in humanoid form each time they transform, or they may hide them entirely.

Society: Kitsune are fiercely independent and have a life cycle demanding their latest stages be taken alone, so kitsune society is a loose, fragmented thing. They claim no kings or lords, only occasional leaders some foxes choose to rally behind—or not.

Kitsune, especially young ones, tend to make dens near others of their kind. These little tribes are essentially neighborhoods where kitsune enjoy company, advice, and limited protection. Kitsune are quick to defend their own against unwarranted attack, but should a kitsune provoke an outsider, it's generally accepted they should take responsibility for the consequences of their actions. Otherwise, the kitsune reason, how shall they learn to keep their meddling under control? A fox unable to contend with possible retribution for mischief is a dead fox.

Kitsune are easy-going and tolerant for the most part but take seriously threats brought down on them by their own. Kitsune who do not understand how their actions affect their own kind can quickly come to find themselves run out of their own den.

Another quirk of kitsune culture, keeping it unorganized, is their fascination with other cultures. It's easy for a kitsune to get swept away in a double life among other races, even marrying in and producing children, all—more often than not—while hiding their true identity. The tragic tale of Red Jack is one that repeats itself all too often among the kitsune, over and over again. (Though, thankfully, there is only the one of said furious, death-infatuated quiddity.)

Relations: Kitsune are seen by many cultures as creatures of ill omen. Their mischief and tendency toward deception has made them unwelcome guests in many areas, though just as many kitsune meddle for the benefit of their targets. It makes no difference—it is the negative that tends to be remembered. Among other fey, kitsune may be respected for their potent magic and wisdom or dismissed for their capriciousness and fascination with mortals.

Alignment and Religion: Despite their poor reputations, kitsune actually trend toward good, albeit a fiercely independent and chaotic good. Evil kitsune are quite rare and are almost always exiles, often victims of a betrayal or injustice that has consumed them with hatred and vengeance or else kitsune that played a malicious trick too many for their tribes to continue tolerating them.

Kitsune are spiritual creatures, and it isn't uncommon for them to forge divine connections, especially with the natural world or with more mysterious forces, given their curiosity.

Adventurers: The bulk of kitsune adventurers are of an age around their fifth tail, when they become consumed with the urge to travel and explore. If mated, they will implore their mate to go with them, but they otherwise break with tribes, seeking adventure on their own. Other kitsune adventurers may be exiles or else curious, younger kitsune often hiding in their humanoid form.

Magic-using kitsune are just as common as are those in roles appealing to their penchant for charm and trickery, such as bards and rogues. Their strong spiritual side may also draw them into roles such as oracles, shamans, and witches.

Age: A kitsune is considered mature by age 100, and most kitsune don't start to see a decline until 200 years of age. Some lucky members of this race might live to 300 years and beyond.

Names: Kitsune collect names the way some mortals collect rocks. They usually acquire a nickname, often mono- or disyllabic, using gruff or chuffing sounds to suit their natural form. They usually transform this name into something appropriate for the region's races they interact with, and they go by that in public, borrowing names of celebrities or folk heroes as needed to fill in gaps or preserve anonymity, slipping off one identity for another as it suits them.

Female Names: Aishi, Cha, Eki, Hibiki, Jun, Miki, Ori, Suza, Waka.

Male Names: Dakki, Goro, Isaku, Kenji, Noku, Ryo, Taru, Yuti.

SUBCLASSES

The fey provide an array of unique qualities and perspectives for creating interesting new characters. Consult your GM before applying these subclasses to other races.

CIRCLE OF THE INARI
(DRUID: DRUID CIRCLE)

Those of Inari associate themselves with agricultural communities, especially healthy harvests and sacred feasts. You derive great meaning in the patterns of crops, the movement of seasons, and the cycle of agriculture. Happy, you are a harbinger of well-fed communities, but scorned, you herald famine and blight.

BONUS CANTRIPS

When you choose this circle at 2nd level, you learn two cantrips of your choice from any class's spell list.

DIVINER OF NATURE

Starting at 2nd level, you learn to see omens of danger in the natural world around you. When you are outdoors or in the presence of ample plant or animal life, you have advantage on initiative rolls, and you cannot be surprised.

CIRCLE SPELLS

You are granted the following circle spells.

CIRCLE OF THE INARI

Druid Level	Circle Spells
3rd	*augury, spike growth*
5th	*plant growth, remove curse*
7th	*blight, divination*
9th	*insect plague, scrying*

PLANTSPEAKER

Starting at 6th level, you can easily influence plants and plant creatures with your magic. You can spend 10 minutes and expend a spell slot to magically alter the plant life in a 500-foot radius around you for better or for worse. If you decide to aid the plant life, it grows twice as fast as it normally would for 1 day per level of the spell slot expended. If you decide to harm the plant life, it does not grow for 1 day per level of the spell slot expended.

In addition, your healing magic is exceptionally effective on plant creatures. Whenever you cast a spell that would restore hit points to a creature with the plant type, that creature regains the maximum number of hit points possible. For example, a 2nd-level *cure wounds* spell would restore hit points equal to 16 + your spellcasting modifier.

NATURE'S CHOSEN

When you reach 10th level, you are immune to poison and disease, and you have resistance to one of the following damage types of your choice: acid, cold, fire, lightning, or thunder. Once this choice is made, it cannot be changed.

NATURE'S MANTLE

Starting at 14th level, your very presence dramatically affects the plant life around you. As an action on your turn, you can cause the rampant growth of any source of plant life or fungus in a 60-foot radius around you. This growth lasts for 1 minute, during which time you can use a bonus action each round to have the growth latch on to a creature you can see. That creature must succeed on a Strength or Dexterity saving throw or be restrained and take 3d8 bludgeoning damage. On a successful save, the creature takes half damage and isn't restrained. Affected plants and fungi return to their normal size and form after 1d4 hours. After activating this feature, you must finish a long rest before you can use it again.

FANGED WARRIOR
(FIGHTER: MARTIAL ARCHETYPE)

Most humanoid races have similar visions of the skilled warrior. An armored knight with longsword and shield. An agile master of the rapier. A brutal wielder of the greataxe. But for certain creatures, a fast bite can prove just as deadly as the most fearsome weapon.

To be a fanged warrior, you must be proficient with a bite attack, for the familiarity you have with this natural weapon cannot be duplicated by any kind of mundane weapon training. As a fanged warrior, you combine the ferocity of close combat with the agility of the most skilled martial artists.

VICIOUS BITE

When you choose this archetype at 3rd level, your bite becomes more vicious. If the damage die for your bite attack is smaller than a d8, it increases to a d8. If the damage die is already a d8 or greater, increase the damage to the next largest die.

Additionally, you can choose to have any bite attack you make deal either bludgeoning, piercing, or slashing damage.

CLOSE-QUARTERS FANGS

Starting at 7th level, you can move through the space of any creature regardless of its size, and that space is not difficult terrain for you. Additionally, whenever you start your turn grappled, you can make a bite attack as a bonus action on that turn. If the bite attack hits, the grappled condition ends on you.

MARAUDER LEAP

Beginning at 10th level, your bite attack strikes sure and swift. Your reach with your bite attack increases by 5 feet.

IN THE FRAY

At 15th level, you have mastered the art of using your foes' positions to your advantage. When you are within 5 feet of a hostile creature that is not incapacitated, you gain a +4 bonus to AC against ranged attacks and a +4 bonus to Dexterity saving throws against area effects.

JAWS OF STEEL

At 18th level, your tenacity in battle makes your bite attacks almost impossible to avoid. When you hit a creature with your first attack on your turn, you can latch onto that creature. Any attack you make against the same creature until the end of your turn has advantage, and such attacks score a critical hit on a roll of 18–20.

FOXMATE
(ROGUE: ROGUISH ARCHETYPE)

Kitsune, more so than most other fey, bear a special fascination with mortals. As a foxmate, you bring this fascination to life through your dedication to being an ideal partner to your allies. The connection you forge is everything to you.

PROTECTIVE

Starting at 3rd level, your rogue talents are most effective when you have an ally or innocent to protect. Choose a nonhostile creature to be your partner (no action required). Whenever a creature you can see attacks your partner, you can use your reaction to attack that creature. When you choose a partner, you maintain that connection for 1 hour or until you choose another partner. You can use this feature a number of times equal to your Charisma modifier (minimum once). You regain any expended uses when you finish a long rest.

ALL EYES ON ME

Beginning at 9th level, you can draw attention to yourself to protect your companions. Whenever you successfully use your Sneak Attack feature against a creature, the target must make a Charisma saving throw (DC 8 + your proficiency bonus + your Charisma modifier). On a failure, the target has disadvantage on attack rolls targeting any creature other than you until the end of its next turn.

SOMEONE TO PROTECT

Starting at 13th level, whenever you use your Protective feature to choose a partner, your connection with your partner grows deeper. Both you and your partner have advantage on death saving throws as long as one of you is still conscious, and you both automatically succeed on Wisdom (Medicine) checks to stabilize one another.

EXCEPTIONAL TEAMWORK

By 17th level, whenever you use your Protective feature to choose a partner, you and your partner can almost read one another's minds in combat. While you are within 5 feet of your partner, you both have advantage on saving throws, and you both gain a bonus to your attack and damage rolls equal to your and your partner's Charisma modifiers combined.

LOVE OF DEATH DOMAIN (CLERIC: DIVINE DOMAIN)

The love of death domain attracts clerics who worship Red Jack as a god and who the fey lord deems worthy of being closer to Death. The quiddity's power helps you kill those deserving of death's cold embrace. You may seek that power to express your rage. You may simply believe that death is the inevitable end of life and desire to understand that endless cycle. You may simply have an ineffable attraction to the mystery of the grave.

LOVE OF DEATH DOMAIN

You are granted the following domain spells.

LOVE OF DEATH DOMAIN SPELLS

Cleric Level	Spells
1st	*create or destroy water, inflict wounds*
3rd	*gentle repose, ray of enfeeblement*
5th	*speak with dead, vampiric touch*
7th	*blight, phantasmal killer*
9th	*cloudkill, flame strike*

BONUS PROFICIENCY

When you choose this domain at 1st level, you gain proficiency with the Survival skill.

SEEKER OF DEATH

Also starting at 1st level, any spell you cast that deals damage to a creature deals extra damage equal to 2 + the spell's level.

CHANNEL DIVINITY: MARK OF DEATH

Starting at 2nd level, you can use your Channel Divinity to mark your prey for death.

As an action, you mark a creature you can see with the symbol of Red Jack. For 1 hour, you can sense the direction to the creature's location, and all your attack rolls against the creature have advantage.

CORPSE SPEAKER

Beginning at 6th level, you ask Death to grant you a few moments with a creature it has claimed. You can ask a corpse a single question as if you had cast the *speak with dead* spell. Once you use this ability, you can't use it again until you finish a long rest.

DEADLY SPELLCASTING

Starting at 8th level, you add your Wisdom modifier to the damage you deal with any cleric cantrip.

GRAY WALKER

Starting at 17th level, you are able to transform into an insubstantial figure of gray mist. As an action, you can gain the benefit of the *gaseous form* spell (no concentration required), or you can change back into your normal form.

NINETAILS BLOODLINE (SORCERER: SORCEROUS ORIGIN)

The magic that flows through your veins stems from a particularly powerful nine-tailed kitsune. While kitsune typically take the shape of a fox, they also possess the power to take human form, and while these creatures are capricious tricksters, they are also steadfast and loyal lovers and parents. Thanks to their supernaturally long lives, they often watch over their bloodline for generations, often retreating later in life to protect their particularly heroic descendants as a secret mentor.

Some particularly mirthful kitsune arrange events to

urge their descendants into a life of adventure and then leave subtle clues to guide those adventurers to them in order to train them in the ways of magic.

SPIRIT TAIL

At 1st level, choose one spell from the bard or druid class list. A spell you choose must be of a level you can cast, as shown on the Sorcerer table, or a cantrip. This chosen spell counts as a sorcerer spell for you but does not count against the number of sorcerer spells you know. If you do not already have one, a fox tail manifests on your body, twitching and behaving exactly as a natural tail might. You can make your fox tail invisible or visible as a bonus action.

Additionally, at 3rd, 5th, 7th, 9th, 11th, 13th, 15th, and 17th level, you gain one new spirit tail spell as an additional tail appears next to the first.

TAILS OF VITALITY

Starting at 6th level, you can spend 1 sorcery point as a bonus action to regain 1d8 hit points. Each time you do, another of your Spirit Tails turns a drab color until you finish a long rest or until you spend 1 sorcery point as a bonus action to restore its color.

You can't activate this feature while all your tails are drab.

MISCREANT'S MISDIRECTION

Starting at 14th level, when you are hit by an attack, you can use your reaction to turn invisible, teleport to an unoccupied location you can see within 60 feet, and create an illusory corpse of yourself in the place you are standing. This illusion is intangible but looks, sounds, and smells like your corpse and with a wound appropriate to the way it was supposedly killed. The double lasts for 1 hour or until you become visible again. The invisibility ends if you attack or cast a spell.

Once you have used this feature, you can't use it again until you finish a long rest.

TAILS OF FLOWING POWER

Beginning at 18th level, you can spend 9 sorcery points as an action to regain one spell slot of up to 6th level.

RED JACK

(WARLOCK: OTHERWORLDLY PATRON)

You have been touched by the mind of Red Jack. His power is your power, and you wield it with great skill. The confidence that comes from your patron often puts you at the center of attention when others are looking to be entertained. But behind your grace and affability is a darkness, for Death itself bolsters your powers and commands your attention. You scare yourself sometimes.

EXPANDED SPELL LIST

Red Jack lets you choose from an expanded list of spells when you learn a warlock spell. The following spells are added to the warlock spell list for you.

RED JACK EXPANDED SPELLS

Spell Level	Spells
1st	*hideous laughter, inflict wounds*
2nd	*blindness/deafness, calm emotions*
3rd	*revivify, speak with dead*
4th	*confusion, death ward*
5th	*antilife shell, contagion*

ONE WITH DEATH

Starting at 1st level, your connection to Red Jack provides you with the ability to transfer the life force of one creature to another. When you reduce a hostile creature to 0 hit points, you can restore hit points equal to 1d4 + your Charisma modifier to one creature within 60 feet of you that you can see. You can use this feature three times. You regain all expended uses when you finish a short or long rest.

IMMEDIATE VENGEANCE

Starting at 6th level, Red Jack grants you the ability to unleash pain on those who harm you. When a creature within 5 feet of you deals damage to you with a melee weapon attack, you can cause that creature to take psychic damage equal to half the damage dealt to you (no action required). Once you use this feature, you must finish a short or long rest before you can use it again.

RED JACK'S BLESSING

Beginning at 10th level, Red Jack shields you from the ravages of death. You gain resistance to necrotic damage. Additionally, your Immediate Vengeance feature can deal psychic damage or necrotic damage, as you choose.

LIVING DEATH

At 14th level, you can use your action to plunge a creature within your reach into a living death. The creature must succeed on a Wisdom saving throw against your warlock spell save DC or be stunned until the start of your next turn. At the start of that next turn, the creature is incapacitated until the start of your following turn. Once you use this feature, you must finish a short or long rest before you can use it again.

BACKGROUNDS

The following backgrounds are especially common in kitsune. At the GM's discretion, other appropriate races may have access to them.

RED JACK DEVOTEE

Growing up, your elders warned you and your peers about what happened to young foxes that misbehaved: Red Jack would pay you a visit, eat your body, and steal your soul. But while the other youngsters shook with fear and hid deep within their dens at the thought, you were intrigued. Could such a creature actually exist? What kind of power would it take to inspire generations of people of all races to fear you so?

As you matured, rather than growing out of such superstitious beliefs, you embraced them. If the old stories are true and Red Jack does exist, he surely must be one of the most marvelous creatures to ever grace the planes. So with your curiosity piqued and your nascent knowledge of Red Jack firmly driving you, you went out into the world to see if you could find him. Are you just beginning your journey to learn more about Red Jack and his secrets, or have you been searching for years? And if you have learned of Red Jack's obsession with revenge and death, has that changed your opinion of him—or does that just draw you closer?

Skill Proficiencies: History, Nature

Tool Proficiencies: Cartographer's tools

Equipment: A map to a recent location of Strangle Grove, a set of common clothes, and a pouch containing 20 gp

FEATURE: THE RED NETWORK

As a devotee to Red Jack, you have met others who have a similar infatuation with the fey lord. You share information and experiences with each other, all hoping to someday meet the object of your obsession. You and your adventuring companions can expect to receive help and solace from other members of the Red Network, as you call yourselves. You can live at a modest lifestyle by drawing upon the resources of the Red Network and performing small tasks or sharing information with your hosts.

You might also have a connection to a specific patron within the Red Network who can offer atypical resources. As long as you and your associates agree to occasionally perform tasks and share information about Red Jack, this patron can offer special benefits, ranging from a safe place to stay to access to rare equipment and services to powerful allies.

SUGGESTED CHARACTERISTICS

Members of the Red Network are generally kitsune, but any creature that has been touched by Red Jack—whether directly or indirectly—can join. Most members are simply infatuated with the stories of his powers. However, a number of Red Network devotees have had closer experiences. These characters are held in the highest regard within the Red Network, achieving celebrity status. Unfortunately, some of those directly touched by Red Jack and his powers have been tainted by the experience—warped by an obsession with death and vengeance and letting those powerful forces control their lives.

d8	Personality Trait
1	I believe in the power of stories—the more fantastical, the more real they are to me.
2	Another reality lingers just behind the one we live in. I must find that alternate reality.
3	When I find a path that leads toward my goals, nothing can stop me from following it.
4	Nothing is more important than power. Without it, you cannot achieve your goals.
5	There is a time for action, but that time comes only when one understands all the nuances of a situation.
6	I will never know as much as I need to know, but I will pretend I know. That way, everyone will defer to me.
7	No one is truly knowable. Even the most terrible creatures are simply misunderstood.
8	Fortune favors the bold. Recklessness is just a word used by those without the will to succeed.

d6	Ideal
1	Knowledge. The world—both seen and unseen—works according to immutable laws. The more I know, the better off I am. (Lawful)
2	Death. A small voice tells me that everything must die. While I do not kill for death's sake, neither do I hold back. (Evil)
3	Vengeance. Unless people understand that actions have dire consequences, the world will continue to be a terrible place. (Chaotic)
4	Power. The more power I gain, the better control I will have. (Neutral)
5	Acceptance. Good and evil are just constructs of small minds. The world and the creatures within it should not be judged outside the context of their actions. (Neutral)
6	Destiny. I am destined to be powerful, inspiring awe in others. (Any)

d6	Bond
1	A sibling or close friend wandered off into the forest one day and never returned. I know they are still alive.
2	An old nine-tail once told me a story of being at the village where Red Jack died. I think she knows more that she is not telling.
3	A new family has arrived, and one of the kits has a mark that makes me think they are a favored of Red Jack. I must watch warily as this young one grows.
4	My life's work is in a collection of scrolls, detailing all my knowledge of Strangle Grove. I would be distraught if anything ever happened to it.
5	As a youngster, I was orphaned when my parents disappeared in the forest. Although my stepparents were of a different race, they raised me as their own.
6	Once when I was supposed to meet a patron with information, I was attacked by strange creatures. I still don't know if I was betrayed or if something terrible happened.

d6	Flaw
1	I spend much of my time telling tales of the fey. Everyone should love my stories.
2	Leisure time is a waste of time. We need to keep moving and working to reach our goals.
3	The real world is an illusion, and its mundane pursuits are irrelevant. I bore quite easily when presented with mundane problems.
4	There are agents, hidden by illusion, trying to stop my pursuit of knowledge.
5	I would do anything to meet Red Jack even once. Anything at all.
6	If Red Jack notices me, I will gain his favor. This means that everything I do must be dedicated to catching his attention.

STRANGLE GROVE SURVIVOR

At some point during your formative years, the fey demesne of Strangle Grove was overlaid onto your homeland. You and your family didn't notice the difference at first, and life in your village went on as normal. Soon, however, unnatural occurrences and monstrous attacks became an ongoing threat, manifesting as shambling undead, strange plant creatures, and spectral visions of horror seemingly dragged from your mind.

Where others died, you survived. Where others' sanity cracked under the barrage of terror, you became a shining point of calm in a maelstrom of chaos. Finally, after years of fear, the phantom world evaporated. Scarred but unwavering, you helped rebuild your village, making sure those left of your friends and family were safe as they readjusted to their former lives.

But what now? Are you determined to learn what happened and make sure it never happens to others? Did you lose someone dear to you when the phantom world dissipated, and now you travel in search of them? Or was a seed of corruption planted in you by Strangle Grove, so you long to return to that nightmare region?

Skill Proficiencies: Insight, Survival

Language: Sylvan

Equipment: A set of traveler's clothes, a healer's kit, and a strange gem worth 30 gp

FEATURE: SEED OF KNOWLEDGE

Your exposure to Strangle Grove left you with indelible impressions of that place and a sense of its many secrets. You might know how to navigate that strange realm or to deal with the creatures that inhabit it. You might have even learned secrets that could threaten Red Jack, and those interested in the fey lord and his demesne might seek you out to offer recompense for your knowledge.

Work with your GM to determine what your knowledge is, when it is to be revealed, and how it might impact the campaign.

SUGGESTED CHARACTERISTICS

Those who spend time in Strangle Grove experience challenges and horrors that few would wish on their worst enemies. However, as with so many dark experiences, those who survive them are left stronger.

d8	Personality Trait
1	For every story someone else has about a rough life, I can top it twice over.
2	Weakness can be stripped away only through the hardest trials imaginable—for me and those around me.
3	Survival has left me rough around the edges. Social niceties are for others.
4	Seeing the suffering of others is unbearable to me. As I once protected those in need, I will do so again.
5	I've led people under the worst imaginable circumstances. I should lead again.
6	Magic cannot be trusted. All my nightmares were the result of magic gone awry.
7	My senses have been on edge for so long that I twitch and jump at every sound and movement.
8	After living such a rough life, I deserve the finest things

d6	Ideal
1	Community. If we all stick together, we are stronger than if we stand alone. (Good)
2	Dignity. I face my problems with grace and stoicism. Those who die with dignity win over those who live in shame and chaos. (Lawful)
3	Tyranny. The powerful must be kept in check at all times. (Chaotic)
4	Survival. I don't have to be the fastest and strongest—I just have to be faster and stronger than those around me when the wolves are at the gate. (Evil)
5	Readiness. Though I cannot be prepared for all contingencies, I can always be prepared. (Any)
6	Vengeance. So much was taken from me by my oppressors, and I will have retribution. (Any)

d6	Bond
1	I found a strange gem in Strangle Grove. I must never be separated from it, though I know not why.
2	I work the land, I love the land, and I will protect the land.
3	A proud fey of the courts once gave me a horrible beating, and I will take my revenge on any bully I encounter.
4	My tools are symbols of my past life, and I carry them so that I will never forget my roots.
5	The kitsune are my people. I will watch over them.
6	I wish my childhood sweetheart had come with me to pursue my destiny.

d6	Flaw
1	I fear nothing, for nothing can ever be as bad as the horrors I survived.
2	I will never be able to live down the terrible things I had to do to survive.
3	Sometimes I forget I have escaped Strangle Grove, and I relive a horrible experience.
4	I never experienced the freedom of youth, so now I overindulge in anything pleasurable.
5	Everyone else is a fool if they think that my opinion is not correct.
6	As I fight to protect the things I love, the rules and laws of society do not apply to me.

ADDITIONAL OPTIONS

The following options are available to kitsune. At the GM's discretion, other appropriate races may have access to some of these new rules.

EQUIPMENT

Kitsune have developed the following equipment according to their specific needs and utilize them to particular effect.

Paw Hooks. This set of four paw wraps contains hooks that help you grip rough surfaces. Generally, you don them while in humanoid form, and they remain in place when you transform into fox form. In either form, they allow you to make Dexterity (Acrobatics) checks to climb rather than Strength (Athletics). While you are a fox, the paw hooks grip small nooks and crannies normally too fine for fox paws.

Tail Ofuda, Decorative. This long strip of silk has bindings for tying onto a long, fluffy tail such as that of a kitsune. Each is inscribed with a symbol or message, most often a prayer to Red Jack or another powerful entity linked to death.

Tail Ofuda, Holy Inscription. You can use a tail ofuda inscribed with a holy symbol or prayer in a language you know as a spellcasting focus for cleric or paladin spells if you are wearing it.

Tail Ofuda, Material Inscription. A tail ofuda inscribed with magical inks that include powdered bits of material spell components can be used to provide material components for spells as long as you wear it. Components can be powdered and added to the ink of a material inscription tail ofuda with 1 hour of work. Using the ofuda to provide material components that are consumed causes the corresponding ink to disappear, which means it must be re-inked to provide the consumed component again. If a component pouch's contents are added to the ofuda, the material component tail ofuda can generally be used to provide any material component without a listed cost.

Tail Ofuda, Verbal Inscription. Wearing a tail ofuda inscribed with the verbal component of a spell enables you to cast that spell while providing its verbal component. Anyone who sees the ofuda can read enough of it to attempt an Intelligence (Arcana) check to recognize the spell. In general, the DC equals 10 + the spell level. If a spell uses the verbal inscription tail ofuda as a component and doesn't otherwise give away its source (as a ray originating from you would), observers might not notice you are casting a spell. Observers must succeed at an Intelligence (Arcana) or Wisdom (Perception) check contested by your Dexterity (Sleight of Hand) or Intelligence (Arcana) check to notice that you are casting a spell.

The verbal inscription is complete enough for a wizard to copy or prepare the spell, but a non-kitsune must succeed on an Intelligence (Arcana) check to do so. The DC equals 10 + the spell's level. Discounts to

KITSUNE WEAPONS

Name	Cost	Damage	Weight	Properties
Martial Melee Weapon				
Tail whip	5 gp	1d4 slashing	1 lb.	Finesse, light

scribing a spell into a spellbook also apply to creating a verbal inscription ofuda. If you are a kitsune and gain a spellbook spell for free (as a wizard does upon gaining a level), you can instead inscribe the spell on a verbal inscription by paying half the ofuda's price.

Tail Whip. Some kitsune adorn their tails with heavy sharp jewelry or rings that give enough heft to attack with. A kitsune wearing a tail whip cannot retrieve objects with the Dextrous Tail trait but can attack with the tail whip as a weapon. Donning or doffing the tail whip is similar to donning or doffing light armor.

KITSUNE EQUIPMENT

Item	Cost	Weight
Paw hooks (set)	25 gp	1/2 lb.
Tail ofuda, decorative	5 gp	—
Tail ofuda, holy symbol	5 gp	—
Tail ofuda, material inscription	+5 gp	—
Tail ofuda, verbal inscription		
Cantrip	100 gp	—
1st-level spell	150 gp	—
2nd-level spell	250 gp	—
3rd-level spell	350 gp	—
4th-level spell	500 gp	—
5th-level spell	700 gp	—
6th-level spell	1,000 gp	—
7th-level spell	1,500 gp	—
8th-level spell	2,000 gp	—
9th-level spell	3,000 gp	—

FEATS (FOX MAGIC)

Kitsune have evolved a style all their own and are quite fond of the following feats. (These feats add to your Fox Magic trait and do not expend spell slots.)

FANG OF THE FOX (FOX MAGIC)

Prerequisite: Kitsune

You are small but ferocious. You gain the following benefits:

- Your speed increases by 10 feet.
- When you damage a creature using your bite attack while having advantage, you can use a bonus action to swap places with an adjacent ally, which does not provoke opportunity attacks.
- When you use an action to Disengage, you can choose to gain the effects of an *expeditious retreat* spell until the start of your next turn,

FOX BREATH (FOX MAGIC)

Prerequisite: Kitsune

You breathe preternatural fire and thin the veil of reality. You gain the following benefits:

- When you make a melee attack against a creature, you can choose to target them with the effects of a *faerie fire* spell until the start of your next turn, whether you hit or not.
- As an action, you gain the benefit of the *see invisibility* spell until the start of your next turn. You can use this a number of times equal to the number of tails you possess. You regain all expended uses when you finish a long rest.

FOX SKULK (FOX MAGIC)

Prerequisite: Kitsune

You are legion. You gain the following benefits:

- On your turn, when you score a critical hit with your bite or reduce a creature to 0 hit points with it, you can make one bite attack as a bonus action.
- You add the *conjure animals* spell to your Fox Magic trait. When you cast the spell, you summon a fox (use a **jackal**) that looks exactly like you. As a move action, you can swap places with it magically. You can cast this spell three times and regain all expended uses when you finish a long rest. You can summon an additional fox each casting for each tail you possess.

UNSEEN PATH (FOX MAGIC)

Prerequisite: Kitsune

There are many path that go unnoticed by most. You gain the following benefits:

- You have advantage on checks made to escape a grapple.
- While you are hidden, you can take a move action to cast *misty step*, remaining hidden.

Matabiri

The confined test subjects continue to develop a unique proto-language based primarily on hand gestures developed before their vocal chords matured. They continue to possess a close attachment to Artifact 357, and their behavior continues to support my Mother Replacement Theory (see Day 14 log for details). Stranger still, the artifact appears to be responding to their language. I believe I am on the cusp of a breakthrough.

—"Day 1815,"

Official Log of Pema the Humanoid Isolator

The matabiri might appear a swimming contradiction to some at first blush. These amphibious fey are cunning and curious, versed in the arts of observation, experimentation, and deduction, yet they live in primitive clay abodes and flooded tunnels. They are given to reason and resourcefulness yet devoutly worship a silent sleeping god. They share a deep and caring solidarity of race but treat all others as chattel, raw material, and food. A deeply arrogant race, they alone have the sophistication to understand the complexity of the multiverse—just ask them.

Physical Description: Matabiri have wide, frog-like faces and large mouths with stretched lips. Their teeth are jagged and in rows. Many matabiri file them into razor sharp points. The only eye color among matabiri is cold black, but their amphibious skin may be cobalt blue or any range of blue-gray shades to a dark, near-black shade of ash. Some matabiri bear mottling along their backs or limbs, and spots, stripes, and gradients aren't uncommon.

Matabiri spend most of their lives in water or muck, so they have little use for clothing. Anatomical differences between a male and female matabiri are difficult for non-matabiri to understand; complicating the issue is their amphibious nature that sometimes causes the matabiri to change genders at some point in a life cycle. So while matabiri may don accessories or adornments to humor the norms of other cultures or as affectations, the few clothes worn by the matabiri always serve a purpose. Even matabiri armor, when it is used, tends to be constructed of local hides and resources.

Society: Despite the malevolence they display to others, matabiri are very communal, emphasizing community needs over personal gain. They rotate their duties and roles on a regular basis of seven lunar cycles. Matabiri are not discouraged from personal expression and development, only expected to set their interests aside

should the needs of current roles demand it.

Matabiri make use of anything around them. They are excellent improvisers, and most matabiri have a few unique "gadgets" on hand, created on the fly to help them with assigned tasks.

The well-oiled machine of matabiri society has two primary directives: to study and comprehend the Dream and to push the boundaries of their scientific understanding. Experimentation in the name of progress is a motto of the matabiri, and they feel no remorse for the tortures they inflict on lesser beings for the sake of knowledge.

Relations: As a culture, matabiri view other races as lesser creatures; even other fey—even other mogwoi—are worthy only of a snide and contemptuous tolerance.

Some do find outsider customs and products curious but never admired. They are users, collectors, and analysts of such things.

Alignment and Religion: The only god the matabiri want or need is Hob. The Dreamer and his infuriatingly esoteric Dream are spiritual puzzles to the matabiri, though ones that can and must be unraveled.

Given their rigorous social structure and philosophies of discipline and order, most matabiri are

MATABIRI TRAITS

Matabiri characters possess an assortment of traits all their own.

- ***Ability Score Increase.*** Your Dexterity score increases by 2, and your Intelligence score increases by 1.
- ***Languages.*** You can speak, read, and write Aquan and Common.
- ***Size.*** Matabiri average 3 to 4 feet tall and weigh about 40 pounds. Your size is Small.
- ***Speed.*** Your base walking speed is 20 feet.
- ***Type.*** Your type is fey. Spells and effects that specifically target humanoids do not affect you. You also gain the mogwoi subtype (see **Appendix**).

- ***Amphibious.*** You can breathe air and water.
- ***Darkvision.*** At home in poorly lit aquatic environments, you have superior vision in dark and dim conditions. You can see in dim light within 60 feet of you as if it were bright light and in darkness as if it were dim light. Underwater, you can see in dim light within 120 feet of you as if it were bright light and in darkness as if it were dim light. You can't discern color in darkness, only shades of gray.
- ***Dream Reading.*** You can recount visions from your dreams and spend 1 reservoir point as an action to glimpse secrets of the past. You learn of the strongest psychic impression left on an object or willing or helpless creature you touch, such as when the last time it was touched by a creature feeling strong emotions, including what those circumstances and emotions were. Momentous events might take precedence over recent events at the GM's discretion.
- ***Fixed Mind.*** You have advantage on saving throws against enchantment spells and any effect that would create a connection to your mind.
- ***Reservoir.*** As a matabiri, you have a number of reservoir points equal to your proficiency bonus. As long as you have at least 1 reservoir point remaining, you can use your action to cast *create or destroy water* and use the create water option. Your spellcasting ability for spells you cast with reservoir is Intelligence. You regain all expended reservoir points when you finish a long rest. Additionally, you use these points to activate innate spells from the Reservoir Caster feat (see **Additional Options**).
- ***Swim.*** You have a swimming speed of 30 feet.

lawful. While fair and reasonable among members of their own race, matabiri treat other races cruelly. Thus the majority are highly ordered and thoroughly wicked with all but members of their own race.

Adventurers: Matabiri adventurers are often scavengers and slavers, searching for scientific truths and slaves to experiment on. Rangers and druids are common among this ilk while monks often lead such bands.

There is a second type of matabiri adventurer, those chasing Hob's Dream. Seekers of a different type, these dream chasers indulge in, interpret, and enact the Dream in an effort to puzzle out Hob's will. The most drastic form of this is Hob's Call, where anywhere between a handful to scores of matabiri flee their community while still asleep—by some method and for some purpose only their deity knows. Few heeding this call ever return. While nearly any matabiri can hear one of these calls, those chasing dreams are typically in the roles of mediums, shamans, spiritualists, and witches.

Matabiri tend to exile rather than execute their own, and those chaotic, blasphemous, and murderous exiles often seek employment as mercenaries, cutthroats, and adventurers.

Age: Perhaps oddly, barring premature death, matabiri all seem to live for 301 years. No longer.

Names: Matabiri choose their own names once borne to the land, often incorporating elements of their environment that capture their attention. There are no family or clan names; instead a matabiri is named after their task or role within society, often as a title, though sometimes as a nickname.

Female Names: Cypree, Jamyan, Lobsong, Maygru, Pema, Sunna, Yontet.

Male Names: Alligan, Dawa, Gyel, Kenchun, Norbu, Tseten, Willwo.

SUBCLASSES

The fey provide an array of unique qualities and perspectives for creating interesting new characters. Consult your GM before applying these subclasses to other races.

DREAMWEAVER (WARLOCK: OTHERWORLDLY PATRON)

Your patron is a being that lives in the world of dreams, manifesting its will in the waking world only through those who dedicate their lives to its power. This patron is frequently the fey lord Hob, known as the Dreamer to his matabiri worshipers, but it may also be a creature of great power that exists only in the Dream or that has been trapped there and now seeks to make pacts with creatures outside the Dream in an attempt to escape.

The Dreamweaver calls you who make pacts with it dreamweavers as well as you become extensions of its slumbering will. You often call your patron the Great Dreamer to distinguish yourself from your patron.

EXPANDED SPELL LIST

The Dreamweaver lets you choose from an expanded list of spells when you learn a warlock spell. The following spells are added to the warlock spell list for you.

DREAMWEAVER EXPANDED SPELLS

Spell Level	Spells
1st	*bane, sleep*
2nd	*augury, blindness/deafness*
3rd	*blink, slow*
4th	*compulsion, phantasmal killer*
5th	*modify memory, seeming*

WAKING DREAMER

Starting at 1st level, you cannot be put to sleep by magical means, and you have advantage on saving throws against effects that would give you the frightened condition.

MERCIFUL MAGIC

When you reduce a creature to 0 hit points with any spell, you can cause the creature to fall unconscious and become stable instead of dying.

WHISPERER IN DREAMS

Also starting at 1st level, as an action, you can touch an unconscious beast, giant, or humanoid. At the start of its next turn, the creature regains 1 hit point and is charmed by you for 1 minute. While charmed by you in this way, the creature obeys your commands to the best of its ability. The creature uses your initiative, and as a bonus action, you can command it to move and take an action or bonus action. The creature cannot take reactions.

At 6th level, you can also use this feature to charm elementals, fey, and monstrosities. At 14th level, you can also use it to charm aberrations, celestials, dragons, and fiends.

Once you use this feature, you can't use it again until you finish a short or long rest.

PSYCHIC REVERBERATION

Starting at 6th level, when you hit a creature with a melee attack, you can call on your patron to assail your target's waking mind. You deal an additional 2d8 psychic damage. If you roll the same number on both d8s, the creature must make a Wisdom saving throw against your warlock spell save DC. On a failed save, the creature falls unconscious until the end of its next turn.

Once you use this feature, you can't use it again until you finish a short or long rest.

UNREADABLE DREAMS

At 10th level, you gain resistance to psychic damage. Additionally, you cannot be targeted by divination magic or perceived through magical scrying sensors.

MASTER OF WOVEN DREAMS

At 14th level, whenever you charm a creature using your Whisperer in Dreams feature, it gains temporary hit points equal to four times your warlock level.

As a reaction when the charmed condition ends for that creature, you can cause it to make a Wisdom saving throw against your warlock spell save DC. On a failure, the creature drops to 0 hit points. On a success, it is stunned until the end of its next turn.

HOB
(WARLOCK: OTHERWORLDLY PATRON)

You have made your warlock's pact with the inscrutable and enigmatic Hob. His aims are believed to be largely unknowable, but you feel his will directing you nonetheless. You might not be a willing agent in Hob's service, but the compulsion to attend him in some strange task or other cannot be ignored.

EXPANDED SPELL LIST

Hob lets you choose from an expanded list of spells when you learn a warlock spell. The following spells are added to the warlock spell list for you.

HOB EXPANDED SPELLS

Spell Level	Spells
1st	*command, silent image*
2nd	*alter self, see invisibility*
3rd	*clairvoyance, slow*
4th	*confusion, control water*
5th	*animate objects, awaken*

CIPHER

Starting at 1st level, you can make yourself undetectable by means of divination magic such as *scrying* or *detect thoughts* for 10 minutes. Once you use this feature, you can't use it again until you finish a short or long rest.

TOUCH OF DISBELIEF

Starting at 6th level, your touch causes creatures to lose their essential connection to the physical world. You make a warlock melee spell attack against a creature you can reach. On a hit, the target has disadvantage on weapon attack rolls and on ability checks and saving throws made using Strength, Dexterity, or Constitution for 1 minute. Once you use this feature, you can't use it again until you finish a long rest.

NULL MIND

Starting at 10th level, you can't be targeted by any divination magic or perceived through magical scrying sensors unless you allow it.

STEP BEHIND THE VEIL

Starting at 14th level, you gain the ability to step out of phase with the real world. As an action, you become invisible for 1 minute. While invisible, you can take no actions other than moving, but you can move through creatures and objects as if they were difficult terrain. You take 1d10 force damage if you end your turn inside an object. You can end your invisibility early by using an action to dismiss it. Once you use this feature, you can't use it again until you finish a long rest.

LEVIATHAN DOMAIN
(CLERIC: DIVINE DOMAIN)

The unseen mysteries of the deep call to your spirit. You are inexorably pulled toward the sea, seeking to bask in its primordial power. The open water speaks to you like nothing else, and you are drawn to explore its uncharted depths.

LEVIATHAN DOMAIN

You are granted the following domain spells.

LEVIATHAN DOMAIN SPELLS

Cleric Level	Spells
1st	*inflict wounds, mage armor*
3rd	*darkness, darkvision*
5th	*vampiric touch, water breathing*
7th	*black tentacles, dominate beast*
9th	*awaken, conjure elemental*

BONUS PROFICIENCIES

When you choose this domain at 1st level, you gain proficiency in the Stealth skill. You also gain proficiency with the trident and the net.

ABYSSAL BLESSING

Also at 1st level, you gain a bite attack that deals 1d6 piercing damage. You are proficient with your bite attack, which is treated as a light melee weapon with the finesse property.

CHANNEL DIVINITY: BENTHIC BLOOM

Starting at 2nd level, you can use your Channel Divinity to summon forth shadowy tentacles and plant life from your surroundings.

As an action, you present your holy symbol, and the area within 30 feet of you becomes difficult terrain for 1 minute. Additionally, for the duration, when a hostile creature enters the affected area for the first time on a turn or starts its turn there, the creature must succeed on a Dexterity saving throw or be restrained by the shadows. A creature restrained by the shadows can use its action to make a Strength or Dexterity check (its choice) against your spell save DC. On a success, it frees itself.

NICTITATING MEMBRANES

Starting at 6th level, you grow nictitating membranes that grant you advantage on saving throws against effects that would blind you and on saving throws against gaze attacks.

DIVINE STRIKE

At 8th level, you gain the ability to infuse your weapon strikes with divine energy. Once on each of your turns when you hit a creature with a weapon attack, you can cause the attack to deal an extra 1d8 cold damage to the target. When you reach 14th level, the extra damage increases to 2d8.

MESSENGER OF THE DEPTHS

At 17th level, you become amphibious, able to breathe in air and water, and you gain a swimming speed of 30 feet. If you already possess a swimming speed, then while underwater, you gain the following:

- You ignore difficult terrain.
- Magical effects can't reduce your speed or cause you to be restrained.
- You can spend 5 feet of movement to escape from nonmagical restraints or being grappled.

MUDBORN
(SORCERER: SORCEROUS ORIGIN)

You were born not from the flesh of a living creature but from the womb of the earth. You emerged from the cold mud, screaming and ensorcelled by the primordial forces of magic. Or perhaps you were simply found and adopted one rainy night by a kindhearted person, cradled in the gutter and swaddled with mud. Alternatively, many centuries ago, your family legends tell that an ancient ancestor emerged from the earth and set your line on the path of destiny.

No matter the specifics of your origin, the power of

earth and water mingle in your blood. Yours is a serene magic that taps into the everlasting endurance of the earth and the slow determination of water.

ELEMENTAL FOCUS

At 1st level, you can choose an elemental focus that constantly enhances the power of your spells, selecting either earth or water. You can switch focuses by finishing a short or long rest. Starting at 14th level, you can switch between elemental focuses as an action.

Earth. When you cast a sorcerer spell using a spell slot of 1st level or higher, your AC increases to 10 + your Charisma modifier (unless it was already higher) for 1 minute. At 14th level, all creatures you choose within 5 feet of you increase their AC to an equal value as well.

Water. When you cast a sorcerer spell using a spell slot of 1st level or higher, you regain hit points equal to the level of the spell slot. At 14th level, all creatures you choose within 5 feet of you regain an equal number of hit points as well.

ELEMENTAL UNITY

Starting at 6th level, you can spend 3 sorcery points as an action to merge your elemental focuses and enter an elemental form for as long as you concentrate (as if concentrating on a spell), up to 1 minute. Your physical form becomes malleable and regenerative, granting you resistance to bludgeoning, piercing, and slashing damage from nonmagical attacks. Additionally, you regain hit points equal to your Charisma modifier at the start of each of your turns while in this form.

You cannot benefit from your elemental focus while in this form.

MIRING SPELL

Starting at 6th level, you gain a new Metamagic option. When you cast a spell with a duration of instantaneous that targets one or more creatures, you can spend 2 sorcery points to reduce the speed of each of its targets to 5 feet until the end of your next turn if that target fails on a saving throw against the spell or is hit by your spell attack with the spell.

You can use Miring Spell even if you have already used a different Metamagic option during the casting of the spell.

EFFIGY OF MUD

Starting at 14th level, when you use Elemental Unity to enter elemental form, you can spend 5 additional sorcery points as a bonus action to create a mud elemental from your own body. It uses earth elemental statistics with the following additional trait.

Mud Form. The mud elemental can enter a hostile creature's space and stop there. When a creature starts its turn in the mud elemental's space or enters it for the first time on its turn, it must make a Strength saving throw against your sorcerer spell save DC, becoming restrained on a failure. The mud elemental can also move through a space as narrow as 1 inch wide without squeezing.

This elemental effigy is physically a perfect replica of yourself and is friendly to you and creatures you designate when it is created. It obeys your spoken commands, moving and acting in accordance with your wishes and acting on your turn in combat. It can cast cantrips you know.

The effigy is destroyed when it is reduced to 0 hit points or after 1 minute passes.

BODILY RECOMPOSITION

At 18th level, whenever you take damage that isn't psychic damage, you can spend 1 sorcery point as a reaction to take no damage instead. Once you use this feature, the sorcery point cost to use it doubles until you finish a long rest.

PATH OF THE BLOODIED SEA
(BARBARIAN: PRIMAL PATH)

You hear the call of the blood-stained sea. It gnaws at your guts, pulling you into its embrace. This is where you feel welcome, even needed. This is what it's all about, the savage freedom. Your bloodlust must be satisfied.

BORN TO THE SEA

At 3rd level when you adopt this path, you gain a swimming speed of 30 feet. If you already have a swimming speed, it increases by 10 feet.

ACCEPTING THE BEAST

At 3rd level, you live to taste the blood on the water. While you're raging, you have advantage on melee attack rolls against any creature that doesn't have all its hit points.

TIDAL HUNTER

At 6th level, you gain the ability to track blood through the water. While within or on the surface of a body of water, you can track any creature in the water, or that passed through the water, at a fast pace if that creature does not have all its hit points. Additionally, while within the water, you can move stealthily at a normal pace.

NO REST

At 10th level, you no longer need to sleep. Instead, you enter a trance, remaining semiconscious, for 4 hours a day. After resting in this way, you gain the same benefit that a human does from 8 hours of sleep. Additionally, magic can't put you to sleep.

SHARKTOOTH

At 14th level, while raging, you gain a bite attack. Your bite attack deals piercing damage equal to 1d6 + your Strength modifier and ignores resistance to piercing damage. On a critical hit, the target has disadvantage on Dexterity checks and saving throws until it finishes a long rest.

SWAMPFOLK
(RANGER: RANGER ARCHETYPE)

The amphibious matabiri prefer the wettest of swamps when they dwell close to land. Though they can breathe both air and water, a swamp's thin layer of water and sticky, muddy terrain limits their greatest advantage over land-dwelling creatures: the ability to swim. Those matabiri that favor swamps undergo specialized training in order to make the most of the environment.

MUCK DWELLER

At 3rd level, you gain swamp as a favored terrain (or a new terrain type of your choice if it is already your favored terrain). Additionally, you can hide while at least three-quarters submerged in water even if the water does not obscure you. If you are obscured while in any water, you also have advantage on Dexterity (Stealth) checks while touching the water.

CROCODILE'S AMBUSH

At 3rd level when you hit a creature with a melee attack while you have advantage on the attack roll, if you have at least one hand free, you can choose to force the target to make a Strength saving throw with a DC equal to 8 + your proficiency bonus + your Strength modifier. On a failed save, you deal 1d8 bludgeoning damage to it, and it is grappled by you. You can use this feature only once per turn.

MARSH BLOODED

At 7th level, you develop a natural resistance to the swamp's toxins. You have resistance to poison damage and have advantage on saving throws against diseases as well as any effects that would give you the poisoned condition.

ENVENOM WEAPON

At 11th level, when you hit a creature with a melee weapon attack, you can expend one spell slot to cause your weapon to ooze venom. The creature must make a Constitution saving throw with a DC equal to your spell save DC. On a failed save, it takes 2d8 poison damage for a 1st-level slot, plus 1d8 per spell level higher than 1st on a failed save, to a maximum of 5d8, and is poisoned for 1 minute. At the end of each of its turns while poisoned, it takes 1d8 poison damage and makes another Constitution saving throw, ending the poisoned condition on itself on a success.

On a successful save, it takes half as much damage and is not poisoned.

CORPSE LIGHT GUARDIAN

Starting at 15th level when you finish a long rest, a will-o'-wisp appears at your side and follows you. This will-o'-wisp is your guardian: its alignment is neutral, it cannot speak but understands the languages you speak, and its hit point maximum is equal to four times your ranger level. It follows your commands to the best of its ability. It takes its turn on your initiative but can only take an action, bonus action, or reaction if you use your own action, bonus action, or reaction to command it to. You can command it to move without using an action.

While you are within 5 feet of the will-o'-wisp, you can use your reaction when you are damaged to shimmer with ghostly light and share its damage resistances and immunities against that damage. If it doesn't have resistance or immunity to the damage, you can instead use your reaction to transfer half the damage (rounded down) to the will-o'-wisp.

If the will-o'-wisp is reduced to 0 hit points, it is destroyed and does not reappear until you complete a long rest.

VIVISECTOR
(ROGUE: ROGUISH ARCHETYPE)

To the matabiri, the ends—of scientific discovery—justify any means. And a disturbing number of mortal alchemists share this belief, going to any ends to advance their understanding of a creature's nature and anatomy. In their philosophy, dissecting and analyzing carcasses is of little value to the enlightened mind. The only way to understand a creature's true nature is to cut it open while it still moves.

BONUS PROFICIENCIES

When you select this archetype at 3rd level, you gain proficiency in the Medicine and Nature skills and proficiency with herbalism kits. If you already had proficiency in either skill, you gain proficiency in another skill of your choice from the rogue list.

OPPORTUNISTIC EVISCERATION

Starting at 3rd level, your thirst for knowledge on the battlefield allows you to gain more from subsequent attacks. When you deal Sneak Attack damage to a creature that you've already damaged within the last minute, that creature has disadvantage on attack rolls until the end of your next turn.

ENSURE SURVIVAL

At 3rd level, you are well-practiced with ensuring the survival of those you operate on. You can use a healer's kit to stabilize a dying creature as a bonus action.

When you reach 13th level, you can use an action and expend two uses of a healer's kit to cause a stable creature within your reach to regain hit points equal to your level. That creature can't regain hit points from this feature again until it finishes a long rest.

BLOODY INVESTIGATOR

At 9th level, you can learn important information in the heat of combat. When you Sneak Attack a creature, you can ask the GM about one characteristic of your choice from the list below. The GM tells you if the creature's characteristic is equal to, better than, or worse than yours:

- An ability score of your choice
- Current hit points
- Maximum hit points
- Armor Class
- Speed (all types)
- Total class levels (if any)

You can also learn one of these characteristics by making a successful DC 15 Intelligence (Nature) or Wisdom (Medicine) check after spending 1 minute examining a creature's carcass.

EMERGENT MEDICINE

At 13th level, your knowledge of how to cut creatures open translates into something approaching knowledge of how to heal. You can tend to up to ten creatures' wounds during a short rest, including yourself, as long as none of those creatures are more than 100 feet away from one another. If any of those creatures regain hit points at the end of the short rest, they regain an additional 1d10 hit points.

GENETIC ALCHEMY

Starting at 17th level, your study of creatures allows you to take on the form of a creature that you have studied. You can cast *true polymorph* without expending a spell slot. The creature you transform into must be one that you have fought before (except for constructs or undead). Once you use this feature, you can't use it again until you finish a long rest.

BACKGROUNDS

The following backgrounds are especially common in matabiri. At the GM's discretion, other appropriate races may have access to them.

FAR CASTAWAY

Whatever your origins, your life has been defined by calamity when you were lost in the planes. Perhaps you simply awoke in a strange land with no idea how you got there or were swept through portal after portal, stranded gods only know where. You might have been rescued in the end or been forced to save yourself, making your own way back to civilization. Whatever the case, your ordeal has scarred you, and you will never be the same.

Work with your GM to determine the general details of your experience, such as the part of the multiverse where your ordeal occurred and what you had left behind at home. How did you survive? Were you forced by circumstance to forsake your values in some way so that you now live with secret guilt? Did you lose people close to you? Were you in some way responsible for the incident that led to your trials and tribulations? Did the experience affect your religious beliefs or your beliefs about people?

Skill Proficiencies: Insight, Survival

Languages: One of your choice

Equipment: A memento reminding you of your ordeal, flint and steel, a dagger, a spool of twine, several fishing hooks, a set of common clothes, and a pouch containing 10 gp

FEATURE: MODEST NEEDS

As a former far castaway, you have learned to make do with next to nothing, and your lifestyle reflects that. When you choose any lifestyle between squalid and wealthy, you pay lifestyle expenses as if you had selected the next cheapest lifestyle category (for instance, maintaining a wealthy lifestyle by paying for a comfortable lifestyle and so forth).

SUGGESTED CHARACTERISTICS

For a far castaway, the trials and tribulations endured while lost in the multiverse leave lasting marks that define one's place in society. Some far castaways never escape the shadow of their ordeal, maintaining habits learned from months or years of living alone. Others reintegrate into everyday society with little difficulty, set apart only by their focus on the skills that once saved their lives.

d8	Personality Trait
1	I am distant and withdrawn most of the time but will sometimes burst into animated speech, startling my companions.
2	I am prone to grave pronouncements, and I always expect the worst to happen.
3	My experiences have made me an eternal optimist, convinced that good will come.
4	I view my time lost as a spiritual journey, and my devotion to that land's deities is profound.
5	I make almost every topic circle back to my ordeal—sometimes with great insight but sometimes to the annoyance of others.
6	The deprivation of my ordeal has given me a lasting appreciation of the difference between what I want and what I need.
7	I hoard items that were necessary for my survival while I was a castaway.
8	I occasionally succumb to bouts of sadness when appreciating some mundane thing I had all but forgotten while lost.

d6	Ideal
1	Order. Maintaining and enforcing order in one's environment is essential to survival. (Lawful)
2	Opportunity. I am always ready to seize any chance for fortune that presents itself, and I make the most of such fortune. (Chaotic)
3	Independence. The concerns of civilization are no longer my concerns. (Neutral)
4	Self-Interest. I will do anything to survive when my life is on the line, no matter how horrible. (Evil)
5	Generosity. I am always ready to aid those in need, remembering the times when I needed the help of others. (Good)
6	Civilization. Having lived like an animal, I have a new appreciation for the world of people. (Any)

d6	Bond
1	Anyone else who survived my ordeal is like a sibling to me.
2	I consider myself kin to the intelligent creatures where I was lost.
3	The mundane item I brought with me from my ordeal carries great emotional weight for me, and I don't know what I might do if I ever lost it.
4	The person who saved me has my complete devotion.
5	I am determined to one day captain the ship that rescued me.
6	Beggars and others suffering deprivation of one form or another can usually count on me for assistance, and word has gotten around about my generosity.

d6	Flaw
1	I am terrified of being alone.
2	My habit of talking about my ordeal sometimes leads to me being considered unlucky by travelers.
3	I have a noticeable disdain for those who have never faced death.
4	I have contempt for clerics devoted to the deities of the lands that tormented me, convinced by my experience that they know nothing of their patrons.
5	I am extremely uncomfortable—and vocal about it—when I am in unfamiliar territory.
6	I have an almost supernatural—and wholly unexplained—belief that I cannot die.

TREASURE DIVER

You have spent time working as a treasure diver—salvaging wrecks, diving for pearls, and the like, a dangerous but potentially lucrative line of work that requires great skill and greater fortitude. The water is your life, and you have no fear of the dangers that lie below the surface. Your work is sporadic, so you fill your downtime with other occupations common to the coast. Fishing, of course, but you might have also tried your hand at smuggling and piracy from time to time.

Skill Proficiencies: Athletics, Perception

Equipment: A piece of whalebone jewelry, an oyster knife, a net, a set of common clothes, and a pouch containing 15 gp

FEATURE: DIVER'S FORM

Your work as a treasure diver has honed your technique when swimming. Whenever you make an ability check for swimming, you can treat a d20 roll of 9 or lower as a 10.

SUGGESTED CHARACTERISTICS

Living a simple life along the water's edge, treasure divers care little for land-dwelling folk and their civilized niceties. With a keen thirst for adventure and a strong sense of competition, a treasure diver makes a capable and focused ally. But at the same time, many treasure divers allow their antipathy for civilization to lead them down dark paths.

d8	Personality Trait
1	I have a carefree outlook on life and never allow myself to be tied down by day-to-day affairs.
2	I am constantly checking the wind, watching the clouds, and staying conscious of the current state of the weather.
3	I have a deep awareness of and concern for the interconnectedness of nature.
4	I have a keen eye for spotting treasure where others see trash and can generally find something worth salvaging in any pile of junk.
5	I am laconic in the extreme, saying little and never repeating myself.
6	I have a love for physical labor and working up a sweat. I am always ready to lend a hand with whatever tasks need doing.
7	My love of excitement borders on mania.
8	My time spent with other divers, sailors, and smugglers has gifted me with a flair for profanity.

d6	Ideal
1	Independence. I've always been my own boss, and nobody tells me what to do. (Chaotic)
2	Child of the Sea. I am attuned to the ebb and flow of life offshore, and the concerns of life on land have never been mine. (Neutral)
3	Gratitude. I'm grateful for every day that I can earn my keep from the sea, and this manifests as a charitable nature. (Good)
4	Avarice. Whatever it takes to get paid, I'll do it. (Evil)
5	Simplicity. My needs can be met with a good knife and a net. I resist anything that complicates that arrangement. (Chaotic)
6	Beauty. My keen eye for treasure extends to other beautiful objects, and I've turned this appreciation into a philosophy of sorts. (Any)

d6	Bond
1	My home is the whole world to me, and I view other places in relation to it.
2	I've developed a fondness for a creature I encounter frequently when diving. I take treats for it and visit it whenever I can.
3	I have a flawed pearl that bears great sentimental value to me. I wear it as jewelry and will not part with it willingly.
4	I have tended a particular oyster bed since childhood and feel a need to check on it as often as possible.
5	My fellow divers are all the family I've ever had, and I'll do anything to help them. This can be tricky as many of them turn to crime to make ends meet during off seasons.
6	I have a vendetta against a pirate, smuggler, or slaver who operates near my home waters. It will end only when one of us is dead.

d6	Flaw
1	My easy-come, easy-go attitude about money frequently finds me coinless or in debt.
2	The hard-drinking ways of my fellows have caught up to me, and I have a mild dependence on spirits.
3	I have a terrible time trying to plan for the future. If I'm in charge of preparation for something other than diving, something will inevitably be forgotten.
4	I am often rude and dismissive of people from inland areas.
5	I know the seabed near my home like the back of my hand but have a shocking ignorance of the world around me.
6	I become violently angry with those who are careless with delicate things.

ADDITIONAL OPTIONS

The following options are available to matabiri. At the GM's discretion, other appropriate races may have access to some of these new rules.

EQUIPMENT

Matabiri have developed the following equipment according to their specific needs and utilize them to particular effect.

Codex Ring Gadget. Matabiri build small, unique gadgets on a regular basis, creating useful and disposable devices to aid in their ability checks. The codex ring is one such example. It is a large, clunky ring made up of different scrap metals and has six movable bands. Each band is etched with different alphabets, grammatical placements, and obscure symbols. If you are proficient with it or if you are a matabiri, the codex ring allows you to apply your proficiency bonus on ability checks to decipher text and allows you to make such Intelligence checks passively even if doing so would normally be impossible. The codex ring comes apart after being used three times.

Matabiri Resin. This yellow substance is similar to tree sap in viscosity and bears a strong odor. It's an alchemical combination of local saps and matabiri spittle, creating a potent acidic adhesive. Each vial of resin contains enough of the substance to cover a 5-inch square of material. The resin does not splash and is ineffective if thrown at a target. As an adhesive, it holds up to 250 pounds and requires a successful DC 15 Strength check or DC 10 Intelligence check with alchemist's supplies to remove anything stuck to it. Its acidic properties trigger when an attempt is made to dislodge it, whether it succeeds or fails. Substances or creatures in contact with the matabiri resin take 3d4 acid damage.

Poison, Hobwink Powder (Inhaled). This sachet of crushed herbs and clay powder comes from specially harvested mud and swamp plants. When thrown, the sachet releases a cloud of earthy-smelling powder that engulfs a creature you hit with the bag. You throw the bag as an improvised weapon. A creature that inhales the powder must succeed on a DC 10 Wisdom saving throw or fall prey to its hallucinogenic properties. Constructs, undead, and other creatures that don't breathe or that are immune to poison automatically succeed on the saving throw. Those who fail the saving throw enter a sleepwalking state and become compliant to nonviolent, reasonable-sounding orders as though affected by *suggestion*. The effect lasts 1 minute but ends immediately for an affected creature that takes damage, no matter the source. A creature can snap an affected creature within 5 feet out of its stupor by sharply jostling it as an action.

Salamander Hide Armor. Named for its dark, smooth appearance, this armor is not actually the hide of salamanders but a combination of several swamp creature hides, including alligator, snake, and lizard. When cured and treated and formed into armor by matabiri armorsmiths, it has very little drag in water, despite its bulk. When you wear it, its slippery texture makes you difficult to grapple. You can make an ability check to escape a grapple by spending half your movement. If you are proficient with medium armor, you are treated as proficient in Strength (Athletics) checks, Dexterity (Acrobatics) checks, and Strength and Dexterity saving throws, but only for the purpose of avoiding or escaping a grapple in salamander hide armor.

MATABIRI EQUIPMENT

Item	Cost	Weight
Codex ring gadget	15 gp	—
Matabiri resin (vial)	20 gp	—
Poison, hobwink powder (bag, 1 dose)	50 gp	1/2 lb.

FEATS

Matabiri have evolved a style all their own and are quite fond of the following feats.

ILLUMINATED PRESENCE

Prerequisite: Matabiri

You have faint stripes or spots just below the surface of your skin, which you can cause to glow as a bonus action. When this bioluminescence is activated, you shed bright light in a 20-foot radius and dim light for an additional 20 feet. You can dismiss your light as a bonus action.

INKY ESCAPE ARTIST

Prerequisite: Matabiri

While you are in water, as an action, you can secrete a cloud of dark liquid similar to squid ink. The ink forms a 30-foot-radius sphere in water, making the affected area heavily obscured. The ink dissipates after 6 rounds or when a current of at least 10 miles per hour disperses it. (Creating the cloud in fast-flowing water results in the ink dispersing immediately.) The ink cloud is ineffective on land. Once you use this ability, you can't use it again until you finish a long rest.

RESERVOIR CASTER

Prerequisite: Matabiri

When you take this feat, you select two of the spells from the following table. You can cast those spells by spending the indicated number of reservoir points. Intelligence is your spellcasting ability for these spells.

You can take this feat multiple times. Each time you do so, you must choose a different spell.

Reservoir Spells	Reservoir Points
conjure elemental	3
control water	2
fog cloud	1
freedom of movement	3
grease	1
water breathing	2

MATABIRI ARMOR

Armor	Cost	Armor Class (AC)	Strength	Stealth	Weight
Medium Armor					
Salamander hide armor	250 gp	12 + Dex modifier (max 2)	—	—	12 lb.

Norns

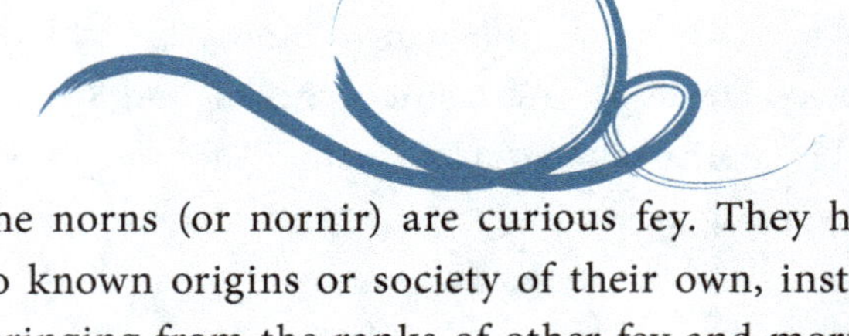

You float on the river of time, and death awaits you. Fail to fight and be dashed upon rocks by rapids. Fight the flow and stay still for a time. Flow with grace and at least choose the rapid and the rock.

—Whisper

The norns (or nornir) are curious fey. They have no known origins or society of their own, instead springing from the ranks of other fey and mortals, especially those who have tampered with destiny. They often lead solitary, transient lives, blind to the sights of the world around them but all too aware of the precise workings of the hand of Fate.

Norns are driven by impulses and visions even they themselves don't comprehend, but like experienced sailors learn to read the mood of the changeable sea, norns become accustomed to living in tune with the demands of destiny.

Physical Description: Norns can look like anyone, but their base form is as the race which they were born from. The only thing markedly different about them is their eyes—clouded, milky white, or absent entirely. They are blind no matter the form they take, so unless attempting to hide themselves, few norns ever bother creating eyes for themselves, just leaving skin in place in the impression of where eyes should be.

Norns have fluid shapeshifting abilities and can even shift between genders. They tend to have a preferred form, at least for a while, but will use whatever shape they feel best serves their current purpose.

A worthy question is how norns can be such accomplished shapeshifters when they cannot see.

The answer has the same root as so many other things about them: they are guided by an intuition that knows exactly what it needs to know and is not beholden to the rules governing mere mortals.

Society: When a norn appears, something momentous is in the offing.

Fey scholars sometimes wryly call the birth of a norn a "twist of fate" because it is an assurance that the local status quo is about to be upended somehow. Norns are not the cause of such events—if anything, their purpose appears to be aiding those involved with navigating the chaos—but such distinctions are lost on most. Norns lead lonely lives and rarely find a home. They tend to be stoic in the face of prejudice; norns sense their greater purpose is more important than temporary discomfort.

All norns tend to be cryptic and have trouble giving straight answers. They don't do this to be frustrating. Norns are so in tune with Fate's movements and the ripples caused by every decision, so it is impossible for them to even perceive a clear and definite future, let alone attempt to explain one. Additionally, many norns have a—possibly rational—fear that any decision they make might affect the future unduly. This makes them wise counselors in times of trouble but infuriating breakfast companions.

Norns will sometimes congregate in small covens of two or three, but they very rarely ever assemble in any larger groups. Norns sense their work is with those struggling with Fate. Despite the seriousness of their inborn mission, norns do have individual personalities, interests, and lives beyond seeking out Fate and aiding others in managing it. It's true that very few ever settle down anywhere for any length of time, but they do marry, raise children, form loyal friendships, and indulge in hobbies.

A great irony of norn existence is that, despite being present at some of the most tumultuous and critical events of a given generation, few norns have any desire for fame and glory. In fact, most norns actively shun it, intuitively sensing that their role is to guide and nurture key players in Fate's games, not to participate directly. In truth, a typical norn secretly longs for a simple, happy life of traveling and meeting new friends,

NORN TRAITS

Norn characters possess an assortment of traits all their own.

- ***Ability Score Increase.*** Your Wisdom score increases by 2, and your Constitution score increases by 1.
- ***Languages.*** You can speak, read, and write Common and Sylvan.
- ***Size.*** Norns stand between 5 and 6 feet tall and weigh around 150 pounds. Your size is Medium.
- ***Speed.*** Your base walking speed is 30 feet.
- ***Type.*** Your type is fey. Spells and effects that specifically target humanoids do not affect you. You also gain the fata subtype (see **Appendix**).

- ***Fluid Identity.*** By concentrating for 10 minutes (as if concentrating on a spell), you can alter your appearance, including height, weight, facial features, sound of your voice, hair length, coloration, and distinguishing characteristics, if any. You can't change your basic body shape or statistics and are always obviously a norn. You can make an Intelligence (disguise kit) check to create a disguise this way even without a disguise kit. At 3rd level, you can change your appearance in 1 minute.
- ***Keen Intuition.*** You have advantage on Wisdom (Insight) checks and on Wisdom (Perception) checks not using sight.
- ***Norn Magic.*** You know the *true strike* cantrip. In addition, you can cast *see invisibility* once without expending a spell slot, but its duration is concentration. When you reach 7th level, you can cast the *arcane eye* spell once without expending a spell slot. Wisdom is your spellcasting ability for these spells. You regain all uses of this trait when you finish a long rest. If you are at least 7th level, you can participate in a norn coven as described in *Along the Twisting Way: Faerie Ring Campaign Guide* (under **norn** in **Appendix: Servitors**).
- ***Second Sight.*** Your eyes are blinded, but your nature yet enables you to take in your surroundings, though through a permanent haze. You treat areas that are brightly lit as though they were lightly obscured and areas that are lightly obscured as though they were heavily obscured.

where they can rely on nothing very exciting happening.

Relations: Norns have surprisingly little to do with most other fey. It's possible the fey's constant internal politics and strife have far less bearing on Fate's ultimate outcomes than they might think, or perhaps the norns are simply unable to intrude on other fey races' complicated ties to Fate. Even norns themselves aren't sure: they simply know that, with rare exceptions, they are mostly called to witness and guide in events among mortals.

Not all mortals are welcoming of such aid however. A norn's cryptic nature can be tiresome, and being confronted with warnings and visions can be frightening. Long-lived races, such as elves and gnomes, are more prone to tolerating or accepting a norn's unusual view of the world, but younger or distrustful races, such as dwarves, half-orcs, and humans, may view them with fear or scorn. The norns' shapeshifting abilities are never so useful as when they are being run out of town.

Alignment and Religion: Norns are predominantly motivated by good as they, perhaps better than anyone, know that evil behavior does not lead to a future anyone wants to live in. The distinction between lawful and chaotic behavior is one they find less useful, and norns tend to follow the rules when it's convenient for their purpose in a place and break them whenever necessary.

The norns know the gods can sway Fate one way or the other, but they are—themselves—also beholden to it. Few norns risk affecting ultimate outcomes by professing loyalty to one god or another, but those with a stronger philosophical bent will gladly embrace concepts of time, fate, and self-determination . . . and argue about them whenever they can.

Adventurers: Norns love to travel and are intuitively guided to people and events of future importance, so it's of little surprise how often they are swept into adventuring parties. Norns are often fascinated with new places and people but tend to take an advising role to encourage their party to consider the ramifications of rash action. Norns frequently play the role of oracle, shaman, or witch, playing on their inherent gifts.

Some are drawn to psychic classes, taking strength from the emotions and fate-weaving around people and items. More disciplined norns may become wizards or even monks.

Names: Norns have a birth name that is standard for their race, and some even keep it. For norns who shift often, they may find their birth name is not utilitarian. Some generate aliases out of thin air, but most develop a nickname or handle of sorts, often related to how the individual norn perceives their relationship with Fate.

Age: Norns reach maturity at around 20 years old. They are immortal, and while they can be killed, time never claims them. They can voluntarily elect to die at any moment of their choosing.

Norn Names: Aquarian, Celestine, Echo, Fathom, Gemini, Journey, Mutter, Orion, Reckon, Stranger, Tarot, Vagabond, Zodiac.

SUBCLASSES

The fey provide an array of unique qualities and perspectives for creating interesting new characters. Consult your GM before applying these subclasses to other races.

COLLEGE OF FATE (BARD: BARD COLLEGE)

You follow the threads of fate, twisting them in defense of your allies and to the detriment of your enemies. Some say that you deliberately alter what you see to your own ends, but none can deny the power you bring to bear on chance and destiny.

BONUS CANTRIPS

When you join the college of fate at 3rd level, you learn the *guidance*, *light*, and *vicious mockery* cantrips. These cantrips count as bard cantrips for you but don't count against the number of bard cantrips you know.

TWIST FATE

Also at 3rd level, you learn to twist the skein of fate in favor of your friends or against your foes. When a creature you can see within 60 feet of you makes a saving throw, you can use your reaction to expend one of your uses of Bardic Inspiration, rolling a Bardic

Inspiration die and adding to or subtracting from the creature's roll. You can choose to use this feature after the creature makes its roll but before the GM determines whether the saving throw succeeds or fails.

TIDES OF FATE

At 6th level, you declare the path that fate has set for a creature and force the creature to walk that path. Choose one creature you can see within 30 feet of you, and choose a course of activity (limited to a sentence or two) for that creature to undertake. This feature functions as the *suggestion* spell, except that it affects creatures that can't be charmed, the target understands the course of action even if you do not speak it out loud, and the target gets no initial saving throw against the effect.

If the target follows your suggested course of action, it gains advantage on the first attack roll or ability check it makes during that course of action, and this effect ends. If the target refuses to follow the suggestion, it has disadvantage on attack rolls and ability checks until the effect ends. The target can make a Wisdom saving throw against your spell save DC at the end of each of its turns to end the effect.

You can use this feature a number of times equal to your Charisma modifier (a minimum of once). You regain all expended uses when you finish a long rest.

GREAT DESTINY

Starting at 14th level, you can pronounce a great destiny for one of your allies. For 1 minute, the ally has advantage on ability checks and gains temporary hit points equal to your bard level at the start of its turn.

Once you use this feature, you can't use it again until you finish a long rest.

FATE COLLECTOR
(ROGUE: ROGUISH ARCHETYPE)

Norns generally prefer to let destiny take its natural course no matter the wait, but you prefer to take the restoration of fate's threads into your own hands. You are an assassin, specializing in reaping fate that creatures attempt to delay or circumvent.

RESTORE THE WEB

When you choose this archetype at 3rd level, you can sense the will of Fate and bring death to those who would avoid it. You gain the ability to cast *detect evil and good* a number of times equal to your Charisma modifier. You regain any expended uses when you finish a long rest.

At the GM's discretion, when you cast *detect evil and good* using this feature, you can also detect any creature that has altered its destiny to avoid death through magic, trickery, negotiation with powerful beings, and so forth. You can then affect such creatures with your Restore the Web, Agent of Fate, Intervention of Fate, and Grim Collection features, regardless of creature type.

SEVER THE THREAD

Also at 3rd level, when you successfully use your Sneak Attack feature against an aberration, celestial, elemental, fey, fiend, or undead and you roll a 1 on any damage die for that feature, you can reroll that die once.

AGENT OF FATE

Beginning at 9th level, you keep an eye on the web of fate at all times, granting you unnatural insight into your target's thoughts and emotions. You have advantage on Wisdom (Insight) checks and Charisma (Intimidation) checks when dealing with aberrations, celestials, elementals, fey, fiends, and undead.

INTERVENTION OF FATE

By 13th level, you have established yourself as an ally of fate, granting you remarkable resilience against those who would kill you before your time. When you use your Uncanny Dodge feature, you can use your reaction to take no damage instead of half damage.

Once you use this feature, you must finish a short or long rest before you can use it again.

GRIM COLLECTION

Starting at 17th level, you become a direct extension of Fate's will. Whenever you successfully use your Sneak Attack feature against a creature, that creature must make a Charisma saving throw (DC 8 + your Charisma modifier + your proficiency bonus). On a failed save, the creature takes 10d10 radiant damage. Aberrations, celestials, elementals, fey, fiends, and undead have disadvantage on this saving throw.

Once you use this feature, you must finish a long rest before you can use it again.

ORACLE
(SORCERER: SORCEROUS ORIGIN)

Your magic arises from the flow of time and the weave of fate. Perhaps you were born under auspicious signs, or your ancestors made a pact with eldritch forces and passed their power down to you. Whatever the reason, you can now see the skeins of fate and have learned to pluck their strands to your advantage.

ORACULAR MIEN

Starting when you select this origin at 1st level, you learn the *thaumaturgy* cantrip. This cantrip counts as a sorcerer cantrip for you but doesn't count against your number of sorcerer cantrips known.

PREMONITION

Also at 1st level, you begin to sense danger a split second before it threatens you. When a creature targets you with an attack or an effect that requires a saving throw, you can use your reaction to impose disadvantage on the attack roll or to gain advantage on the saving throw.

You can use this ability a number of times equal to your Charisma modifier (a minimum of once). You regain all expended uses when you finish a long rest.

FOREWARNING

At 6th level, you can let the future flow through you to guide your actions. If you are surprised at the start of combat and aren't incapacitated, you can spend 2 sorcery points at the start of your turn to act normally.

READING THE SKEIN

Beginning at 14th level, you see the paths of fate twisting before you. You can spend 4 sorcery points to cast the *divination* spell without needing material components.

FORESIGHT

Starting at 18th level, you learn the *foresight* spell. This spell counts as a sorcerer spell for you but doesn't count against your total number of sorcerer spells known.

WATERBEARER
(SORCERER: SORCEROUS ORIGIN)

Magical pools and fountains of water are often associated with divination and fate. You take this association even further, connecting the waters to your norn legacy. You can spontaneously generate waters infused with destiny, whether to aid or hinder.

DIVINING WATERS

Starting at 1st level, you are able to peer ahead into the near future while you meditate during a long rest. At the end of your long rest, roll a d20 and record the result as a foretold roll. You can then replace any d20 roll you or another creature makes with that foretold result (no action required). You can choose to use this feature after the roll is made but before the GM determines whether the roll represented a success or failure. You gain 1 additional foretold roll per long rest at 7th and 15th level. You can use only one foretold roll per turn. You regain any expended foretold rolls when you finish a long rest.

MALEFIC VISIONS

Starting at 6th level, you gain the ability to share your disjointed visions with other creatures, causing confusion and pain. As an action, you can spend 2 or more sorcery points and force a creature you can see to make an Intelligence saving throw equal to your spell save DC. On a failure, that creature takes 1d8 psychic damage per sorcery point spent and is stunned until the end of its next turn. On a successful save, the creature takes half as much damage and is not stunned.

AQUATIC AFFINITY

Beginning at 14th level, your sorcerous abilities grant you advantages when you are in your element. You gain a swimming speed equal to your base walking speed, and you can breathe underwater.

Perfect Prescience

Starting at 18th level, you are occasionally gifted with the exact knowledge of how to alter the future in any manner you choose. When you determine your foretold rolls with your Divining Waters feature, you can roll twice and take the preferred result.

Way of the Unseen Path
(Monk: Monastic Tradition)

You focus on seeing beyond the physical. You hone your inner awareness—the Sightless Eye—until you no longer require mundane sight. Once able to gaze beyond, you can send your spirit along the unseen path to strike against foes.

Opening the Sightless Eye

Starting when you choose this tradition at 3rd level, you begin to transcend the illusion of sight. While you are blinded, you don't suffer disadvantage on attack rolls, and attackers don't gain advantage on attack rolls against you. You still fail ability checks requiring sight and suffer other mundane effects of being unable to see.

Additionally, as a bonus action, you can spend 1 ki point to impose disadvantage on all attack rolls made against you until the start of your next turn.

Unseen Spirit Strike

Starting at 6th level, your spirit can walk the unseen path to strike foes from afar. When you take the attack action, you can spend 2 ki points to strike at range. Until the end of your turn, your unarmed strikes have a reach of 30 feet and deal psychic damage. Your spirit strikes as an invisible attacker.

Sightless Vigil

At 11th level, your awareness of other creatures and your surroundings intensifies. You have advantage on Wisdom (Insight) checks.

Additionally, you can spend 3 ki points to cast the *find traps* spell.

Staring Beyond

Starting at 17th level, you can spend 5 ki points to gain blindsight with a radius of 60 feet for 1 minute. During this time, you can see ethereal creatures within the range of your blindsight, and your unarmed strikes can hit them.

Wyrd
(Sorcerer: Sorcerous Origin)

Your path is a dark one, filled with acrid cauldron-smoke and the faint, omnipresent echo of discordant chanting. Like other norn witches, you have taken the appellation "wyrd" and have developed inborn talents for fate magic and powers that allow you to influence the destiny of the creatures around you. But the curse of the wyrd is that no matter how hard you may try, your magic can never change the fate set for you at birth. Be it weal or woe, that destiny is written in stone.

Severed Thread

At 1st level, when you cast a cantrip that deals damage, you can cause the spell to reduce each creature's hit point maximum by an amount equal to the damage the target takes. This reduction lasts until the creature finishes a long rest. If you reduce a creature's hit point maximum to 0, it dies. When you reach 6th level, you can spend 1 sorcery point when you cast a spell using a spell slot to have it reduce each target's hit point maximum this way.

Premonition of Danger

Also at 1st level, you can sense danger before it materializes. You have advantage on initiative rolls.

Fatechanger

Starting at 6th level, as a reaction when a creature you can see that is not yourself makes an attack roll, ability check, or saving throw, you can spend 3 sorcery point to cause it to roll an additional d20. You can choose to spend a sorcery point after the first d20 is rolled but before you know if it is a success or failure. You choose which of the d20s the creature uses.

Eyes of the Seer

At 14th level, you gain truesight with a range of 30 feet and are immune to being blinded.

SPECTER OF FATE

Starting at 18th level, you can cause your physical body and the equipment you're carrying to become incorporeal until the end of your next turn as an action. You can maintain being incorporeal as long as you use your action on each of your turns to continue using this feature.

While incorporeal, you can move through other creatures and objects as if they were difficult terrain. You take 1d10 force damage if you end your turn inside of an object. You also gain resistance to acid, cold, fire, lightning, and thunder damage as well as bludgeoning, piercing, and slashing damage from nonmagical attacks. You cannot be grappled, restrained, or knocked prone while incorporeal. While you are incorporeal and a creature you can see makes an attack roll, ability check, or saving throw, you can spend 5 sorcery points to apply your proficiency bonus as a bonus or penalty to the roll after you know whether it has succeeded or failed but before any effects are applied. This bonus or penalty can change whether the roll succeeded or failed.

BACKGROUNDS

The following backgrounds are especially common in norns. At the GM's discretion, other appropriate races may have access to them.

AGENT

Unknown to those around you, you are the eyes and ears of an unseen master. Often undercover or otherwise incognito, you insinuate yourself into a group to watch, listen, and gather information about its activities. At the same time, you might be called upon to mislead, distract, and otherwise provide misinformation to those you supposedly follow. It's a dangerous life, but you wouldn't have it any other way

Skill Proficiencies: Deception, Perception

Tool Proficiencies: Disguise kit, vehicles (land)

Equipment: A disguise kit, a set of common clothes, a small blank book, a piece of charcoal, and a leather belt pouch containing 5 gp

ALLEGIANCES

When you choose this background, work with the GM to decide what organization or group you were assigned to watch and what organization or master you secretly serve. Organizations can be chosen from the table below.

Think about your current assignment and whether you're set up to simply gather information or to subvert. How long have you been on the inside, and how much misinformation have you spread? Consider whether members of your target organization are aware of the subversive or disloyal element within their ranks or if you're having second thoughts about which side is right.

d8	Organization
1	Local government
2	Thieves' guild
3	Merchant cartel
4	Law enforcement
5	Foreign government
6	Church
7	Military
8	Cult

FEATURE: WOLF IN SHEEP'S CLOTHING

You maintain a dual allegiance, serving your true employer or organization as well as the group you have infiltrated. You can move freely within both groups, even if they are at deadly odds with one another. You know of other members of each group that you can call upon for information or minor aid, and you might be able to gain entry to restricted or private areas meant only for members of either group.

Other characters aware of your true allegiance watch you for signs of disloyalty, and those in the group you've infiltrated won't react well if they discover the truth about you.

SUGGESTED CHARACTERISTICS

Agents develop a flawless gambler's face early on, or they don't last long in their chosen profession. You keep your cool even when it seems like the game is up, never giving anyone what they're looking for. Instead, you make them take it. Still, you are constantly conflicted as you try to maintain two sets of loyalties as genuinely as possible, knowing that your life depends on it.

d8	Personality Trait
1	I have a short temper with people who question my motives.
2	I always keep my ears open when others are talking, even if they aren't talking to me.
3	I always have a story ready to go if someone confronts me about what I'm doing—and an escape plan just in case.
4	Whenever I enter a new place or new group, I try to pick up local habits as quickly as possible.
5	I get suspicious of anyone who shows more than a passing interest in me or my actions.
6	I love talking with new people.
7	New friends are great cover, so I try to keep a few handy at all times.
8	Sometimes plans fail, and you have to improvise.

d6	Ideal
1	Instability. I seek to topple the icons of power, so I can rise in their place. (Evil)
2	Learning. Acquiring new information and experiences is the only way to truly grow. (Any)
3	The Job. My mission is all that matters, and I'll see it through to the end. (Neutral)
4	Freedom. I go where I want, and I don't let locked doors stop me. (Chaotic)
5	Greater Good. I play a dangerous game to keep the people I care about safe. (Good)
6	Faith. My superiors have more information than I do, and I trust that they'll make the right decisions with it. (Lawful)

d6	Bond
1	A friend went missing while on a mission, and I won't stop until I discover what happened.
2	A great enemy threatens my home. I'll face deadly risk to gain an advantage in the fight.
3	My contact in my true organization is my lifeline.
4	I have a secret that I'd die to protect, even if it means failing my mission.
5	I can't take revenge on the people who actually hurt me, so I'll make sure those connected to them pay the price.
6	I owe my organization a debt that I can't ever fully repay, but I'll try my best for as long as I can.

d6	Flaw
1	I've gotten too deeply connected with someone I'm supposed to be watching and reporting on.
2	If it ever comes down to saving my skin or saving the mission, I'm not sure I'll make the right choice.
3	I'll do anything to climb the ranks of the organization I'm infiltrating, even if it means becoming the thing I hate.
4	My loyalty has flipped, and when my previous employers find out I've turned the tables, they'll be out for blood.
5	Despite my success at living in two worlds, I have trouble holding my true feelings in check, and it's only a matter of time before the wrong people notice.
6	I see double agents everywhere I look, and I don't trust others because of what I've done.

BROKER

You've spent your life watching others, learning what they desire and bringing those desires to life for a price. Perhaps you were raised in a merchant family where you learned the art of the bargain, compiling your first list of potential clients from your family's patrons. You might have been attached to people in high places, working as a servant to a wealthy noble. Or were you desperate for survival, chancing into a meeting with an underworld facilitator who saw your potential and cultivated it for her own purposes? Either way, you track the flow of commerce, goods, and services, lending or selling your insight to those who need it.

Skill Proficiencies: Deception, Insight

Languages: Two of your choice

Equipment: A set of traveler's clothes, a small notebook containing names of contacts, a quill and ink, a merchant's scale, and a pouch containing 10 gp

FEATURE: DESIRE FOR DESIRE

Your greatest strength lies in being able to find what one person wants, then connecting them with someone who has it. You maintain an extensive list of contacts in different places and walks of life. When you have a specific service, commodity, or object in mind, you can spend time canvassing your contacts and working with the GM to find someone who has it. Whenever you work as an intermediary for others, you can use their station, reputation, or title as your own as long as you're working to acquire the thing they want.

SUGGESTED CHARACTERISTICS

Brokers hang their hats on the idea that there's always something that someone wants, and if they can provide it, everything will work out. Some work to promote cooperation and understanding while others don't get out of bed unless the finder's fee is right. But all must be shrewd businesspeople and keen observers of others, knowing that many people hide their true desires behind shame, propriety, fear, or greed.

d8	Personality Trait
1	Everybody wants something, and I'm here to help them find it.
2	I'm always polite, even to people I despise.
3	I deal fairly with everyone, at least long enough to get the measure of them. Then I use that to my advantage.
4	It's not what you know but who you know. I try to know as many people as possible, so I can profit later.
5	I lose patience with people who aren't interested in making a deal.
6	I like to talk to fill up gaps in the conversation. As long as people are listening to me, my chances of cutting a deal stay alive.
7	I defer my own preferences to those of my clients.
8	I can flex my personality to fit in with any group of people.

d6	Ideal
1	Connection. Connecting people is what it's all about, and I work to break boundaries for the good of my clients. (Any)
2	Benefit. I work as a go-between to help worthy people get what they otherwise might never find on their own. (Good)
3	Free Trade. I despise any law or regulation that restricts who can do business and what that business is allowed to sell. (Chaotic)
4	Objective. When I broker a deal between two clients, I want both sides to walk away with the best terms possible. (Neutral)
5	Greed. There's no deal to be made unless I come out ahead. (Evil)
6	Professionalism. I have a reputation to uphold, and I do that by keeping my word and dealing in good faith. (Lawful)

d6	Bond
1	My family worked as intermediaries for powerful people, and they taught me everything I know.
2	All the connections I forge are the foundation of something greater. One day, the world will recognize the work I've done bringing people together.
3	I live for the deals that seem impossible. The harder I have to work to bring two parties together, the happier I am.
4	Helping someone achieve a goal soothes the memory of my own failures, at least for a short time.
5	I have a dark past that I'm trying to leave behind, and I'll do anything to prove I'm no longer the person I once was.
6	Someone once helped me find the thing I'd been desperately searching for. Now, I live to make that happen for others in any way I can.

d6	Flaw
1	It's a struggle not to take advantage of my clients. It would be so easy.
2	I can't abide anyone who tries to stick their nose into my business dealings.
3	Every deal I make is a step to something greater—and I sometimes don't see the risks I take in making those deals.
4	I would do anything to one day control all the trade I see going on around me.
5	I have a vice that I must indulge, and my business connections keep me supplied.
6	I have trouble trusting even close friends, always suspecting that everyone else is looking for the best angle.

INVESTIGATOR

Details are your life. You can look at the state of a room and understand what happened there hours before just as clearly as if you had been there. Every person's story is just another set of details, revealing themselves to you as a map of intention, deceit, and desire.

A person with your talents is a valuable resource to a wide array of people. Law enforcement is the most obvious, and perhaps you search out the perpetrators of crimes to bring them to justice or speak for their victims. Or you might work for yourself, taking jobs from private citizens or wealthy patrons who value discretion and who all require someone who knows how to read the world as you do.

Skill Proficiencies: Insight, Investigation

Tool Proficiencies: Thieves' tools

Languages: One of your choice

Equipment: A magnifying glass, a set of common clothes, a badge of office or a writ to practice licensed investigations, and a pouch containing 5 gp

FEATURE: EYE FOR DETAIL

You have a knack for taking in the details of a scene and drawing connections between seemingly insignificant elements. When you spend 1 hour investigating an area, you determine a general overview of events that took place in the area within the previous 24 hours. You can't learn the exact identities of creatures in the area without finding specific clues to their identities, but you can tell if an area was the site of a scuffle or a fight, if magic was used there, if a murder was committed, and so on.

Likewise, you have a preternatural insight into others' behavior and can sense when a creature's will has been overridden. After talking with a subject for 10 minutes, you can automatically tell if the creature is not acting of its own volition, whether because it is subject to mundane blackmail, has been affected by magic that has charmed it, and so on. You can also determine if a creature was similarly manipulated during previous events by examining detailed accounts of those events.

SUGGESTED CHARACTERISTICS

Investigators are often quiet people, rarely inserting themselves boldly or directly into social situations. Instead, they listen, pose short questions to encourage others to speak or steer conversations in subtle ways. The eyes and ears of an investigator are always open, and many investigators seem flighty or distracted to those unfamiliar with their methods. They have little time for dallying and can come across as blunt or crass as they focus more on events than on the people caught up in them.

d8	Personality Trait
1	I listen and watch more than I talk.
2	I get impatient with small talk and other unnecessary pleasantries.
3	Everyone has something to hide.
4	When others are subtle, I tend to spell things out.
5	I speak only when I feel the need to encourage others to speak.
6	I can't help but poke around whenever I'm in a new place.
7	A detail out of place always draws my attention.
8	Any bit of information is potentially useful.

d6	Ideal
1	Independence. We can never understand all things, so we have no choice but to follow the whims of fate. (Chaotic)
2	Improvement. Learning from the mistakes of the past is what gives us the tools to build a better future. (Good)
3	Truth. I'm a servant of the truth, whatever the outcome of revealing that truth might be. (Neutral)
4	Order. Misdeeds harm more than just their immediate victims; they undermine the well-being of all. (Lawful)
5	Knowledge. Knowledge is power, and it gives us the tools to move through life. (Any)
6	Power. Secrets provide leverage over others, too often forcing them into subservience. (Evil)

d6	Bond
1	I work to protect a certain group of people.
2	I'm drawn to uncover the truth behind mysteries because a mystery from my own past still haunts me.
3	Too many people hide what they've done—just as I tried to do in the past. I won't let them get away with it.
4	I lost something precious to me because I overlooked a crucial detail.
5	The people who taught me my investigator's skills are the most important figures in my life, and I hone my craft to honor them.
6	I never let a mystery pass uninvestigated.

d6	Flaw
1	I drink and smoke to dull the details of my life and work that I yearn to forget.
2	Suggestions of wrongdoing or would-be crime scenes are irresistible to me.
3	I hear secrets and lies hidden within every conversation.
4	I am overwhelmed with jealousy when anyone solves a puzzle before I can.
5	I hold other people to a nearly impossible standard—and hold myself to standards even higher.
6	I lose all sense of risk and self-preservation when following a lead.

ADDITIONAL OPTIONS

The following options are available to norns. At the GM's discretion, other appropriate races may have access to some of these new rules.

EQUIPMENT

Norns have developed the following equipment according to their specific needs and utilize them to particular effect.

Destined Armor. The norn can create armor attuned to surviving a specific creature's attacks by mixing a piece of the target's body (such as hair, nails, or blood) into the metal as it is forged. While the item itself is not magical, the tides of fate protect the wearer from that creature's attacks. When you are struck by a creature's attack while wearing destined armor designed to withstand that creature, the creature rolls an additional die of the weapon's damage and discards the highest die roll. Destined armor costs 100 gp more than normal armor of its type.

NORN WEAPONS

Name	Cost	Damage	Weight	Properties
Martial Melee Weapon				
Norn war spindle	10 gp	1d6 slashing	7 lb.	Finesse, reach, special, two-handed

Destined Weapon. The norn can create a weapon attuned to a specific creature's doom by mixing a piece of the target's body (such as hair, nails, or blood) into the metal as it is forged. While the weapon itself is not magical, it finds its mark on that creature more readily. When you hit a creature with a destined weapon that is that creature's destined doom, you roll an additional die of the weapon's damage and discard the lowest die roll. A destined weapon costs 150 gp more than a normal weapon of its type.

Norn War Spindle. This sharpened, spindle-shaped spinning weight is attached to a 10-foot rope. You can use a norn war spindle to make a special shove contest against a creature within the weapon's reach. You use either your normal attack bonus with the spindle or a Dexterity (Acrobatics) check contested by the usual Strength (Athletics) or Dexterity (Acrobatics) check by your target. If you succeed at a shove contest with a norn war spindle, you can knock your target prone or drag your target 5 feet closer to you, but you can't push it away.

NORN EQUIPMENT

Item	Cost	Weight
Destined armor	+100 gp	—
Destined weapon	+150 gp	—

FEATS

Norns have evolved a style all their own and are quite fond of the following feats.

COVEN SIBLING

Prerequisite: Norn

You can form a connected group called a coven with up to two other norns. You must initially meditate with the other norns with whom you wish to connect for 8 hours. Once a coven is formed, when any member of the coven casts *arcane eye* using the Norn Magic trait, any other member of that coven within 30 feet of the caster can use a reaction to expend one use of their Norn Magic or to expend a spell slot of 4th level or higher. Doing so empowers the first norn's *arcane eye.*

Each member using this reaction benefits from the first member's *arcane eye* as if having cast the spell. Each member is considered the caster of the spell, though its movement remains under the control of the original caster. Any in the coven can maintain concentration on the spell to maintain it up to its full duration.

If one norn uses this reaction, the range of the *arcane eye*'s normal vision and darkvision increases to 60 feet.

If two or more norns use this reaction, the vision granted by *arcane eye* gains the benefit of the *see invisibility* spell.

FLESH SCULPTOR

Prerequisite: Norn

Your natural ability to mold your body is enhanced beyond that of your kin's, allowing you to add the *alter self* spell to your Norn Magic trait. You can cast this spell once with that trait and regain the ability to do so when you finish a short or long rest.

PERSONA SHIFTER

Prerequisite: Norn

Your ability to change shape lets you fully immerse yourself in a new identity. Whenever you take on a new form (whether using your Fluid Identity feature or any other means), choose two skill or tool proficiencies. You can use those proficiencies as long as you remain in that form.

SEER

Prerequisite: Norn, Wisdom 13 or higher

By gazing into the near future, you can shift events to ensure or avoid the fate you glimpse. You gain the following benefits:

- Increase your Intelligence or Wisdom score by 1, to a maximum of 20.
- Each time you take a long rest, you see glimpses of what the next 24 hours might bring. Roll a d20, and record the result. When you or a creature you can see makes an attack roll, an ability check, or a saving throw, you can use your reaction to force the creature to use the result you recorded instead of its own roll. You can use this ability after the roll is made but before the GM determines if the roll succeeds or fails.

Putti

You are so pretty! Your bark is smooth—and soft like a petal. Your juices are red as roses but warm like the sun. What a precious thing you are! I surely hope Korapira doesn't kill you.

—Lotus (upon meeting her first human)

The putti are more than the curious little plant creatures they seem. Korapira created them to someday be the tools of her annihilation of all animal life, the putti themselves born from the agonizing pain and death of sentient creatures. This horrific provenance belies their innocent, child-like appearance and shy behavior. In truth, despite their origins, the putti lack Korapira's bloodthirst—but that should not be confused with any kind of regard for other life. Besides other putti and plants, the putti simply don't comprehend other living things much at all.

These whimsical and distracted fey are interested in how anything and everything works, but their social interactions are difficult. As they mature as a race, some are outgrowing Korapira's simplistic agenda of destruction. These restless putti philosophize and wonder: is this all there is, and what is our place in the world?

If Korapira cannot satisfy these questions for them, she may find herself at odds with her own children.

Physical Description: All putti emerge fully grown from the bloom of a flower of sheol. Their creation involves the painful death of a sentient creature inside the tree, breaking the victim down and transmitting its component parts into the creation of the putti. The putti emerge with will and imagination but no other apparent remnants of the creatures used to create them.

Putti are androgynous in appearance and have no gender distinctions, though once out in the society of other cultures some may adopt a preferred gender to ease integration. They are generally small, purple-skinned—of some varying shade—and resemble nothing so much as slightly bloated, oversized, floating infants with shimmering, entirely green eyes. (Though as more cultivars arise, their appearance shows much more variation.) Clothing, when putti bother to wear any, is usually cobbled together from plant material.

Society: Putti society is still emerging. They have no childhoods or formative years, no need for self-reproduction, and no towns or cities.

There are no individual family units; all putti are—together—family, and the only creatures the putti truly bond with are other putti. Still in a nascent phase as a race, the putti have regarded Korapira as their only leader, and her agenda as their only purpose.

The putti are highly intelligent however—more so

PUTTI TRAITS

Putti characters possess an assortment of traits all their own.

- ***Ability Score Increase.*** Your Intelligence score increases by 2.
- ***Languages.*** You can speak, read, and write Common and Sylvan.
- ***Size.*** Putti average about 3 feet in height and weigh roughly 10 pounds. Your size is Small.
- ***Speed.*** Your base walking speed is 25 feet. (Though you cannot walk, you use this speed to determine your movement while floating.)
- ***Type.*** Your type is fey, but you also count as a plant for certain purposes. If a spell or effect functions only on fey or only on plant creatures, it functions on you. If it treats fey and plant creatures differently, it treats you as a fey. Spells and effects that specifically target humanoids do not affect you. You also gain the mandragora subtype (see **Appendix**).

- ***Darkvision.*** Accustomed to the shade beneath the canopy of forest and jungle, you have superior vision in dark and dim conditions. You can see in dim light within 60 feet of you as if it were bright light and in darkness as if it were dim light. You can't discern color in darkness, only shades of gray.
- ***Floating.*** You float through the air as if always under the effect of a *levitate* spell. You cannot float more than 5 feet above a solid or liquid surface. If you somehow attain a greater height above a surface, you descend slowly toward the surface as if under the effect of a *feather fall* spell. While floating, you can propel yourself at your walking speed without pushing or pulling on objects or surfaces.

  This trait is suppressed if you are encumbered, and you can suppress it as a bonus action. When this trait is suppressed, you can move only at a speed of 5 feet.

  While you are floating, you cannot be knocked prone.
- ***Limited Telepathy.*** You can telepathically communicate with any creature within 30 feet of you as long as you share a language with that creature.
- ***Photosynthetic.*** Exposure to at least 2 hours of sunlight per day serves the same purpose for you that a full ration of food serves for a humanoid. For each day you spend with no exposure to sunlight, you must succeed on a DC 15 Constitution saving throw or gain one level of exhaustion. You require the same amount of water per day as humanoids.
- ***Plant Telepathy.*** You can telepathically communicate with any plant creature or putti within 30 feet. You can also cast *speak with plants* without expending a spell slot once per day; when you do, the duration requires concentration unless you are at least 5th level. You can communicate with the affected plants telepathically.
- ***Strange Mind.*** You have advantage on saving throws against being charmed, and magic can't put you to sleep.
- ***Subrace.*** The putti are evolving into different cultivars (or subraces), reflecting the environments into which your kind has spread. Choose one of these cultivars (see **Cultivars**).

than their flighty natures and social behavior might suggest—and over time, they've begun to consider the world beyond Korapira's Green Expanse and their purpose within it. A growing philosophical trend among them is seeing Korapira, their beloved creator, as unfortunately limited by her hatred of animal life, and to slavishly fall in line behind her desires is to limit their own growth. The putti are not abandoning Korapira however; most still support her in their experiments and discoveries. A growing number are simply asking questions and are beginning to go beyond the Green Expanse to find their answers.

Putti long to know their place in the world, but to know that, they must learn the world. They travel and conduct experiments on the way, testing boundaries, learning, and seeking understanding. The putti are not socially adroit and have no natural empathy, but neither are they innately cruel or violent. They simply regard other living creatures with about the same amount of empathy and respect as most living things give to grass and trees. There is no need for them to harm anyone—until there is.

Putti share psychic bonds with one another and show other putti respect and even affection. Such warmth may surprise other creatures who are almost never subject to this side of them.

Relations: The putti understand they are off-putting to most other sentient creatures, so they are shy and cautious in initial meetings with non-putti. Their curiosity ultimately overpowers their concern however, and they can be found interacting with virtually any society that accepts them, even grudgingly. New experiences are what they are after, and they flit from interest to interest, asking questions all the while: "what is this?" and "how does this work?" Once they've absorbed a great deal of knowledge, they can grow meditative for some time as they reconcile what they've learned with what they know and then attempt to connect to their own existence.

The putti are not malicious by nature, but their insatiable curiosity and curious philosophizing can go from endearing to terrifying when they determine they need to examine a living creature's response to a stimulus to better learn—especially when that stimulus is deadly. All moral considerations bow before a putti's quest for knowledge, assuming the putti has even learned enough of other societies to comprehend morality in the first place.

Alignment and Religion: The putti begin their lives as absolutely true neutral. Morality, if they learn it at all, is a concept taught to them by other societies. Most putti as they mature find even Korapira's morality puzzling and self-limiting. Extraordinary events may sway a putti one way or the other, but ultimately, a putti must see the benefit of accepting a limiting morality—usually it happens because one morality seems to hold the key to understanding their existence.

Curious putti may play at faiths and worship, but they are unable to truly synthesize religion without having some form of moral breakthrough. There are exceptions; putti certainly understand the importance of nature and death for example and follow these portfolios more than any other.

Adventurers: Putti have always trickled away in small numbers to seek greater purpose, but over time, these numbers have become larger and larger as their questions get bigger and go unanswered. Given their unmistakably fey appearance and difficulties with social integration, many become adventurers to pursue their vision.

Innately psychic, putti are strong in classes that depend on strength of mind more than body. Their ties to nature make them potent druids as well.

Age: Putti are fully mature from the moment of their birth, but their average lifespan is difficult to determine. The oldest putti known is only 26 years old. (The singular Eolelo Ai being the exception, and they are currently 148.)

Names: Korapira used to name every new putti herself, but as time has gone on and their numbers have grown, the putti have taken over naming the fledglings. Using Korapira's words and the first psychic impressions each new putti broadcasts, other putti bestow a name upon them.

Putti First Names: Anakoni, Elipeka, Haunani, Iokua, Kale, Leiomi, Mele, Nanani, Pua, Uilani, Wilolia.

Putti Second Names: Ai, Ea, He, Ia, Kee, Loa, Mei, No, Puk, Ui, Waka.

CULTIVARS

Putti are venturing out from the jungles of their birth and are reflecting the changes in their environments.

DESERT PUTTI

Once a traveler on the liminal outland of Zerzura, you are hardier than your jungle-dwelling kin. As a desert putti, you possess several adaptations that benefit you in your primary environment.

Ability Score Increase. Your Constitution score increases by 1.

Dowser. You can cast the *create or destroy water* spell, requiring no material components. Once you use this ability, you can't use it again until you finish a long rest.

Natural Armor. You are covered in a thin layer of bark. Without armor or a shield, your AC equals 12 + your Dexterity modifier.

JUNGLE PUTTI

Jungle-dwelling putti reflect the dangerous and vibrant world to which the putti were first adapted.

Ability Score Increase. Your Dexterity score increases by 1.

Camouflaged. Your skin reflects the hues and tones of the flora of your home, though the range of those colors is extensive. In jungle, swamp, or woodland environments, you have advantage on Dexterity (Stealth) checks, and you can attempt to hide when you are only lightly obscured by foliage.

Pollen Cloud. As an action, you exude a cloud of pollen around you. Any creature within 5 feet of you must succeed on a Dexterity saving throw (DC 8 + your proficiency bonus + your Constitution modifier) or become blinded until the end of its next turn. The cloud then dissipates. Once you use this ability, you can't use it again until you finish a long rest.

SUBCLASSES

The fey provide an array of unique qualities and perspectives for creating interesting new characters. Consult your GM before applying these subclasses to other races.

CIRCLE OF THE GREEN EXPANSE (DRUID: DRUID CIRCLE)

You are wholly devoted to Korapira's vision of verdant destruction, and you traverse the wilderness of countless planes to work the will of your mistress, killing in her name, hastening and encouraging the crumbling of civilization, only to disappear into the wild. Your single-minded dedication makes you unfriendly toward druids of other circles, whom you view as trespassers. The magic you wield is an extension of the deadly power of your mistress.

PLANT FORM: MANDRAKE ROOTLING

When you choose this circle at 2nd level, you can use your Wild Shape ability to transform into a mandrake rootling (see below and see *Along the Twisting Way: The Faerie Ring Campaign Guide* for more on mandragoras).

MANDRAKE ROOTLING

Small fey (mandragora), neutral

Armor Class 13
Hit Points 18 (4d6 + 4)
Speed 20 ft., burrow 10 ft.

STR	DEX	CON	INT	WIS	CHA
8 (−1)	7 (−2)	12 (+1)	4 (−3)	10 (+0)	11 (+0)

Damage Resistances piercing
Condition Immunities blinded, deafened
Senses blindsight 30 ft. (blind beyond this radius), passive Perception 10
Languages understands Sylvan but can't speak
Challenge 1/4 (50 XP)

False Appearance. While the mandrake rootling is buried, only a sprout is visible above ground, and it is indistinguishable from the surrounding flora.

ACTIONS

Multiattack. The mandrake rootling makes 1d4 Touch of Delirium attacks.

Touch of Delirium. *Melee Weapon Attack:* +2 to hit, reach 5 ft., one creature. *Hit:* 2 (1d4) poison damage, and the target must succeed on a DC 13 Constitution saving throw or be poisoned for 1 minute. Until the poison ends, the target is confused (behaving as if under the effects of the *confusion* spell). The target can repeat the saving throw at the end of each of its turns, ending the poison on itself on a success.

REACTIONS

Screech. When pulled from the ground or caught by surprise, the mandrake rootling emits a screech audible within 300 feet of it. All non-plant creatures are deafened while in this area. The mandrake rootling continues to screech until the disturbance moves out of range and for 1d4 of the rootling's turns afterward.

CIRCLE SPELLS

You are granted the following circle spells.

CIRCLE OF THE GREEN EXPANSE SPELLS

Druid Level	Circle Spells
3rd	*darkness, spider climb*
5th	*plant growth, slow*
7th	*freedom of movement, grasping vine*
9th	*cloudkill, tree stride*

PLANT FORM: CHITTERING CREEPER

When you reach 6th level, you can use your Wild Shape ability to transform into a chittering creeper (see *Along the Twisting Way: The Faerie Ring Campaign Guide*).

STRIKE FOR THE MISTRESS

Starting at 6th level, when you use Wild Shape to take plant creature form, your attacks count as magical for the purpose of overcoming resistance and immunity to nonmagical attacks and damage.

ELEMENTAL WILD SHAPE

At 10th level, you can expend two uses of Wild Shape at the same time to transform into a shambling mound.

SEEK THE GREEN

At 14th level, you gain the ability to teleport yourself and up to eight willing creatures to the nearest full acre of dense vegetation. You do not need to have previously visited the location or even know of its existence. There is no guarantee that the destination will be safe.

If you use this ability while already in an area of dense vegetation, it instead informs you of the direction and distance to the nearest portal to the Green Expanse. Either use of this ability requires an action.

CIRCLE OF THE SUN
(DRUID: DRUID CIRCLE)

You bring light to dark places, healing plants that have grown withered and gnarled beneath over-thick canopies and allowing life to flourish where it could not otherwise. You harness the sun, causing flora to bloom even in places where it should not, creating artificial suns and spreading overgrowth wherever you go. As steward of nature's balance however, you also use your power to ensure that plants do not spread where they are not meant to or overpower others. You wield the sun's blazing fire to destroy all which upsets the delicate balance of nature.

BONUS CANTRIPS

At 2nd level, you learn the *light* and *sacred flame* cantrips. They are druid spells for you and don't count against your number of druid cantrips.

SUN'S INVIGORATION

Starting at 2nd level, when you spend Hit Dice to regain hit points upon finishing a short rest while in an area of direct sunlight, you and all creatures of your choice within 30 feet of you that also spent at least one Hit Die to regain hit points regain additional hit points equal to your Wisdom modifier (minimum 1). One of those creatures (which can be you) also gains temporary hit points equal to your Wisdom modifier (minimum 1) until that creature finishes a short or long rest.

CIRCLE SPELLS

You are granted the following circle spells.

CIRCLE OF THE SUN SPELLS

Druid Level	Circle Spells
3rd	*flaming sphere, scorching ray*
5th	*daylight, hypnotic pattern*
7th	*fire shield, wall of fire*
9th	*flame strike, greater restoration*

BEACON OF SUNLIGHT

Starting at 6th level, when you cast a spell that deals fire or radiant damage, blinds creatures, or creates an area of bright light, you can empower it using one of the following options:

- Double the radius of its area, including both its bright and dim light. Any light it sheds is sunlight.
- All fire damage the spell deals is instead radiant damage.
- All saving throws against the spell are made with disadvantage.
- When you roll dice to determine how much radiant or fire damage the spell deals, choose up to a number of those dice equal to your Wisdom modifier (minimum one) and reroll them, taking the new result in place of the old result.
- You make any spell attack rolls for the spell with advantage. If you score a critical hit, the target is blinded until the start of your next turn.

Once you use this feature, you can't use it again until you complete a short or long rest.

RADIANT WILD SHAPE

Starting at 10th level, you can expend two uses of Wild Shape to become a sun sprite, a sphere of golden light 5 feet in diameter. While in this form, you take on the statistics of a will-o'-wisp with the following changes:

- When you transform, you gain temporary hit points equal to your level in this class.
- You are a Medium fey instead of a Tiny undead, and your alignment does not change to chaotic evil.
- You do not gain the Consume Life trait.
- You and any creature standing within the light you shed from your Variable Illumination trait is resistant to bludgeoning, piercing, and slashing damage from nonmagical attacks and regains 5 hit points at the end of each of your turns, up to a total of 5 hit points regained across all creatures per level you have in this class.
- Your Shock attack deals radiant damage instead of lightning damage. You can use your shock to attack twice, instead of once, when you use the Attack action.

GOLDEN CORONA

At 14th level, when you cast a spell of 1st level or higher that targets one or more creatures, you can choose one of the following effects:

- When you cast the spell, all creatures affected by it take radiant damage equal to your Wisdom modifier (minimum 1) and must succeed on a Constitution saving throw against your spell save DC or be blinded until the start of your next turn.
- When you cast the spell, all creatures affected by it regain hit points equal to your Wisdom modifier (minimum 1) and gain resistance to cold damage until the start of your next turn.

You can use this feature four times. You regain all expended uses when you finish a long rest.

COLLEGE OF GOD'S VOICE
(BARD: BARD COLLEGE)

You are not merely a secular storyteller or minstrel—you are godkin. Many sing ancient hymns to the gods and ballads of heroes that did great deeds in the name of their divine sovereign. You take this a step farther, claiming to speak with the voice of a god itself, using your own charisma to attract followers like a messiah.

Some putti embrace the full responsibilities of being a favored child of Korapira. These individuals lead a cult of followers to help ensure the destruction of the known world and its rebirth of wood and sap to carry through the will of their demented sovereign.

BONUS PROFICIENCIES

When you join this college at 3rd level, you gain proficiency in three of the following skills of your choice: Deception, Insight, Religion, Sleight of Hand, and Stealth.

CULT OF PERSONALITY

Starting at 3rd level, when a friendly creature you can see makes an attack roll, saving throw, or ability check, you can use your reaction to make the same kind of roll, using your ability scores, proficiency bonus, and other modifiers. The creature that made the first roll can choose whether or not to use your result in place of its own.

You can use this feature after the first roll is made but before you know if it is a success or failure. If the roll is an attack roll, you must make the same type of attack roll (such as a ranged weapon attack or a melee spell attack).

Once you use this feature, you can't use it again until you finish a short or long rest.

INCITE FERVOR

Starting at 6th level, you can expend one use of Bardic Inspiration to grant a Bardic Inspiration die to all creatures of your choice within 30 feet of you that can hear you and that do not already have a Bardic Inspiration die. The die must be rolled and added to each creature's next attack roll or saving throw (your choice). This choice applies to all affected creatures.

EMBODIMENT OF GOD'S VOICE

Starting at 14th level, your voice carries gravity superior to your mortal stature. Whenever you or a creature you can see makes a spell attack roll or Charisma saving throw, you can expend one use of Bardic Inspiration to roll a Bardic Inspiration die and add the number rolled to the result.

GREEN WARDEN (RANGER: RANGER ARCHETYPE)

You travel the world with your living plant companions as emissaries of the natural world. While not a druid, you have been trained in the druidic arts, either by a druidic master or by one who has stolen and betrayed the secrets of a druid circle. As part of your training, you form a bond with the natural world that allows you to draw power from nature as long as you swear to protect it.

Some wardens gain their powers from Korapira's Green Expanse and work to undermine civilization by sowing the seeds of the plants that will destroy it. Others call these zealots green ravagers. Not all wardens hate the ravagers enough to hunt them down, but most resent them for spoiling their reputation as protectors of nature's balance.

PLANT COMPANION

At 3rd level, the natural world grants you a companion to fight alongside you as a sign of your compact. This awakened plant can be no larger than Medium and must have a challenge rating or 1/4 or lower. This plant companion gains the following benefits:

- Its Intelligence score increases to 10, and it learns one language of your choice that you speak.
- It adds your proficiency bonus to its AC, attack rolls, damage rolls, and to any saving throws or skills it is proficient in.
- Its hit point maximum increases to four times your ranger level unless its current hit point maximum is already higher.
- Its walking speed increases to 20 feet unless its current speed is already higher.

Your plant companion takes its turns on your initiative and follows your commands to the best of its ability, though unless you are incapacitated it can't take an action unless you use your action to command it (either verbally or by signs it can see) to take the Attack, Dash, Disengage, Help, or Hide action. Once you can use Extra Attack to make multiple attacks with a single Attack action, it can make two attacks when you command your companion to attack.

Your plant companion is native to one of your favored terrains. While in its native terrain, your plant companion can appear to be a normal plant as long as it remains motionless. You have advantage on Dexterity (Stealth) checks while hiding in or behind your plant companion.

If your plant companion dies, the natural world provides you with a new one native to your current region at next dawn.

GREEN TONGUE

Also at 3rd level, you can touch a plant as an action to imbue it with limited sentience and animation for 10 minutes or until you use this feature again, giving it the ability to communicate with you and follow your simple commands. You can question the plant about events within 30 feet of it that occurred within the past 24 hours, gaining information about creatures that have passed, weather, and other circumstances.

The plant might be able to perform other tasks on your behalf, at the GM's discretion. While your touch doesn't give a plant the ability to uproot itself and move about, it does allow it to freely move its branches, tendrils, or stalks.

To touch a plant creature, you must make an unarmed melee weapon attack. If you hit, you can communicate with it as if you shared a common language, but you gain no magical ability to influence it.

WARDEN'S INSTINCTS

At 7th level, whenever you take the Dash, Disengage, Help, or Hide action, you can command your companion to take one of those actions as a bonus action. In addition, when a creature within 5 feet of you attacks your plant companion, you can use your reaction to impose disadvantage on the attack. Whether the attack hits or misses, your companion can make a single attack against the creature.

NATURE'S STING

Starting at 11th level, whenever your plant companion hits with an attack, it deals an additional 1d10 poison damage. If the target is a creature, it must succeed on a Constitution saving throw against your ranger spell save DC or be poisoned until the start of your next turn.

LEECHING BLIGHT

Starting at 15th level, when your plant companion is reduced to 0 hit points, you can use your reaction to cause it to release a plume of noxious rot. When you do, all creatures of your choice within 30 feet of your companion must make a Constitution saving throw against your ranger spell save DC, taking 8d8 necrotic damage on a failed save or half as much damage on a successful one. If this damage reduces a creature to 0 hit points, your plant companion regains half its maximum hit points at the end of your next turn.

Once you use this feature, you can't use it again until you finish a long rest.

WARPED NATURE DOMAIN
(CLERIC: DIVINE DOMAIN)

Your worship of Korapira reflects her embodiment of nature's deadly power. Natural poisons and thorn-bearing flora are holy to you, and you make liberal use of both in your ceremonies and rituals. Your mandate is clear: fauna must make way for flora, and the bloodier that process is, the better. Rarely do your purposes coincide with those of civilized folk, but among certain of the fey and the intelligent creatures of the wild, you are seen as an ally—provided your wrath remains focused on common enemies.

WARPED NATURE DOMAIN

You are granted the following domain spells.

WARPED NATURE DOMAIN SPELLS

Cleric Level	Spells
1st	*detect poison and disease, entangle*
3rd	*barkskin, spike growth*
5th	*plant growth, vampiric touch*
7th	*blight, grasping vine*
9th	*awaken, tree stride*

BONUS PROFICIENCY

At 1st level, you gain proficiency in one of the following skills of your choice: Intimidation, Nature, or Stealth.

ACOLYTE OF KORAPIRA

Also at 1st level, you learn one druid cantrip of your choice.

CHANNEL DIVINITY: CHARM PLANTS

Starting at 2nd level, you can use your Channel Divinity to charm plants. As an action, you present your holy symbol and invoke Korapira. Each plant creature that can see you within 60 feet of you must succeed on a Wisdom saving throw or be charmed by you for 10 minutes or until it takes damage. While it is charmed by you, a creature is friendly to you and other creatures you designate.

CHANNEL DIVINITY: CAMOUFLAGE

At 6th level, you can use your Channel Divinity to camouflage yourself and creatures of your choice within 30 feet of you. Each affected creature gains a +10 bonus to ability checks made to hide or use Stealth while in an area lightly obscured by moderate foliage. In addition to yourself, you can grant this benefit to a number of creatures equal to your spellcasting ability modifier.

POISON STRIKE

At 8th level, you gain the ability to infuse your weapon strikes with magical poison. Once on each of your turns when you hit a creature with a weapon attack, you can cause the attack to deal an extra 2d6 poison damage to the target. When you reach 14th level, the extra damage increases to 4d6.

SOW THE SEED

At 17th level, you gain the ability to grow a seed pod inside your body. After 1 hour of gestation, the pod appears in your mouth at which point you can plant it in the ground to cause a clone of yourself to grow from the soil over the next 120 days. This ability functions as the *clone* spell, except that it has no material component, and the clone grows beneath the ground rather than in a sealed vessel.

WAY OF THE WINDSTORMER (MONK: MONASTIC TRADITION)

You move like the wind itself, manipulating your ki to harness the speed of the gale, to embody the power of the hurricane, unfettering your body from the earth and moving through the sky with the grace and majesty of a bird. You are able to leverage your natural bond with nature and your lightness of being to bend the reality of the winds around you. You focus on using the very air to aid you in your travels and grant you deadly powers.

SILVER ZEPHYR

Starting when you choose this tradition at 3rd level, you can spend 2 ki points as an action to surround yourself with a silver wind. For the rest of your turn, your movement does not provoke opportunity attacks, and you can move through spaces occupied by hostile creatures of any size. Their spaces do not count as difficult terrain for you. At the end of your turn, every creature whose space you moved through that turn must make a Strength saving throw. On a failed save, it takes damage equal to your Martial Arts damage + your Strength or Dexterity modifier (your choice) and falls prone. On a successful save, it takes half as much damage and does not fall prone.

UNFETTERED MISTRAL

At 6th level, your connection to the wind allows you to dodge direct attacks with ease. When a creature makes a melee attack against you, you can spend 1 ki point as a reaction to impose disadvantage on the attack roll before it is made. If the attack misses you, you can spend an additional 1 ki point to gain one of the following benefits as part of that reaction.

Dancing Leaf. You can move up to your speed in any direction. This movement does not provoke opportunity attacks.

Frigid Tramontane. You make a single melee attack against the creature that attacked you. On a hit, this attack deals additional cold damage equal to your Martial Arts damage.

UNBOUND BY THE EARTH

Starting at 11th level, the wind buoys your every movement. You gain a flying speed equal to half your base speed (rounded down to the nearest 5 feet). If you already had an equal or faster flying speed, you gain the option to hover. (Putti also gain the option to hover.) At 17th level, your flying speed becomes equal to your walking speed.

BULWARK OF AIR

At 17th level, you can surround yourself with a shielding cocoon of raging wind that hedges out the effects of all other winds and gases. The shell also allows you to fly and breathe even underwater. You can dismiss this wind or restore it as a bonus action. While surrounded by this cocoon, ranged weapon attack rolls against you have disadvantage, and you have advantage on Dexterity saving throws against spells and effects that deal damage in an area.

While surrounded by this cocoon, you can spend 3 ki points to cast *wind wall* as an action or as a bonus action, without expending a spell slot. While concentrating on this spell, you sacrifice the benefits of your cocoon.

BACKGROUNDS

The following backgrounds are especially common in putti. At the GM's discretion, other appropriate races may have access to them.

PLANAR PILGRIM

Whether you wandered through a planar passage connecting the jungle of your birth to other lands or traveled along with a wandering liminal outland, you have drifted far from home. Those who know you see you as something otherworldly and strange. Some might fear you, but others value the knowledge you have gained in your travels.

Consult with your GM to determine what odd insight you might have attained in your travels through the extraplanar wildernesses that connect to Korapira's demesne, and why you have wandered so far. Were you simply curious and daring? Did you flee your birthplace for fear of its mistress? Or did she send you out across the planes for some mysterious purpose?

Skill Proficiencies: Insight, Survival

Tool Proficiencies: Herbalism kit, woodcarver's tools

Languages: One of your choice

Equipment: A blowgun, 50 blowgun needles, a vial of poison (basic), a carved wooden trinket, a set of common clothes, and a pouch containing 10 gp

FEATURE: NEVER EXPOSED

Your familiarity with harsh environments has taught you the value of always being able to create shelter for yourself. Given two hours, you can piece together a makeshift tent from the surrounding foliage in any wooded environment. The tent is capable of sheltering up to eight creatures of Medium or smaller size. Once built, the structure cannot be moved.

SUGGESTED CHARACTERISTICS

Planar pilgrims are oddities among the putti race. They develop a sense of detachment when it comes to places and things, instead focusing on intellectual pursuits and theories. They make remarkably useful companions though, always prepared for any contingency and possessed of a wealth of information gleaned from the places they have seen.

d8	Personality Trait
1	I experienced something while traveling alone that made a profound impact on me. I continue to draw lessons from my experience and attempt to share with others.
2	My urge to wander makes me reticent to put down roots. On the other hand, I'm an ideal traveling companion.
3	I have learned the value of always having the right tools on hand. It is difficult for me to pass up something potentially useful.
4	Being used to the closeness of the wilds, I feel exposed in wide-open spaces.
5	I take a "live and let live" attitude toward the religious views of others.
6	I am aware of my strangeness, and I use it to make memorable introductions.
7	I never go charging straight into a dangerous situation but prefer instead to gauge things carefully beforehand.
8	I am curious when encountering other travelers—even unfriendly ones—and will learn what I can from them.

d6	Ideal
1	Freedom. I am not content to stay in one place for long. (Chaotic)
2	Practicality. Preparation is the key to survival, and I will see to it that my companions and I are properly outfitted. (Lawful)
3	Relativism. My wanderings have shown me the mutability of morality. I reserve judgment on many topics, accepting some views that others find difficult to accept. (Neutral)
4	Charity. I am generous when I can afford to be, knowing that one day I might benefit from the same attitude in others. (Good)
5	Indifference. Having witnessed the deaths of both noble and humble creatures, I am capable of dispassionately allowing horrors to occur. (Evil)
6	Skepticism. I accept nothing at face value. I need to know how things truly work. (Any)

d6	Bond
1	I want nothing so much as to benefit my people somehow.
2	I don't form bonds easily—but once I do, I will risk life and limb for a friend.
3	I loathe my creator, Korapira, and will do what I can to thwart her.
4	After a brief captivity as an exhibit in a noble's menagerie, I bear great malice toward aristocrats.
5	I am a dedicated member of a secret society, and I can't talk about it.
6	My knowledge of the Green Expanse is a closely guarded secret.

d6	Flaw
1	I am a horrible judge of character.
2	Others often find it too easy to talk me into stupid plans.
3	I occasionally forget how the laws of physics work on the plane where I find myself. And sometimes it's hilarious.
4	I have an extreme dislike for a common domestic creature.
5	I cannot take a joke and have an embarrassing need to get even when one is played on me.
6	My lack of concern for material wealth combines poorly with my odd love of gambling.

ADDITIONAL OPTIONS

The following options are available to putti. At the GM's discretion, other appropriate races may have access to some of these new rules.

EQUIPMENT

Putti have developed the following equipment according to their specific needs and utilize them to particular effect.

Bottled Sunlight. This alchemical gel absorbs sunlight and then releases it when the bottle is broken, making a point on a hard surface or object it touches shine brightly for 1 hour. A 60-foot-radius sphere of bright light shines from this point. The sphere sheds dim light for an additional 60 feet. The light moves with the object and can be blocked by opaque coverings.

Forest's Embrace. This alchemical perfume attracts plants to it with alarming speed. Applying a vial of perfume is an action. While you wear it, any plant who approaches within 30 feet of you must succeed at a DC 10 Charisma saving throw or be charmed by you for as long as it remains within 30 feet of you while the perfume lasts. In addition, you treat all areas within 5 feet of non-creature plants as difficult terrain. When you begin your turn within 5 feet of non-creature plants, you must succeed at a DC 10 Strength saving throw or be restrained. When you are restrained, you can escape as an action by succeeding at a DC 10 Strength check.

Forest's embrace can be thrown as an improvised weapon; if you hit a creature, it is treated as wearing this perfume. If you miss with a vial, it lands and breaks a number of feet shy of the target equal to the difference between your attack roll and the target's AC. Touching the surface where the vial broke automatically exposes a creature to it. Forest's embrace lasts for 1 hour.

Poison, Tears of the Green Mind (Injury/Ingested). This poison must be harvested from a gland in a putti's neck, dealing 2d10 slashing damage to the putti in the process. A creature subjected to this poison through injury must succeed on a DC 15 Constitution saving throw or take 7 (2d6) poison damage and become poisoned for 1 minute. While poisoned in this way, the creature is paralyzed. The creature can repeat the saving throw at the end of each of its turns, ending the effect on itself on a success.

A creature subjected to this poison through ingestion must succeed on a DC 17 Charisma saving throw or be poisoned for 2d6 hours. On a successful save, the creature is poisoned for 1d6 hours. The poisoned creature is paralyzed, but if the save was successful, it also gains the ability to telepathically communicate with plants while poisoned, as if under the effect of a *speak with plants* spell.

PUTTI EQUIPMENT

Item	Cost	Weight
Bottled sunlight	300 gp	—
Forest's embrace (vial)	25 gp	—
Poison, Tears of the Green Mind (vial, 1 dose)	500 gp	—

FEATS

Putti have evolved a style all their own and are quite fond of the following feats.

CHOSEN OF NATURE

Prerequisite: Putti

You strengthen your plant-like nature to help you shrug off effects that would hinder your body and mind. Choose one or two of the following conditions or effects:

- Charmed
- Paralyzed
- Poisoned
- Stunned
- Being transformed into a new form by the polymorph spell or similar magic

If you chose two conditions or effects, you have advantage on saving throws to resist the chosen conditions or effects. If you chose one condition or effect, you are immune to the chosen condition or effect.

You can select this feat multiple times. Each time you do so, you must choose different conditions or effects.

DIVINELY TOUCHED

Prerequisite: Putti

As a bonus action, you force each creature within range of your limited telepathy to succeed on a Charisma saving throw (DC 8 + your proficiency bonus + your Charisma modifier) or perceive you as a holy being. For 1 hour, you have advantage on Charisma checks made against affected creatures. You can end this effect on one or more creatures as a bonus action.

Once you use this ability, you can't use it again until you finish a short or long rest. A creature that successfully saves cannot be affected again for 24 hours.

MASTER TELEPATH

Prerequisite: Putti

The range of your telepathy increases by 30 feet. You can select this feat multiple times.

MIND READER

Prerequisite: Putti

Choose a creature within the range of your telepathy. That creature must succeed on a Charisma saving throw (DC 8 + your proficiency bonus + your Intelligence modifier) or expose its thoughts to you for 1 minute as if targeted by the *detect thoughts* spell. On a successful saving throw, the creature is immune to this ability for 24 hours. Once you use this ability, you can't use it again until you finish a short or long rest.

TELEKINETIC

Prerequisite: Putti

You can use the *telekinesis* spell, except the range is equal to the range of your telepathy, and you can affect only Medium or smaller creatures or objects weighing up to 200 pounds.

When you direct this ability against a creature, you can use your reaction to force the creature to succeed on a Strength saving throw (DC 8 + your proficiency bonus + your Intelligence modifier) or take bludgeoning damage equal to your proficiency bonus.

Once you use this ability, you can't use it again until you finish a long rest.

UNTETHERED

Prerequisite: Putti

You have a vastly improved control of your float bladder. You gain the following benefits:

- As an action, you activate the ability to float higher than normal using your Floating trait. For 10 minutes, you are not limited in how high you can float above a solid or liquid surface. However, if you rise more than 5 feet above a surface, your horizontal movement is limited to a speed of 20 feet. If you are encumbered, you sink to the surface beneath you as normal. Once you use this ability, you can't use it again until you finish a short or long rest.

Teras

Mommy! Wait . . . would you prefer I call you Daddy? Hey look, this is as disorienting for me as it is for you . . . quit trying to emotionally blackmail me, Dad! I know *you carried me for three months. You can't hold that over me forever!*

—Ogremaw the Dread, Junior

The fey are alien to most other species; the teras, however, are alien even among fey. Born as spores seeking a host, the teras duplicate what they can of their host bodies and then improve upon it. Other species viewing the results, however, may not agree on the word *improve*.

Teras can be difficult to identify, let alone define. By nature, they defy definition. They are fey of change, of mutability, of a world unto themselves in complete flux. They sometimes seem beset by curses such as tumors, growths, or warped biology, but the teras take such deformities and transform them into gifts. These fey believe all change is to be embraced, even if that change may initially seem undesirable.

Physical Description: Teras defy description. Pureblooded teras—that is, those who use another teras as a host—are easiest to identify by a willowy, fragile-appearing stature, luminescent, hairless skin, and elaborate bone growths. Pureblooded teras tend to have an unearthly, alien beauty about them that mortals may find fascinating.

Teras born from a different host race mostly resemble a member of that host's species but with some form of mutation. The exact form of mutation varies widely, but tumors, bone growths, withered limbs, conjoined twins, and so on are only some of the possibilities.

Mutations need not be visible: some teras have rearranged bodily organs—or extra ones—or hollowed spaces within their bodies. Some bleed honey or require a diet of only raw meat. The point is that the teras cannot resist coming into contact with a species without tweaking it in some way. Making it different. In their eyes, making it better.

Teras are androgynous, though non-purebloods may visually possess various gender characteristics of their host race.

Society: A teras begins existence as a parasite bursting from the flesh of a host creature whose genetic material it borrows to make its body. Luckily for the host, the magic of a teras prevents this traumatic experience from killing the host or inflicting much permanent damage. (Usually.) Once emerged, the teras is full-grown, resembling either its "parent" species or a pureblooded teras, but always "improved."

In New Pelora, Oleron's domain, the pureblooded teras rule and

dictate the day-to-day, everchanging laws of the realm and jockey with one another for Oleron's favor. The echelons of power are filled with debauched, psychic fey willing to break any taboo or commit any atrocity just for the fleeting feeling of not being bored. Teras tire of anything quickly once they experience it and must push further and further to feel interest. Boredom is like a death of the mind to a teras.

Teras of other lineages—often with "births" arranged by purebloods to test out new mutations—fare less well in New Pelora, often relegated to the menial tasks no pureblood would inflict upon themselves. The most common job for non-purebloods is to go to the planes and bring back living creatures as amusements. Some teras choose not to return from these jaunts, desiring to feed their own experiences instead of catering to another's.

Teras born outside of New Pelora attempt to integrate with their host's society as well as they can. They are no less driven by a need for new experiences—nor any less prone to growing jaded—than purebloods, but they instinctively work to keep their natures hidden.

TERAS TRAITS

Teras characters possess an assortment of traits all their own.

- ***Ability Score Increase.*** Your Dexterity score increases by 2, and your Constitution score increases by 1.
- ***Languages.*** You can speak, read, and write Common.
- ***Size.*** Pureblooded teras vary widely in size and build while those born from other races tend toward the build of that race. Your size is Medium.
- ***Speed.*** Your base walking speed is 30 feet.
- ***Type.*** Your type is fey. Spells and effects that specifically target humanoids do not affect you. You also gain the morph subtype (see **Appendix**).

- ***Adaptive Physiology.*** Your body is remarkably resilient and adaptable to your surroundings. As a reaction when you are damaged, you can spend one Hit Die to heal as if you had just finished a short rest. You can use this reaction even if the damage would incapacitate you. If you are at least 5th level, you can spend up to half your Hit Dice this way. Once you use this feature, you can't use it again until you finish a long rest.
- ***Blood of Oleron.*** Through your veins flows the wildly mutable blood of Oleron himself, making your body particularly susceptible to magic that unnaturally alters its composition. You have disadvantage on saving throws against transmutation spells. In addition, any transmutation spell affects you as if cast from a spell slot one slot level higher than it actually used.
- ***Darkvision.*** Adaptable to almost any environment, you can see in dim light within 60 feet of you as if it were bright light and in darkness as if it were dim light. You can't discern color in darkness, only shades of gray.
- ***Teras Magic.*** Your form is always in flux. By concentrating for 10 minutes (as if concentrating on a spell), you can alter your appearance, including height, weight, facial features, sound of your voice, hair length, coloration, and distinguishing characteristics, if any. You can't change your basic body shape or statistics, but can resemble a member of another race of your size. You can make an Intelligence (disguise kit) check to create a disguise this way even without a disguise kit. At 3rd level, you can change your appearance in 1 minute.
- ***Unnerving Presence.*** You have proficiency in the Intimidation skill.

Besides appeasing their cravings for novel stimulation, teras work to affect change and upset the status quo in their surroundings—sometimes to good ends. For every teras openly leading charges against tyrannies and stagnant kingdoms though, there is another in the shadows killing innocents to study death or whispering in the ear of a high priest to change the church's dogma to exterminate rather than tolerate the unworthy—just to see what the faithful will do and what will happen.

Relations: The teras have no true prejudices or biases against others, though they do feel a certain amount of pity for species locked into static forms. Luckily, anyone can change with will and a little magic, and teras are glad to work with other races in "improving" their minds and bodies if they wish. With some exceptions, teras prefer to have permission before working changes on sentient creatures, but if it is obvious—to the teras—that a change is direly needed, they might not bother with permission.

There is some tension among the teras themselves with pureblooded teras considering their form to be the true shape of evolution and other teras to be useful tools in manifesting new, never-before-seen mutations. Of additional consideration are the caterpillar-like membras and the powerfully psychic yet frail terani; while teras are accepting of their many evolutionary branches, their lineage can prove perplexing even to other fey and provide a mistaken view of the teras as a whole.

This is the secret other species must know to understand the teras condition: there is no teras "as a whole."

Alignment and Religion: Chaos is the lifeblood of the teras. Laws are interesting only for about as long as it takes to devise them. Teras build things only to tear them down and try something else. They are intelligent and do not literally go about transforming things on a whim—like their progenitor, Oleron, they understand that while they may want to change everything, constant chaos will eventually leave the ultimate stagnation of *nothing* in its wake—but they are ever mindful for opportunities where instigating change will have the broadest, most interesting effect.

As for religion, some teras, particularly purebloods, worship Oleron with zealot-like fervor. Teras mostly do not find gods and religions as supportive enough of personal evolution, but those deities closest to chaos with constantly changing forms and dogma may find teras faithful away from New Pelora.

Adventurers: Teras make natural adventurers with their adaptability and devotion to leaving things much different to how they found them. Arcane and psychic classes—particularly those with a transmutation focus—account for a large number of teras adventurers, but the innate variance within teras means they can be found in any class—even monks and paladins, though very few teras have the willingness to remain in such disciplined vocations for long.

Age: Theoretically, teras are immortal, and while they can be killed, time never claims them. Their physiologies are basically just sacks of cancer—immortal cancer, growing forever. That said, it is common for random mutations to prove lethal, so a teras could on the one hand live forever, or they could die unwittingly at any point in their lives. They are born fully mature.

Names: A standard name scheme does not exist for the teras. Non-pureblooded teras may have any sort of name, usually taken from the culture of their host. Purebloods tend to borrow words from Aklo or Sylvan or other language Oleron currently favors and use them as names until they decide to change them.

SUBCLASSES

The fey provide an array of unique qualities and perspectives for creating interesting new characters. Consult your GM before applying these subclasses to other races.

FACELESS

(ROGUE: ROGUISH ARCHETYPE)

Legends of the Faceless are repeated only around campfires late at night and in particularly disturbing nursery rhymes. Few earnestly believe the stories of killers with perfectly blank faces, but the seed of fear grows into a weed that is hard to uproot. Wise are those who remember the tales of hooded beings that can change their faces into that of anyone they see and steal the face of anyone they kill.

Of course, you are more than a mere spook in a faerie tale. You use your chilling mutagenic powers to imitate your targets, becoming a master of disguise by literally transforming your appearance.

MIMIC

Starting at 3rd level when you choose this archetype, you can use your action to change your physical appearance to perfectly match one humanoid that you have seen in the past 24 hours. This is a physical change, not an illusion, and it holds up to physical inspection. You can only adopt the appearance of creatures that are the same size as you (so you cannot transform into a Small creature if you are Medium, for example). If that creature has uniquely identifying features that you have not seen, such as a hidden scar or birthmark, your transformation does not include those features.

This transformation alters your voice to sound like the person you are imitating but does not grant you knowledge of their mannerisms or syntax. A creature interacting with you who has interacted with the original can notice something is strange if its passive Intelligence (Investigation) score is at least equal to your Charisma (Deception) check. If you have interacted with the original for at least 1 minute outside of combat, you have advantage on Charisma (Deception) checks to impersonate that individual.

This transformation lasts for 1 hour or until you end it as a bonus action. You cannot adopt the form of a creature you have already transformed into until you finish a long rest.

MIMIC'S AMBUSH

Also at 3rd level, you have advantage on attack rolls against creatures that believe you are the person you are mimicking and that are not hostile to that person. The first time you attack such a creature, a hit is automatically a critical hit. You also have advantage on attack rolls against any creature that has not yet acted during the current combat.

MIND SIPHON

Starting at 9th level, you can cast *detect thoughts* as a bonus action, requiring no components. Once you cast this spell in this way, you can't cast it again until you complete a short or long rest. Your spellcasting ability is Intelligence, and the save DC is 8 + your proficiency bonus + your Intelligence modifier.

THIEF OF FACES

Starting at 13th level, you can steal the faces of those you kill. As a reaction when you kill a humanoid of any size category, you can absorb their physical appearance, rendering their corpse featureless and smooth. Once you use this feature to steal an appearance, you can't steal another until you complete a short or long rest.

Additionally, you can use your Mimic feature to transform into a creature whose appearance you have stolen. This transformation perfectly mimics all of the chosen creature's physical features. This transformation lasts until you end it as a bonus action, and you can assume this shape as many times as you wish without needing to complete a rest.

GROTESQUE TRANSFORMATION

At 17th level, you gain the ability to morph into monstrous, powerful forms. You can cast *true polymorph* on yourself to become a specific creature you have observed, requiring no components and without expending a spell slot. Once you cast this spell in this way, you can't cast it again until you finish a long rest.

OATH OF THE UNFETTERED (PALADIN: SACRED OATH)

For some teras, the mutability of their bodies extends to their very psyches, allowing them to act as both beneficent protector and wrathful engine of destruction in the name of their deity. The ever-shifting nature of these fey make it difficult for them to commit to the rigid tenets of a typical paladin's oath. Instead, they have committed to embodying and fostering change and growth while also destroying limitations.

The oath of the unfettered is a polarized one, flitting back and forth between altruism and selfishness, creation and destruction, hope and wrath, and allows you to pursue your goal of making the world more colorful, creative, diverse, and ultimately interesting. Many unshackled knights, as you are known, are fluid in their presentation of gender and might even change gender as often as they change between creative and destructive roles.

TENETS OF THE UNFETTERED

The tenets of the unfettered are customized to each paladin, focusing on breaking the limitations that individual believes to be most onerous and nurturing the freedoms deemed most vital.

Encourage Innovation. Support, protect, and aid those working for change, progress, mutation, and creativity.

Care for Yourself. Showing your most dazzling and memorable idiosyncrasies encourages others to tear away the pointlessly confining rules of society. Care for and protect yourself, for you are responsible for your own uniqueness.

Laws are Made to be Broken. Rebel against and destroy unjust and abused authority when you can.

OATH SPELLS

You gain oath spells at the following paladin levels listed.

OATH OF THE UNFETTERED SPELLS

Paladin Level	Spells
3rd	*bane, bless*
5th	*alter self, enlarge/reduce*
9th	*bestow curse, remove curse*
13th	*freedom of movement, locate creature*
17th	*mass cure wounds, mislead*

RIGHT-HAND AND LEFT-HAND PATH

When you choose this oath at 3rd level, you embrace duality. Your right hand represents creation and order; your left hand represents destruction and chaos.

When you complete a long rest, choose the right-hand path or the left-hand path (or determine it randomly with a 50 percent chance of choosing either path). When following the right-hand path, you gain the Right Hand of Light Channel Divinity option. When following the left-hand path, you gain the Left Hand of Darkness Channel Divinity option. If you have a fluid expression of gender, the magic of your path helps you to easily present as a different gender when you change your path, potentially even transforming your body (as determined by your own personal oath).

Right Hand of Light. You can use your Channel Divinity to call the light of creation into your right hand. As an action, you can touch a creature and end one disease, poison, spell, or other magical effect currently affecting it. Additionally, this touch allows you to use your pool of healing power as if using your Lay on Hands feature. Each point you spend from this pool heals 2 hit points when spent in this way.

Left Hand of Darkness. You can use your Channel Divinity to call the forces of darkness into your left hand. As an action, you can touch a creature and impose a curse upon it. That creature must succeed on a Wisdom saving throw against your spell save DC or be blinded, deafened, frightened of you, or poisoned (your choice) for 1 minute. It can repeat the saving throw at the end of each of its turns, ending the effect on a success. Additionally, this touch allows you to use your pool of healing power as if using your Lay on Hands feature. Each point you spend from this pool deals 2 points of necrotic damage when spent in this way, up to an amount of damage equal to twice your level in this class.

AURA OF TWIN VIRTUES

Beginning at 7th level, the power of your chosen path radiates from you like a beacon. While you are following the path of light, you and friendly creatures within 10 feet of you have resistance to necrotic damage and have advantage on saving throws against being charmed. While you are following the path of darkness, you and friendly creatures within 10 feet of you have resistance to radiant damage and have advantage on saving throws against being frightened.

At 18th level, the range of both of these auras increases to 30 feet.

FLUID DUALITY

Starting at 15th level, you can shift between left-hand and right-hand paths as a bonus action. When you choose the left-hand path, you have advantage on attack rolls until the start of your next turn. When you choose the right-hand path, you have advantage on saving throws until the start of your next turn.

BEYOND DUALITY

At 20th level, you can embrace both the left-hand and right-hand paths at once, becoming something greater than them both. Your appearance becomes graceful (and potentially genderless), wreathed in both light and shadow.

You can take this combined path as an action. For 1 minute, you gain the following benefits:

- You instantly gain 2 uses of your Channel Divinity and can use either Channel Divinity option granted by this oath. These extra uses of Channel Divinity disappear after 1 minute if not used.
- Both of the auras granted by your Aura of Twin Virtues are active at once.
- You and friendly creatures within 30 feet of you are resistant to bludgeoning, piercing, and slashing damage and to damage from spells.
- When you use your Fluid Duality, your choice changes which path you return to after Beyond Duality's benefits end but doesn't cause you to leave your combined path. You still get the benefit for your path choice (advantage on either attack rolls or saving throws).

ONCOMANCER
(SORCERER: SORCEROUS ORIGIN)

It's not unusual for a teras to form semi-intelligent tumors in their unpredictably mutable bodies. But through some combination of science and magic, some of these tumors develop enough awareness to communicate in limited fashion.

You can manipulate your tumors, changing your bodily make-up to become more resistant to ailments, conditions, and disease but at a physical cost.

Somewhere on your body is a pronounced tumor—an unwholesome mass that is always immediately visible unless concealed by bulky clothing or magic. This tumor cannot be removed or healed by any means short of divine intervention or a *wish* spell. You immediately lose all your oncomancer abilities if deprived of your tumor.

SENTIENT TUMOR

Your tumor is sentient but counts as a part of you. It shares your hit points and cannot be individually damaged or targeted. It uses your ability scores but cannot make attack rolls or ability checks on its own.

Starting when you choose this origin at 1st level, your tumor offers you protection against harmful bodily effects. You have advantage on saving throws against poison, and you have resistance to poison damage.

TWO MINDS ARE BETTER THAN ONE

At 1st level, your tumor magically pursues its own studies and can assist you in its areas of expertise.

Choose two of the following skills of your choice: Arcana, History, Nature, or Religion. You become proficient in those skills if you are not already, and your proficiency bonus is doubled for any ability check you make that uses either skill.

DEFENDING TUMOR

Beginning at 6th level, your tumor becomes more adept at defending your body with magic. You have advantage on Intelligence, Wisdom, and Charisma saving throws against magic. In addition, when you would take bludgeoning, piercing, or slashing damage, you can use a reaction to spend 1 sorcery point and gain resistance to all those damage types until the end of your next turn.

IMPROVED STUDY

Starting at 14th level, your tumor furthers its studies. You gain proficiency in any two skills of your choice.

SYMBIOSIS

Beginning at 18th level, the magical protection your tumor offers you becomes even more powerful. You gain immunity to poison.

In addition, your tumor can shroud you in powerful defensive magic. As an action, you can spend 5 sorcery points to draw on this power, gaining the following effects for 1 minute or until you lose your concentration (as if you were concentrating on a spell):

- At the start of each of your turns, you regain 10 hit points.
- You have advantage on all saving throws.
- You gain a +2 bonus to AC.

PATH OF THE MUTANT (BARBARIAN: PRIMAL PATH)

All teras are mutants by nature, but their most barbaric warriors manifest their mutations in powerful and unpredictable ways. Though no teras knows the origin of these incredible mutant warriors, most suspect that the wildly changeable and adaptable blood of these barbarians traces to a powerful teras elder or to Oleron himself.

UNSTABLE BLOOD

At 3rd level when you choose this path, your blood changes when you rage to take on a new and caustic form. Choose one of the following options; once you select a feature, you cannot change it until you gain a level.

Adhesive Ichor. Once per turn when you take damage while raging, you can engulf the creature that damaged you in a sticky web of your own blood. The creature must succeed on a Strength saving throw (DC 8 + your proficiency bonus + your Constitution modifier) or be restrained until the end of your next turn or until a creature uses its action to break the web with a successful Strength (Athletics) check with the same DC.

Corrosive Blood. Once per turn when you take damage while raging, you can cause the creature that damaged you to take acid damage equal to your Constitution modifier (minimum 1). Additionally, the attacker suffers a cumulative –1 penalty to damage rolls with that weapon after dealing damage. If its penalty drops to –5, the weapon is destroyed. Magical weapons cannot be corroded in this way.

Psychoactive Essence. Once per turn when you take damage while raging, you can cause the creature that damaged you to be covered in a bubbling, iridescent, but seemingly harmless fluid. Whenever the creature covered in this fluid attacks a creature that isn't you, you can use your reaction to cause the creature to take psychic damage equal to your level in this class. The fluid remains on the creature until you mark a new creature or until it wipes it off as an action.

MUTATING MIND

Your mind is constantly changing, learning and forgetting things that other creatures would consider part of the core of their beings. At 6th level, you learn one language or gain proficiency with one tool, and you gain proficiency in one skill of your choice.

Whenever you finish a short rest, you can choose to forget the language or lose the tool proficiency and learn one new language or gain one tool proficiency of your choice. When you finish a long rest, you can choose to lose the skill proficiency to gain a new one in its place.

WRATHFUL MUTATION

At 10th level, your body changes and warps when you rage. Choose one of the following options; once you select a feature, you cannot change it until you gain a level.

Grotesque Visage. Your face morphs into a hideous mask of alien hatred. While raging, enemy creatures within 5 feet of you have disadvantage on attack rolls against creatures that are not you. Creatures immune to being frightened are immune to this feature as well.

Spiny Carapace. Spikes like daggers burst from the chitin shell that forms around your skin. While raging, your AC increases by 2, and any creature that either enters your space for the first time on its turn, starts its turn in your space, grapples you, or starts its turn in a grapple with you takes piercing damage equal to your Constitution modifier (minimum 1).

Tentacle Arm. One of your arms transforms into a tentacle. While raging, your reach increases by 5 feet, and you have advantage on Strength (Athletics) checks to grapple other creatures with it.

MUTANT REGENERATION

Starting at 14th level, your constantly morphing body can regenerate its own tissue. At the start of each of your turns while raging, you can choose to spend one Hit Die to regain hit points equal to the number rolled on the die plus your Constitution modifier. If you don't, you instead gain 5 temporary hit points. You cannot regain hit points or gain temporary hit points in this way if you took any acid or fire damage between the end of your last turn and the start of your current turn.

SCHOOL OF MUTABILITY (WIZARD: ARCANE TRADITION)

For some teras, their bizarre internal chemistry emerges through their magic rather than their bodies. As a mutable mage, you gain the ability to fundamentally alter your own magic and that of others.

Your school emphasizes that all magic is subject to change at any point, and you have honed your abilities to fundamentally alter spells. You may be an experimenter, trying to combine various magical effects for your studies. Or an anarchist, bringing chaos and destruction with you wherever you go.

MUTABLE MAGE

Beginning when you select

this school at 2nd level, you gain the ability to focus on the basic qualities that are common to all magic. When you finish a long rest, choose one other school of magic. Until your next long rest, the gold and time you must spend to copy a spell from that school into your spellbook is reduced by one third.

BRINGER OF CHANGE

Starting at 2nd level, your ability to magically alter objects and spells grants you insight into their inner workings. You gain proficiency in the Arcana skill, and you gain proficiency with one type of artisan's tools of your choice. Your proficiency bonus is doubled for any ability check you make that uses the Arcana skill or the selected tools.

MUTABLE MAGIC

Starting at 6th level, you can alter the area of effect of any spell you cast to a different area as long as the spell affects the same number of squares or fewer than the original. For example, a spell with a 30-foot line effect could be mutated into a 15-foot cone, and a 30-foot cone could mutate into a 15-foot-radius burst. This ability has no effect on spells without a defined area of effect, and it cannot be used to change a spell that emanates from the caster into an area of effect that does not.

ELEMENTAL FLEXIBILITY

Beginning at 10th level, you can quickly and instinctively change the nature of your spells. You can change the appearance of any of your non-illusion spells that have visual components, such as making a *shield* spell resemble a tower shield or making *mage hand* appear as a hag's claw. This does not change any other features of the spell nor can it render a spell effect invisible.

In addition, when you cast a spell that deals acid, cold, fire, lightning, or thunder damage, you can use your reaction to change the damage type to another of those five damage types. You can use this feature a number of times equal to your Intelligence modifier (a minimum of once). You regain any expended uses when you finish a long rest.

TWISTED ARCANA

Starting at 14th level, you gain the ability to warp the spells of your enemies to such a degree that you can effectively control them. When a creature you can see within 60 feet of you casts a spell that targets a creature or an area, you can use your reaction to force the creature casting the spell to make an Intelligence saving throw equal to your spell save DC. On a failure, you change the caster's intended target or point of origin to any other legal target or point of origin for the spell. Once you use this feature, you must finish a long rest before you can use it again.

WAY OF THE TENTACLE
(MONK: MONASTIC TRADITION)

A monk uses every part of their body as a weapon, but a limb as unusual and powerful as a tentacle can be transformed into a weapon deadlier than any humanoid limb. The first teras to "improve" their humanoid hosts by replacing their arms with tentacles founded this martial art—and a few humanoids unlucky enough to have mutated into a tentacled form, such as yourself, have eagerly accepted their training.

TENTACLES FOR ARMS

Both of your arms are transformed into thick tentacles. These new appendages lack fingers and are longer than your original arms but are somehow just as dexterous. Starting when you choose this tradition at 3rd level, your reach increases by 5 feet.

TENTACLE TECHNIQUE

At 3rd level, you develop techniques that can only be performed with your new appendages. Whenever you hit a creature with an unarmed strike, you can spend 1 ki point to impose one of the following effects on the target:

- If it is no more than two size categories larger than you, the creature must succeed on a Dexterity saving throw or be grappled by you. This can allow you to grapple a creature normally too large for you.
- If it is no more than two size categories larger than you, the creature must succeed on a

Strength saving throw or be knocked prone, taking damage equal to your Strength or Dexterity modifier (your choice). This can allow you to trip a creature normally too large for you.

- The creature is covered in a sticky slime, halving its movement speed until the start of your next turn.

GRASPING ARM

At 6th level, your arm becomes powerful enough to manipulate creatures while grappling them. While you grapple a creature, you can use a bonus action to perform one of the following techniques:

- You immediately end the grapple by slamming the creature against a surface, object, or creature within reach, dealing damage to the grappled creature equal to your Martial Arts die plus your Strength or Dexterity modifier (your choice). If the other target is a creature or an object, you must make a melee attack against it. If the attack hits, it takes the same damage as the original target.
- You tighten your grip, constricting the target, dealing damage to the creature equal to your Martial Arts die plus your Strength or Dexterity modifier (your choice). The creature takes this damage at the start of each of its turns until it is no longer grappled by you.
- You immediately end the grapple by throwing the creature a number of feet upward equal to your Strength or Dexterity score (your choice) or twice that far horizontally. If it hits a surface before traveling the full distance, it takes 1d6 damage per 10 feet it has not yet traveled. Otherwise, it takes 1d6 bludgeoning damage plus 1d6 damage for every 10 feet it fell vertically from the highest point in the throw.

LEECHING TENTACLES

Starting at 11th level when you hit a creature with an unarmed strike, you can spend 2 ki points as a bonus action to regain a number of hit points equal to the damage the creature took.

CLARITY THROUGH PAIN

Starting at 17th level when you take damage, you can use your reaction to regain a number of ki points equal to half your monk level. Once you use this feature, you can't use it again until you finish a long rest.

BACKGROUNDS

The following backgrounds are especially common in teras. At the GM's discretion, other appropriate races may have access to them.

EXILE

You were cast out of your homeland and have been forbidden to return on pain of imprisonment or worse. With no other recourse, you set out to find a new home in a new land, searching for a place of your own in the world beyond the only home you ever knew.

When you choose this background, work with the GM to decide what society or organization you were cast out of and where you found yourself. What happened to see you exiled? How serious was your transgression, and how high up does the malice against you run? Do you deserve your exile, or are you a victim of mistaken identity or secret plots?

Skill Proficiencies: History, Insight

Tool Proficiencies: Disguise kit

Languages: One of your choice

Equipment: A disguise kit, a set of traveler's clothes, a small memento of home, and a pouch containing 5 gp

BANISHMENT

You can work with your GM to decide the exact nature of your exile, or you can choose or roll on the following table to determine the reason for your banishment.

d8	Banishment
1	I was a member of the ruling class, but a coup overthrew the government.
2	I am guilty of a heinous crime but was connected enough to avoid a death sentence.
3	I hold beliefs branded heresy by the church.
4	I am the illegitimate child of the land's ruler.
5	Members of my family were involved in an act of treason. Most are now dead.
6	A prophecy foretold that I would bring great devastation to my homeland.
7	I escaped prison and fled to avoid recapture.
8	I was wrongfully accused of a crime.

FEATURE: EXPATRIATE

After fleeing your homeland, you've settled in a new place, even if only temporarily. No matter how many times you move on or where you end up, you are adept at integrating yourself into the local culture. After one week of living in a new place, you adapt to local cultural expectations and suffer no penalties to social interaction arising from your foreign origins. Similarly, you can gain access to services without any of the difficulties that other outsiders might face, even in extremely xenophobic cultures.

SUGGESTED CHARACTERISTICS

Exiles must adapt to survive, so they are often malleable in social situations. They shift to fit prevailing attitudes, the better to avoid drawing undue attention to themselves. Though they might not be able to fade away completely, exiles can mitigate the worst consequences of being a stranger in a strange land. But all the while, they must be wary of people from their former lives who might be hunting them.

d8	Personality Trait
1	I am suspicious of anyone from my former homeland.
2	I am always trying to build a life similar to the one I held before my exile.
3	I use the details of my past to create interest and opportunity when dealing with new people.
4	I just want to blend in as best I can.
5	I'm wary of government workers, soldiers, and other official figures.
6	I enjoy learning new things.
7	Foreign languages are fascinating to me.
8	I'm comfortable in a mixed group of people where I can see different attitudes and perspectives at work.

d6	Ideal
1	Vengeance. Any harm done to me, I will return it many times over. (Evil)
2	Discovery. Learning more about the world forces me to learn more about myself. (Any)
3	Survival. Better to accept a situation and move on than risk lives upholding principals. (Neutral)
4	Freedom. I don't let anything hold me back. (Chaotic)
5	Protection. Leaving my homeland was the right choice to protect those close to me. (Good)
6	Society. Keeping the structure of a society functioning is more important than demands placed on the individual. (Lawful)

d6	Bond
1	Someone unknown is responsible for my exile, and I won't rest until I find out who.
2	I'm drawn to new people and things, particularly if I can learn from them.
3	I know more of my fellows are out there, banished. I must find them, keep them safe.
4	I'll go out of my way to discover news from home.
5	A few people from my past keep in touch, and I send them information from time to time.
6	I use my past experience as an asset, making use of my former skills and standing whenever I can.

d6	Flaw
1	I've broken my exile to secretly return home, and that truth will be my end if it comes out.
2	My banishment hasn't dissuaded me from the behavior that inspired my exile in the first place.
3	No one is harder on me than I am, despite my exile being deemed full punishment for my transgressions.
4	I have something the people who banished me want—and I'm looking forward to them coming after me to try to take it.
5	I believe my own culture is superior to all others. The longer I talk to people, the more likely that is to come out.
6	My distrust of power makes it hard for me to deal with the authorities—and to obey their edicts.

PARAGON OF FORM

Since you can remember, you've sought nothing less than physical perfection. You train and adventure constantly and for no other reason than to improve yourself, to be more powerful than you were yesterday, to realize your unlimited potential. Others admire your accomplishments and your exploits, and they consider you someone of importance, holding your adventures in their hearts with awe, respect, or envy.

Skill Proficiencies: Acrobatics. Athletics

Tool Proficiencies: One type of gaming set

Languages: One of your choice

Equipment: A memento from your youth (a reminder of your goals) or a small sack of oddities (each chosen as a meditation on form), a mirror, a set of weighted clothes and some training equipment (hand weights, juggling balls, or a jump rope), and a belt pouch containing 10 gp

FEATURE: WORD GETS AROUND

You (and your companions) are always welcome into public gatherings of adventurers and other like-minded souls, often at an inn or tavern. In such a group, you are privy to all sorts of gossip and the collected secrets that adventurers are want to pass around, so long as the tales of your exploits and displays of your prowess are plentiful. And you probably won't ever have to pay for your food and drink, though you may have to contend with competition from the occasional up-and-comer trying to show you up.

SUGGESTED CHARACTERISTICS

Whether you're mysterious and brooding or magnanimous and larger than life, you command attention with your very presence. You are strong and agile and confident in your abilities. Others are attracted to you and your single-minded focus on pushing yourself. You easily get drawn into tales of your many exploits.

d8	Personality Trait
1	I am energized by my audience and encourage their participation with my stories. Their admiration keeps me going.
2	I exercise constantly, such as by always moving and random calisthenics.
3	I don't like to brag, but I'm willing to let my companions tell the tales of my exploits.
4	I make friendly challenges of those I meet, like arm wrestling and foot races and such.
5	I train with kids on my travels to get them started on the right path.
6	I make little wagers with myself when I do small feats, pushing for better the next time.
7	I have a daily exercise regimen that I won't let anything interfere with.
8	I say little, preferring to lead by example.

d6	Ideal
1	Power. Any who stand in my way will fall before my might. (Evil)
2	Potential. Pushing myself is the only way to know what I'm capable of. (Any)
3	Independence. One must be able to fend for themself and control their destiny. (Neutral)
4	Excitement. The thrill of exertion and risking my life is all I need to keep going. (Chaotic)
5	Protection. There is something big coming, threatening all I hold dear, and I need to be ready. (Good)
6	Duty. I owe it to those depending on me to be better. (Lawful)

d6	Bond
1	Someone in my past was my role model, and everything I do is for their memory.
2	I owe it to myself. I'm worth the effort.
3	There is someone I'm competing against, and someday we'll have to square off.
4	My fans deserve the new stories I can bring.
5	I must be the best. Losing is not acceptable.
6	The people need my power. If not me, who?

d6	Flaw
1	I resolve arguments with my fists.
2	I take stupid risks to not show weakness, often putting others in danger.
3	I am my own worst critic, perpetually dissatisfied with my level of progress.
4	I am obsessed with my appearance, admiring my reflection religiously and marking my physical accomplishments.
5	I push far too hard, starving myself and training to exhaustion. I am a danger to myself.
6	Feelings of inadequacy lead me to make bad choices, always afraid of being ignored or left behind.

ADDITIONAL OPTIONS

The following options are available to teras. At the GM's discretion, other appropriate races may have access to some of these new rules.

MUTATION FEATS

The following mutation feats are available only to teras. You may swap out any mutation feat for another mutation feat whenever you gain a level.

ANTENNAE (MUTATION)

Prerequisite: Teras

A pair of antennae extend from your head, allowing you to take on a more tactically oriented role:

- You gain telepathy to 30 feet and can maintain contact with one creature at a time that you share a language with.
- You can use your action to enable an ally within 30 feet to use the Attack, Dash, Disengage, Dodge, or Help action on your turn. You can use your movement to enable an ally within 30 feet to move your speed.
- When an ally within 5 feet of you misses with a melee attack, you can use your reaction to allow them to repeat the same attack against another creature of your choice.

EXAGGERATED MUSCULATURE (MUTATION)

Prerequisite: Teras

Your muscles bulge and twist in strange proportions, enabling you ever greater control over your physical form:

- Increase your Strength, Dexterity, or Constitution score by 1, to a maximum of 20.
- Whenever you make a Strength, Dexterity, or Constitution check, you can treat a d20 roll of 9 or lower as a 10.
- You have advantage in any contest where you and your opponent are both making Strength, Dexterity, or Constitution checks.

EYE FLOATERS (MUTATION)

Prerequisites: Teras; Intelligence, Wisdom, or Charisma 13 or higher

Your eyes can leave their sockets, acting as familiars (per the *find familiar* spell), turning them into independent eye companions. Your eyes become fey creatures with the statistics of an octopus, except they gain a flying speed of 30 feet and can only convey visual information. Replace the octopus's traits with the following traits.

Amorphous. Your eye companions can move through spaces as narrow as 1 inch wide without squeezing.

Amphibious. Your eye companions can breathe air and water.

You can release one or both of your eyes from their sockets at once. As an action, you can see through one or both eye companions until the start of your next turn, but in either case, during this time, you are blind to your own senses; if both eye companions are released, then you remain blind with regard to your own senses until one or both have returned. If an eye is destroyed, it will regenerate in its socket after a long rest.

IRON VISCERA (MUTATION)

Prerequisite: Teras

Your internal organs are adaptable to effects that might debilitate a creature of lesser resiliency:

- You have resistance to poison damage, and you have advantage on saving throws due to being poisoned.
- After each long rest, you gain temporary hit point equal to twice your constitution modifier (minimum of 2).

MAGIC POLYP (MUTATION)

Prerequisite: Teras

A fleshy polyp with an eye on the end appears on your body, gawking and surveying with a mind all its own:

- Increase your Intelligence score by 1, to a maximum of 20.
- As a bonus action, your polyp can take over for you in order to maintain concentration on a spell. It must be able to see any targets.
- Your polyp can cast any cantrip you know as a bonus action without impacting your ability to cast spells.

POLYCHROMIC STARE (MUTATION)

Prerequisite: Teras

Your eyes display a mesmerizing range of colors while providing you a shifted view of the world, almost as if everything is in slow motion compared to you and giving you an uncanny presence on the battlefield:

- Increase your Charisma score by 1, to a maximum of 20.
- When a hostile creature attacks you, you can use your reaction to move up to your speed without provoking opportunities attacks.
- When a hostile creature misses you with a melee attack, you can use your reaction to force that creature to repeat the same attack against another creature (other than itself) of your choice.

PROBING TENDRIL (MUTATION)

Prerequisite: Teras

You grow a thin 15-foot tendril that seems to possess a curiosity all its own and allows a greater range of effect:

- You can use your action to control the tendril. You can use the tendril to manipulate an object, open an unlocked door or container, stow or retrieve an item from an open container, or pour the contents out of a vial. The hand can't attack, activate magic items, or carry more than 10 pounds.

- ❖ When taking the Help action, you can aid a friendly creature in attacking a creature within 15 feet of you.
- ❖ You have advantage when making opportunity attacks.

REACTIVE MUTATION (MUTATION)

Prerequisite: Teras

You have some measure of control over your body at a cellular level, allowing you to adapt to different stressors:

- ❖ Increase your Constitution score by 1, to a maximum of 20.
- ❖ When you finish a long rest, you may swap out any mutation feat for another mutation feat with 10 minutes of meditation, instead of at each new level.

SENTIENT GROWTH (MUTATION)

Prerequisite: Teras

Your volatile cells have formed a pulsing, semi-intelligent tumor that can sense when danger threatens and activate your body's natural defenses in response:

- ❖ You take 1 less damage from the first attack that hits you in a round.
- ❖ If you are hit with a melee attack by a creature, you no longer provoke opportunity attacks from that creature until the end of your next turn.
- ❖ If you're subjected to an effect that grants a second saving throw to avoid a secondary effect or an extended duration, you can use your reaction to automatically succeed on the saving throw.

SHIFTING FLESH (MUTATION)

Prerequisite: Teras

Your flesh is deceptively malleable, foiling attackers from taking advantage of a dropped guard or a slipped footing:

- ❖ You are immune to the extra damage from critical hits and sneak attacks.
- ❖ After a creature hits you with a critical hit or sneak attack, if it attacks you again before the end of its next turn, it's first attack roll is made with disadvantage.

STABILIZING PODIA (MUTATION)

Prerequisite: Teras

Your flesh spontaneously projects small tubular growths, sprouting from your flesh where needed to staunch bleeding and escape tight spaces:

- ❖ If damage reduces you to 0 hit points and fails to kill you, you become stable. While stable, if you fail to take any additional damage prior to your next turn, you regain 1 hit point.
- ❖ You have advantage on ability checks to escape being grappled.

TRACKING SPORES (MUTATION)

Prerequisite: Teras

You emit a cloud of specialized spores that relays limited information back to you about your surroundings:

- ❖ You have advantage on passive Wisdom (Perception) and passive Intelligence (Investigation) checks.
- ❖ Creatures don't gain advantage on attack rolls against you as a result of being hidden from you.
- ❖ Your ranged weapon and ranged spell attacks ignore half cover and three-quarters cover.

VESTIGIAL APPENDAGE (MUTATION)

Prerequisite: Teras

A strange, underdeveloped, alien-looking appendage sprouts from somewhere on your torso, aiding you in certain tasks:

- ❖ Increase your Strength or Dexterity score by 1, to a maximum of 20.
- ❖ Opportunity attacks against you are made with disadvantage.
- ❖ You have advantage on Strength and Dexterity saving throws and ability checks to avoid being moved or knocked prone.

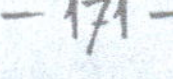

Twilight Children

Are you cold, child? Hungry? Alone? These are funny nonsense words where I'm from. Like stories told before a fire with a full belly and dear friends. Take my hand, dear heart, and never feel need again.

—Avasule,
Duchess of Waking Nightmare

These fey are changelings, the offspring of fey dalliances, the lost children in the wilds, and the babes stolen from cradles and raised in magical demesnes with fey creatures as their family, friends, or masters. The lives of twilight children may be enchanted or nightmarish, depending on the fey who finds or steals them. Some are treated as guests or fey children, others are slaves or playthings. No matter their upbringing however, the twilight children never quite belong with the fey but neither can they ever go home again.

Physical Description: Twilight children are irrevocably changed by their lives immersed in fey magic. They retain much of the general look of their original race but change according to the sorts of fey they primarily associate with—so they may develop the horns and hairiness of a faun or the razor teeth and bat ears of a gremlin or the dusky skin and tail of a darkling, for a mere few examples. More so, the process of becoming a twilight child can easily change the normal expectations for the physical appearance of a given heritage, creating an individual who is significantly taller or shorter, heavier or lighter, and so on, than normal.

Regardless of parentage and environment, there is always something a little ephemeral and frail about the twilight children. They all bear the look of someone caught between the real world and a dream.

Society: There is no unified society of twilight children. Given that one twilight child can be completely opposite from another, there are no guarantees that their own kind will be any more familiar than other fey.

Most have only dim memories of their lives before they lived in the fey realms, if they were even old enough to form memories. Those kidnapped from loving homes may still remember the feeling of a safe, warm family that even well-intentioned fey can't replace. By contrast, some twilight children came to the fey by becoming lost while running away from abusive homes or after being orphaned, so becoming a changeling was perhaps for the better.

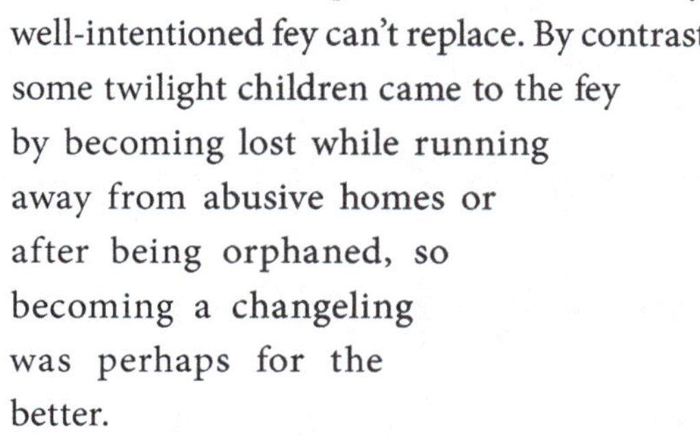

Not all fey bear benevolence for their little captives though. Some are experimented on, transformed, and tortured; some are raised as servants, slaves, or consorts; some are abandoned in a wild demesne and left to their own bid for survival. It is these cases most likely to produce a twilight child who has lost all life meaning but to hunt and kill fey.

Twilight children raised among fey in happier circumstances are still seldom totally accepted; they are still too different, too limited by their form. The

TWILIGHT CHILD TRAITS

Twilight children characters possess an assortment of traits all their own.

- ***Ability Score Increase.*** Your Intelligence score increases by 2, and two other ability scores of your choice each increase by 1. The ability scores you choose must be ones that would increase for a character of your humanoid origin (see **Inheritance** below). If your origin would have increased only one score, that score instead increases by 2.
- ***Languages.*** You can speak, read, and write Common, Sylvan, and one other language representing your humanoid origin.
- ***Size.*** Twilight children vary in height and build depending on their humanoid parentage. Your size is Small or Medium, depending on your humanoid origin.
- ***Speed.*** Your base walking speed varies according to your humanoid origin: 25 feet if you are Small or 30 feet if you are Medium.
- ***Type.*** Your type is fey. Spells and effects that specifically target humanoids do not affect you. You also gain the changeling subtype (see **Appendix**).

- ***Darkvision.*** Accustomed to living in shadows, you have superior vision in dim and dark conditions. You can see in dim light within 60 feet of you as if it were bright light and in darkness as if it were dim light. You can't discern color in darkness, only shades of gray.
- ***Fey Kin.*** Choose one option from the following list, representing the fey individuals or region responsible for your transformation: Bite (bitterclaw), both Darkling Magic and Sunlight Sensitivity (darkling), Fixed Mind (matabiri), Glow (goodfellow), either Gnomekin Magic or Illusion Resistance (black hat or far darrig), Keen Smell (kitsune), Mark Prey (fir bolg), Norn Magic (norn), Teras Magic (teras), Two Worlds (see below).
- ***Inheritance.*** As a twilight child, you retain a number of features from your original humanoid race, including size and a racial tag indicating your parent race. You are considered both a fey and a member of your original race for the purpose of targeting effects or attuning magic items. If a spell or effect applies to both fey and humanoids but differently, it treats you as a fey.
- ***Shadowskin.*** You have proficiency in the Stealth skill, and you can take the Hide action as a bonus action when you are in dim light or darkness.
- ***Twilight Strike.*** Whenever you score a critical hit with a weapon attack, you add 1d6 cold damage to the extra damage of the critical hit. If you are Small, shadows seem to cling to your small frame, and you cast a shadow as if you were Medium. If you are Small, whenever you hit with a weapon attack, you add 1d4 cold damage.
- ***Two Worlds.*** If you choose this option for your Fey Kin trait, you have advantage on saving throws against spells and effects from fey and from humanoids that share the racial tag of your Inheritance.

changelings may be friends, sidekicks, or treated as favored pets but never as equals, and it is a rare and cunning twilight child that achieves any power in fey courts. This can be particularly galling for twilight children who are born of a union between fey and mortal, sometimes even of a sovereign like Manitou. They find their blood accounts for nothing, and some develop an obsession with their fey parent—either wishing to know the parent and plead their worthiness to best their lot or for vengeance at being created and abandoned.

Returning to their home planes has little more to offer. They are strangers to their own former kin and viewed with the same distrust and awe the mortal races have for fey yet do not possess powers or agendas as fey do. Thus they are locked out of thriving in mortal communities as well.

Relations: Most twilight children are hungry for friends or at least allies. Other half-species, such as aasimars, half-elves, half-orcs, and tieflings, understand better than most the frustrations of being born between two worlds and never really belonging in either. Gnomes can be comforting influences to a twilight child as these little fey tend to be happy to treat twilight children as equals and take them along on their (often bizarre) adventures.

Other fey races may be viewed warmly or as enemies, depending on the nature of their foster fey. Twilight children have little power for the most part in the fey courts, but they tend to be the best informed—raised among fey yet not viewed as rivals, twilight children hear more secrets and gossip than their unassuming origins suggest. Clever twilight children stay behind the curtain of fey court intrigues but pull more strings than the proud fey would ever believe.

Alignment and Religion: Much like the diversity in their originating race, the alignment and religion of the twilight children varies widely. For every twilight child embracing fey customs and beliefs, another shuns them entirely. Twilight children can be vulnerable to suggestion at times in their desire to fit in and may adopt the ethos and faith of a companion who treats the twilight child respectfully. When that respect is given out of manipulation and not sincere appreciation however, the twilight child can become a duped cultist or patsy.

Adventurers: On the edge of two worlds, the twilight children often turn to adventuring in the hopes it will help them discover something they are missing. In the process, some twilight children are lucky enough to find belonging as a valuable, respected member of a group of companions. Others seem doomed to wander the Material Plane or the fey lands, never attaining a true sense of belonging anywhere.

Any adventuring class may appeal to at least some twilight children. Their fey aspects make them particularly well-suited as bards and sorcerers, and some "foster families" of fey may orient them more to certain classes, but they can be found in all vocations.

A specialized sort of twilight child adventurer is the fey hunter. Often rangers and the like, these changelings are devoted to slaying either any fey they can find or a particular kind of fey that has particularly earned their enmity. The most ambitious fey hunters are after a sovereign's head.

Age: Twilight children reach maturity at the same rate as their original race. Regardless of their heritage though, all twilight children can live to be over 300 years old.

Names: Due to their various origins, names among the twilight children vary substantially. Some have been given or adopted fey names while a select few have retained their birth name from their originating culture. Once achieving adulthood, some twilight children forego all prior names and choose one of their own; having usually had so little control over their lives before, some decide they can at least exert their will on what they should be called.

SUBCLASSES

The fey provide an array of unique qualities and perspectives for creating interesting new characters. Consult your GM before applying these subclasses to other races.

COLLEGE OF THE KNOWING SEELIE

(BARD: BARD COLLEGE)

You are often quieter than your more musical colleagues. You, as an agent of the courts, harness talents of observation, investigation, and interrogation in order to provide your masters with secret intelligence. You are often known as seelie detectives to the fey public.

(The Seelie and Unseelie of course share some characteristics, and the college of the unseelie would provide the same class features. That said, both sides employ other agents that vary greatly from one another.)

BONUS PROFICIENCIES

When you become a seelie detective at 3rd level, you gain proficiency with medium armor, shields, and martial weapons.

SECRET IDENTITY

At 3rd level, your connection to a fey lord allows you to assume a secret identity. As part of your secret identity, choose a location of residence, a lifestyle (such as Poor, Wealthy, or Aristocratic), and a vocation. You are provided with at least one set of clothing appropriate to your vocation and lifestyle along with documentation (real or false) to prove that the details of your secret identity are true. This documentation appears real under casual observation.

As long as you spend at least 1 day of downtime each month living as your secret identity, you can maintain up to five contacts that believe your secret identity to be indisputably true. If a creature suspects something is fishy about your identity while interacting with you, it can attempt to make a Wisdom (Insight) check contested by your Charisma (Deception) check. On a success, it may not realize the extent of your lie, but it does recognize that some part of your identity is false. You can expend a Bardic Inspiration die after rolling your check but before knowing your opponent's result, adding the die roll to your result.

A creature that wants to investigate your secret identity can spend 8 hours researching one aspect of your identity. At the end of those 8 hours, it can make a DC 20 Intelligence (Investigation) check, uncovering the truth about the object of its suspicion on a success. At 6th level, this DC increases to 25, and it increases again to 30 at 14th level.

Work with your GM to determine the details of your identity and your contacts. You can change your secret identity by spending seven days of downtime to establish a new false history, vocation, and contacts.

STYLISH RECOVERY

At 6th level, when you fail on an ability check or miss with an attack roll, you can spend a use of Bardic Inspiration. Roll a Bardic Inspiration die, and add the number rolled to the result, possibly turning a failure into a success or a miss into a hit. You can choose to do so after you roll the die for the check or attack but before the GM determines the result of the roll.

ILLUSORY REINFORCEMENTS

Starting at 14th level, you can summon illusory duplicate agents to confuse your enemies. As an action, you choose two points within 60 feet of you. An illusory double of yourself appears at each of these points. These doubles seem completely real, including mimicking your sounds, smells, and temperature. You can choose to instantly and unnoticeably switch places with one of the doubles when they first appear or as an action on your turn.

The illusory doubles mimic your every action as accurately as possible, passing through physical obstacles if necessary. When you move, each illusion can move up to your speed. When you make a melee attack against a creature adjacent to you, a double also makes a melee attack against a creature adjacent to it, with a bonus to hit equal to your proficiency bonus + your Dexterity modifier + your Charisma modifier. If the attack hits, the target takes psychic damage equal to 4d6 + your Charisma modifier. The difference in damage does not allow observers to tell which of you is real.

The doubles each have an AC equal to 10 + your Dexterity modifier + your Charisma modifier. A double disappears if it is hit by an attack but does not disappear if caught in a spell or effect that affects an area or if it passes through damaging terrain. The doubles also disappear when you cease concentrating (as if concentrating on a spell), up to a maximum duration of 10 minutes.

Once you use this feature, you can't use it again until you finish a long rest.

DARKNESS DOMAIN
(CLERIC: DIVINE DOMAIN)

The fey aren't known for their veneration of gods, but twilight children bring much with them from their previous lives. You find solace in your veneration of darkness, of shadow, granting its special gifts to those, like you, caught between worlds. You develop mastery over the chill left behind when light fades and over the shroud of darkness itself.

DARKNESS DOMAIN

You are granted the following domain spells.

DARKNESS DOMAIN SPELLS

Cleric Level	Spells
1st	*bane, sleep*
3rd	*darkness, darkvision*
5th	*fear, protection from energy*
7th	*black tentacles, ice storm*
9th	*cone of cold, dream*

BONUS CANTRIP

When you choose this domain at 1st level, you gain the *ray of frost* cantrip. This doesn't count against your total number of cantrips known.

SWALLOWED BY NIGHT

Also at 1st level, you can always attempt to hide while in a lightly obscured area created by dim light, even while you are being observed.

CHANNEL DIVINITY: NIGHTFALL

Starting at 2nd level, you can use your Channel Divinity to unleash a wave of frigid darkness. As an action, you present your holy symbol. Any magical light within 30 feet of you is dispelled, and nonmagical light sources are snuffed out. Additionally, each hostile creature within 30 feet of you must make a Constitution saving throw, taking cold damage equal to 2d10 + your cleric level on a failed saving throw and half as much damage on a successful one. A creature that has total cover from you is not affected.

CHANNEL DIVINITY: SHROUD OF NIGHT

At 6th level, you can use your Channel Divinity to partially shroud your allies from sight, protecting them from harmful spells. As an action, you present your holy symbol, and a wave of shadowy energy spreads out in a 30-foot radius centered on you. You and all your allies in the area are treated as being invisible for the purpose of being targeted by spells. You and your affected allies can see one another normally.

POTENT SPELLCASTING

Starting at 8th level, you add your Wisdom modifier to the damage you deal with any cleric cantrip.

MIDNIGHT CLOAK

At 17th level, you can use your action to activate an aura of chilling darkness that lasts for 1 minute or until you dismiss it using another action. You radiate darkness in a 60-foot radius. Your enemies in the darkness have disadvantage on saving throws against any spell that deals cold or necrotic damage. You and your allies can see through this darkness normally.

GIANTSLAYER
(FIGHTER: FIGHTER ARCHETYPE)

When you are small, any creature larger than you appears to be a giant. You accentuate your small stature, building on every advantage you can. No one will ever call you weak. Using guile, cunning, and resourcefulness, you are able to fell creatures easily ten times your own size.

THE HARDER THEY FALL

Starting at 3rd level, you deal additional damage when fighting creatures larger than you. Whenever you hit a creature with a melee weapon attack or a ranged weapon attack from within 30 feet, you deal an additional 1d6 damage if your target is larger than you.

You can only deal this extra damage to a single creature, once per turn.

UNSEEN INTRUDER

Starting at 7th level, creatures larger than you have disadvantage on Wisdom (Perception) checks made to see or hear you.

WRESTLER OF GIANTS

Starting at 10th level, you can grapple creatures regardless of size category, and creatures larger than you have disadvantage on Strength (Athletics) and Dexterity (Acrobatics) checks made to grapple you.

SPECIALIZED FIGHTING STYLE

At 15th level, your core fighting style evolves to be even more effective against larger foes. You gain one of the following benefits when fighting creatures larger than you, based on which Fighting Style you chose at 2nd level. Only that Fighting Style you gained through this class is improved by this feature.

Archery. Your ranged weapon attacks now deal an additional 1d10 damage if the target is larger than you. You can only deal this extra damage to a single creature, once per turn.

Defense. When you are hit by an attack from a larger creature while you are wearing armor, you can use your reaction to gain resistance to bludgeoning, piercing, and slashing damage from the attacks of creatures larger than you until the end of the current turn.

Dueling. When you are wielding a melee weapon in one hand and no other weapons, your weapon attacks against creatures larger than you score a critical hit on a roll of 19 or 20.

Great Weapon Fighting. When you hit with an attack you make with a melee weapon against a creature larger than you, you can attempt to shove the target as a bonus action. You have advantage on the Strength (Athletics) check to shove the creature, and if you succeed, you deal the target 2d6 bludgeoning damage. The weapon must have the two-handed or versatile property for you to gain this benefit.

Protection. When a creature larger than you that you can see attacks a target other than you that is within 5 feet of you, it makes the attack roll with disadvantage as long as you are not incapacitated—you need not use your reaction. You must be wielding a shield.

Two-Weapon Fighting. When you engage in two-weapon fighting against a creature that is larger than you, you have advantage on your attack roll with the second weapon.

SLIPPERY DODGER

Starting at 18th level, creatures larger than you have disadvantage on attack rolls against you.

LOST CHILDREN
(WARLOCK: OTHERWORLDLY PATRON)

When a humanoid child dwells for long in the fey realms, they eventually cast off some of their humanoid self and become fey. This process often cleaves shards or echoes from their souls. Over the centuries, this fragmentary collective consciousness of these countless lost children has amassed considerable magical influence over these alien realms. As one, the Lost Children possess incredible psychic power but lack the maturity to control it. Many entering pacts with the Lost Children are but children themselves, entering into an arcane contract with an immature yet impossibly powerful psychic presence.

You have promised to lead these echoes, these memories and shed identities of lost children, back to the mortal world, and you can tap into their depthless wellspring of arcane potential.

EXPANDED SPELL LIST

The Lost Children let you choose from an expanded list of spells when you learn a warlock spell. The following spells are added to the warlock list for you.

LOST CHILDREN EXPANDED SPELLS

Spell Level	Spells
1st	*alarm, color spray*
2nd	*rope trick, web*
3rd	*haste, major image*
4th	*confusion, conjure woodland beings*
5th	*animate objects, telekinesis*

ETERNAL YOUTH

Starting when you make a pact with this patron at 1st level, you stop physically aging as every second you age is split among uncountable thousands of souls. You still die when your time is up, but magic can't age you.

VIGOR OF YOUTH

At 1st level, you can target yourself or touch another willing creature as an action to bestow upon it the blessing of youth. For 1 minute, that creature gains the following benefits:

- They gain temporary hit points equal to your level in this class.
- Each of their speeds increase by 10 feet.
- They have advantage on Dexterity checks and Dexterity saving throws.

Once you use this feature, you can't use it again until you finish a short or long rest.

BURDEN OF AGE

Starting at 6th level, you can call upon your patron to inflict the pain of countless centuries of loneliness upon a target you can see within 30 feet. That target must make a Wisdom saving throw. On a failure, it suffers the following effects for 1 minute. It can repeat this saving throw at the end of each of its turns, ending the effects on a success:

- They have disadvantage on Dexterity checks and Dexterity saving throws.
- Each of their speeds are decreased by 10 feet.
- At the start of each of their turns, their hit point maximum is reduced by 10 until they finish a long rest. If their hit point maximum is reduced to 0, they die.

Once you use this feature, you can't use it again until you finish a short or long rest.

COLLECTIVE IMMORTALITY

Starting at 10th level, you can call upon your patron to sacrifice some of its collective life essence to save your own. As a reaction when you are reduced to 0 hit points, you can regain hit points equal to twice your level in this class. Once you have used this feature, you must finish a short or long rest to use it again.

LOST FOREVER

Starting at 14th level, you can draw a creature into the endless faerie maze that your patron wanders for eternity. You can cast *maze* without using a spell slot. You must use your action on each of your turns to maintain concentration on the spell, to a maximum of 1 minute. The target also takes 1d6 psychic damage at the start of each of its turns while lost in the maze.

Once you use this feature, you can't use it again until you finish a long rest.

PATH OF THE GLOAMING ROAD
(BARBARIAN: PRIMAL PATH)

You walk the shadow of two worlds. Yet it is within the untamed wilds that you find your defining purpose and the clarification of solitude. You want nothing more than to feel the dirt between your toes, to smell the damp earth, to be free of all ties and obligation. You call the trees and creatures of the night your closest friends.

WHAT LIES BENEATH

At 3rd level when you adopt this path, you gain tremorsense out to 30 feet as long as you remain barefoot.

CONSUMING EMBRACE

Also at 3rd level, just as the land holds tight to what it claims, you do not easily relinquish your prey. While you're raging, any creature you grapple has disadvantage on attempts to escape the grapple.

SHADOW'S SPLENDOR

At 6th level, the shadows are family to you. You (and up to ten other creatures you choose) can use Stealth at a normal pace rather than a slow pace.

COMMUNION

At 10th level, you channel the majesty of the wild and can bestow it upon others. You can cast the *awaken* spell, but only as if it were a ritual.

SHADOWS WITHIN

At 14th level, the shadows fly to your aid. When a hostile creature attacks you while you're raging, you can use your reaction to suddenly blend in with your surroundings. You become invisible until the start of your next turn.

PATH OF THE NIGHTWALKER
(BARBARIAN: PRIMAL PATH)

You walk the night, seeking communion with the dark spaces, with the creatures that thrive on the other side of day. Nocturnal by nature, the darkness frees you, gives you permission to be what you are.

You travel the isolated stretches, avoiding the well-worn paths, and stick to the shadows to find your peace.

WILD SERENITY

At 3rd level when you adopt this path, you gain the ability to cast the *silence* (the effect is centered on you and moves with you) and *speak with animals* spells, but only as rituals.

NIGHT'S SOUNDING

Also at 3rd level, your senses adjust to a life nocturnal. While you're raging, any creature you damage can't hide from you as long as you aren't deafened.

SWIFT SURETY

At 6th level, you act with an instinctual grace. You can wear any armor without having disadvantage on Dexterity (Stealth) checks, and you have advantage on Dexterity (Acrobatics) checks made to keep your balance and to avoid obstacles.

WILD PASSAGE

At 10th level, the trees acknowledge your entreaties. You can cast the *tree stride* spell, but only as if it were a ritual.

NIGHT'S FLEET WINGS

At 14th level, you react with preternatural swiftness. While raging, the first time on your turn that you leave a hostile creature's reach, you don't provoke an opportunity attack from the creature.

SHADOW CASTER
(WIZARD: ARCANE TRADITION)

You eschew the wizardly study of a single school of magic, preferring instead to weave your spells with the essence of shadow to create strange and unpredictable effects that defy explanation. You are often distrusted for your association with "dark magic," and not without good reason. You are a trickster after all, hiding a darkness within, and you understand that shadow is a tool like any other form of magic, to be used as you see fit.

SHADOW AFFINITY

Beginning when you select this arcane tradition at 2nd level, you learn the *minor illusion* cantrip if you don't already know it. The cantrip doesn't count against your number of cantrips known.

SHADOW WEAVE

Also at 2nd level, when you target one or more creatures with a spell of 1st level or higher, you can choose to shroud one of those creatures in darkness. Until the start of your next turn, the creature can't make opportunity attacks and has disadvantage on Wisdom (Perception) checks involving sight. The creature is not affected if it has some means of seeing through magical darkness or if it can't be blinded.

BENIGHTED EYES

At 6th level, you learn to manipulate shadow that would obscure your sight. As a bonus action, you gain the ability to see in normal and magical darkness out to a range of 30 feet until the start of your next turn.

You can use this ability a number of times equal to your Intelligence modifier (a minimum of once). You regain all expended uses when you finish a short or long rest.

SHADOWPLAY

Beginning at 10th level, you can twist the shadows around your magic to change one spell into another. When you cast a spell, you can choose to instead cast a different spell of the same school. The different spell must be in your spellbook, but you need not have it prepared. You must complete the full casting time of the new spell if it was longer than the casting time of the original spell. The new spell is cast at the same level as the original spell.

You can use this ability a number of times equal to your Intelligence modifier (minimum of once). You regain all expended uses when you finish a long rest.

INFUSION OF SHADOWS

Starting at 14th level, you can infuse your damaging spells with raw shadowstuff that heightens your attacks. Whenever you cast a spell that deals damage, you can choose to roll half the spell's damage dice to deal cold damage. If the spell allows a saving throw, any creature that takes cold damage from the spell and that fails its saving throw also has disadvantage on attack rolls and ability checks until the start of your next turn.

After rolling the infused spell's damage, you can reroll a number of cold damage dice equal to your Intelligence modifier (minimum of 1). You must use the second roll.

Once you use this ability, you can't use it again until you finish a short or long rest.

BACKGROUNDS

The following backgrounds are especially common in twilight children. At the GM's discretion, other appropriate races may have access to them.

AMBASSADOR

You've always had a knack for finding resolution during disputes, whether involving yourself or third parties. Steering a conversation comes second nature to you as does making a reasoned appeal designed to bring others around to your way of thinking. Whether you wanted it to or not, this talent has landed you in the middle of many confrontations.

Perhaps you came from a family rife with squabbling, developing these skills as a survival tactic. You might have studied at a university or temple or with advisors to nobility. Maybe you enjoy the feeling of helping to defuse conflict—or perhaps you get a thrill from manipulating the feelings of others without their notice, steering them toward the outcome you wanted all along.

Skill Proficiencies: Deception, Persuasion

Tool Proficiencies: Forgery kit

Languages: One of your choice

Equipment: A forgery kit, a set of traveler's clothes, a writ or letter of introduction from someone you previously assisted, and a pouch containing 10 gp

FEATURE: IMPARTIAL MEDIATOR

Your skill at settling conflicts allows you to ingratiate yourself to people embroiled in disputes. If the disputing parties will listen to you long enough for you to make your case, you can insinuate yourself as their arbiter, and those involved will abide by your judgment as long as it's generally fair. But if you show overt bias or selfish interest, they might well walk away.

Your reputation can result in individuals seeking your services as a mediator, and you can leverage an audience with powerful individuals you might otherwise be unworthy to meet. Your mediation skill might even allow you safe passage through areas of conflict if you reveal your intention to negotiate a resolution to that conflict. The GM has the final say on determining what you can accomplish with this feature and how successful you might be.

SUGGESTED CHARACTERISTICS

Ambassadors understand that to get things done, they have to figure out what everyone wants. They know how to modify their behavior to fit almost any situation, ingratiating themselves to the people they're dealing with. Motivations for ambassadors vary wildly from profoundly selfish to purely service oriented. Most ambassadors fall in between, showing a genuine affinity for settling disputes but always having some personal stake that makes the effort worthwhile.

d8	Personality Trait
1	I work hard to cultivate a reputation for fairness.
2	I never turn away someone asking for my help.
3	I always use clear language and take time to make sure my listeners understand me.
4	People who can't settle their own affairs irritate me, and I step in just to make it stop.
5	The wrong word at the wrong time can spell disaster. I always choose my own words carefully.
6	Being able to save or destroy a relationship with a few words is power I relish.
7	I shift my approach depending on who I'm talking to.
8	I take great pains to remain calm, especially in the face of looming hostilities.

d6	Ideal
1	Aspiration. I constantly seek to improve by challenging myself to achieve larger victories. (Any)
2	Peace. Only through understanding one another can we end pointless conflict. I will usher in that understanding. (Good)
3	No Boundaries. Bottling up tension and conflict just makes that conflict more likely to explode. Better to spread it around and snuff it out quickly. (Chaotic)
4	Impartiality. I must not favor any side in a dispute, giving equal weight to all. (Neutral)
5	Ambition. Every squabble I settle is another piece in the puzzle of my advancement. (Evil)
6	Precedent. There's always a rule or law that we can apply to settle a dispute. (Lawful)

d6	Bond
1	The mentor who taught me to be the voice of reason is the most important person in my life.
2	Everything I do is simply preparation to return to the person I love. To win over that person's family, I'll need every bit of help I can get.
3	There are two places in the world that I love more than anything, but I don't know how to choose one over the other.
4	When I settle a dispute, it quiets the turmoil inside me. At least for a while.
5	Other people once put their lives on the line to help me. I repay them a little bit each time I keep a conflict from escalating to violence.
6	I lean toward others who are also pulled between two groups or who are caught between two ways of life.

d6	Flaw
1	I spend so much time between conflicting parties, I never feel like I fit in.
2	I only accept another person's judgment of a situation if it agrees with my own opinions.
3	When others offer their assessment, I'm quick to voice any disagreement I have.
4	My temper flares if anyone challenges my rulings.
5	One day, I will have to choose between two things I love, and I'm putting that day off for as long as possible.
6	When I feel uncomfortable, I try to insinuate myself into a group—and often go too far when I do so.

COMMANDO

The regular soldiers in an army fight and live in a regimented, structured fashion. That wasn't your life. Though you were a member of the military, you were one of the elite, specializing in reconnaissance and scouting, wilderness exploration, ambush, or sabotage. Whether a member of a standing army, a mercenary company, or a temple militia, you were chosen for your talents and trusted with autonomy—but that autonomy sometimes bred conflict when it set you at odds with your superiors.

Skill Proficiencies: Stealth, Survival

Tool Proficiencies: Thieves' tools and one type of artisan's tools

Equipment: A set of artisan's tools (one of your choice), a set of camouflage traveler's clothes, a hunting trap, and 5 gp

FEATURE: AMBUSH AND SABOTAGE

You are trained in setting traps and snares using tools and materials at hand. With 2d3 hours of work, you make a Dexterity (Survival) check to fashion traps in an area 30 feet on a side. The traps you can create include snares (which function as single-use hunter's traps), shallow pits, and deadfalls. Any trap you create with this feature deals a maximum of 1d6 bludgeoning, piercing, or slashing damage, as appropriate to the trap.

Work with your GM to determine the specific nature of snares and traps you can set given your circumstances. Detecting your handiwork requires a Wisdom (Spot) check contested by your Dexterity (Survival) check.

Additionally, you know how to sabotage simple machines. With appropriate tools and 2d10 minutes of work, you can render wagons, doors, pulleys, cranks, and other simple devices nonfunctional. Unless carefully inspected, your sabotage isn't obvious until someone tries to use the object.

SUGGESTED CHARACTERISTICS

Commandos are often independent personalities prone to rely on their own judgment. This isn't to say they don't form relationships however since most commandos work in small groups of like-minded individuals. Commandos understand that there's always a bigger picture underlying a specific mission. But all that matters to them is the part of the mission for which they're responsible, and that responsibility takes priority in all day-to-day actions and decisions.

d8	Personality Trait
1	If I seem quiet, it's because I'm watching for danger.
2	I use simple sentences and try to convey my meaning quickly.
3	When I move, I make as little sound as possible, no matter what the situation.
4	I trust a few people close to me. Everyone else has to work to earn that trust.
5	I'm uncomfortable sleeping indoors, so I usually find a place out under the stars.
6	I like to come at enemies from where they least expect it. The direct approach is for fools who want to get killed.
7	I enjoy breaking things just a little too much.
8	If you're going to do something, make it count the first time. Don't take three clean strikes if one dirty blow will end the fight.

d6	Ideal
1	Necessity. I'll do whatever it takes to get the job done, and sometimes that means disobeying orders. (Chaotic)
2	Service. Someone has to step up and make the hard choices to keep others safe. (Good)
3	Loyalty. When we're on our own against the world, it's crucial to remember why we're doing what we do. (Lawful)
4	Comrades. The people fighting beside me are what matter most. (Neutral)
5	Commitment. I'll get the job done because I'm the best at what I do. (Any)
6	Fear. What I do strikes terror into my enemies, and I thrive on that. (Evil)

d6	Bond
1	I saved someone's life a long time ago, and I still feel responsible for them.
2	I'm most comfortable when the only people around me are those few who I trust and keep close.
3	The insignia from my old unit keeps me grounded, and I'll never willingly part with it.
4	The site of my last mission will haunt me for the rest of my days, but I still long to go back.
5	I saw something I shouldn't have during a mission. I'm still trying to make sense of it.
6	The place I trained is the only place I've ever felt at home.

d6	Flaw
1	Plans and schemes don't mean much in the moment. If any part of a mission changes, I improvise.
2	I won't trust people from the other side of the war I fought in, no matter what.
3	Sometimes I have trouble balancing greater orders or needs against the well-being of the people close to me.
4	Getting close to people I was trained to hate, I learned more about them. Now I know we aren't so different, and it gets in the way of what I have to do.
5	I continually rail against authority and get myself into trouble for it. That's why I prefer people around me who understand what I'm going through.
6	I disobeyed direct orders to save my companions, and someday I'll have to pay for it.

ADDITIONAL OPTIONS

The following options are available to twilight children. At the GM's discretion, other appropriate races may have access to some of these new rules.

EQUIPMENT

Twilight children have developed the following equipment according to their specific needs and utilize them to particular effect.

Fey Claw. This claw dagger acts as an extension of your body, like bear or cat claws. Three muted gray blades, 4 inches in length, protrude from the fey claw's horizontal handle. The lowest inch of each blade is dull, ensuring you don't cut yourself while wielding it. When you hold the handle in your fist, the blades extend out to resemble claws. Fey claws are often wielded in pairs. Being prone doesn't impose disadvantage on attack rolls with fey claws. You have advantage on ability checks you make to hold onto a fey claw despite attacks or hazards.

Poison, Ironblood (Ingested/Injury). This dull-gray powder is a blend of pure iron dust and rare minerals and herbs. You can conceal it in food as an action. Its flavor and smell are faint, requiring a successful DC 20 Wisdom (Perception) check to notice. Ironblood poison remains active in food until the food spoils. When a fey creature consumes the poisoned food, the fey must make a DC 15 Constitution saving throw 1 hour later or be poisoned. While the poisoned condition lasts, the fey can't cast spells or use other magical abilities. Every dawn, the fey must make another Constitution saving throw. On a success, the creature regains its magical abilities but remains poisoned; if it had already regained them, instead the poisoned condition ends. On a failure, the fey's Constitution score is reduced by 1d4 until the poisoned condition ends and it finishes a long rest thereafter. The fey dies if this reduces its Constitution to 0. If the fey had recovered the use of its magic, failing a subsequent saving throw against ironblood poison makes it lose the use of its magic again. If the creature is not fey but has fey ancestry, it gains the poisoned condition but is immune to losing its magic or having its Constitution score reduced by the poison.

As an action, you can coat a weapon or three pieces of ammunition with ironblood poison. A coated weapon in ironblood poison remains coated for 1 minute. A fey struck by the coated weapon or ammunition must make a DC 15 Constitution saving throw, taking 2d10 poison damage on a failed save or half as much damage on a successful one.

Twilight Charm. This simple wooden charm resembles a circle broken into two pieces. On both sides of the charm, half of the circle is painted while the other remains bare wood. The charm symbolizes the dual heritage of the twilight children and is instantly recognizable by other twilight children. If you are a twilight child, you can show the charm to another twilight child to gain advantage on the next Charisma check you make to influence that twilight child. You can't use a twilight charm to gain advantage to influence that twilight child ever again.

Twilight Shield. A twilight shield is made from metal subjected to similar environmental extremes of transition between the fey realms and the Material

Plane as the twilight children. As a result, they have a silvery sheen to them, mottled with black swirls. In bright light or darkness, a twilight shield's bonus to AC is +1, but its bonus increases by 2 for a total of +3 in dim light.

TWILIGHT CHILD EQUIPMENT

Item	Cost	Weight
Poison, ironblood (vial, 1 dose)	500 gp	—
Twilight charm	10 gp	—

FEATS

Twilight children have evolved a style all their own and are quite fond of the following feats.

COMPANION TO SHADOW

Prerequisites: Twilight child; Intelligence, Wisdom, or Charisma 13 or higher

You can cast the *find familiar* spell but only as a ritual. When you cast the spell, instead of conjuring a spirit in animal form, you infuse your shadow with a sliver of consciousness, turning it into an independent companion. Your shadow becomes a fey creature with the statistics of a commoner, except it can make only unarmed strike attacks (dealing 1 damage) and can't speak. Additionally, your shadow companion has damage resistance to cold, fire, lightning, and thunder and to bludgeoning, piercing, and slashing from nonmagical attacks, plus the following traits.

Amorphous. The shadow companion can move through a space as narrow as 1 inch wide without squeezing.

Sunlight Weakness. While in sunlight, the shadow companion has disadvantage on attack rolls, ability checks, and saving throws.

While your shadow companion roams free, you don't cast a shadow. This is unnerving to other creatures and imposes disadvantage on any Charisma check you make against a creature not familiar with your shadow companion. When the shadow companion moves with you, you can disguise it as a normal shadow with a Dexterity (Stealth) check opposed by the passive Perception of any observers.

DUSK HUNTER

Prerequisite: Twilight child; the ability to cast at least one spell

You use the shadows to close on enemies, attacking with impunity and dispatching with cold efficiency. You gain the following benefits:

- When a creature within 5 feet of you makes a melee weapon attack against you, you can use your reaction to cast a spell with a casting time of one action and targeting only that creature.
- When you're concentrating on a spell, creatures have disadvantage on attack rolls against you.
- You have advantage on spell attack rolls against creatures within 5 feet of you.

TWILIGHT CHILD ARMOR

Armor	Cost	Armor Class (AC)	Strength	Stealth	Weight
Shield					
Twilight shield	100 gp	+1 (+3 in dim light)	—	—	5 lb.

TWILIGHT CHILD WEAPONS

Name	Cost	Damage	Weight	Properties
Martial Melee Weapon				
Fey claw	5 gp	1d4 slashing	2 lb.	Finesse, light, special

FADE INTO THE BACKGROUND

Prerequisite: Twilight child

You traverse the shadows with ease. You gain the following benefits:

- Increase your Dexterity score by 1, to a maximum of 20.
- While in dim or dark conditions, you have advantage on passive Wisdom (Perception) and passive Intelligence (Investigation) checks.
- If no one has attacked you since the beginning of your last turn, you can use your Move action to hide with advantage on your check.

FAMILIAL ENEMY

Prerequisite: Twilight child

Your hatred for one side of your lineage burns hot. Choose either fey or the humanoid race you chose for your Inheritance feature. You gain the following benefits:

- Increase your Strength or Dexterity score by 1, to a maximum of 20.
- When you hit a creature of the chosen type with a weapon attack or a spell attack, you can use your reaction to reduce the target's AC against your next attack by an amount equal to your proficiency bonus.
- Your critical hits against creatures of the chosen type deal an extra 1d8 damage of the type dealt by the original attack.

LIMINAL STRIDE

Prerequisite: Twilight child

You wear the shadows like a cloak, deflecting would-be attacks and confusing your enemies. You gain the following benefits:

- Your speed increases by 10 feet.
- If a creature attacks you, use your reaction (before you know whether the attack would hit) to try to swap places with another creature within 5 feet of you. To swap places, try to shove the creature, except you can make a Dexterity (Acrobatics) check, and if you win, you swap places and that creature becomes the target of the original attack.
- When you take the Disengage action, you gain half cover from ranged attacks, or three quarters cover in dim and dark conditions, until the start of your next turn.

MARKED BY MANITOU

Prerequisite: Twilight child

All twilight children of Manitou have small horns, but yours have grown to an impressive size. An unarmed strike with your horns deals 2d4 piercing damage and scores a critical hit on a roll of 19 or 20. Additionally, choose either the Intimidation or Persuasion skill. If you are proficient in the chosen skill, you can add double your proficiency bonus to ability checks involving that skill.

QUICKLING STEP

Prerequisite: Twilight child

You harness a preternatural speed and agility, drawing from your fey heritage. You gain the following benefits:

- Your speed increases by 10 feet.
- When jumping, you can add your Strength and Dexterity scores together (or the modifiers in the case of a high jump) to determine the distance achieved.
- When you move at least 10 feet, you have advantage on Dexterity saving throws until the start of your next turn.

SELF-SUFFICIENT

Prerequisite: Twilight child

Your difficult life has taught you that you must be able to rely on yourself to get by. You gain the following benefits:

- If you start your turn with 0 hit points, you can choose to forgo your death saving throw to regain 1 hit point. If you do, you also gain three levels of exhaustion. You can't use this feature if you are already exhausted.
- When you finish a short rest, you gain temporary hit points equal to your Constitution modifier (minimum of 1). Any remaining since the previous short rest are lost.

Appendix

The following present optional kith subtypes for use with your fey characters. You can find additional information on them and additional subtypes in *Along the Twisting Way: The Faerie Ring Campaign Guide.*

KITH SUBTYPES

Between the rule of power and the ties of blood, there lies the pull of kith, where it's sometimes easier to know where you stand.

Changelings are born to the mixed union of fey and non-fey creatures or created in some way from non-fey creatures. They might include mortals exposed to fey magic for sufficient periods of time, twilight children, or unique circumstances. Changelings are diverse and tend to maintain traits related to the creature's original type. (You may take an additional kith subtype.)

Fata are touched by destiny for good or ill, and their eyes are open to the weave of fate. They are set on a path toward a certain destiny and cannot stray from it without severe consequences.

Fomorians are brutal masters of nature and enemies to the sídhe. They revel in the untamed wilds, celebrate under the open sky. They revere the hunt and take sacrament in blood.

Gnomekin are cousins to the gnome humanoid race, but being fey, they are more closely tied to the original gnome fey race for which they all distantly claim heritage.

Mandragoras are animated flora given mobility and some measure of intelligence (not so unlike a "plant homunculus"). A creature with the mandragora subtype possesses both the plant and fey types.

Mogwoi are among the eldest of the fey and innately bound to the Material Plane.

Morphs are strange, alien fey that grow from spores implanted in other races, sometimes willingly so and sometimes not.

Shadows are natives to the Shadow Plane or otherwise touched by ancient primordial darkness.

Sprites are free-spirited, often fitting closely to the "trickster" persona so often attributed to fey. They tend to have some domain that they like to call their own and to place most of their attention, whether that be their wreath or some location or type of environment, plant, or object.

Yokai are at home in the wilds of the Material and Preternatural Planes. Though they vary greatly, they often have animal-like features and many are shapechangers. They have a strong connection with the spirit world.

OPEN GAME LICENSE Version 1.0a

The following text is the property of Wizards of the Coast, Inc. and is Copyright 2000 Wizards of the Coast, Inc ("Wizards"). All Rights Reserved.

1. Definitions: (a) "Contributors" means the copyright and/or trademark owners who have contributed Open Game Content; (b) "Derivative Material" means copyrighted material including derivative works and translations (including into other computer languages), potation, modification, correction, addition, extension, upgrade, improvement, compilation, abridgment or other form in which an existing work may be recast, transformed or adapted; (c) "Distribute" means to reproduce, license, rent, lease, sell, broadcast, publicly display, transmit or otherwise distribute; (d) "Open Game Content" means the game mechanic and includes the methods, procedures, processes and routines to the extent such content does not embody the Product Identity and is an enhancement over the prior art and any additional content clearly identified as Open Game Content by the Contributor, and means any work covered by this License, including translations and derivative works under copyright law, but specifically excludes Product Identity. (e) "Product Identity" means product and product line names, logos and identifying marks including trade dress; artifacts, creatures, characters, stories, storylines, plots, thematic elements, dialogue, incidents, language, artwork, symbols, designs, depictions, likenesses, formats, poses, concepts, themes and graphic, photographic and other visual or audio representations; names and descriptions of characters, spells, enchantments, personalities, teams, personas, likenesses and special abilities; places, locations, environments, creatures, equipment, magical or supernatural abilities or effects, logos, symbols, or graphic designs; and any other trademark or registered trademark clearly identified as Product identity by the owner of the Product Identity, and which specifically excludes the Open Game Content; (f) "Trademark" means the logos, names, mark, sign, motto, designs that are used by a Contributor to identify itself or its products or the associated products contributed to the Open Game License by the Contributor (g) "Use", "Used" or "Using" means to use, Distribute, copy, edit, format, modify, translate and otherwise create Derivative Material of Open Game Content. (h) "You" or "Your" means the licensee in terms of this agreement.

2. The License: This License applies to any Open Game Content that contains a notice indicating that the Open Game Content may only be Used under and in terms of this License. You must affix such a notice to any Open Game Content that you Use. No terms may be added to or subtracted from this License except as described by the License itself. No other terms or conditions may be applied to any Open Game Content distributed using this License.

3. Offer and Acceptance: By Using the Open Game Content You indicate Your acceptance of the terms of this License.

4. Grant and Consideration: In consideration for agreeing to use this License, the Contributors grant You a perpetual, worldwide, royalty-free, non-exclusive license with the exact terms of this License to Use, the Open Game Content.

5. Representation of Authority to Contribute: If You are contributing original material as Open Game Content, You represent that Your Contributions are Your original creation and/or You have sufficient rights to grant the rights conveyed by this License.

6. Notice of License Copyright: You must update the COPYRIGHT NOTICE portion of this License to include the exact text of the COPYRIGHT NOTICE of any Open Game Content You are copying, modifying or distributing, and You must add the title, the copyright date, and the copyright holder's name to the COPYRIGHT NOTICE of any original Open Game Content you Distribute.

7. Use of Product Identity: You agree not to Use any Product Identity, including as an indication as to compatibility, except as expressly licensed in another, independent Agreement with the owner of each element of that Product Identity. You agree not to indicate compatibility or co-adaptability with any Trademark or Registered Trademark in conjunction with a work containing Open Game Content except as expressly licensed in another, independent Agreement with the owner of such Trademark or Registered Trademark. The use of any Product Identity in Open Game Content does not constitute a challenge to the ownership of that Product Identity. The owner of any Product Identity used in Open Game Content shall retain all rights, title and interest in and to that Product Identity.

8. Identification: If you distribute Open Game Content You must clearly indicate which portions of the work that you are distributing are Open Game Content.

9. Updating the License: Wizards or its designated Agents may publish updated versions of this License. You may use any authorized version of this License to copy, modify and distribute any Open Game Content originally distributed under any version of this License.

10. Copy of this License: You MUST include a copy of this License with every copy of the Open Game Content You distribute.

11. Use of Contributor Credits: You may not market or advertise the Open Game Content using the name of any Contributor unless You have written permission from the Contributor to do so.

12. Inability to Comply: If it is impossible for You to comply with any of the terms of this License with respect to some or all of the Open Game Content due to statute, judicial order, or governmental regulation then You may not Use any Open Game Material so affected.

13. Termination: This License will terminate automatically if You fail to comply with all terms herein and fail to cure such breach within 30 days of becoming aware of the breach. All sublicenses shall survive the termination of this License.

14. Reformation: If any provision of this License is held to be unenforceable, such provision shall be reformed only to the extent necessary to make it enforceable.

15. COPYRIGHT NOTICE

Open Game License v 1.0a Copyright 2000, Wizards of the Coast, Inc.

System Reference Document 5.1 Copyright 2016, Wizards of the Coast, Inc.; Authors Mike Mearls, Jeremy Crawford, Chris Perkins, Rodney Thompson, Peter Lee, James Wyatt, Robert J. Schwalb, Bruce R. Cordell, Chris Sims, and Steve Townshend, based on original material by E. Gary Gygax and Dave Arneson.

Along the Twisting Way: The Faerie Ring Prelude. © 2010, 2017, Zombie Sky Press, www.zombiesky.com.

Along the Twisting Way: The Faerie Ring Campaign Guide (5E). © 2018, Zombie Sky Press, www.zombiesky.com.

Along the Twisting Way: The Faerie Ring Player's Guide (5E). © 2020, Zombie Sky Press, www.zombiesky.com.

BROKEN
eye
BOOKS

by faerie light

www.ingramcontent.com/pod-product-compliance
Lightning Source LLC
Chambersburg PA
CBHW081140300726
48982CB00006B/1020
* 9 7 8 1 9 4 0 3 7 2 5 1 8 *